Dating Trouble

A GROVER BEACH TEAM BOOK

ANNA KATMORE

GENRE: YA/CONTEMPORARY ROMANCE

DATING TROUBLE
Fourth book of the
GROVER BEACH TEAM series

Cover Design by Marie Graßhoff

Edited by Annie Cosby, www.AnnieCosby.com

First Publication: January 2015

www.annakatmore.com

To Silje Victoria

For being the best beta reader one can find on this planet!

And because she loves Chris as much as I do. ;-)

Dating Trouble

Chapter 1

I BANGED MY head against Ryan Hunter's shoulder. "Kill me now!"

"Aw, why so tragic, booklover?" Hunter wrapped an arm around me and dragged me through the gate to the soccer field behind our high school. "It's only for ten weeks. Grab a nice tearjerker, drool over Edward Twilight, and time will fly by."

"Cullen."

"What?"

"His name is Edward Cullen, not Edward Twilight." I rolled my eyes. "And I read that one years ago."

"Right. Whatever." My team captain, with the teddy bear brown eyes and roguish half-smile that made girls faint in droves when he walked past, patted my back. "I'm sure you'll find another great book to keep yourself busy until you can play soccer with us again."

I cast him a sharp sideways look. "Do you honestly want to know how many books I'll have to read in that time to keep me sane?"

Ryan grimaced, running a hand through his chaotic, black hair. "Um, no."

"Five hundred and seven—and then some." *Gah*! "I hate Doctor Trooper. How could he do this to me?"

A laugh escaped Ryan. It was typical for him to sound so chilled out. Nothing fazed him, no matter how huge the problem. "Come on, Miller. It's really not the end of the world."

"You only say that because you don't have to sit over there!" I pointed a thumb over my shoulder at the bench on the sidelines. But at the sight of Ryan's helpless look and shrug, I forced down my frustration. It wasn't his fault my leg was out of order for the winter season. That was courtesy of a girl player from the Riverfalls Rabid Wolves. She'd nearly kicked my kneecap into outer space during a recent match. Boy, that had hurt. I'd wanted to bawl like a baby. Except, there'd been too many guys around to really do that.

Ryan released me, stooped down, and pulled his left sock higher to cover his shin guard. While he retied the laces of his cleats, he angled his head to look up at me and squinted against the sun of this late November afternoon. "Will you stay and watch practice? Lisa's supposed to show up later."

I grinned. "That was my plan." His girlfriend, Lisa Matthews, was one of my best friends, and we'd talked on the phone before I came down here.

"Good." Ryan jogged over to Tony Mitchell, Alex Winter,

and Nick Frederickson—all members of the Grover Beach Bay Sharks. I wiggled my fingers at them when they glanced my way, before I headed for the single bench in front of the bleachers on the sideline. I *did* bring a book today, and it was *not Twilight*, but I also wanted to watch my friends practice.

The coming ten weeks were bound to be pure torture. Since last summer, soccer had become a solid part of my life. Not that I was any good at it, but I loved the team sport. It was also nice how I had transformed from a lazy bookworm into an athlete who could actually run three miles without dying of breathlessness during Hunter's excessive training schedule.

Speaking of physique, there was one effect better than all the rest, even if it had nothing to do with soccer training at all. Straightening my light blue shirt, which was a tight fit, I looked down at my front and smiled, because I'd finally grown the curves nature had denied me when puberty struck. *Phew.* No girl should get her driver's license before her boobs. That's just cruel.

As I reached the bench, I looked up again and—what the hell—I stopped dead.

A guy was sprawled out along the seat, his head pillowed by his folded arms, gazing at the sky. Or maybe he was asleep. I couldn't tell, because he'd pulled the rim of his ball cap low on his forehead. Headphones were plugged in his ears. The sound of Volbeat drifted to me, even from five feet away. Hmm, he had good taste in music. In clothes...not so much. Dark brown sneakers, brown shorts, and a yellow tee gave him a crazy *Peanuts* look.

I didn't know who he was, or why he was occupying my seat, but since I was still part of this soccer team and he was *not*, it was only fair to shoo him away. There were enough empty seats on the bleachers where he could continue his Monday afternoon nap.

I walked up to his side, slapped his knee with the back of my hand, and waited until he pulled the earphones out; well, one of them at least. "Hey, Charlie Brown, this is my seat." The sharpness in my voice left no room for discussion, or so I hoped. I wasn't your typical commanding person. That was my friend Simone's job. She had it down to the last bat of her eyelashes. Today, however, I thought I'd pulled off a pretty good imitation.

The guy angled his head toward me, took off his cap, and raked a relaxed hand through his short hair, which was the color of sunlight hitting glass. He blinked his cornflower-blue eyes a couple of times. A slow smile crawled across his face. "Sorry, I didn't know the bench had your name on it."

Hah! "Well, if you look again, you'll find it carved into one of the boards somewhere." Simone Simpkins and I had eternalized ourselves here sometime last summer. We'd tried to talk Lisa into it, too, but she'd only rolled her eyes. She'd always been the most reasonable of us.

The guy's smile morphed into an intrigued expression, as one of his eyebrows wandered upward. "Is that so?" he drawled.

I dumped my backpack next to my gray vintage boots and crossed my arms over my chest. Charlie Brown finally worked up the decency to sit up. The longer I looked at his face, the more familiar it seemed. I might have seen this guy at one of

Hunter's parties but, for the love of Christ, I couldn't fish his name from my mind.

However, he didn't leave, which grated on my nerves. He pulled out the second earpiece, scooted down to one end of the bench and, without words, offered me a spot beside him. With a snort, I accepted the offer.

Nine days after the accident, I didn't need crutches any longer, was able to drive a car, and could climb stairs again without awkwardly dragging my injured leg behind me. But sitting down on something as low as this bench caused me trouble. My knee still hurt a little when I bent it more than a full right angle. So, as usual, I kept my right leg as straight as possible and slumped in slow motion down onto my butt.

The *Peanuts* copy had put his cap back on and the cable of his headphones around his neck. Right now he was ogling me in a peculiar way—I could see that from the corner of my eye.

"You're Susan Miller, aren't you?" he said over the noise still coming from his headphones.

My gaze got stuck on the red shark grinning from the ten-by-ten-foot poster on the other side of the soccer field, and I nearly choked on air. Slowly, I turned to him. "And just which little bird told you that?"

"Not a bird. Your knee did." He rubbed his neck and lowered his glance in a way that made me think of how guilty I'd felt when Mom told me I'd fried my ant farm at age six, because I'd let them take a sun bath on my windowsill on a dramatically hot August day. "And unless I'm totally mistaken," he continued, managing to look sweet even as he grimaced, "I'm your replacement."

"You. Are. *What?*" I jumped up in horror—not very gracefully—and planted my fists on my hips. "Hunter!" I yelled across the field and turned back to Charlie Brown, blowing air out of my nose like a bull in an arena. "Listen, just because I'm temporarily out of order doesn't mean you can come and take my place. *Hunter!*"

The guy rose to his feet, placating me with his palms up, but I didn't give him a chance to speak. "I'll be back to my awesome normal in just a few weeks and able to play soccer again! No need for anyone to jump in for me. HUNTER! Get your sorry ass over here, *now!*"

Charlie Brown bit his bottom lip. "Ryan said the news probably wouldn't go down well with you. I'm surprised he hasn't told you yet."

Oh no, he hadn't told me. What the hell? I was unable to play for a while, not forever. No need to run off and find the next best guy to replace me—no matter how cute that guy looked, by the way. "What's going on here?" I huffed as my team captain finally drew up beside me.

Ryan sucked in a breath between his teeth, his expression sheepish. "Er...did I forget to tell you that I found someone to play with us for the time that you can't?"

"Obviously so!" At my murderous gaze, Hunter took a step back. Wow, I didn't know I was that good. I could have let a sly grin slip right now, but I didn't.

"Calm down, Susie," the guy in brown shorts said in a soothing sort of way and reached out to touch my arm. He cast

Ryan a look befitting a Boy Scout and a subtle nod. Gah, did he really think I hadn't seen that? The next second, Ryan took off, back to the others.

"No one calls me Susie," I growled at Charlie Brown and pulled my arm away.

"Okay. Don't bite my head off, and it won't happen again." He winked at me and, to my total surprise, it cut me silent.

With my head slightly cocked, I gazed up those few inches he had on my five-foot-eight frame. He smiled all the way to his ears. Because of how sweet he looked when he did so, I was willing to give him ten seconds to say whatever was on his mind.

"I'm not going to take your place. I used to play soccer a few years ago, and when Ryan asked me to play for a while, I said yes to do him a favor." Carefully, as if not to be too forward, he placed his hands on my shoulders, moved me back to the bench, and helped me sit down. He squatted in front of me, elbows resting on his thighs, so we were eye to eye. "I promise to be gone the day your leg is fine and you can take over again. How's that?"

He smelled like lemongrass and Coke popsicles. Awesome.

I drew in another deep breath and finally let my frustration sail off on the ship of sighs. With my index finger, I shoved my glasses farther up my nose. I normally didn't bring them to soccer practice, but since I wasn't going to play only read today, I'd had no choice. "I guess that's okay."

"Great." He clapped his hands once, stood up, and placed his white iPod on the bench next to me. "Take care of this for me?"

I nodded and noticed that he hadn't turned the music off.

He headed away, but after only a few steps, he twisted to me again, walking backward. "I'm Ethan, by the way." He shrugged and grinned. "Just in case you wanted to know." Ethan grabbed his cap, turned it backwards, and ran off toward the rest of my team.

I sat rigid with my gaze transfixed on his back. My hands, which were usually cold as ice bags, were now sweaty. Why the heck were they *sweaty*? I wiped them on my white jeans and ground my molars together. Replacement player, my ass. Hunter would have to answer a few questions for me after practice.

More aggressively than I'd actually intended to, I pulled the zipper of my backpack open and fished for the book I'd brought today. It was *The Fiery Cross*, an *Outlander* novel. Over the past couple of weeks I'd become addicted to that series, but this was already book five of eight, and the series would hardly keep me busy much longer than a few more days. Yeah, that's the problem when you devour books like your friends munch popcorn—you run out of good stuff pretty quickly.

In the distance, I heard Hunter introduce Ethan as their temporary teammate. Most of the guys and girls seemed to know him already, which wasn't a big surprise. Everyone who knew Hunter also knew his friends. Well, apart from me, obviously.

I didn't pay attention and buried my nose in the book, but with the music still coming from Ethan's iPod, I just couldn't concentrate. Maybe he'd left it on for a purpose? Most likely to continue getting on my nerves. For a moment, I considered switching the music off or at least turning the volume down, but when I reached for it, my hand developed a will of its own and plugged one of the headphones into my ear. Fine, I was curious. Before, there'd been a song from one of my favorite bands playing, so maybe there were more of my favorites.

Right now, Aerosmith was playing, which actually wasn't bad. I picked up the white iPod and skipped a few songs forward, then searched through the library. Apart from that one song, there was no more Volbeat, which was a shame, but the other music was good enough to keep listening. Some metal, some rock, and even Ed Sheeran—that was totally my thing.

Turning down the volume, I put the second headphone into my ear and continued reading where I'd stopped before. Twenty pages flew by to the voices of Kings of Leon. Only once or twice did I sneak a peek at the soccer field to see how Charlie Brown was shaping up—and holy moly, he was *good*!

He'd just headed the ball past Frederickson—who'd gotten an award for best junior goalkeeper in North California—for an amazing goal. He cut a fine figure when he ran, too. Not like Kyle Foster, who thundered across the lawn like an engine on steroids, or like Alex Winter, who seemed too lazy today to even tie his shoelaces. In fact, Ethan was some serious competition for Hunter. He looked like he owned that field in a very natural, very comfortable way.

Sasha Torres high-fived him on his goal, and that was when Ethan looked my way.

Have you ever been caught gaping at someone, like really ogling in awe? You know how it makes your cheeks heat with embarrassment, right? Unfortunately, it wasn't only my cheeks.

Heat crawled all over my face, right up to my hairline, as Ethan called me out on my staring with a tight-lipped smirk.

I wanted to hide behind my book and whine, and yeah, maybe that's what I actually did, but only after he'd turned away and engaged in the game again. I was listening to his music, I was ogling him, and I certainly was glowing red as a stop sign. Could it get any worse? If only time machines were real. I would go back thirty minutes exactly and never walk up to this bench.

As something touched my shoulder, I jumped right out of my skin, jerking my head around and screeching. The iPod, connected to the headphones in my ears, slid off the seat and landed on the ground before I could grab it.

Shoot! With my heart drumming like I was leading a battalion of soldiers, I tossed my book aside and picked up the iPod, quickly checking whether Ethan had seen what I'd done to his stuff. His back was turned to me. I breathed again and pulled the headphones out of my ears, dropping them in my lap together with the iPod. Finally, I faced Lisa, who'd lowered down next to me on the bench.

"Hey," she said and laughed. "A little skittish today, are we?"

Still fumbling to turn off the music, I made a wry face and got right to the point. "Did you know your boyfriend replaced me?"

For the length of a drawn-out breath, Lisa frowned at me. She shoved a hand through her long brown hair. "Susan, you're not speaking my language right now."

Good, she had no idea. Knowing and *not* telling me would

have been a major breach of trust. It didn't stop me from wailing, though. "He brought in Charlie Brown to play soccer instead of me!"

Pushing up the sleeves of her pink blouse, Lisa laughed again. "He did what?"

"Yellow shirt," I whined and nodded toward the soccer field. When Lisa spotted Ethan in the middle of a sea of blue jerseys and the truth dawned on her, an *Oh* was all she gave me.

"Yeah, exactly. *Oh.* Ryan told him he could take my place because, obviously"—I lifted my eyebrows to a duh expression—"I'm not good enough to play for the team anymore."

"Come on, that's not true and you know it. Ryan loves having you on the team. I'm sure he and the guys can't wait till your knee is better and you can play again. And until then, why not bring in a temp?" As she glanced at the guys again, a grin that said *girls' business only* spread across her face. "Also, he's cute."

Who cared? It didn't give him the right to take my place.

"Who is?" Simone's voice startled us. We both turned around to find her and Allie Silverman behind us, scanning the soccer field with spiked interest. Both of them had hair that reached to the end of their backs, only Simone was a natural Scandinavian blonde with big curls, while Allie's hair was as black and straight as a raven's coat. Like Lisa, they were both on the cheerleading team—the team that usually cheered for us soccer players. Only now, they'd cheer for Ethan instead of me.

"The guy who's dressed like a rotting banana," I muttered in answer to Simone. "But I guess *cute* is a term that can be argued. I don't like him. He's playing my position on Hunter's team."

Allie gasped. "Permanently?"

"Temporarily," Lisa corrected quickly. "Until Susan is fit to play again."

"Oh, that's not too bad." Simone shoved her beautiful curls over one shoulder and snickered. "He's quite the eye candy. What's his name?"

Simone was the girlfriend of one of the guys on my team, and the two of them usually stuck together like glue, so her remark made us all chuckle. She'd never—not in a million years—dump Alex Winter for another guy.

"Ethan," I told her.

"Did you talk to him already?" Allie wanted to know.

"A little. Before practice started. Why?"

"Because he's looking at you right now," Allie and Simone said at once with grins in their voices.

"What?" Oh man, shoot me, because I did exactly what you shouldn't do at such a moment. I whirled around to check. And of course, I met Ethan's gaze, which was indeed focused on me. While my expression was dull, if not a little surprised, the corners of Charlie Brown's mouth tilted up before his attention returned to the other players and the ongoing match.

I slapped both hands to my face, groaning with my eyes squeezed shut. "I hate you guys! Now he must think I'm checking him out."

"Are you?" Lisa giggled.

"No." Granted, I'd done it before, but this time it was a

total accident. I wanted to dig a hole all the way to China to hide in.

When I opened my eyes, thank God, there was a light at the end of the tunnel. Samantha Summers—the girl that inhaled cherry lollipops like others inhaled air and who had become my closest friend since she'd moved to Grover Beach only three weeks ago—marched through the gate and strolled over to us. She was tiny and funny and I loved her like a sister. She would back me up against the gossiping hens surrounding me.

Sam sat down Indian-style in the grass in front of us and made a face. "Susan, you look miserable. What did I miss?"

"Ethan," the other three told her at once.

"Who is Ethan?"

"I'll tell you if you promise not to turn around and look," I said before anyone else could point out my replacement to her.

Sam's face scrunched, and it made her look absurdly intrigued. "Promise." After I gave her the same story I'd given the others, her face split with a grin. "Okay, now you got me all curious. I *have* to turn around, Susan, I just *have* to!" She got all fidgety on the ground.

"No! You can't. He already noticed us watching him," I hissed, keeping my gaze determinedly away from the players. If she turned around, I'd pull her back by a fistful of her short, black, messy hair—that was a promise on my end.

"You're crazy, Susan," Lisa teased and added, "But there's no need to turn around, Sam. You're lucky—he's coming over here."

What? I froze at her words...gulped...and saw the soccer

ball rolling toward us. It stopped right by Sam's leg. She picked it up and sure enough, Charlie Brown was jogging our way.

"Hiii, Eeethan," the girls sang out in unison as he took the ball from Sam.

Appalled, I stared into his wicked eyes. When he started to grin, I wanted to shout at him: *I told them your name, so what?* Only, I couldn't make my mouth form coherent words because embarrassment had wired my jaw shut.

"Hey, girls," he greeted the others like a perfect charmer. His gaze landed on my lap. On his iPod still *in* my lap, to be exact. "You like my music?" He chuckled but didn't give me a chance to answer as he turned around and headed back into the game.

"Thanks a lot!" I spat through gritted teeth at my supposed friends. A moment later, however, I was snickering along with them, because aside from all the embarrassment, the situation *was* funny. If I were one of them, I'd have acted equally as stupid for sure. I'd just never been at the receiving end before.

Sam leaned back to prop herself on her elbows and stretched her legs out in front of her. She was the smallest of us, all right, but always wearing camo pants and black Doc Martens, she was also the most dangerous-looking of us five—even if her appearance was deceiving. Samantha was the nicest girl I'd ever met. Right now, she let go of a long sigh. "Take it easy, Susan. So he's playing your position." She shrugged it off. "It's only for a while, and he's cute. It's really not a drama."

Yeah, she was right; it wasn't. And Sam would know a thing or two about dramas herself. Only a week ago her cousin

Chloe had almost succeeded in making her parents send Sam back to Egypt, where Sam's parents still lived. Because her father was a general in the U.S. Army and garrisoned in Cairo for three more months, Samantha had been allowed to move ahead to Grover Beach at the beginning of November to stay with Chloe and her family, so she wouldn't have to move later, during the school year.

No one could have guessed that Chloe still had a crush on Tony Mitchell, the guy from my soccer team who Sam had hooked up with. It had caused a pretty nasty scene a week ago when Chloe wrecked her car and later almost drowned herself in the sea. We had quite an eventful fall.

Admittedly, none of us had liked Chloe Summers much before. But after what happened, we all looked at her with different eyes now—even though she never looked at any of us, ever. It seemed she felt really bad and sorry about what had happened. And now, knowing all the facts, it wasn't hard to forgive her, whether she asked for it or not.

On the weird side, none of us had ever seen Tony as radiantly happy as he'd been since the day he and Sam became a couple. He spent every minute of his free time with her, so it didn't surprise me when he came over to us during timeout. Stopping behind Sam, he bent down and stole a kiss. He did that every so often, and most of the time, he didn't come alone. Hunter normally couldn't stay away from Lisa either, but today he kept away.

Noticing, Lisa pouted at Tony. "Why isn't Ryan coming over?"

"He's scared." Tony chuckled. "After the thing with Ethan, he's afraid Miller will bite his head off."

"Ha, ha," I said. But there was a grain of truth in that joke. I flashed a tight-lipped smile across the field at Ryan. Catching my gaze, he rubbed his neck and laughed out loud, knowing that Tony had just ratted him out.

With only a short time left for practice, Tony headed back to score another goal against Ryan's team. Watching the two of them out on the field was always a delight. Hard to say which of them was the better player. Since it was Ryan's final year at Grover Beach High, I often wondered if he would nominate Tony for captain of the team when it was time for him to leave. But that was still a few months off and no one talked about it just yet.

Practice ended at quarter to four, and my friends immediately fanned out to their guys on the field. Being seventeen and still as single as could be, I stayed put and shoved my book into my backpack. It was then that I saw Ethan walking toward me and my mouth dried out. Why? Because he'd taken off his shirt and was wiping his face with it. Before he shook it out and put it back on, I got an exclusive glimpse at his rock-hard abs and shapely chest. I was pretty sure the real Charlie Brown didn't look anything close to this beneath his yellow shirt.

Determined not to get caught staring again, I quickly turned my head away and rose from the bench. The backpack was already on my shoulders and I was about to walk off in the opposite direction when Ethan called out to me, "Hey, Susan, can you wait up a minute?"

Startled, I pivoted to him again. He loped over and stopped so close to me that a whiff of his sweat caught me square in the face. Luckily he'd put on enough deodorant that it didn't smell bad at all. Maybe it was just his shower gel, I couldn't tell. In any case, it smelled manly and...*nice.*

Still slightly out of breath from practice, he sat down and glanced up at me. His cheeks were red and he'd tossed his ball cap aside, displaying a disheveled thatch of blond hair. He resembled a little boy, which was quite a cute look. It suited him.

"What's up?" I asked, feeling a bit awkward because of my previous gawking. Hopefully that wasn't the reason he wanted to talk to me. I'd put his iPod back on the bench without a scratch, too.

When Ethan reached out for my hand and pulled me down next to him, I didn't protest. "I need to talk to you about my joining the team," he said.

"You stole my place, end of story," I answered, a little sullen now. "What more is there to talk about?"

He grimaced and released my wrist. "Hunter says I can stay, if you say I can."

"Oh." My gaze skated over the soccer field to find Hunter with Lisa some sixty feet away. When I lifted my eyebrows, he started to walk toward us, but Lisa quickly grabbed his arm and said something to him that made him stop and smile. She cast me a brilliant grin, gave me two very unsubtle thumbs-up, and dragged Ryan away to the parking lot. I rolled my eyes. Did she think she was Grover Beach's new matchmaker all of a sudden?

It was a miracle Ethan hadn't seen them sneaking off. He was still gazing at me. "So what do you think? Do I make a worthy player for the Bay Sharks?" His voice sounded awfully hopeful.

Dropping my gaze to the ground, I coughed to get rid of the annoying dryness in my throat. "How would I know?" I mumbled. "It's not like I watched you play today."

For a few seconds, Ethan just stared at me. The feeling was aggravating. As I turned to him again, the corners of his mouth tilted up in a slow grin and he drawled the word, "Liar."

The heat of embarrassment rose in my body and here I was, once again wishing for a time machine. Since that wasn't going to happen, all I could do was laugh. I don't know why, it just burst out of me, and rather hysterically, too. I sounded like a hyena. Yeah, that was sexy Susan Miller at her best.

But sexy or not, the anger and tension from the past hour slipped away from me. I could look Charlie Brown straight in the eye and didn't even blush. "Okay, you're right. I did check you out, but I had to see what Hunter came up with to replace me. And"—while we were at it—"the thing with the girls before was totally stupid, but I'm not saying sorry for that."

Ethan had watched me, fascinated, when I had my laughing fit, but now he chuckled, and the sound of it was quite delightful. "You don't have to. It's sweet that you couldn't wait to tell your friends my name."

I rolled my eyes. "Yeah, right. Like that was the only thing on my mind since you introduced yourself." *Yeah, right. Like that wasn't the truth.* A shrug rolled off my shoulders, and suddenly I felt I could be honest with him. "As for joining the team—only temporarily, of course—you're actually a passable player from what I saw. Your long passes are excellent. I guess Hunter could use you. And yes...I like your music." Now I stuck out my tongue at him.

Man, I needed to stop before I talked myself into a frenzy which, hands down, happened more often than not, especially when I started to feel comfortable with someone. I couldn't tell why exactly he made me feel so at ease, but I'd obviously slipped past the point of no return already. "You have a lot of good stuff on your playlist. And it was your fault anyway; you didn't turn off the music when you left." Duh!

A little surprised, either over my swell of words or about my taste in music, he tilted his head. "You like Aerosmith?"

"Not so much, but I kinda inhale Kings of Leon day and night. Sadly, there's not enough Volbeat on your iPod. That's my second favorite band in the world."

Ethan turned to me on the bench, putting one leg on the other side to straddle it. An excited gleam appeared in his eyes. One that I knew all too well from myself, when I talked about books or music. "Yeah, they're awesome," he gushed. "I've only just discovered them, and I'm going to get all the CDs they have. Call me weird, but when I really like a band, I just don't want to download their music. I'm like a –"

"Hoarder? That's totally what I do."

"Yeah, something like that. Only, the music shop in town isn't very well stocked. I'll have to order a few things online."

"I have all their CDs, and DVDs. Their best one is *Live*

from beyond Hell. You can borrow it if you want." When he nodded, I made a mental note to find it tonight and bring the CD to school tomorrow. "Guess what! I even got them to sign my hoodie after a concert last winter."

"You're kidding me! You've met them? How cool is that?"

"Veeeeery." I pulled my backpack down from my shoulders and fished for my phone before thumbing euphorically through the thousand pictures on it. When I found the right one, I held the phone out to him so he could look at the screen. My proud grin reached from Utah to Ohio. The picture showed me with the singer from Volbeat, his arm casually draped over my shoulders, both of us smirking at each other rather than into the camera.

"Holy cow! That's awesome!"

"Yeah. And he smelled so terrible, all sweaty and worked up after the show—" I laughed. "But, for the life of me, I couldn't bring myself to shower that night."

Ethan nailed me with a calm stare. "I totally understand. I wouldn't have washed Michael Poulsen's DNA off either, if it was pasted on me."

Oh boy, could it be that Charlie Brown and I spoke the same language? I'd known him for what, five minutes? And I already felt like I'd met my soul mate. We raved endlessly about the bands we loved, those with a natural talent for singing, and ranted about others who apparently thought they needed to strip naked in a video to draw attention.

It struck me dumb how much Ethan and I were in tune. Okay no, it didn't—nothing ever rendered me speechless, but it was amazing. None of my friends felt so strongly about my taste in music, so this boy in front of me was definitely a keeper.

When my phone went off after some time, we were so deep in conversation that I didn't answer until the fifth or sixth ring. Absently, I said, "Yeah?"

"Susan? Where are you?"

My mother's impatient voice dragged my attention away from Ethan's shiny blue eyes. "Still at the soccer field," I answered warily. "Why?"

"It's after seven. Your great aunt Muriel is here. We've been waiting for you to start dinner for over half an hour."

I brought the phone down quickly and glanced at the display to check the time. She was right—it was five past seven. Crap! Being with Ethan, I'd totally forgotten my grandfather's sixty-eighth birthday. His slightly senile, hard-of-hearing sister Muriel had come from Pasadena to celebrate with us tonight. I was supposed to help Mom cook dinner. Just where had the time gone? We couldn't possibly have been talking for three hours. My face felt like the color just vanished from my cheeks. "Sorry, Mom. I got caught up," I said into the phone and promised to be home in a few minutes.

"You have to go?" Ethan asked after I hung up.

"Yes. Family celebration." Grimacing, I packed my stuff and stood up. "I can't believe I forgot about that."

Ethan rose with me. "It's crazy. I wouldn't have thought we were talking for more than twenty minutes." He walked with me to the exit of the field, matching my slightly slower than normal pace. As we reached the parking lot, he stopped by a blue Ford

Mustang and unlocked the doors with the punch of a button on his key ring. Looking back and forth between the car and me, he asked, "Need a ride home?"

I shook my head. "It's not far. Only five minutes."

He said, "Okay," but it sounded like: *What a shame*. And it was exactly how I felt about having to go home now. I hadn't enjoyed anything as much as talking to him in a long time. In fact, my mouth and throat had gone so dry from talking that I constantly had to swallow now to keep my voice smooth.

We looked at each other for an extended moment as if neither of us wanted to say goodbye first. When I decided I would be the one, Ethan beat me there, but what he said was, "Um, that was nice. Maybe we should do it again. What do you think? Tomorrow after school? We could go get a soda together somewhere."

I ran a hand through my hair and played with the ends that hung in front of my chest. "What...you mean like—"

"A date?" He shrugged. "Yeah, I guess. Three o'clock at Charlie's Café?"

A very funny feeling spread in my stomach. One that was usually reserved for when I was watching a movie with Zac Efron in it. "Okay."

"Okay," Ethan repeated with a smile, already opening the door of his car.

I waved at him instead of saying goodbye and turned around, grinning like a lunatic. But before I could walk away, he shouted after me, "Hey, wait." As I pivoted once more, he asked, "What should I tell Hunter about me playing on the team?"

I laughed and again found a strand of my hair to twirl around my finger. “Well, I said yes to the date, didn’t I?” And with that I hurried home, hoping to get a piece of Granddad’s birthday cake before Aunt Muriel ate it all.

Chapter 2

MONDAY NIGHT WAS a fight night in my house. It started right after dinner when Gramps had blown out the thousand candles on his birthday cake and Dad cut it, then handed him a piece.

"Richard, you know my father shouldn't be eating sweets," my mom scolded him through gritted teeth. "Remember his diabetes, for goodness' sake."

"Come on, Sally," Dad wheedled. "It's his birthday. You didn't make this cake to have the birthday boy watch the rest of us eat it."

After that conversation starter, it was clear to me that I'd be sleeping with a pillow over my head tonight—like so many times before. Granddad cut me a wary look from across the table just before I got up and went to the fridge to get a glass of milk. No idea why I did that. I didn't even like cold milk. But each time my mom and dad got in an argument, I felt the need to dash out of the room and find something else to do.

I gulped down some milk right from the carton, then went to the sink and washed away the cow-ish taste in my mouth with a glass of water.

"...it will take a ton of insulin until he's back at his normal sugar level! Why can't you be reasonable for once in your..."

My mom's angry shouts drifting from the dining room were drowned out by Grandpa's deep rumble behind me. "Have a glass for an old man, too?"

With a smile that I didn't have to force as much as expected, I turned around and found him sitting at the small, square table in the middle of the yellow room, his wrinkled hands folded in front of a huge piece of cake. I filled a glass for him, then another, as my great aunt Muriel joined us with a confused expression on her face.

"Are they always like that?" she asked, pointing a finger over her shoulder.

A sigh escaped me. "Most of the time."

Muriel pulled out a metal folding chair next to my granddad and sat down. Her hair wasn't as white as his yet, but otherwise they couldn't deny being siblings. Same big nose, the thin lips, and a healthy rosy color to their cheeks. I must have gotten my green eyes from my mother's bloodline, too. Fetching three forks, I joined them, and we ate the cake to the background music of my parents having their second go at each other this week—and it was only Monday.

*

Mom and Dad were decent enough to stop fighting for a moment when Gramps and Muriel said good night and thanked them for the invitation to dinner. My grandfather's house was next to ours. When my folks' fights escalated at night, I used to walk over and knock on his door—no matter what time—dressed in my PJs and armed with my alarm clock. Gramps always let me sleep on the couch. Tonight, however, due to Muriel's visit, I had to suffer through an argument that found its climax at twenty minutes past midnight with banging doors and my mother shouting, "What is wrong with you? Do you want to wake Susan?"

Thanks, Mom. Only took them four hours of nonstop shouting at each other to remember they actually had a daughter. I pressed the pillow harder over my ears and tried counting sheep to escape the mad reality downstairs. It didn't work, and soon the sheep turned into soccer balls being kicked over a fence by Ethan. I watched him do that for some time and concentrated on the warm feeling that spread in my stomach. It was the thought of seeing him again that had my insides in a funky twist.

Oh boy, I was so going to put on nail polish tomorrow. Simone did it all the time, and she was the most beautiful girl I knew. I wanted to look pretty for Ethan. Remembering how he'd smirked and called me a liar today released a shot of adrenaline inside me. Getting really excited, I flashed a smile in the dark. Three p.m. couldn't come fast enough.

Sleep must have claimed me, because when the alarm went off next to my face, I jerked upright to bright morning light in my room. Rushing to the bathroom, I showered, put on some tropical-smelling body lotion, combed and tied my wavy, light brown hair in a high ponytail, and fished for the untouched set of ten little bottles of nail polish in the cabinet beneath the sink. It was a giveaway prize from one of my favorite authors some time ago. Each color of the spectrum was in that box, from yellow to deep purple. I tried the soft pink one to match the pink shirt I'd put on after the shower.

Except, when I was done, the result looked nothing like Simone's ever pretty nails. Maybe because hers were always perfectly manicured and hyper long, and mine were as short as could be from biting them in French class. No way was I going to leave the house looking like I'd been finger-painting. The only problem: the gift set came without nail polish remover.

Mom was my last resort. She always did her nails, so she would have some remover, too. Grabbing my schoolbag and also the CD for Ethan, I rushed downstairs to find my life-saver but stopped dead in the doorway to the kitchen when I saw her sitting at the small table where Gramps, Muriel, and I had held our own little celebration last night. She was wrapped in her dressing gown, a cup of steaming coffee in front of her, and the pretty auburn hair I always envied tied in a messy knot at the back of her head. When she looked up at me, dark rings dug deep into her skin underneath her green eyes. Obviously, the fighting hadn't been over with the door-banging.

Mom smiled at me. A smile that drew forgiveness from

everyone so easily. Including my dad. He came in at that moment and kissed her on the top of her head before he left for work. But first he came toward me and planted a kiss on my forehead, too. "I'm late," he said. "See you sweeties tonight."

"Bye, Dad," I called after him. When he was gone, I sat down across from my mom. "You look tired."

"I'm all right." She reached across the table to squeeze my hands. "I'm so sorry for yesterday, honey. We didn't mean to ruin the evening for you and Gramps."

"It's okay." That was a lie, but she looked sorry enough; I didn't want to add to that. "We ate the cake in here while you and Dad wrestled it out in the living room. And guess what?" I gave her a teasing smile. "Gramps didn't die of a sugar rush."

That made her laugh and eased the tension a little. "I know it was a silly reason for an argument. Dad and I will try to be better, I promise."

I nodded, giving her the encouragement she needed. The problem was, all their fights started with silly reasons and I'd given up hope for a change a long time ago.

When she dragged my hand toward her and planted a kiss on my knuckles, she noticed my failed experiment and her forehead creased to a frown.

"Yeah," I whined. "That was an accident. Can you help me fix it before I have to go?"

Mom brought out her first aid kit, which was actually a whole damn bag full of nail polish and stuff, and started rubbing drenched cotton pads over my nails until they were as clean as ever. "I've never seen you put nail polish on before," she said, concentrating on the task at hand. "Why today?"

Grinning, I waited until she looked up and caught me pausing for a dramatic moment to announce my news. "I have a date today."

"You don't say!" All of a sudden, her face lit up like a light bulb. "Who is he? Do I know him? Is it Nick?"

"Frederickson?" I grimaced. "God no!" He was just a good friend. Even though there was this one moment when I'd thought I was falling for him. We'd just won a soccer match and Nick wrapped me in a bear hug, twirling me around. My stomach had filled with that butterfly feeling you always hear about, but it turned out to be just a burp from the soda I drank after the first half—which I suppressed of course. The moral of that story: Don't let somebody shake you after you drink something bubbly.

"His name is Ethan," I told my mom. "After school, we're going to meet in town. He's playing soccer in my place for a while. You know, because of my knee. We talked all of yesterday afternoon and he invited me to have a drink with him today."

Mom stopped rubbing the nail of my pinky. Her face fell. "Did you say after school?"

"Yes. Three o'clock."

"Honey, we have to pick up the car from the shop this afternoon. Did you forget?"

Hell, yes, I had forgotten. Dammit. The car had been in the shop for over two weeks, and Mom needed me to drive her out to Nipomo in my dad's car, so she could bring hers home. I blamed Ethan for the recent black hole in my memory, since I normally had no trouble remembering anything like that...or my granddad's birthday, for that matter.

"Can't we pick it up tomorrow?" A whiny sigh escaped me. "I really want to go on that date. It's my first, Mom."

"Oh dear, I'm so sorry, but I need the car tonight."

"What about Grandpa? Can't he drive you?"

"He's going to take Muriel back to Pasadena. She has an appointment she can't miss."

"Noooo." With a loud thud, my forehead knocked against the table.

"We'll be back around four. Maybe you can ask Ethan to meet up later?"

"Fine," I muttered, fogging up the metal tabletop with my breath. What other choice did I have, anyway?

After Mom was done cleaning up the mess on my nails, I snagged a donut from the kitchen counter and left for school, eating on the way. The trouble with the nails had cost me too much time to sit through my usual breakfast of toast, eggs, and OJ this morning.

Licking my fingers after the last bite, I walked through the doors of Grover Beach High and headed to my first class—science. Pushing through the crammed corridors always proved a little hard in the morning. I shouldered my way through to my locker and got my science book out. As I banged the door shut and spun the lock, I caught a familiar figure in the corner of my eye. My heart started breakdancing. Crazy, I'd never had that feeling before, and it really felt as exhilarating as it was so often described in the many romance books I'd read. I stood there nailed to the floor for a moment, savoring that new experience down to the core. Eventually, I inhaled deeply a couple of times and walked up to Ethan.

He was surrounded by a group of people, three guys and two girls exactly. They all looked like seniors, a class above me, and I knew none of them. Ethan didn't see me approaching. He was talking to one of the girls, a Thai supermodel lookalike—all long legs, delicate features, and yards of black hair.

The first thing I noticed about Ethan was his clothes. The white shirt and battered jeans fit him a lot better than the Charlie Brown outfit of yesterday. His short blond hair was styled to a casual Mohawk, his lips curving into a flirtatious smile directed at the girl.

A small sting in my chest made me aware of how much I disliked the sight of the two of them together, but I refused to read too much into this display and stopped next to him.

"Hey," I said to catch his attention and gripped the CD I'd brought for him a little harder.

When Ethan turned his head to me, his smile wavered. He looked as if he was unsure whether I'd just spoken to him or to someone else. It didn't escape me that he didn't say hi. That caused my throat to dry out a little.

"Um, I brought you the CD," I continued, my voice going from steady to hesitant within a couple of heartbeats as I held out the Volbeat album to him.

Now that he couldn't deny I was speaking to him any longer, he turned to me fully, one hand in his pocket, the other wrapped around the strap of his backpack he carried on one shoulder. He still said nothing, and he didn't take the damn CD, either. Instead, his gaze wandered from my head to my toes in a skeptical once-over. Heck, what was wrong with him today? And the worst thing about this was that all his friends were staring at me like I was some kind of alien.

I hated how a feeling of insecurity crept into me at Ethan's considering look. Where was the chatty, fun guy from yesterday? Could he really forget me so easily, or was he just playing stupid? Well, there was one way to find out. Clearing my throat, I straightened my spine. "Listen, I can't meet you at three today, something's come up. So maybe we can postpone the date until a little later? Would five work for you?"

Ethan's eyes widened. Folding his arms over his chest, he actually had the nerve to laugh. "Sweetness, what made you think you and I would be going out together?"

The air froze in my lungs. As a round of chuckles erupted from his friends, I wanted to vaporize like a vampire in the sun. He was nothing but an ass who'd been nice to me yesterday because he needed my *Yes* to join the soccer team. Nothing else. My hand with the CD dropped to my side. I swallowed hard, shock freezing my body, but I refused to let him have the last say. He could dump his crap on someone else.

"Obviously I got it wrong. Sorry, my bad," I snapped, flipping him off as I whirled about and strode away.

From behind, a humored female voice drifted to me—the pretty Thai girl, I supposed. "What was that?" There was also the sound of a soft smack on someone's shoulder, arm, or wherever it was that she hit him. "Are you dating that girl?"

"Ow, you're breaking my heart, Lauren!" Ethan half whined and half laughed. "You're the only one I'm dating tonight. I don't even know who she is." That was the last I heard before I let the voices of the other students around me drown him out.

And to think I'd even tried to paint my nails for him today... Agh.

But deep down it still stung.

Walking straight to science, I found my seat close to the window and slumped down with my arms crossed and chin dipped low. It took all of ten seconds until Sam and Nick made a beeline toward me. Sam sank into the vacant chair at my side, while Frederickson parked himself on the corner of my desk. "Wow, Susan, you're wearing the face of a badger. What has you so wound up?"

"Ethan!" I spat.

"What about him?"

"He's a complete and utter blockhead."

Nick exchanged a wary glance with Sam before he replied, "Are you serious? From what I heard this morning, you and Ethan seemed to have quite a nice time after practice. Hunter mentioned that Ethan said you'd told him he could play."

"Did he lie?" Sam demanded.

"No... I did say that." Sort of. "But when you see Hunter again you can tell him I changed my mind. If he cares about my feelings even a little, he won't let Ethan play my position."

Nick sucked air in through his teeth, scrunching up his face. "Ooh." He lifted his hands, rising from my desk like a fire had broken out. "I'll leave you girls alone, so you can talk this out."

The moment we were to ourselves, Sam lifted her eyebrows, prompting me to clarify. I would have done so, if the bell hadn't cut our plans short. Sam, who sat next to Nick in science, vacated the chair beside me for Trudy Anderson. But as soon as the teacher had come in and started the lesson, I got a text from Sam asking for the full story.

Hiding my cell beneath the desk, I typed in the most important deets about my recent encounter with Ethan and sent the message off. Her reply was a sad smiley face, but another text followed soon. She suggested we skip lunch with the guys in the cafeteria today, get the girls together instead, and go into a huddle out on the campus grounds. This sounded exactly like what I needed. I looked up from my phone and over to her, pressed my lips together, and nodded. In a final text, I asked her not to tell Nick what had happened. The guys didn't need to know everything, though they might find out soon enough. Once they met Ethan, he'd certainly spill the amusing story of how he embarrassed Susan Miller.

With Sam, Lisa, and Simone in most of my classes, the morning went by quickly enough. They were all taken aback as much as I was when they heard what had happened. When lunch break came and we found a place outside in the sun where we ate the sandwiches that Sam had picked up at the cafeteria, I could finally rant in a volume fit for a situation like this. It felt so good to just let it all out and not whisper behind cupped hands anymore.

"He's such a moron! You should have heard him, oh my *God*! 'What made you think you and I would be going out together?'" I reiterated in a dull imitation of his voice, then dropped my forehead to my folded arms on my knees and moaned. "He just used me. Pretended to like me so I'd say he could play."

"Cheer up," Simone said, placing her hand on my shoulder. "We'll get even and make you feel better."

I lifted my head. "How?"

"Simple. First, Lisa will tell Hunter to kick Ethan off the team. And then we go shopping."

"Shopping?" Lisa laughed. "Is that your answer to everything?"

"That's my answer to boy trouble. It'll help Susan get in a better"—she leaned forward in a conspiratorial way—"mood."

And it was the best answer she could have come up with. Buying new books always did to my soul what conditioner did to frizzy hair. There was only one problem. "I can't. I have to drive out to Nipomo with my mom after school to pick up her car."

"Fine, we'll meet you in town when you get back," Simone stated. "It can't take you all day to drive those thirty miles."

"No. We should be home around four. I'll call you." And already, my old smile was back in place.

Chapter 3

THE GOOD THING was that Mom and I made it out to Nipomo and back in record time and I was free to go book shopping, or whatever it was that Simone had in mind, by three forty. The bad thing was that just before I left the house, my father called and said he'd be late this evening. That was going to end in another argument. Mom worked as a nurse at the French Hospital Medical Center in San Luis Obispo. She was on duty tonight, so it was Dad's turn to cook dinner for us and make sure that Gramps took all his pills and the insulin injection.

At seventeen, I was old enough to cook dinner for myself, and Gramps wasn't a helpless, senile old man, either. He could look after himself very well. But since my gran had died of a heart attack two years ago, Mom had become hyper-careful and overly protective of him. Nobody said it out loud, but I believed she blamed my father for my grandmother's death.

That particular day, Dad had begged on his knees for Mom to go with him to a very boring, very late charity banquet his boss had invited him to. She thought if she'd stayed home that day, she might have been able to save her mother.

Honestly, I didn't see how. Grams was sitting at her sewing machine when it happened. She just slumped forward and was dead. It was over within seconds, the doctor had told us. She didn't suffer or even cry out for help. No way would Mom have heard anything, given that we lived next door. Still, that was the time when the fights had begun. And they had never stopped.

Whatever the cause, Mom and Dad would argue again as soon as they were together, but at least it wouldn't happen until tomorrow morning. I'd learned to treasure those rare occasions when only one of them was home. Reading in a silent house was the best thing I could think of. And I planned to do that right after shopping with the girls today.

At ten to four, I met my friends in front of Charlie's Café. We'd agreed on starting the shopping trip with a hazelnut latte deluxe, which Charlie, the middle-aged owner, had recently added to the menu.

We filed in one after the other, me being the last to walk through the door. Just as it slid closed behind me, I heard the first traitorous gasp from Simone. Another followed instantly from Sam and Lisa. Sam was small enough that I could look over her head, but it took Simone, who was as tall as me, stepping aside for me to catch a glimpse of the person who had stunned them into silence.

Ethan sat at the bar.

My heart pounded like a bass drum—not from excitement to see him, but from anger. He turned around, maybe because he'd been waiting for someone and heard us enter, or because my friends' loud gasps drew his attention. Whatever it was, when he saw me, he cracked a goddamn smile.

I gritted my teeth and just followed the others past him. Strangely enough, Ethan seemed to be expecting me to stop by him, so when I didn't, his smile vanished and a confused frown took its place.

"Hey, Susan," he said in a wary voice from behind me.

Now look who remembered my name when his friends weren't with him.

Simone stopped walking and cast me a quick glance full of questions over her shoulder, but I shook my head, so she went to the low, rectangular table in the back. I, on the other hand, turned around and folded my arms over my chest. "What?" I snapped.

He peered at me, tongue-tied, for a couple of seconds. His brows furrowed even more as he slid from the bar stool to stand before me. "Um, I thought we had a date at three?"

"Excuse me?"

At my harsh tone, the guy behind the bar, who Ethan had been talking to when we'd come in, cast a surprised glance at me. He was a pretty boy with dark hair and even darker eyebrows. His name was Ted, and I knew him from my journalism class.

Ignoring Ted, I concentrated on Ethan as he murmured,

"I've been sitting here the past hour, waiting for you to show up, and now you come with your friends and don't even say hi?"

"Whoa, dude, you've got some nerve. Maybe you should've been thinking about that before you dumped all that shit on me." I paused and put on a sugary smile. "Have a good day, Ethan." Spinning on my heel, I stomped off to my friends.

Man, payback felt so good.

By the time I sank into one of the dark rattan chairs and picked up the menu just to have something to hold on to, Ethan had disappeared from the café and the door slowly drifted closed on its own.

"What did he say to you?" Sam hissed, shoving the menu down so it was no longer hiding my face.

"That he was waiting for me."

"He did? That's weird."

I grimaced. "It is, isn't it?"

Ted came over to take our orders and hushed us into silence. Only when we were alone once more did Lisa demand, "So, what are you going to do?"

"Nothing. He's a moron, obviously with multiple personalities, and I don't have to stand for that."

She let out a thoughtful sigh. "I just don't get it. I'm sure I saw Ryan hanging out with him a few times and, even though we were never officially introduced, he seemed like a nice guy to me."

"Whatever problems he has, it shouldn't ruin our shopping, so let's not talk about him anymore," I said. Ted returned then and served each of us a hazelnut latte deluxe. I took my cup and lifted it in a salute to my friends. "He was a short chapter in my book. Very short, indeed." I took a sip, dipping my lip into the hot milk foam, and wondered why Ted was still standing by our table.

When our gazes locked, he said, "Your drink's on Ethan. He paid for it before he left. And he says sorry for whatever shit he supposedly dumped on you."

Choking on my mouthful of latte, I put the cup down before it spilled over my pants. Sam smacked me on the back until I could breathe again.

I wiped the foam off my mouth. "You're kidding me!"

"Nope." With a smirk that made him appear several years older, Ted turned around and went back behind the bar.

Was Ethan really that crazy? How could he forget what he'd said to me this morning? "Serious mental issues," I thought out loud, shaking my head. "Can any one of you make sense of this?"

All three shook their heads. A great help they were.

I moaned. "Here I finally find someone seriously sweet"—someone who could measure up to any fictional character I'd ever been in love with—"and he turns out to be just a weirdo."

Leaning back in her chair and lacing her fingers over her stomach, Sam chewed on her bottom lip. "What if it was all just a big misunderstanding? Maybe he's on some anti-amnesia meds and simply forgot to take his pills this morning."

I let out a throaty laugh. "Watched some Sci-Fi with Tony last night, did you?"

"Why?" She looked at me innocently. "Things happen."

"In what universe?"

"Fine, don't believe it." She stuck her tongue out at me. "But I think, for the latte alone, he deserves a second chance."

"You can't be serious." I grabbed a sugar pack from the glass bowl in the middle of the table and ripped it open. Adding the sugar to my latte, I stirred until it sank into the foam. "He totally embarrassed me this morning. How does that deserve a second chance?"

Sam raised her eyebrows, grinning. "Tony was a complete douche when I met him. Now we're happy together. Just saying."

Fair enough, she had a point. And the side I got to know of Ethan yesterday made me want to spend more time with him. It was as if we were on the same wavelength. Maybe there did exist some weird explanation for his behavior this morning. There were certainly no anti-amnesia pills involved, though. I'd rather believe Ethan was abducted by aliens. Finding out the truth tempted me... Only, was it really worth the effort?

I doubted it, yet I wanted to hear my friends' opinions. In eleventh grade, you didn't make such serious decisions all by yourself. "All right. Let's vote. What should I do?"

Simone said, "Forget him."

Lisa said, "Forget him."

Sam said, "Talk to him."

"That's two against one." I shrugged. "Sorry, Sam, you're out." And that was that. I wasn't going to talk to Ethan ever again. With that decision made, I could finally enjoy my hazelnut latte deluxe, which I didn't even have to pay for. Win-

win.

The shopping afterward was pure delight. I found a dozen books to add to my TBR stack, a pair of skintight blue jeans, a picture frame—which I had no idea how to fill but needed to have because of the beautiful seashells on it—and some accessories for my hair. Satisfied, exhausted, and happy, I sank against the door when I got home and reveled in the silence in the house.

My new books found a place on the giant shelf my dad had built for me some years ago and which reached from wall to wall on one side of my room. The bags with the other stuff I'd bought today, I dropped on my desk. There was no time to put them away. Quiet nights were as holy to me as Christmas Eve. I didn't intend to waste even one minute of it. Armed with a book, I settled on my bed in the corner next to the window and stuck my feet under the crochet blanket that my grams had made for my eighth birthday. Bambi was on that quilt. It was my most valued treasure.

Before I began to read, I leaned as far out of my bed as I could without falling. My arm was just long enough to reach the top drawer of my desk where I kept a pack of liquor-filled chocolate pralines. Placing them on the mattress next to me, I shoved a piece into my mouth. The pralines would keep my hunger in check, because no way was I going to stop reading for dinner alone.

Around nine, Dad came home and knocked on my door to say hi. I was lucky he didn't make it past the threshold or kiss me good night, because from all the pralines I'd consumed, my liquor breath might have gotten me into trouble.

I waved from the bed and when he closed the door again, I finished this volume in my now-favorite series. As I turned off the light a couple of hours later, I hoped to dream of the Scottish Highlands.

Instead, I dreamed I was swimming in a pot of caffè latte while Ethan sat on the edge of the pot and repeatedly shouted down at me, "You can't even play soccer right now! What made you think that you and I would be going out together?"

Since my paddling didn't seem to be getting me out of the pot, I stopped at some point and drank up the five thousand liters of coffee instead. Afterward, I walked up to Ethan and spit it all at his face. "That's for playing my position!" I yelled at him.

Luckily, I woke up after that. To say I wasn't done with Ethan yet was a vast understatement. The guy seemed stuck in my mind like a toothpick in a cheese cube. So how could I get him out of there?

Sitting at the kitchen table and shoving a spoonful of scrambled eggs into my mouth, I wondered if it was better to evade soccer practice for a while. At least until my knee was fine and Ethan would have to clear the field for me again. Not seeing him seemed like the easiest way to forget about him. I toasted myself with my glass of orange juice on that decision and washed the eggs down with a sip, then I got ready for school.

A few minutes before the bell rang, I slipped into the building and headed straight for my first class. Certain that Sam would be the first to grill me this morning on the subject of

Ethan and how I felt about him today, I was surprised to run into Lisa in the hallway.

"Susan, wait," she hissed with an urgent look. "I have to tell you something." Only problem—she was talking to a teacher and had to finish that little chat first. Patiently, I waited at the corner of the hallway, off to the side, for a couple of minutes, until a familiar voice carried to me—and caused the hair at the back of my neck to stand on end.

I cast a look over my shoulder. In front of the restrooms, Hunter and Ethan were engaged in a chat. It looked like one had just come out and one was about to walk into the restrooms, but both had too much to tell the other to move on.

Instantly, I shielded my face with one hand and lowered my head. Right, as if Hunter wouldn't recognize me the second he looked over. And probably Ethan, too. Rolling my eyes at myself, I ducked around the corner fast, so they wouldn't see me, but their voices kept drifting through the corridor.

So much for not going to soccer practice to avoid Ethan. I'd have to skip school, too! Seeing him today totally ruined my intention of getting the blockhead out of my mind. And heck, yesterday's free hazelnut latte still had my emotions in a knot. Maybe we needed to talk it out once and for all—just so I could stop thinking about him and hopefully sleep better.

But with my nerves in this state, I could hardly walk over and confront him. *Gah*! What misery, and before first period even started. Frustrated, I banged my head against the wall behind me, pulling at my hair.

Lisa, who was standing with her side to me, must have

caught my angst. She shot me a puzzled look, which I returned with a nod in Ethan's direction. She bit her lip, so obviously wanting to tell me something, but the stout woman wasn't done talking to her yet. I had no idea which subject Lisa had with her, but they seemed on very close terms. Man, what would I give to spring my friend from her teacher's clutches and consult her about my trouble with Ethan.

Since that obviously wasn't going to happen anytime soon, I steeled my nerves and stepped around the corner, facing the guys in front of the restrooms. My breakfast rolled around in my stomach, but I ignored that queasy feeling and walked straight up to Hunter and Ethan, gaining speed and courage as I went.

Ethan saw me first. Though he kept talking to Ryan, his eyes focused on me alone. Only when I stopped a couple of feet before him and stared at him did he cut off mid-sentence.

"Okay, explain," I snapped.

Surprised, Hunter turned to me, too, but I ignored him.

"Explain what exactly?" There was that same dismissive edge in Ethan's voice as yesterday. As he cocked his head then, a taunting grin replaced his frown. "Sweetness, are you stalking me?"

That caught me off guard and I coughed an outraged laugh. "Oh my *God*! What's wrong with you?"

"Excuse me? You're the one who keeps chatting me up."

Hunter chuckled. "Susan..." I wouldn't have paid him any attention, if he hadn't put an arm around my shoulders, too. "Susan..." he said again and waited until I tilted my head in his direction.

Ryan had all my respect as team captain and I valued him as a really good friend, but right now I wanted to wipe that smirk right off his face. "What?" I snarled.

He put his other hand on my shoulder and turned me to face Ethan again. "Meet Chris."

"Chris who?"

"Donovan," Ethan said.

"Ah right." I folded my arms over my chest, adopting a cynical look. "And you're Ethan's alter ego, or what?"

The guy who looked like Ethan smirked at me. "Brother."

"Brother..." My face fell.

Ryan leaned closer and whispered into my ear, "Twins."

"Twins." A second passed and the information sank in like a hot dog in a bun. "*Twins*?" I pivoted to Ryan, banging my head against his chest. If only I could knock myself out this way.

The duplicate of the nice guy I met Monday afternoon started to shake with laughter. "So you met Ethan? Hell, now I get it."

I didn't care if anything made sense to him. He was a jerk for how he'd talked to me yesterday, and I wanted to be as far away from him as I could. And, holy guacamole, I had to find Ethan and sort out this terrible misunderstanding. After all, I still had the live album of Volbeat in my backpack.

"See you later," I growled at Hunter and said nothing at all to Chris, but turned and trudged off, mentally banging my head on a brick wall for not realizing what was going on. Moments later, though, it hit me that I might not find Ethan or—worse—I might mistake Chris for him again.

To avoid another disaster, I stopped in my tracks, spun around, and walked back to the guys. Hunter was laughing, but Chris still had his eyes on me. I must have made quite the impression. Not a very good one, I was sure.

As I stood in front of him once more—and boy, the brothers did look incredibly alike—I fished a pen from my schoolbag and reached for Chris's arm. Explaining myself wasn't going to help me much, I supposed, so without a word, I shoved the sleeve of his white sweatshirt up to his elbow and pulled his forearm to me. Then I scribbled my number on him.

It was funny how he let me write on his skin and didn't even budge. Maybe my behavior startled him into silence. Good. I suppressed a sneer as I said, "Tell Ethan to call me." I was about to walk off again when I remembered the CD and fetched that from my backpack, too. I pushed it at his chest. "Give him that and tell him thanks for the latte."

Chris blinked twice. His eyes were the same cornflower-blue as Ethan's. Beautiful and captivating. He let a smirk loose that sped up my pulse. "Pleeease," he drawled.

"Pleeease," I repeated, faking my sweetest smile. As I turned and walked away, I banged straight into Lisa. My schoolbag slipped from my shoulder and landed on the floor.

"Am I too late?" Lisa whispered as I bent to pick up my backpack.

I made no effort to keep my voice low like hers. "For what?"

"To tell you that this isn't Ethan and that I figured it all out."

I straightened and cast a crotchety look over my shoulder at the guys. Chris's scrutinizing gaze bored into me like a lance. "Yep. Too late."

Chapter 4

IT TOOK UNTIL five o'clock this evening for Ethan to finally call me. I knew it could only be him when an unknown caller ID flashed on my phone, and I picked up with a galloping heart. "Hello?"

"Hey, sweetness," the guy at the other end said, and with a shudder slithering down my spine I knew I had been wrong. This was not Ethan. He wouldn't call me *sweetness* in that wicked drawl.

I moaned, disappointed and twice as frustrated. "Why are you calling me, Chris?"

"Because you gave me your number," he teased

"I didn't give it to *you*."

"No? The handwriting on my forearm objects."

I took off my glasses and rubbed between my eyes, where a hard throbbing had started two seconds ago. "Fine. I didn't give it to you to *call* me. Where's your brother?"

"Last time I checked, he was in his room."

"Get him on the phone, please, will you?"

"Hmm. That means I have to get up and walk over there. I don't think I'm in the mood to do that just now." Was he actually chuckling?

"Then why did you call me?" There was only a heartbeat between that and me banging my head on the keyboard of my computer where I was doing homework.

Chris laughed, and he sounded amazingly sweet when he did. Just like Ethan had when we'd first met. "I told you, because you gave me your number," he explained.

"Not that again," I whined.

"Fine." He paused. "Then maybe to ask you to go out with me?" By the sound of it, a smirk came with that question.

"What?" This was so unexpected that I jerked around in my swivel chair and slammed my knee on the desk. Ow, crap, that hurt. Thank God it was my good knee. The pain came and faded quickly. "You must be kidding me."

"Nope. Why would I?" Was he teasing me again?

"Because I want to talk to your brother and not you, to begin with. And aren't you supposed to be dating Lara?"

He hummed into my ear. "Who's Lara?"

"Asian supermodel? Long black hair?" I pointed out with an annoyed snarl.

"Oh, you mean Lauren? Well, I did date her yesterday. And I might again sometime. But there's always a free spot in my calendar to squeeze you in, sweetness."

"Are you actually mental?"

"I hope not," he answered with the same seriousness that I had put in my voice. "Why? Are you not a safe girl to date?"

"I'm the *perfect* girl to date, just not for you, dumbass!"

"Aw, don't say that, little Sue. You don't know me yet."

"And God willing, I never will. Please, go get Ethan now and stop wasting my time."

Chris laughed again. It was so loud I had to pull the phone away from my ear. "All right, you win. But tell you what," he said. "If it doesn't work out between you and Ethan, which I know it won't, you let me take you on a date. Deal?"

There was only one answer to give. "When hell freezes over."

His voice turned serious—too much so for the next line to pass as a casual remark. "That happens more often than you think, sweetness."

An odd chill started at the back of my neck and spread way down into my limbs. The strangest thing was, the chill didn't feel at all uncomfortable.

I heard some rustling at the other end of the line, a knock, and the faint sound of a door being opened. "Call for you," Chris said, but from a distance now. More rustling and a smack followed.

"Hello?" Ethan said moments later. I wondered if Chris had tossed him the phone.

"By the way, she said thanks for the latte!" I could hear Chris's last comment, followed by his chuckle and a door slamming shut.

"Hi, Ethan. It's me. Susan." I felt so awkward I could burn a hole in my chair from embarrassment.

"Hey, Susan," he said, with surprise ringing all the way from his house to mine. A moment of silence passed. Then a deep breath—my breath—and finally a laugh from the other end. "You're welcome."

I frowned at the stack of books on my desk. "Welcome for what?"

"For the latte. I guess it's what you ordered at Charlie's yesterday, right?"

"Um, well. Yeah." Charlie's... Did I have to apologize now? But how could I have known they were twins? They were the ones who had messed around with me. Heck, Ethan should have figured all that out way before me—before I made a complete idiot of myself. "It's not my fault that you have a twin, Charlie Brown," I blurted out and rose from my chair. Walking to the window, I gazed at the street below.

"Ah, so it's mine?" Ethan laughed at me, the same sweet sound I'd heard from his brother a minute ago. "I don't see how exactly I could have prevented *that* from happening."

"You could have tried in an embryonic stage."

"And kick my brother out of my mom's womb? Yeah, I would have liked that."

"You could have told me," I said a little calmer now, but more sulkily, and swirled around, facing my room instead of the sun outside.

"There was no reason to. It usually doesn't come up as the first thing I say when talking to a cute girl."

He thought I was cute? I squeezed my eyes shut and suppressed a silly little squeal. My hand curled so tightly around the phone, I was surprised it didn't crack.

"Susan? Are you there?"

"Um, yeah. Yeah, of course." Dammit, he'd heard the smile in my voice. It made him chuckle.

"Hey, I was thinking..." he drawled, and all I heard was: *Go out with me, go out with me!* "Maybe you want to hang out a little. Today. You know, to make good for standing me up yesterday." There was a teasing note in his voice.

When I said nothing—because, frankly, I was too giddy from his request—he continued, "I can come over to your place, if you'd like that. Or you can come over to mine."

It was five o'clock, my mom was home, and my dad would be here in another ten minutes. They hadn't had a chance to finish the fight that started yesterday with Dad's call about coming home late, so that would be flashing over our house like a sign of doom for the rest of the evening. I didn't want Ethan to get here and find himself in the middle of my daily horror show.

"I think I'll come to yours. My folks are a little busy tonight." I hurried across the room, tripped over my own feet in my excitement, which was spreading throughout my entire body, and fell against the door. My cell dropped to the floor with a clang. Crap!

Picking up the phone and wildly cursing at myself in a voiceless stream of f-words, I heard Ethan's laugh. "Susan? Did you just hurt yourself?"

Rubbing my head, I moaned, "Only a little." Maybe I'd

pop a chill pill before I left. Stumbling around his house this way was not an option for making up for our missed first date. "Give me your address, and I'll be there in ten."

I jotted down his addy in the back of *Harry Potter and the Prisoner of Azkaban*, which was the first thing I grabbed in my current state of mega-nervousness. After I hung up, I went downstairs to ask my mom for her car.

"Where are you going?"

"To Ethan's."

"Be home by seven." She lifted her finger in my face with the keys dangling from her hand. "And no forgetting about it again!" She only said that because of my excited flush.

"Promise." I crossed my heart and headed out with one last check of myself in the mirror. My hair was in a perfect ponytail, skin a healthy pink—too pink—no leftovers from lunch between my teeth, and there were no stains of any sort on my light green tee. *Ethan, here I come!*

Taking a deep breath, I sank behind the wheel of my mom's car and stalled the engine twice before I got my nervous foot to dose the gas just right to drive off. Now I knew why the girls all had anxiety attacks before their first dates. Not that this was really a date, it was merely *hanging out with Ethan*. Alone. At his place. A snicker escaped me, which didn't matter because no one was there to call me a nutcase. Heck, I was so going to title this a date later when I called Sam and told her everything about it.

Ethan's house, though small and squeezed in between equally sized bungalows, was easy enough to find. They didn't have an exclusive drive or a garage to park their cars, but from where I stood, the white bungalow with the dark brown roof, windows, and door looked cozy and inviting. And my CD was playing somewhere in that house. A smirk slipped to my lips. I rang the doorbell and waited while the first line of *Ode to Joy* played out, drowning out my music.

When the door opened, I found myself face to face with a woman who looked set to run me over like a bus. She pushed her arms through the sleeves of a beige trench coat, slipped into a pair of black pumps, flicked her amber hair over her shoulder, gave me a smile, and slid the strap of her purse up her arm, all at the same time.

"Hello, sweetie, what can I do for you?"

Uh, did I look like a Girl Scout trying to sell cookies? I swallowed, feeling the nervous pit in my stomach again. "I'm Susan. Is Ethan home?" Immediately, I wanted to slap myself for that question. He was listening to my music and he'd told me to come over not fifteen minutes ago, so of course he was home. But honestly, what else was I to say?

"Yes, he's in his room." She shouted over her shoulder, "Ethan!" Then she grabbed a scarf that was way overdoing her attire considering there was just a light breeze today, but it complemented her outfit, which had me thinking she was going to an important meeting. She left me standing in the entrance, excusing herself. Obviously, she was running late.

The door slammed shut behind me, but there was no sign of Ethan. In fact, the music was all that was to be heard for the next twenty seconds. I felt a little stupid being left alone in this house and considered walking outside to ring the bell once more. Eventually, I shook my head and tracked the sound down the hallway to the back of the house.

There were two doors next to each other at this part of the bungalow. One of them must lead to Chris's room. A shudder skittered down my spine at the memory of our chat on the phone. Luckily, it wasn't hard to tell from which room the music was coming, so I knocked on that door and when no one answered, I hesitantly entered. No wonder Ethan didn't hear me. The loud music blasted away my every thought as soon as I opened the door.

Sprawled in a comfy chair close to the wide, square window that must be overlooking their garden, Ethan was reading what looked like a textbook for Spanish class, because there was a smiling boy wearing a sombrero and shouting *HOLA!* in a speech balloon on it. Immediately, drool formed in the corner of my mouth because, oh my freaking Jesus, he was wearing sweats. *Only* sweats—totally with nothing on top and no shoes or socks either. He knew I would be coming, so was he doing this on purpose to set my heart in a flutter for a greeting? If so, he'd totally succeeded.

Ethan didn't hear my hoarse "hi," nor did he notice me standing in his room. I had to reopen and slam the door to get his attention, but when he looked up, his lips formed a smile. Not instantly. It took him a couple of seconds to get rid of that frown, so I guessed the textbook was really captivating and I'd just ripped him out of some serious studying for finals or something.

Ethan didn't say anything. It wouldn't make much of a difference anyway with the volume turned up like he was trying to give a bunch of aliens a signal. He rose from his chair, put his textbook away, and lowered the volume of the music, his eyes glued on me all that time.

When the room was quiet enough for us to hear our own voices, I said rather fast because of my nerves as I gushed over his toned body, "Um, hi. Sorry for breaking into your room...sort of." I shrugged. "Your mom let me in."

Ethan came toward me slowly, I'd like to add, like some sort of tiger on a prowl. He still said nothing, so I blabbered on, and not only because it gave me something to do other than staring at his oh-so-naked chest where a set of two silver chains glinted. "She called you but with that noise fending off the cats and dogs of the neighborhood, I get it that you didn't hear—"

Ethan placed his hand over my mouth, cutting me off mid-sentence. He put his index finger in front of his lips in a sexy *shh* gesture. The urge to plant a kiss on his palm took hold, but I managed to resist. What would that have made me look like? A horny dork?

His blue eyes raked over me for a moment, and all I could do was swallow hard. What was his plan? Maybe his brother was napping next door and he didn't want to wake him.

Yeah, sure, with the music blasting the roof away just a second ago.

My ragged breath was dampening the back of his hand as I tried to keep from swooning by breathing deeply through my nose.

Ethan took his hand away from my lips. "I didn't expect you to jump at my offer so fast...especially after you turned me down so mercilessly on the phone."

What in the world— My brows furrowed to a baffled V, then it dawned on me and I groaned. "Nooo. Chris?"

"The very same." His smug grin pricked my nerves like little needles.

"Why are you listening to my CD?"

"I could tell you, but you might not like the answer."

I dared him to explain with my lifted eyebrows.

Chris leaned a little closer and said softly in my ear, "Because you gave it to me."

The guy was driving me up a wall. I wanted to knock myself unconscious with a hammer, but maybe that was a bad idea, considering I stood in the door of Don Juan's room. Not only equipped with the body of the infamous seducer, Chris clearly had the ego to match.

"That, as well as my number," I growled, keeping a lid on my anger, "you should have passed on to Ethan. Why didn't you?"

He twirled a swath of my hair around his finger, almost stroking my cheek with the move. "I wanted to learn what taste you have in music, so I know what to put on when we make out on my bed."

I smacked his hand away. "In case you haven't figured it out all by yourself, let me make it clear now: You have a screw loose. More importantly, it's considered rude to hit on someone who actually came to see your brother."

"Why? You think he'll be mad?" His mouth curved up. "You think he'll date you?"

Well, he invited me over and called whatever we missed yesterday a date. So, yes, I was under the impression, which is why I came over today. What I said out loud, though, was, "Why, don't you?"

Chris stroked his chin with his thumb and index finger. "In fact, I think I'll just watch for a while and let myself be entertained by how things go from here." He winked at me, grabbed my shoulders, and spun me to face the door. As he leaned around from behind to open it, I caught a whiff of mint that must have been his breath way close to my face. Steering me out into the hallway and to the left, he opened the other door and gently pushed me into the room.

The exact copy of the guy behind me, only dressed in a washed-out, green t-shirt and actual jeans, sat on the bed in the corner playing some video games. When he looked up and saw me, his mouth stretched into an immediate smile.

"You've got a visitor," Chris taunted and moved me farther into the room. He let go and left without another word, but erupted into fits of laughter on the way out.

I shut the door behind him and dropped against it, releasing a long exhale and making a mental note to never again enter the room on the left in this hallway.

"Hey there, you okay?" Ethan asked and got off his bed, walking toward me with a puzzled frown.

"Mm-hmm." I nodded but still felt too shaky to leave my safe spot by the door. Now I couldn't hang out with Ethan ever again without imagining that exact same six-pack on him that Chris had displayed. Crap.

"You look a little out of breath."

"I walked into the wrong room."

"Why?"

"Why do you think?" I folded my arms over my chest and scowled, blaming him for misleading me. "He's playing my music. Why did you give him the Volbeat album?"

Ethan laughed at me as he parked his butt against the corner of his desk. "I didn't. You did."

Jeez, could these guys stop rubbing it in already? "But only so he'd give it to you."

"Well, he refused to. At least he's playing it loud enough that I can listen, too."

As if that was his cue, Chris turned up the music in his room again. We could hear it at a low volume through the wall. "See?" Ethan flashed a brilliant half-smile that I just so happened to fall in love with that minute.

"So, um, what do you want to do?" I asked, to take my mind of the encounter with Chris, and tucked my fingers in my tight pockets with a shrug. He clearly hadn't put much thought into that part of me being here when he'd invited me over. His face was a blank wall. He pursed his lips thoughtfully to one side, but not so much as a single idea came out.

Straining my neck, I glanced over his shoulder at the widescreen TV a little away from the foot end of his bed. "What were you playing?"

"*FIFA*. You know what that is?"

"Are you kidding me? I play it all the time with Nick. Care for a match?"

Ethan's eyes started to glow. "Sure. Make yourself comfortable. I'll get you something to drink and"—he paused and studied me like I was a whole different race—"popcorn?"

When I looked at him in those baggy pants and the washed out t-shirt, I was thinking *Peanuts*, but I didn't say that out loud. "Popcorn would be great."

While he was gone, I settled on his bed, took the controller, and continued the game he'd started. He came back with a bottle of mineral water, soda, and a bowl of warm, buttered popcorn. Yum. I made room for him to join me on his bed and he picked up a second controller, placing the bowl between us.

"Don't think just because I'm a girl you stand a chance at winning," I bantered and picked my team—the Netherlands.

Ethan picked the Ukraine. "I'd never dare to think that." He shoved me with his elbow and chuckled.

We played for a while. It was one of the funniest afternoons I'd had in a long time. And I hadn't exaggerated when I told him I was good at this game. Ethan was going down in flames! Only, he was a sore loser and tried to cheat by reaching for my controller.

"Hey, stop that, you!" I tossed a single kernel of popcorn at his face.

Charlie Brown took that as a challenge, grabbed a handful from the bowl, and called out, "Eat that, Miller!"

Lips pressed shut, I tried to wiggle away, but he didn't let me. His controller dropped to the floor, mine slid between the bed and the wall, and the bowl went flying with popcorn snowing down on us. I laughed so hard that I opened my mouth and was immediately fed popcorn.

"Go away!" I shouted, chewing what he managed to shove into my mouth.

"Only when you admit that I'm the winner."

"Some loser you are! I won this game fair and"—I grinned—"easy. You totally suck!" That was a mistake, though. Ethan pursed his lips. He wagged his brows once, and I knew whatever was to come wasn't going to be good. His fingers found my sensitive sides and he started tickling me until I was choking from laughter and coughing out popcorn crumbs.

I shoved hard at his chest, but my *hard* was *cotton soft* for him, because he didn't budge an inch.

"Surrender!" he demanded, smirking down as he lay half on top of me, pinning my wrists on the mattress now.

"Never!" I screamed at his face, only it didn't come out as a scream at all. It was a hoarse whisper, induced by the hot tingle his nearness caused inside me. We both stilled. His face was close enough that our noses would have rubbed against each other at the slightest movement. His eyes were as wide as mine, but they switched down to my mouth the next instant. I didn't know why, but this made me lick my lips. And he did the same.

My heart jumped from a light jog into race mode. Oh my freaking goodness, this was it. Ethan was going to give me my first kiss. How in the world was that happening on our first date? And it wasn't really a date anyway, but just us playing some stupid Wii.

All of a sudden, Chris's words pressed back into my mind. *I wanted to learn what taste you have in music, so I know what to put on when we make out on my bed.* I was crazy to think about that right now, but the memory of his smirk when he'd said it wouldn't go away.

And here I was, about to make out with his brother. A mocking *na na na na na na* chanted though my head—and Chris deserved it for being so overly bold and arrogant. Swallowing, I focused back on Ethan.

The moment for my first kiss couldn't be more perfect, though I wished Ethan wouldn't lie on top of me like this, because now he would notice each of my hitched breaths and find out exactly how nervous I was. He would know in an instant that I hadn't been kissed ever before, and somehow that made me freak out even more. Looking at this perfect copy of a god above me, all I could think of was how many girls he must have kissed already in his life. Nice girls, good kissers, no wallflowers like me. What if I sucked at kissing?

Ethan's gaze moved back to my eyes. His breathing came a little strained as well now and the tiniest crease formed between his brows. He hesitated.

I didn't know much about kissing in reality, but I did know that one should look excited, smitten, or even relaxed when about to do it—not wary. "I'm sor—" he began, but he never got to finish the sentence, because there was a sharp knock on the door and it opened at the same time.

"Hey, E.T.," Chris said in a casual voice as he walked into

the room. "I'm going to order pizza—" That's where he stopped not only speaking but walking too, and gaped at us with his chin smacking against his chest. "You're shitting me."

Hello? Could you find anything more awkward to say?

With a cough, Ethan sat up, letting go of my wrists, and ran nervous hands through his hair. I scrambled up, too.

For some reason, Chris couldn't stop staring at us like he'd just caught his brother making out with a monkey. What the hell was his problem? A mere hour ago, he was the one predicting he'd have me next on his list.

Since he'd successfully ruined this perfect moment, could he please get out now? But then I remembered Ethan's reluctance and wondered what his brother really had interrupted.

"I'm sorry, I didn't know you were still here," Chris told me in a shaken voice, something that made absolutely no sense to me—especially since it was so far away from the arrogant, confident voice he'd had when I was in his room. Finally turning on the spot, he walked out.

Ethan stumbled to his feet and shouted after him, "Pizza sounds good." He turned to me and freaking *forced* a smile. "Want to eat with us?"

Is that what happens when a kiss goes wrong? Everyone behaves weird afterward? "Um..." I glanced at my watch and, with a jolt, shot off his bed. It was six minutes to seven. "Dang!"

"What's up?"

"I have to go."

Ethan followed me out of his room to the front door. He sounded troubled when he said, "Look, if it's because of what—"

"No, it's not," I assured him quickly, trying to save us both from an embarrassing situation. However, part of me wondered if he actually might kiss me if I stayed longer. "Mom needs the car and I've got about three minutes to make it back home."

"Oh." An easy smile slipped to his lips and his cheeks turned a soft pink.

Somehow I had the feeling I should be the one blushing after what had happened in his room, but I was too stressed out right now, so I blurted, "Hey, it was nice. We should totally do that again." Playing Wii, of course, not fooling around on his bed with no real outcome. Crap, I wanted to slap my forehead for that thought. "I mean—I—"

Chris leaned around the corner from a different room, maybe the kitchen, with a skeptical expression—one I didn't appreciate. Could he just keep his nose out of this, please? "Ah, heck, I guess I'll see you," I said to Ethan and pulled the door open, but I didn't get a chance to leave. He grabbed my wrist and held me back, swinging me around to face him once more.

"It was nice, Susan. Come over again tomorrow?" His smile was unsure. "Or let's go have that soda we talked about."

After a halfhearted sigh, I nodded. "Okay. Call me after school." I smiled back at him and pulled my hand out of his. Remembering who had actually called me today, I nailed Chris with a scowl down the hallway. "Give him my number, dickhead!"

Chris, who was still staring at his brother like he'd lost his marbles, nodded, and I walked out the door.

Chapter 5

ON THURSDAY MORNING, I repeated to Lisa and Simone all the details about my visit to Ethan's, which I'd already told Sam on the phone last night—minus the encounter with Chris. That was just too embarrassing to mention. My friends squeezed my hands and squealed like little guinea pigs, full of hope that there might be something budding between Ethan and me. Considering the fluffy feeling in my stomach when I chased that thought, I couldn't even blame them for their outburst of excitement. If only they'd be a little more subtle about it. Half the crowd in the hallway was giving us sidelong glances.

It was a good thing their guys came along and pulled the girls away so I could head on to science. Only, I wasn't walking alone for long. As I rounded the corner, someone casually draped his arm around my shoulders and said, "Hey, Sue."

Looking up, I found a set of flashing, blue eyes trained on

me. My smile was inevitable, but the next instant I stiffened in wariness. *Careful, Susan*, I told myself. So with a distrustful frown, I asked, "And you are…"

"Chris." He rolled his eyes as if tired of me not being able to tell him and his brother apart. Heck, how could I? It was like trying to tell one grain of sugar from the next. Impossible—until one of them opened his mouth, I thought grimly.

"What do you want, Chris?" I snapped, not bothering to hide my disappointment about walking through the hallway with the wrong guy by my side. And to make my point clear, I picked his hand up with two fingers and removed his arm from my shoulders.

Instantly, Chris slid in front of me, blocking my way. He leaned against the metal door of a locker and folded his arms. Sporting a black leather jacket and ragged jeans, he didn't look like a *Peanuts* character one bit, so maybe that was the way to tell them apart.

"I'm curious," he said with a crooked smile that rendered me speechless for a second.

Uh-oh. One look at his face, and I knew he was trouble. I got that bad feeling deep down in my gut, almost like when you're facing a Rottweiler and you know it's going to bite you at your next move. Maybe it was just his black leather jacket producing that visual, but most of it probably had to do with his wicked invitation to make out on his bed.

He tilted his head, locking gazes with me. "Did you and Ethan kiss yesterday?"

"Keep your drool in, Spike," I managed to say after I

figured out how to use my vocal cords again. "What happens between your brother and me isn't any of your business."

Chris only laughed at that. "I knew it. He didn't have the guts."

What the hell was that supposed to mean? The longer I stared at Chris's face, the more he got on my nerves. Or maybe the little chills did, the ones he ignited with his look. Anyway, I decided not to question that last comment but pushed past him, knocking against his shoulder with mine.

"Have a nice day, little Sue," he cooed after me, and I was once again tempted to flip him off over my shoulder. Ah, actually, why not? My middle finger was the last thing he saw of me before I rounded the corner.

Unfortunately, my history teacher, Miss Hayes, saw it too, and she didn't hesitate to pull me aside and tell me I had detention.

Punished because of that moron, Chris Donovan? I was steaming with fury as I slipped into science class, my face hot and red also because I was terribly embarrassed by the prospect of having to sit through an extra hour after school for the first time in my life.

I didn't tell Nick or Sam about it, but I was still angry when first period was over. Outside class, I hooked my arm through Sam's and walked down the hallway with her, trying to shake off Nick for a moment. "Ethan's brother is a dick," I snarled.

"Chris? Why?" Sam asked.

"Because he thinks Ethan doesn't have the guts to kiss me."

And because he got me in freaking detention, for Christ's sake!

Sam's messy, layered hair swung around her chin as she cut a glance at me. "How do you know?"

"He waylaid me before class and said some crap about yesterday. About when he caught Ethan and me on his bed."

"And you think he's right—about not having the guts, I mean?"

I let my arm slip out from hers when we had to part for our next classes. "I don't know. But I hope not, because I really, *really* want Ethan to be my first kiss. He's cute," I whined, "and super sexy, and he makes me laugh." Hopefully, he'd stick to his promise and meet up with me again after school today. Well, after school *and* detention.

With drooping shoulders and a growl erupting from my throat, I went to second period, which was French with Miss Lewis. Oh joy. I chewed on my nails twice as hard in her class this morning.

No more incidents occurred before lunch, which gave me some time to cool off and accept my doom. It wasn't so bad after all, was it? I'd probably meet Alex Winter there. He was in detention all the time for either forgetting his homework or talking in class. At least that's what I'd heard about him.

The girls and I headed into the cafeteria together. A line had already formed in front of the food counter, and it would take us ages to get there. Luckily, Nick, Tony, and Ryan stood quite a bit ahead in the line. They called to us, offering to take our food on their trays, so we didn't have to line up at all.

"Pizza and kiwi for you?" Nick asked me, reciting my

usual.

"Yeah, but grab an extra kiwi, please," I told him, following my friends to the long table by the window that was known by all as the soccer table. Hoping Ethan would join us, since he'd temporarily taken my place on the soccer team, I searched the room for him and found him sitting with a bunch of seniors, two rows away from the science club table. On the way to my seat, I had to pass him. It was nice how he cracked a smile when he saw me. He also reached for my hand and stopped me.

"Meet at Charlie's today?" he asked and winked.

Yeah, I have to admit, I kind of melted a little right on the spot. The sigh that came out of my throat was unintentional, but it couldn't be taken back. "Five okay?"

"Want me to pick you up?"

A million thoughts shot through my head at once, all of them connected with my parents having another argument and Ethan walking into the middle of it. No way! "Um, why don't we just meet there? I need to get a few things from town anyway."

"Cool. See you then. And please, Susan..." At his dragging out my name, I swooned a little more. "Don't stand me up again."

Our short conversation earned him some curious looks from his friends, but none of them said a word. At least not in front of me.

"I won't," I said with a smile and headed off to my friends.

In my usual place, Nick had already put down a plate with two slices of Hawaiian pizza—ham and pineapple, my usual toppings. "What's the extra kiwi for?" he asked me as he tossed both fruits, one at a time, across the table.

Flames of shame licked at my face. Lowering my head, I mumbled, "It's for later."

"What's later?"

Since I couldn't just ignore his question, I said with some hesitation and my voice as low as possible, "I have detention."

"You *what*?"

I swear all the kids at the table turned their heads and their disbelieving gazes on me.

"Very subtle, guys," I muttered, aware of other heads now turning in our direction as well. Grabbing the fork on my plate, I scattered the heap of pineapple pieces on my pizza, put the fork down and took a bite. "Miss Hayes caught me saluting someone with my middle finger this morning, so she put me in detention. It's no big deal." The food in my mouth muffled my voice. "Alex is kept after school every other day."

Alex Winter laughed at me. "But I'm not flipping people off in the hallway."

"Yeah, and that's totally not like you," Lisa said. "What happened?"

I swallowed and sipped from my bottle of Sprite. "Some dick got on my nerves. Never mind."

"Ooh, language, Miller," Tony said and chuckled as he bumped his shoulder against mine. "All you need now is a tacky tattoo in a striking place and you'll have a rep as the school's new bad girl."

Everybody burst out laughing at that visual. Only Ryan

kept it low with a chuckle and a teasing look at me, as though he might have an idea about just who the mentioned dick was. I neither denied nor agreed to his suspicion but kept munching my pizza. Once done, I peeled and cut one of the kiwis into slices. The other one I slipped into my backpack.

Simone and Lisa pestered me about my punishment in PE until I told them how it was Ethan's stupid brother who got me into trouble. Loyal friends they were…they giggled their heads off again.

My final class of the day was journalism. Lisa was in it with me. We sat down in our front-row seats and watched the rest of the students filing into the room. Ted came in last. He said "hi" when he passed and took the seat behind me.

"Hey," I replied, turning around, and tilted back with my chair, leaning one arm on his desk. "Are you working at Charlie's today?"

"Yep, all week through Friday."

"Cool. Ethan and I are swinging by this afternoon."

"What?" He gave me a mocking smile. "You and Ethan are showing up *together* this time?"

"Ah, shut up, you." I stuck out my tongue at him and faced front again just as the teacher walked into the room.

The lesson went by fast enough and while most of my friends went home after seventh period, I trudged through the hallway back to the room in which Mr. Ellenburgh usually taught English. Now he was sitting at his desk, keeping an eye on renegades like me.

"Hi, Mr. Ellenburgh." I waved when I entered.

As he looked up from his newspaper, he did a double take. "Susan! What in the world are you doing in this class?"

I grimaced. "I guess I belong here. If you check your list, I'm sure you'll find my name on it."

Mr. Ellenburgh ran his finger from top to bottom on a sheet under his newspaper and, certainly enough, said in a baffled voice, "Susan Miller. Here it is." His gaze skated back to me. "What reason did Miss Hayes have to send you here?"

The wrong ones, obviously. At this point, I was pretty sure if I told Mr. Ellenburgh it was all a mistake and I did nothing wrong, he would let me walk right out the door. But I wasn't a liar. "She caught me in a weak moment. Don't you worry, Mr. Ellenburgh"—oh, my favorite teacher of them all—"I don't intend to make this a habit."

"Fine. Take a seat then, Susan." As he gestured for me to choose a place in the room, his compassion for my unfortunate situation showed in his eyes, and it made me like him even more.

I kept my gaze low as I walked down the aisle between the rows of desks, so nobody would notice or recognize me. Of course, that was a stupid thing to hope for, but I just couldn't look at any of these gangsters' faces. It gave me a feeling of complicity.

In the far back, I sank into a chair and pulled out my math book to do my homework. All around me, the guys and girls started to chatter away, having a great time.

Mr. Ellenburgh didn't call them to order or make them shut up. Obviously, at this time of the day, no one really cared what people did. Who knew that detention wasn't all about punishment and discipline but could be fun? I started to grasp why Alex never complained about being kept after school. It was a shame he wasn't here with me today, but getting a head start on my homework was fine with me.

I'd started working on the second algebra problem when something orange teased the corner of my eye. A moment later, a basketball slowly rolled across my desk, from right to left. It was so surreal that I didn't even think about stopping the ball and instead gave a tiny shriek of surprise when it dropped with a bang to the floor, bouncing up and down a few times next to me. My pen had slid from my fingers, too, and rolled over the edge of the desk.

I bent down to pick up both the pen and the ball. When I straightened again, one of the Donovan twins stood in front of me, and by his roguish smirk I decided it had to be the infamous and less likable of them.

"Hey, Sue," Chris said and took the ball from me. "Never seen a basketball?" His white muscle shirt sported a flashy green *Grover Beach Dunkin' Sharks* brand across the chest, accompanied by the image of a cartoon shark tearing a basketball with its teeth. So, on a wild guess, I assumed he was on our school's basketball team.

It could've been that he was also one of the guys who got a little rowdy every now and then and played basketball in the halls during school hours, which was an absolute no-no. The thugs on the other side of the room grinning at him—definitely his friends—confirmed my assumption.

"My name is *Susan*," I corrected him with a growl. His calling me Sue, or even worse, "sweetness" was becoming a real pain in my neck.

The chuckle that followed was proof enough that he didn't give a damn about my name. "I'm wondering...does my brother know that his girlfriend is in detention?"

"If you tell him, I'm going to shoot you." My glare manifested my intention of really doing that. "And I'm not his girlfriend," I added with a huff.

"Yeah. I know that." Chris stated this with an odd inflection in his tone, which made me wonder what he really meant by it.

I decided I didn't care and hoped he'd leave me alone, but instead he slid into the seat next to me, tipped back to balance the chair on two legs, and stacked his feet on the desk. He started to spin the ball on his finger. "So, what got you in here?"

Since there was no getting rid of him, I put my pen down, turned to him, and crossed my arms over my chest. "You, in fact."

"*Me*? Wow." Chris caught the ball with both hands. "How?"

"My history teacher saw me flipping you off this morning."

"Yeah"—he furrowed his brows, totally faking a hurt look, when he very obviously had trouble holding back a laugh—"that was actually rude." For good measure, he waggled a finger at me. "We really need to work on your manners if you're going to keep going out with my brother." As he spun the basketball again, his toned biceps twitched underneath perfectly smooth skin, and I wondered why he'd abandoned his leather jacket. It might have stopped me from staring. Chris certainly was a dick, but there was no denying he looked just as mouthwatering as Ethan. Duh!

"Speaking of which," he continued with an innocent look I didn't trust—not one bit! "Are you two going to meet up again today?"

"Why are you so interested in your brother's privacy? You should stop poking your nose where it doesn't belong. Especially when it's also concerning *my* privacy, because I'm not going to tell you shit."

"Ah, such a cute mouth and such bad words. Now I get why you've been put in detention, Miss Miller. Must be a soccer thing with the language, eh?"

When I didn't get his meaning and pulled my face into a frown, he shrugged one shoulder. "It was a surprise to see you sitting with the Bay Sharks at lunch today. I assumed you'd be with the geek squad."

"Why would you think that?" I felt like I'd knocked into a wall. But then it dawned on me. "Oh, no, let me guess. The glasses, right? You really think because I'm wearing them I'm a nerd?"

Wary, Chris hummed a sigh. "That was the idea, yes."

"And Ethan didn't tell you that I was—*am*"—I rolled my eyes at my own slip—"on the soccer team?"

"Ethan doesn't say much these days."

"For good reason. It's none of your business."

"Maybe. But now I'm curious." Chris made a face as if he'd

left one detail totally out of sight. “Why does he suddenly go to soccer practice?”

“If you must know, he’s taking my place for a while because I hurt my knee.”

He sucked his lips between his teeth, and I swear, if it was Ethan doing that in front of me, I’d feel the need to throw myself at him this instant. But this was Chris, and I decided I felt nothing. Not even when his blue eyes turned a shade darker and a bit more mysterious. “Is that so?” he drawled.

“Yes, that is so,” I replied, mocking his lilt. “And for your information, just because someone’s wearing glasses doesn’t mean he or she’s a geek. I only need them for reading, not for playing. And now, if you don’t mind, go and grate on someone else’s nerves. I’ve got homework to do.” I shooed him off with a wave of my hand.

With a laugh, he got to his feet and clamped the ball under his arm. “Just tell me if he kisses you. I’d really like to know.”

“The hell I will. Now go away.”

Chris tossed the basketball to one of his friends, who must have been watching because he was prepared to catch it. Then he leaned across the table toward me and pulled my glasses off my nose, staring straight into my eyes. “My offer for a date in a week is still on.”

He must be crazy. That was the only possible explanation. I reached for my glasses, but he pulled them out of my reach in time. “Give them back, dickhead! And I’ll never go out with you,” I snapped. “Not today, not next weekend, and not in ten thousand years.”

For an infinite moment, Chris studied me. Eventually, he began to smile. "You *will* go out with me, sweetness. And I'll show you how fast hell can freeze over when I want something."

If nothing else, his reducing me to *something* should have made me kick out under the desk and hit his shin. Maybe it was his smile that hammered all the way through my barriers or his dangerously sweet purr in my face. Who knew, but for that moment I was immobilized, except for the twitch in my throat when I gulped.

"You see?" Chris teased and put my glasses on the desk in front of me, never breaking eye contact. "The fire's already reducing to a soft glow." He nudged my chin lightly with his knuckles then straightened and walked away as if he'd just borrowed a pen from me and not made my insides quiver with an unholy foreboding.

With a shake of my head and a hard mental slap, I got a grip on myself again. I knew his kind—he was trouble, the kind that drew looks from every corner when he walked through the hallways and that could turn a girl's brain to mush with just a dimple in his cheek. But not with me. I was not going to be the next name on his checklist and I wouldn't let him ruin something as important as my first kiss because he just smelled easy prey.

After I found my dignity again, I cleared my throat and called out, "Hey, Chris!"

Folding his arms on the backrest of the chair he'd straddled by his friends, he cast me an intrigued and self-assured glance over his shoulder. I didn't give him the time to even think about the word "sweetness" leaving his mouth, but continued, "It takes a little more than a cute smile to get on my good side, and luckily your brother comes equipped with the whole package." I flashed a sardonic grin that hopefully stung his ego in front of his gang. "You want to freeze hell? Go ahead and try. It'll get you nowhere with me."

For a stunned moment, Chris gazed at me. My snappiness had certainly terminated his interest in me. After all, he seemed to be someone after an easy lay and a jolly good time, nothing more. Especially not if that *something* proved to require serious effort. Right?

Wrong. The left side of his mouth tilted up so slowly that a shudder made it through my entire body before he was done with the smirk. He blinked and ran his tongue along the inside of his bottom lip. The whole class had stilled and all eyes were on him and me now, gazes darting back and forth.

With an audience to quote him later, he stated, "Game on, little Sue."

Chapter 6

WITH THE RING of the bell, I was out of detention and hurried to get home and ready for my date with Ethan. But being trapped in a room with Chris for the past hour had me on edge. His smirk, his voice, and even his vile announcement of making me his next big catch haunted me. It meant nothing, so why the heck couldn't I get this jerk out of my head?

What bothered me even more than his ego, which was obviously too big to fit in a ballroom, was his remark that his brother was not going to kiss me. Did he really think that Ethan didn't want to go that far with me? Today was the third day in a row that Ethan had asked me to hang out with him. There must be at least *some* interest from his end. No one expected him to propose with a ring straight away, but a kiss should be in the stars for us. I'd read too many romance books not to feel it coming.

But just to help things a little, I consulted the expert—my friend, Simone. She came to my place after I called her and prepped me in a way I'd never done before.

"You go shower and blow dry your hair," she commanded, clearly in her element. "In the meantime, I'll see what your closet has to offer." She was already flicking through the hangers bearing the mostly unworn dresses in my wardrobe as I headed out of my room. When I came back, she sat on my bed with a lurid red dress draped over her legs and a wraparound smile that she might as well have stolen from a Disney movie.

"You don't really want me to wear that, do you?" I said with a skeptical frown.

"Do you want to get kissed tonight or not?" That seemed to be her standard answer to any veto I brought forth that afternoon. With it, she brushed away my protest and put mascara on my lashes, smeared apple-flavored gloss on my lips, and smoothed my waves with a flat iron. When she was done, my hair hung like liquid honey down my shoulders. Kudos to her for knowing what she did. I liked the new me. The girl in the mirror looked slightly older and, heck, tons more sexy.

Now it was time to stuff my slim self into a dress I'd owned since tenth grade but hadn't worn once. My former lack of boobs would have ruined the effect. The dress had long sleeves but was quite short and showed a darn lot of my legs.

"It's sending out the right signals," Simone assured me, when I gave myself a sidelong look in the mirror. "Ethan will be drooling all over you tonight. If that doesn't earn you a kiss at the end, I don't know what would."

Kissing Ethan... I didn't know what I could want more in the world right now.

It was half past four—time to go if I didn't want to be late for my date. Gathering my nerves, which were suddenly all over the place, I slipped into my black ballerina flats, picked one of the seventeen purses Simone had brought to match with a possible dress, and headed downstairs.

Mom gave me a hug when she saw me, all new and shiny. "You look beautiful, honey." She held me at arm's length with her hands on my shoulders and added in a stern voice, "Curfew at eight. It's a school night."

"Ten," I whined. "Please."

After a deep sigh, she offered, "Okay, nine then."

"Oh, come on, Mrs. M.," Simone rushed to my rescue. "It's almost the weekend. Nine thirty? They need time for a good-night kiss. It's Susan's first, after all."

While Simone beamed with hope for my mom to give in, I burned with embarrassment. How could she mention my first kiss in front of my mother? But her plan worked out and Mom let me off with a smile. "All right, nine thirty. But I don't want you to walk home by yourself in the dark. Make sure Ethan takes you."

"He will!" Nodding, I shoved Simone out the door so as not to give my mom a chance to change her mind. "See you later."

Outside, Simone stopped in front of her car. "Want me to give you a ride?"

"No, thanks. I'll walk. My nerves need a cool-down before

I meet up with Ethan." I hadn't been this nervous since Dad and I got in line for a hug from Mickey Mouse in Disneyland when I was five. And kissing Ethan would be so much better than getting squeezed by a giant stuffed mouse in red shorts.

I was so deep in thought as I ambled down the road to Charlie's, concentrating on the small craters in the concrete, that I didn't notice someone falling in step beside me until I heard Ethan say my name. With a gasp, I jerked my head up, then cursed under my breath, and tried to rub away the twinge in my neck.

Ethan's brows came down in a sympathetic grimace. "Sorry, I didn't mean to make you jump. I just wasn't sure if it was, well, *you*."

"Huh?"

He gave me a quick once-over. "You look different." From his voice it was impossible to say whether he meant *good* different or *bad* different. Because insecurity trampled over me like a running herd of antelopes, I didn't want to find out the answer.

"Where did you park your car?" Yes, very clever and very subtle change of topic, I know.

"Um, I didn't drive here."

"You walked?" That must have been two miles or more. "Did your car break down?"

"No." A soft laugh escaped him and now it was his turn to rub his neck, but not because of an obvious kink. He seemed bashful all of a sudden. "I was getting a little nervous this afternoon, so I took the long walk here to kill time."

Smiling, I clutched Simone's purse to my chest. "You were nervous?"

Ethan nodded and shoved his hands into the pockets of his black jeans. "I—" He broke off as suddenly as someone would do when realizing he was talking to the totally wrong person. With his gaze on me, he took two deep breaths which might have been accompanied by a racing heart from the look of it. Was he in shock?

"I wasn't sure if I'd find you here or if you were going to stand me up again. I don't fancy sitting at the bar alone," he told me in a more controlled voice, his gaze lowered to his toes.

That was definitely not what he wanted to say before. A frown crept over my face but faded away fast. To nag him about it would only ruin the beginning of our date, and I didn't want that to happen. It would probably have killed me to be stood up like that, too, so I blew some stray hairs off my forehead that had gotten static from the straightening, and said, "Good that you're not alone today then."

We reached the café and Ethan walked in before me. I took the chance to check my reflection in the glass door. Some of my hair on top was still floating up like Simone had rubbed a balloon on my head instead of using a straightening iron. Quickly, I licked my fingers and brushed my hair down, making it stay put.

Puzzled by my delay, Ethan turned around, scrutinizing me with lifted eyebrows. I dropped my hands and gave him an innocent grin.

We sat down at a round table for two near the bar. Ted

waved at me when he saw me, then he nodded at Ethan in greeting. Since there wasn't much going on weekday afternoons, Ted wasn't only bartending but also bussing tables, something that Tony Mitchell did on weekends. Charlie, the owner of the café, was nowhere to be seen. Since he could rely on his staff a hundred percent, he took more and more days off lately.

Ted came around the bar with a smile, draping a dishtowel over his shoulder in a casual move. "So you brought company today," he teased Ethan.

For the briefest moment, Ethan looked at me. He turned a sweet shade of pink and lowered his gaze to the pack of sugar he'd started to play with after we sat down. "Yeah, seems all the misunderstandings have been eradicated," he replied in an awkwardly low voice.

Ted studied him for a silent second and finally said, "Good for you." He turned to me next, and that's when I saw that he'd lost his smile. Of course, he made sure to pick it up again immediately. "So what can I get you? A hazelnut deluxe?"

"Mm-hm." I nodded, my mouth already watering for the caffè latte.

"And for you?" Ted asked Ethan.

"I think I'll take a cappuccino. Whipped cream, no foam, please."

Ted gave a quirky arch of his eyebrows, as if this order was especially interesting for him. Why, I couldn't figure out.

As soon as we were alone again, Ethan leaned forward, propping his elbows on the table, and put on a shit-eating smirk. "Now, spill. What got you in detention?"

Oh my freaking Jesus! That put even my obvious change of topic to shame. I gulped and gritted my teeth. "I'm going to kill your brother."

"For telling me?" Ethan laughed. "He wasn't the first. Alex and Tony said something about it today at soccer practice, though they wouldn't tell me the reason."

My list of people to deal with tomorrow morning had just expanded by two names. Avoiding Ethan's gaze, I shrugged it off. "It was nothing."

"You know you're just making me all the more curious by saying that," he teased me. "I'll just end up thinking some really funny shit about you."

"Yeah? Like what?"

"Like you've been flashing your hot teacher in class or you've been spraying graffiti in the hallways."

I laughed out loud and smacked him on the shoulder. "You're crazy, you know that, right?"

"It's all in your hands."

"Fine, hear the full story then. One of my teachers saw me flipping off your brother this morning."

In an instant, Ethan's amused expression went blank. "Why'd you do that?"

"He seems a little too interested in what you and I do together," I answered, trying for a casual voice to keep the mood light.

Ethan stroked his index finger over his chin. "Is he now?"

"You don't have to worry. I told him he wouldn't hear crap from me." Somehow, this sounded strange even to myself, so I added quickly, “Anyway, what’s there to tell? I mean we’re friends, that’s all, right?”

Maybe that would change tonight, though. In a heartbeat my hopes got really high again, sending fleecy little balls of excitement down into my gut.

“Yeah.” Ethan leaned back so Ted could put our coffees on the table and murmured, “Thanks.”

I said thanks, too, but Ted only looked at Ethan and nodded.

I scooped up some of the foam in my spoon then squeezed my eyes and lips together and rubbed my nose because my static hair was tickling me again. Ethan reached across the table, surprising me when he twirled a bunch of my hair around his finger and tucked it behind my ear. There was, however, not half as much sensuality in this move as there was yesterday evening when Chris had done the same thing.

So Ethan was probably a practical-thinking guy, not a ravisher like his brother. All the better. Chris had the charm of a skunk and... Hell, I shouldn’t even be thinking about him right now. What was wrong with me?

Shaking off the chill that had stolen over me remembering Chris’s perfectly shaped torso, I anchored myself in the present by focusing on Ethan’s warm gaze. Silky as my hair was from straightening, it didn’t stay behind my ear for long, and after three more tries of hooking it behind my ear, I simply ignored the strands coming down again over my right eye.

“What did you do with your hair?” Ethan wanted to know.

“My friend straightened it for me.” I rolled my eyes. “She

thought it would make me look good for a date."

"I like it how you usually have it," he told me in a sheepish voice.

Immediately, I thought *Oh, thank goodness* because—wanting to look good or not—the itchy strands had started to get on my nerves. With a relieved sigh, I brushed my hair out of my face and tied it at the back of my head with a hair tie from my purse. That gesture was enough to take away ninety percent of the tension that had built inside me this afternoon and, all of a sudden, I could breathe again. "Ah, this feels so much better." Way more myself.

"But I like the idea that you did this for me," Ethan said playfully, and one corner of his mouth tilted up.

"It was an experiment and it failed, so let's pretend it never happened," I teased back and poured some sugar into my caffè latte.

Ethan, playing along, adjusted the collar of his shirt in a perfect mockery of Elvis Presley. He lifted his eyebrows and screwed up his mouth. "I have not the slightest idea what you're talking about."

Did I say how much I loved this guy when only his natural self shone through? Never would I have thought that someone could make me feel so comfortable with such little things. I started to believe we weren't only soul mates, but actually twin souls. Why in the world had I been so nervous all afternoon?

Soon enough, the conversation returned to our favorite topics: music and books. For most of the time we were sitting in the café, we discussed what a great job New Line Cinema had done with the adaption of *The Lord of the Rings* and the epic film music. We also talked through some *Harry Potter* and *Sherlock Holmes*, which we both adored, but I couldn't get him to like *Twilight*. That was okay with me, only it slowed down our conversation until it came to an awkward standstill.

Note to self: never mention sparkly vampires again.

I ran my index finger over my bottom lip, biting my nail, and cut a glance at the next table, where a girl was playing a game on her phone. "Know what I'd love to do right now?" I mumbled.

Ethan laughed. "Hopefully play *Mario Kart*, because that's what I was thinking."

My mouth stretched to a broad grin. "Let's go!"

Ethan got up and pulled his wallet from his back pocket. He tossed a few dollars on the table for our drinks plus tip and offered me his arm. Laughing, I looped mine through his.

"Your place or mine?" he asked.

My place was out of question because of the fighting we'd get from my parents, but this time at least I had a proper excuse. "I don't have a Wii."

"So it'll be my place. If we're lucky"—he cast a glance at his watch—"we'll be just in time for dinner, too. Are you hungry? I'm always hungry," he ended with a guilty look.

With the nervousness gone, I realized I actually *was* hungry and smiled. "As long as it isn't spinach or liver."

A noticeable quiver fizzed through Ethan. "God forbid."

Even though it was a two-mile walk to his house, the time flew by way too fast for me. He hadn't let my hand slip away from his arm even once, and I relished the nearness. His body, so warm and firm next to mine, made me think I had reached my own personal heaven.

As soon as he opened the front door of his house and ushered me through, he called over my head, "Mom, we've got a guest for dinner. Is that okay?"

Mrs. Donovan came out of the kitchen and brought a spicy smell with her. "Of course," she said and offered me her hand with a smile. "Sorry, I was in a bit of a rush last time we met. I'm Beverly."

"This is Susan," Ethan told her before I could introduce myself, so all I said was, "Nice to meet you."

"Come on." Ethan tugged at my hand. "Let's have a race before dinner is ready."

I followed him to the back of the house, but before we reached his room, the door at the very end of the hallway opened and, to my total surprise, Lauren, the black-haired supermodel came out. Of course, Chris slipped out right after her and he laced their fingers.

His hair was a mess and so was his shirt. He'd obviously been distracted while buttoning it up. *Jerk*! Could he be any more obvious and disgusting? He would *so* not get me next with that kind of stuff, I thought, rolling my eyes. But then a different image crossed my mind. My hands in this chaos of hair as he kissed me deeply. Oh no, not him but Ethan...when Ethan kissed me deeply. A strange heat lit my body at that visual and suddenly I had trouble breathing.

In a dreamlike haze, I'd stopped in the hallway when Ethan

was already inside his room, not even caring about greeting his brother or his friend. My inability to take my eyes off Chris as he passed me right after Lauren made me want to kick myself awake.

Aware of my staring, Chris winked at me. My knees buckled, but it was all I needed to realize my mistake, and I hurried after Ethan, banging the door shut a tad too hard.

Ethan was already on his bed, a controller in the shape of a steering wheel in his hand, holding a second one out to me. *Mario Kart. Right!* I made myself comfortable next to him, but no matter how much fun this game was and no matter how much Ethan and I laughed while he totally brought me to my knees, the visual of my hands in Chris's—no, no, in Ethan's!—hair haunted me. God, sooner or later this twin issue was going to drive me insane.

Ethan had just beaten me for the fourth time in a row when a knock rattled the door and Chris called from the other side, "Feeding time!" We stopped the game and joined him and Beverly in the kitchen, which was also the dining room, with a round, cherry wood table at one side. I wasn't exactly sure why, but realizing that Chris must have taken Lauren to the door to see her off when we'd met them in the hallway earlier was a relief. It would feel awkward to face his catch of the week after how grossly he'd hit on me today.

I had to give him credit for playing the innocent son and nice brother in front of his family. He didn't let slip one word about how he intended to add me to his long list of bad rep, and I appreciated it. I didn't think I could handle sitting through dinner with his *normal* self. A shiver rattled me. Then again, maybe he had a real liking for Lauren and had forgotten about our challenge already.

I made myself useful by carrying the plates and cutlery that Beverly had placed on the island unit over to the table and laying it out for four people. No one bothered to bring in a fifth chair and a fifth plate was missing, too. Warily, I sided up to Ethan, who put down a bowl filled with potatoes. "Isn't your father coming home for dinner?"

Ethan gave a bitter laugh. He didn't bother to keep his voice low like mine when he told me, "My father lives in L.A. with his former secretary. He hasn't been home for dinner in almost six years now."

"Oh," I breathed, turning a little hot in the face.

"No worries," he said, playing it off. "Take a seat."

I sat down and was about to reach for the glass of water near my plate, when Chris came around the table and took my hand. Without a word, he pulled me up, moved me one seat to the left, and sat down in the chair I had vacated. Okay, every house had its own rules, I guessed, grimacing as I looked at Ethan, who lowered on Chris's other side, across from me. He shook his head and smiled, easing my trepidation.

Beverly dished out fried fish and buttered slices of toasted baguette for everyone. When she took the seat to my left, we started eating. The boys immediately fell into easy conversation, telling their mother about their day at school. So this was what a normal family did when they ate together. It was the most relaxing thing to just listen to them and for once not have to deal with arguments and death glares at the dinner table. Jeez, it had been so long since we had peace in my house that I'd totally forgotten what it felt like.

Of course, the time came when Beverly started grilling me, but in a friendly way. She was most interested in how and when her son and I met and, funnily enough, in what kind of house I lived. It was a challenge to describe our two-story house to her so she'd get a real visual.

"Don't mind her," Ethan told me when I reached my limit trying to come up with a year of construction. He handed me the basket with the bread slices to grab another. "She's like that with everyone. Mom's a real estate agent, always on the hunt for houses to sell."

"Wow, that's a cool job," I said to her. "Must be awesome to see so many houses from the inside."

"It's the best job in the world. I love houses," she rhapsodized.

"Me, too." Especially the quiet ones, but I didn't say that out loud.

We kept chatting long after we'd all finished eating. I felt like I'd been part of this cozy little group forever—another sign that Ethan and I were meant to be together. And if Chris continued behaving like that, I might even get used to him as the brother of my future boyfriend.

When a grandfather clock chimed eight somewhere in the house, Beverly rose from the table and clapped her hands once. "All right, guys. Dishes to do. Go play it out."

What kind of cryptic announcement was that? But

obviously the twins knew what she meant, and Ethan complained, "Oh, come on, Mom. I've got a guest."

"Yeah, right," Chris backed him up, giving me a mocking smirk. "*She* can do the dishes."

"Your brother's girlfriend won't be doing your chores," Beverly told him off with a finger pointed at his face.

My breath caught in my lungs as I shot a glance at her and noticed from the corner of my eye that Ethan did the same. We looked at each other then, and I gulped. Ethan's cheeks turned an adorable shade of lovely. "Mom, she's not my girlfriend," he murmured.

"See? She's not his girlfriend." Chris rose from his chair. "She *can* do the dishes." He tried to slip out of the room, but Beverly caught him by the collar of his black shirt, which he'd buttoned correctly by now, and pulled him back, laughing.

"No way, buddy. You do your job first."

"Ah, all right, I'll do it," he surrendered and chuckled. He started to pile the plates on the table. When he winked at me as he grabbed mine, I knew he was just taunting me all along. And it was okay. Nice, even. What in the world had happened to the jackass I met at school? Did he store his insufferable outdoor manners in the closet as soon as he got home?

Chris carried the dishes to the sink and shouted over his shoulder, "Dessert in twenty!"

That was the cue for Ethan to rise, and I followed suit. He pulled me back into his room for another game of *Mario Kart*.

"What did your mom mean by 'play it out'?" I asked while I picked my character for the race.

"We have a deal in this house. When Chris and I cook, she has to clean the kitchen afterward, and when she cooks, one of us has to. Usually, we play a game of basketball in the backyard." He grinned. "Loser has to do the dishes."

That was so sweet my heart melted a little for this family, but what really caught my attention was something different. "Wait. Did you say when you and Chris cook?"

"Yeah. It's something I enjoy a lot. We both do." Ethan waited for the red light on the screen to switch to green, then we both raced off, and he continued, "A couple of years ago, we actually had this plan to open a restaurant together one day and call it *The Twin Chefs* or something."

"That's a great idea."

He nodded. "I'd still love to do that, but I think Chris is more into basketball than cooking now. He wants to play in college, maybe go pro."

The sad note in Ethan's voice loomed over us like fog over San Francisco, so I suggested, "But you can do that restaurant thing on your own, as well. You could be *One Amazing Half of the Twin Chefs*."

"Right, and you could come test my food."

"I'd be there every evening, I swear." Quickly, I crossed my heart before I grabbed the wireless steering wheel again and tried to beat Ethan in this race. Not a chance. "Well, if your dream of the restaurant doesn't work out," I said, "you can always pursue a career in car racing."

"And spray the name Super Mario on my cart?" He laughed.

I shrugged and put my controller down. That was enough defeat for one evening. "Where's the bathroom?"

"Past the kitchen, second door on the right." Ethan pulled back his legs so I could get off the bed, while he started a single player race.

Out in the hallway, music drifted to me from the kitchen. I sneaked a peek inside on my way. Instead of the mount of dishes getting smaller in there, it seemed the stack had doubled after dinner. Chris was pouring what looked like cream into four dessert bowls on the kitchen island, singing along to Sam Smith's "Stay With Me." He didn't notice me at all. His body moved gently, as though he was tapping his heel to the rhythm. Next, he grabbed some fruits from a bowl behind him, started to peel them, and I went to find the bathroom.

I could hear his singing even in here. It gave me goosebumps of fascination. Ethan had been right; busying themselves in the kitchen gave the twins a happy time. This was so weird because it was so different from how I pictured them—especially Chris. Maybe I was wrong and he wasn't an insufferable moron after all? To say he confused me was the understatement of the year.

On my way back to Ethan's room, I slowed my steps, only because I hoped I could listen to Chris's singing a little more. Maybe that was a mistake, because when I dared another glimpse into the kitchen, he looked up. Never stopping his singing, he crooked a finger at me and beckoned me to come to him.

Why I followed his invitation, I don't know.

His black shirt hung over the backrest of one of the kitchen chairs and the t-shirt he was wearing now was a snug fit, showing off his dancing muscles while he cut more fruit. The dessert bowls he was preparing each had a different name painted on it. *Ethan* was scrawled on the green one. The blue one spelled *Christopher*, but somebody had crossed out the *opher* with a sharpie and written *ian* above. The yellow bowl was for *The best mom in the world*, and tonight I was obviously *Milk*.

When I stopped across from him at the island unit, he sang to me, "*Oh, won't you...stayyy with meee... 'cause you're...aaall I need,*" and dipped a slice of peach into the cream in his own bowl. When he held it out to me with a tempting look, I shook my head. I didn't like peaches.

Unimpressed, Chris shrugged his shoulders and bit off the creamed tip. He put the peach slice away and reached for another fruit. I could do nothing about it when the corners of my mouth tilted up as his hand hovered above a kiwi wedge, and Chris noticed. Knowing he'd finally found my week spot, he smiled, too. He kept singing, "*This ain't love, it's clear to see, but darling, stay with me,*" while he dipped that little piece of fruit into his bowl. He held it out to me across the kitchen island once more.

With the cream on it, there was no chance I could take it from him with my hands. But that was probably not his intention anyway. If I wanted it, I had to let him feed it to me. My mouth watered. That was okay, considering it was kiwi, my favorite fruit, he was offering. But why my heart had flung itself into a beating race was unclear to me. Our gazes locked above his outstretched arm. He was patiently waiting for my next move which, frankly, could have been an off remark as well as me catching the kiwi with my teeth.

At this point, neither of us knew which option I was going to choose. What I noticed, though, was that he'd stopped singing while the song played on.

A silent argument started inside my head.

This is kiwi. You want kiwi.

But this is also Chris. I don't want his fingers to touch my lips, even by accident.

Screw his fingers. This is kiwi! And there's cream on it.

Still...it's Chris.

Pretend it's Ethan, then.

Oh hey, I could do that.

Pressing my lips together for a brief moment, I started to lean forward, never breaking eye contact. I swallowed then parted my lips, and Chris cracked the tiniest smile. He dipped his chin a little lower which resulted in his gaze getting all the more intense as I carefully caught the kiwi between my teeth.

I thought I was prepared for the moment when my lips would inevitably brush against his fingers, but I was not. I didn't know why it was such a big thing, because it was for the shortest possible time, but a hot sizzle of adrenaline rushed through my body nonetheless.

What made this even more awkward was the way Chris's gaze remained fixed on me as he withdrew his hand and licked the remaining cream from his thumb and index finger. It was the thought of my lips brushing exactly these spots that ignited another prickling rush through my veins.

Unable to stay a second longer in this room, I spun around and left with a determined stride. Chris's laughter followed me, then he continued singing, an amused note in his voice.

Chapter 7

THE DONOVAN FAMILY and I came together again at the table five minutes later. Chris placed the dessert bowls in front of us and took the seat to my right again. He played it cool, no remark about feeding me in the kitchen at all. It would hardly be the right thing to do, anyway, with his brother being present and all. But hearing him whistle the tune of "Stay With Me" as he placed a dessert bowl in front of me still felt like a taunt.

My cheeks warmed with the memory of how he'd tempted me to take the fruit he held out...my lips brushing his fingers.

Because of my nerves, I hadn't even had a chance to savor the taste of the kiwi wedge dipped in cream. Now, however, I realized that the dessert wasn't actually just bland vanilla cream with fruit, as I had expected. In fact, Chris had created an awesome coconut-lemon cream. And though various types of fruit slices floated in my bowl, I couldn't find a single peach slice.

How very considerate of him. But I'd have rather bitten off my tongue than tell him that.

After dessert, Ethan offered to drive me home, and not a minute too soon. If I was late, my mom would ground me for at least a week. We headed out to his car where he made me swoon a little when he opened the door for me like the last gentleman left in Grover Beach. The drive didn't take half as long as I'd wished, but on the plus side, Ethan cut the engine in front of my house.

Was this it? The moment when he'd lean across the center console and kiss me? My heart pounded like it was trying to bulldoze a way out of my chest.

Ethan turned to me, a half-smile on his lips. I was breathing so fast that in another couple of minutes we wouldn't have any air left in the car. My knees shook as I shifted in my seat to face him, too. "Thanks for a lovely evening," I said with what little control over my voice I had left.

"Mm, it was really nice." Instead of leaning toward me, he dipped his head back against the headrest. "It's funny how my mom took a liking to you in an instant," he continued, his voice still light but coy. Then he laughed, a heartwarming sound. "Chris and I always suspected she wanted one of us to be a girl."

"You can't be serious." It came out as playful banter, but inwardly it felt like a complaint about his making small talk rather than kissing me.

"I am."

Yeah, I'd figured as much. My heart sank as my longed-for

first kiss drifted farther and farther away. What was happening here? Hadn't we had a great time together? It was our second official date—or whatever—and three minutes past my curfew. Not that I wanted to rush anything, but it was *now* or *never*!

As the seconds ticked by, "never" seemed to be the more likely outcome of the above.

A grim thought sneaked into my mind. When Chris drove a girl home, he probably didn't waste a minute on words. Gee, why was Chris in my head right now, when I wanted Ethan to kiss me?

Frustration seemed a reasonable answer to that one. The thought of my first kiss had clearly wound me up. Ethan was a great guy: gorgeous, polite, sweet...and seductive when he didn't think about it. Hm, maybe that was the whole problem. Were we both overthinking it?

"Hey, I really like hanging out with you," Ethan said next, and I could sense that this was going in the direction of another date. At least I hoped as much. A small stone dropped from my chest.

"You're only saying that because you beat me at *Mario Kart* tonight," I teased him, not knowing what else to say, since I didn't want to be the one to ask him out.

"Yeah, that, and because your feet don't smell like my other friends' do," he joked.

We both shook with laughter, and I poked him with my elbow. "Thanks for that visual, Ethan. It's really what a girl wants to hear after a second date."

He smirked at me. "Oh, you should hear what I come up

with for the third one."

Was there going to be a third? The question must have been written in my eyes, because he cleared his throat and stammered, "Want to, er...do something again this weekend? If you're already bored of video games, we could go to the movies."

Truth be told, I had spent way too much time with Nick Frederickson, and he'd spoiled me in an irreparable way. "Are you kidding me? I could never get bored of playing Wii! But a movie sounds good."

"Saturday night? We could even do both. Come to my place, and we can play some games before we go out. But no *Mario Kart.*" He nudged me with his shoulder, a chuckle rolling off his chest. "I don't want you to get too frustrated to see me again."

"That won't happen." Even without getting kissed, I enjoyed the time with Ethan a lot more than being the third wheel in Sam and Tony's relationship—or in any other relationship, for that matter. Ethan would make an awesome boyfriend, but he was a cool friend, too. "Call me about Saturday." I fumbled with the door until it finally opened. After a deep sigh, I told him good night and climbed out.

Swallowing hard as I adjusted my dress, I gazed after his car until the red taillights turned around the corner.

Mom was waiting for me on the couch in the living room. Dad was in the kitchen, pouring himself a glass of Scotch. The current silence in the house was deceiving. If Dad was knocking back a drink before bedtime, it was an indicator of two things. One, the fight they'd had in my absence was one ranking quite high on my self-made scale of severity. And two, Mom would have another reason to attack Dad—for getting drunk, even if he wasn't going to be wasted from only one glass. Anyway, it would drive me out of my bed and next door tonight.

"Hey, Mom, I'm back," I said.

She rose from the couch and came toward me with a smile. Kudos to her for keeping me out of their fights and always having a loving tone for me, even during their loudest arguments. Both of my parents did. That was the reason I could never be mad at either one of them, even if the nightly shouting hurt my eardrums and I'd end up on a therapist's couch before my twenty-fifth birthday, telling him where my insomnia stemmed from.

Mom ran her soft hand over my hair. "How was your date?" She was probably as excited to hear whether Ethan had kissed me as Simone was.

"Quite nice. I'm going to see Ethan again this weekend." That was the most detail I'd give her. I mean, come on, she's my mom. You don't tell all the sickly sweet details about a date to your parents. Especially when those details aren't as sickly sweet as you'd hoped for in the first place.

Upstairs in my room, I stripped out of my dress and put on a tank top and flannel bottoms. After brushing my teeth, my bed tempted me, but Simone expected a call and it would be impolite to make her wait. My phone lay on the nightstand, and I picked it up while I crawled under the covers. The screen lit up at a swipe of my thumb. There was a surprise text waiting for me.

It wasn't from any of my friends, but I knew the number of

the sender. Earlier this afternoon, I'd saved it as *Arrogant Dick* in my contacts.

My first thought was to delete the message from Chris unread. No court in the world could convict me for that after how he'd confronted me in detention today. But the image of him singing in their kitchen and holding out a cream-dipped kiwi pressed back into my mind. Curiosity got the better of me so, with a snort and a shake of my head, I opened the message and read: *Not like a geek.*

Who in the world was supposed to make sense of that? Was there something missing? Scratching my head, I typed: *What?* And sent it off.

While waiting for his explanation, I keyed in a quick update about tonight for Simone, but also added Sam and Lisa to the receiver line. As soon as that text had gone out, my phone started to ring. My first thought was that one of the girls had been really quick to read my text and wanted to talk about it, but checking the display, it said that a certain *Arrogant Dick* had dialed my number.

What in the world— "Chris, why are you calling me?" I groaned into the phone. But I'd probably run right into that one when I decided to respond to his text.

"To wish you a pleasant night and to answer your question," Chris replied with a chuckle.

An irritated sigh escaped me. "Does your brother know that you're talking to me?"

"No. He just came in...too soon after he drove you home, if you ask me." He added with a tease in his voice, "Does that mean he, once again, didn't kiss you?"

Teeth clenched, I snarled, "None of your business."

"Come on, it's a simple yes or no question." An amused laugh drifted through the line. "I'll sleep a lot better if I know the answer."

What did I care if he slept well? "Why don't you ask him yourself if you want to know so badly?"

"Okay... Since you told me to..." There was a pause and the sound of a door opening which added ten extra degrees to my blood. He wasn't really going to— "Hey, Ethan!" Chris called out, cutting my thought short. "Did you kiss Susan tonight?"

"No. Why?" The answer came from far away. My heart sank with Ethan's flat voice. Then a door banged shut somewhere in Chris's house.

"Ethan said no," he rubbed it in, as if I hadn't heard the news myself. "I wonder why he didn't." His voice had adopted a thoughtful edge that was one hundred percent fake. "Could it be that he's just not interested?"

Much as his suggestion stung, I was wondering it myself. But it was too early to give up hope just yet. *Third time's a charm*, the saying chanted in my mind as I said to Chris, "FYI, he asked me on another date."

"Aw, playing video games again? Is that really your idea of a successful date?"

"We're going to the movies." *And might play some video games before that*, but I didn't mention it. "*Your* idea of a successful date is probably coming out of your room with bed hair and a messy shirt."

Chris waited a second. There was an unmistakable smirk in his tone when he purred in my ear, "I knew you noticed that." His voice became even lower and a quantum more seductive. "Did it bother you?"

"Why the hell would it?"

"Because, for one," Chris didn't hesitate a beat to explain, "I look exactly like my brother and, from what I can tell, you're totally into him. Means you're totally into me, too. And two, only one out of us seems to be dying to snatch a kiss from you these days."

His explanation, or whatever the heck that was, sent my thoughts into complete chaos. It was silent enough to hear a pin drop in my room.

"You stopped breathing, Sue." There was, for once, not the slightest edge of teasing in his tone. Rather astonishment. But that faded away quickly and a chuckle carried through the line. "I guess that means you agree with me on both points."

Did I? The likeness of the twins was striking and not something one could overlook. Since I thought Ethan was the cutest boy in the world, it would make sense to assume I thought the same about Chris. Except that Chris was lacking charm, manners, courtesy, and my fabulous taste in music. Although his singing "Stay With Me" had stroked a sense of admiration awake in me.

"Chris, tell me one thing," I whispered, not at all sure if I really wanted an answer. "You had the most beautiful girl in your room this afternoon. Why do you want to kiss *me*?"

"Because Lauren, like most other girls, is an easy catch." After telling me this in the most nonchalant way, he made a dramatic pause. "You, on the other hand, challenged me today—and in front of my friends, too."

"So you want me because you can't have me?"

"Who says I can't have you?"

"I do."

"Oh, okay. So yes, then I definitely want you."

His logic made me laugh, but there was more frustration than humor ringing in it. "You need to understand that I could never kiss a guy without having true feelings for him...which I don't have for you, Chris."

"Really?" His voice went up like he was scrunching up his face. "I've kissed more than twenty girls the past few months, and it was lots of fun. But not one of them made me *feel* anything. Well, other than—"

"Stop it!" I shouted, squeezing my eyes shut. "I don't want to hear it."

"Okay, okay," he laughed. "Anyway, there's another reason why I want you."

"What's that?"

"You looked *way* hot in that dress today. Definitely not like a geek, which should answer your question to begin with." I thought he couldn't sound any more seductive than that, but a moment later, he proved me wrong, as his voice dropped another notch and picked up a layer of heat. "If I'd been the one driving you home tonight, I would have kissed you. And you would have liked it."

Chills ran down my back and arms like a melting scoop of ice cream. Not unpleasant, but awkward, anyway.

"Sleep tight, sweetness," he breathed and hung up.

My mouth snapped open as I lowered my hand and dropped the phone into my lap. I knew he was saying these things for only one reason...and I was *not* going to be taken in by them. He might have caught me in a weak moment when he fed me the kiwi, but if he thought I was going to fall for him because of such a trivial thing, he was in for a surprise. My hair wasn't black, I wasn't called Lauren—and most of all, I wasn't a random chick waiting for him to pick me up at a corner and enjoy for an evening, maybe two.

Gorgeous? By God, he was. I couldn't deny that when I was head over heels for his twin brother. But it took more than good looks to be really attractive, and Chris needed to clear his ego before it swallowed him whole in a bubble of delusions.

Damn, why hadn't I thought of that comeback when he was still on the phone? "Super, Susan, just super," I muttered and slapped my brow. Finally, I scooted lower under the covers and turned off the light.

But sleep? I wish.

As I had predicted, my parents took stuff out on each other again so loud one might have thought they were giving a rock concert. A bit before midnight, I was so fed up with their noise that I grabbed my phone, which served as my alarm clock, and sneaked out of the house. Grandpa kept a spare key under the potted plant on the windowsill so I didn't have to wake him when I went over for refuge and crashed on the couch.

He was up long before me in the morning and kissed me on the forehead when I said my mandatory thanks and returned to my own rackety home. Mom looked sheepish when she saw me coming in. Dad had already left for work.

"When are you ever going to stop that shit?" I wanted to yell at her as I grabbed a donut from the plate on the counter. But instead, I broke off a bite and shoved it in my mouth. There was no point in discussing it. Some things never changed.

Avoiding talking with my mother at all, I got dressed, packed my stuff, and beat it to school.

On the up side, it was Friday and the first day this week that Ethan sat with the soccer team at lunch. I was sure Ryan had invited him over, but it was also obvious that Lisa was the puppet master. She beamed like a streetlamp at midnight as we walked to the table and squeezed my arm a little too tight.

I didn't complain about her matchmaking ambitions this time. In fact, being near Ethan for the entire lunch hour was the highlight of my day, even if we didn't talk much because Alex engaged him in a discussion for most of the time. It didn't matter, I got a kick out of staring at him just as well.

When the break was over and we all had to go to our afternoon classes, Ethan promised to call me tomorrow to make plans for the evening.

And he kept his promise.

Saturday afternoon, my phone went off, ripping me out of the last chapter of another *Outlander* book. This unknown number belonged to Ethan, and right after our chat, I saved him in my phone as Charlie Brown. He'd suggested we meet in his room as soon as I was done reading, which made me fly over the final pages twice as fast. Ten minutes later, I tossed the book away and got ready to go out.

Since the red dress had gotten me nowhere with him on Thursday, but had only given Chris some funky ideas, I decided to roll with more comfortable clothes today. Jeans and a white blouse over a strappy blue top. On the way downstairs, I had a merry whistle on my lips, for once not making the success of this date dependent on a kiss.

Since my father was the first one I ran into downstairs, I asked him, "Could you drive me over to Ethan's house, please?"

He folded the newspaper he was reading and rose from the table, fetching his keys. I liked Mom's car a lot better than Dad's, and as always when I climbed into the black Toyota, I pinched my nose, trying not to gag. Four months post purchase, this vehicle still bore the typical new car smell that I just couldn't seem to get used to. Rolling down the window, fresh air slapped me in the face and gave me a chance to refill my lungs before I turned blue.

After I gave my dad clear directions where to take me, he said, "So who is this guy? Ethan." He was trying to sound casual, as if he hoped this question didn't bear the stamp of a worried father.

Major fail, Dad!

"He's a guy from my school and soccer team. We went out a couple of times."

"The guy from Thursday, right? Your mom told me about him."

"Really?" I teased. "With all that fighting, there was a moment when she could squeeze that in?"

I didn't mean it in an accusing way. Heck, if I could joke about this with one person in the world, it was my dad. But he heaved a deep sigh anyway. "It's not easy for you right now, huh?"

I shrugged. "What kid likes listening to their parents' endless arguments?"

After a short pause at a crossing, Dad patted my knee. "We're trying to find a way to deal with it. It *will* get better. I promise."

Deal with it how? With Scotch and more arguments? "Come on, Dad. You know it won't get any better. She'll always find reasons to attack you. She just never got over Grams."

"We talked about seeing a marriage counselor this morning."

Did they? Or did *he*? I couldn't imagine my mother doing anything like that. Not when she wouldn't accept the true problem and reason for their fights, even after two years. "That sounds like a good idea," is what I said out loud.

A moment later, Dad pulled up to the curb in front of Ethan's house. Thank God, because talking about my parents' issues was starting to depress me. We both looked out through my window, silently regarding the cozy-looking bungalow. No fights in there. Was he thinking the same?

Suddenly, my Dad surprised me when he chuckled. "I've got the feeling I should get out with you and introduce myself to this boy."

"Dad!" I rolled my eyes.

"What? Isn't that what considerate fathers do?"

"It's what fathers do when they want to embarrass their daughters and brand them as dorks for life. Please, don't be that guy."

Laughing, my dad reached behind my neck, pulled me forward, and placed a kiss on top of my head. "Have fun, sweetheart. Curfew is midnight."

I nodded and cast him a smile. "Bye, Dad."

While he reversed in the broad, empty street, I jogged up the two steps to Ethan's door and rang the bell. One of the twins opened it, striking me with his smooth appearance. Washed out jeans and a white polo shirt, hair in a cute mess; this could be either of them. Not even the warm and welcoming smile was enough to assure me I was facing the right one.

"Hi, Susan," he said.

I took my time, just staring.

He folded his arms over his chest and regarded me with delight. "You're trying to figure out who I am, aren't you?"

"Nope, I just got the answer," I replied and shoved past Chris. "Is Ethan in his room?"

"Yes." He closed the door and ran after me, successfully holding me up in the hallway. "How did you figure it out?"

"Simple." I reached to his collar and picked up the massive silver chains around his neck that I had seen on him the other day, when I entered the wrong room. I wound them around my finger until they were almost choking him. "Your *I rule* chains gave you away." With a smug smile, I dropped them and flicked him on the forehead.

Chris frowned at the soft attack but wouldn't step aside to let me pass. "Hey, that's rude."

"What? The flick or calling your chains what they are?" I laughed and flicked him a second time.

"Both," Chris snarled. He grabbed my arm and spun me around so fast that I had no chance to realize what was going on until my back was flush against his chest. His arms built a firm cage around my torso. "And if you do that one more time," he growled into my ear, "I'll give you a hickey the size of Ohio...right here." As he dipped his head a little lower, his breath feathered against my neck an instant before he touched that very spot with his lips.

Little electric fire bolts zipped through my body, starting right where his mouth was. I could feel the shivers way down to my toes. A gasp escaped me, so full of shock that I couldn't savor the traitorous feeling of excitement trying to take over. Writhing in his hold, I landed a weak jab to his chest with my elbow. "Go away, Chris! You're disgusting!"

He chuckled, but the iron cage around me eased, and he let me slip away. For a moment, I used the wall for support, struggling very hard to catch my breath after that sensual assault. "Never...do that again!"

"Why?" The tilt of his eyebrows mocked me. "Afraid you might get addicted to it?"

"Yeah, either that"—I rolled my eyes and made a gagging sound—"or throw up."

"Every addiction starts with denial, so I'll let you believe that."

I was having trouble resisting the urge to kick him, but the sudden change in his expression kept me frozen.

"Why did you come here, anyway? Are you coming to my basketball game tonight?" he asked, a frown marring his face.

"What? No."

"Then why are you here?"

"Movies? Ethan and I?" I made a duh face. "I told you on the phone, remember?"

When I decided Chris had wasted enough of my limited time in this house and took another step down the hallway, he lifted his arm and braced his hand against the wall in front of me. "Wait. That's today?"

"Yes." Why did that shock him?

"But you can't."

Hah, you wait and see! I was so about to tell him just *how* we could do that, only I never got a chance to. Chris whirled about and stormed to Ethan's room, entering without a knock.

"Hey, what's this crap about you going to the movies tonight?" he snapped.

Over his shoulder, I caught a glimpse of Ethan sitting at his desk, looking up from whatever he was doing there. "I'm going with Susan. What's your problem?"

"My problem is that it's my last game this year. The big rematch against Clearwater High. You were supposed to come."

Oh my God, if Chris sounded any more like a sulking little boy, I might take him in my arms and cuddle him for comfort. He was seriously hurt over his brother blowing him off. I'd always suspected that every person had a weak spot, and basketball was clearly Chris's.

"You promised," he added, frozen in Ethan's door with his shoulders sagging. His voice dropped another sulky notch. "Mom's coming, too."

All right, I was officially undone. It might sound terribly cliché, but it was true. If there had ever been a playboy on his knees, it was Chris Donovan, right now, all because his brother had driven the proverbial lance through his heart. I couldn't stop my own hand from lifting and carefully touching Chris's arm. "If it means so much to you, we won't go to the movies tonight. Ethan can go to your game."

Both the twins' gazes zapped to me. Ethan asked, surprised, "I can?" while at the same time Chris pulled his brows to a frown and said warily, "He can?"

"Yes," I answered them both, feeling a little ridiculous, because they were obviously making this depend on me. "The movie won't run away. And if it's the last game before winter break, you really should go. It would kill me if my family didn't come to my big games."

"Okay, but you have to come, too," Ethan demanded.

Uh. Basketball was really not my thing, but in order to spend more time with Ethan, I would put up with any trial. Pressing my lips together, I gave a helpless shrug. "Basketball it is."

A grin stretched Chris's mouth wide and he looked for a moment as if he was going to lift me in an effusive hug. Not because he was being a dick again and wanted to rile me, but because he was genuinely happy.

He thought better of it, however, which I had to give him credit for. Nevertheless, turning to me so that only I would see his face, he mouthed, “I owe you.”

Oh, I had a feeling I might take him up on that sometime.

Chapter 8

"THAT WAS REALLY nice, Susan," Ethan told me a little later. And he didn't just mean my strike in Wii Bowling. "Sometimes basketball seems to be everything to Chris."

"Well, I have my soft moments," I teased, but I was wondering if it really was all about basketball for his brother. To me, it seemed like family played a big role for him, too. Otherwise, he wouldn't have been so hurt that Ethan had found something else to do.

I aimed another virtual shot at the screen. "When does the game start?"

"In forty-five minutes," the answer came from the door. Chris peeped inside the room, pressing his lips together and arching his brows. "Mom is ready and we're leaving in five. If you two want a ride, you better finish this fast."

The ball rolled down the line on the TV and knocked out

all the pins in a sensational strike that won me the game. Beaming, I whirled around and rocked on the balls of my feet, hands clasped behind my back. "I'm done. We can go."

Stabbed by my gloating, Ethan folded his arms over his chest and narrowed his eyes at me, all but tapping his foot. "I don't care how much you complain...next time it's *Mario Kart* again."

"Fine with me." As long as there was going to be a next time, I was the happiest girl in the world. Smiling brightly, I met Chris's interested smirk and wondered if, at that moment, he was reading my mind.

As we all came out of Ethan's room, Beverly slipped on her black pumps and a cardigan that matched her burgundy wool dress. It's not what I would wear to a basketball game at my high school, but I couldn't imagine her wearing tattered jeans topped with a too-long jersey and wielding a foam finger, either.

Outside, she stopped in front of a black SUV and faced us, holding out the keys. "Does anyone want to drive?"

That offer certainly didn't include me, but with a look at her heels, I thought I knew the reason she wasn't so keen on driving tonight. Chris didn't hesitate to grab the keys and get behind the wheel. With Beverly riding shotgun, I had Ethan all to myself in the backseat. Three minutes in the car with him, and his smell was already making me gaga, evoking the wildest dreams. I hadn't seen him put on cologne before we left the house, but I might just have missed it while tying my shoes. It was a mix of something herbal and exotic, very boyish and very bewitching.

"Susan, darling," Beverly said shortly before we arrived at the school parking lot. "How long can you stay out tonight?"

"Um...my curfew on weekends is usually midnight," I told her, leaning forward so she could hear me over the faint music drifting from the radio.

"Great!" She shifted a little in her seat and half-faced me. "You know, we have a little tradition on game nights. If the Sharks win, I take my boys out to the St. James Steakhouse in Oceano. If they lose, my boys have to take me out to Burger King in Arroyo Grande. Whichever it is, you're in for a treat tonight."

My heart melted. A soft laugh escaped me, and I turned to Chris. "I better cheer for your team tonight, so you and Ethan get a proper meal, huh?"

"He and I," Chris teased, with a brief skip of his gaze to me then back at the road, "...and you."

I noticed two things at that moment. One, from the sound of it, Chris was happy to have me going out with them after the game. And two, the amazing smell in this car didn't come from Ethan. It must have been Chris who put on the exotic-smelling cologne. Staring at the side of his face, I took another couple of deep breaths, suddenly not wanting to lean back in my seat anymore.

"What?" he said when he noticed my puzzlement, an obvious smile in his voice.

"You smell nice." Oh my freaking Jesus, I did *not* say that out loud, did I? Please, no!

Chris chuckled, and so did the other two. "Well, thanks,"

he said, and I melted back into my seat, wishing my raised temperature was enough to burn a hole for me to hide in.

Ethan, of all people, cut me an amused look. "Hey, if I'd known you like Axe, I'd have put some on as well." Shouldn't he be mad that I—his sort-of date for tonight—complimented his brother instead of him? If he was, he was a damn good actor. But I was starting to believe Ethan didn't care at all whether I was interested in him. Of course, I'd just made such a fool of myself that he probably pitied me more than anything.

Glad when we all got out of the car and the evening breeze cooled my still-burning face, I sidled up to Ethan and set a pace that would give Chris and his mom a chance to walk a little ahead of us.

Reveling in the smell of my great love's only brother wasn't cool. But getting past the cash box at the school entrance free of charge because we knew one of the players definitely was.

In front of the locker rooms, Beverly hugged Chris and wished him luck. Ethan smacked him on the shoulder, stating, "I want a steak, bro." When it was my turn to say something, I shrugged and cast him a playful smile. "You made us all come watch you tonight, so you better try not to slip out there on the court."

His laughter bounced around in the hallway as he shouldered his black duffle bag and walked through the door into the boys' changing room.

The rest of us found a spot in the middle of the bleachers with a great view of the court. Music boomed down from the loudspeakers on the ceiling and mingled with the noise of people talking to each other, some shouting across the rows of seats. The crowd, a milling mass as they swarmed in through the two double doors at either end of the gym, slowly settled down and the whole place started smelling of hot dogs.

It didn't take long for the pop song to change to an excited fanfare. Students, teachers, and outsiders alike cheered as my high school's basketball team rolled in like they'd already won the game. I clapped my hands along with the others, and winced when Ethan whistled with his fingers next to me because Chris had dunked a ball into the basket for warm-up.

The opposing team stormed in shortly after ours, and they received the same welcome blast from the guest section across from us. Their dark blue jerseys created a strong enough contrast to the Dunkin' Sharks' white ones that there wouldn't be any trouble keeping track of the players.

I'd never heard of the other team's high school, but they brought their mascot—a lion. At the beginning, the guy in a lion suit motivated the guest supporters to sing and clap for their team, but he soon sank onto the low bench on the sideline and rested his chin in his mighty paw, bracing his elbow on his thigh. No one could blame him for his drooping confidence when the Sharks were leaving his team behind like a Ferrari zooming ahead of a moped.

That changed, however, after the first half. Their coach took out three players. On our team, no one was replaced. The new guys, all tall hunks with feet as big as boats, turned the game around with a far more aggressive technique. Though not all moves were fouls, there was a lot more scrambling for the ball

all of a sudden. Every time one of our guys got blocked or tossed off balance and skittered along the floor, the sound of skin rubbing on linoleum made the little hairs on my arms stand on end. I'd experienced the burn of such a fall, and it was nothing I wished upon anyone, be it our team or the other. The rest of the audience obviously felt the pain, too, because a collective "ow" sounded from the bleachers each time a guy tripped.

While the opponents sank one after the other, most of our team's shots were easily caught before the ball could even touch the basket. Team *Lion* evened the score in record time.

Chris found himself blocked by a guy who towered above him by about a head. This one brought man-marking to a whole new level, and soon enough Chris was displaying more burns on his legs and shoulders than most of the other players put together. But it didn't take away any of his determination. If anything, it made him attack harder and dive for the ball more. He and one of his teammates sank two shots each shortly before the end of the fourth quarter, which made the crowd rampage and cheer. But the Lions evened that out before the referee blew his whistle.

I turned to Ethan. "Twenty to twenty. What now?"

"They play five minutes overtime," he told me.

The Lions managed two more points, and I was biting my nails in agony as the huge scoreboard beneath the ceiling counted down the final seconds of extra time.

With nine seconds to play, Chris caught the ball from one of his friends. In a mad run, he dribbled toward the opposite basket, but right as he tossed the ball, his shadow from team

Lion rammed a shoulder into his back. With a groan that I could hear all the way to where I sat, Chris landed on his knees. He looked irritated for a moment, but thankfully not severely hurt. And the amazing thing was, even with being fouled, he'd scored the two points they needed to get even with the Lions again.

Basketball rules were a riddle to me, and to be fair, I always had to look at the scoreboard to check how many points a basket was worth after one team scored. But I had played enough soccer this year to know such a foul wouldn't stay unpunished, even if the playing time was officially over now.

Chris was given the ball.

"It's a free throw. If he gets the damn ball in the basket now," Ethan told me, all tense and focused on his brother, "he wins the game. If he misses, there'll be five more minutes of overtime."

Good to know. I crossed my fingers, pressing my hands under my chin. When Chris tossed the ball, taking a light jump, my eyes grew wide and I traced the path of the basketball with my gaze until it slid smoothly through the hoop.

The display switched. 23 to 22.

The Dunkin' Sharks had won! I sucked in air to cheer along with the rest of the crowd and only now realized I'd been holding my breath all through his free throw.

While most of the people who'd come tonight slowly fought their ways toward the exits now, some headed down the bleachers to congratulate the players. Ethan, Beverly, and I did, too.

Chris spotted us on the sideline. Slapping some of his

friends on the shoulders, he detached from them and came barreling at us like a bouncing ball drenched in Red Bull. It was cute to see him worked up and happy like that, his cheeks all red from playing. His mother didn't even grumble when he crushed her in a hug that reeked of man sweat and euphoria.

Although I didn't let him get anywhere near me when he tried to wrap an arm around me while he laid the other over Ethan's shoulders, I wasn't a complete spoilsport and still congratulated him on their win. "That was pretty cool," I said, mirroring his smirk.

He leaned close and purred in my ear, "How about a kiss for the winning team?"

"Yeah...I actually think I'd rather kiss that stuffed loser lion over there, thanks."

"So you have a thing for wild cats?" he mocked me quietly. "What the hell are you doing with Ethan then?"

I shoved against his shoulder. With another grin, he rushed back to his team. As they headed for the showers, he shouted to Beverly, "Fifteen minutes!"

We sat down outside the changing rooms and watched as the hallway rapidly emptied. Ethan asked me, "How did you like your first ever basketball game?"

"That was quite extreme." I scrunched up my face. "It hurt me so much each time one of them bruised a knee or something. It feels like I've gotten more abrasions on my legs now than any of them."

Beverly laughed at my confession. "They can be really rough sometimes. At least I only have to worry about one now and not both my boys." She rubbed Ethan's back in a loving way.

I gave Ethan an incredulous look. "What, you played basketball, too?"

"Mm-hm," came his answering mumble.

"Why did you stop?"

He shrugged one shoulder. "I had my reasons."

And that was that. He didn't say more, and I could tell by his averted face that it wasn't the time to knock a hole in his head with questions. Instead, I fell silent and we just waited for Chris to come out of the changing room. Yet his promised fifteen minutes stretched into twenty, then twenty-five, and when he wasn't out after half an hour, I started wondering if he'd traded steak for a party with his friends in there tonight.

Ethan got impatient, too. He stood up, suggesting he'd find him and haul him out of the locker room if necessary. Before he reached the door, though, it opened and a guy came out, freezing him on the spot. Since Ethan blocked my view, I could only see a black sweatshirt and jeans, but from the muffled voice it was Chris. "Let's go," he said, already walking toward the exit. He'd pulled up his hood, probably because his hair was still wet from the shower and he didn't want to get brain freeze outside.

Beverly and I got up and rushed after him. His angry stride gave me a horrible sense of foreboding.

"Chris, wait," Beverly called and snatched him by the sleeve. "What's up with—"

When she broke off, I froze on the spot. Ethan slowly walked up to me. He'd already seen what was wrong with Chris, but to me it was a shock that nailed my tongue to the roof of my mouth.

There was a small cut above his right eyebrow and a bit of a tissue stuck in one of his nostrils. It had completely soaked with blood, and some more was pooling at the corner of his mouth. Nausea churned my stomach. Without thinking, I pulled a tissue from my pocket and dabbed at the smudge of blood on his brow. Chris turned his startled gaze on me, his right eye sporting a real shiner.

"Sorry," I mumbled, having no idea how to get myself out of this. All I knew was that Chris was hurt, and I didn't like it. He grasped my wrist and leveled a long look at me. Trying to cover up my worry, I told him, "I don't like seeing anyone hurt."

"I'm fine," he murmured.

Heat flooding my face, I hastily dropped my hand and stepped back. Ethan said nothing, just moved closer to me, for which I was grateful.

Beverly's voice hitched as she grabbed Chris's chin and turned his face into the light. "What in the world happened?"

Chris pulled away with a sigh. "Leave it, Mom. It's nothing. Can we go now? I'm hungry."

"No, we certainly cannot go. Look at you! Who did this?"

Ignoring his mother, Chris walked through the double glass doors, but Beverly wouldn't let it go. She stormed after him and we followed, the cool breeze once again welcome. She cornered him by the car, snatching the keys from his hand.

"Where do you think you're going?" Beverly snapped.

"To Oceano...as was the plan," he growled back.

"But not with that black eye. And we're not leaving until you tell me what happened."

"Someone had to shut up Will Davis, that's what happened."

Beverly took a surprised step backward. "What?" she whispered. "You started it?"

I rubbed a sudden chill from my arms, wishing I could get out of here somehow with nobody noticing.

"I didn't start it, no," Chris replied. "He got on my nerves, and I broke his face." He cut a quick glance at Ethan, eyes so narrow they couldn't even be called slits any longer. As he reached for his mother's keys again, I saw that his knuckles were bruised, too. Pulling the bloody piece of tissue out of his nose, he tossed it into the street and added, "He deserved it, so can we drop it and go eat?"

"What restaurant do you think will let you in with a bloody face like that?" Beverly shot back, coming to the end of her patience. "Certainly not St. James Steakhouse! And what will Susan think of you now? We promised to take her out to celebrate your team's and *your* victory tonight."

What? Why did she have to drag me into this? An ice-cold shiver zoomed through my body. It intensified and turned sizzling hot when Beverly forced Chris to look at me again. "You will apologize to your brother's friend this minute for ruining our evening. And she even tended to you."

Jeez, I'd only wiped the blood from his face. I didn't want him to apologize. But I was too stunned to croak even one syllable as our gazes locked in the dark parking lot.

Chris gave me a look that made my heart pound painfully against my ribs. "I'm sorry."

I bit my lip and moved even closer to Ethan. That made Chris's frown grow. Something was off, but I couldn't quite put my finger on it. Whatever his mother had said made sense to him, even when it was all so confusing to me.

When I finally located my vocal cords and found enough air in my lungs to speak, I stepped forward and placed a hand on Beverly's arm, unable to look at Chris now. "Really, there's absolutely no need to apologize to me. I don't care much for fancy restaurants anyway. We can just leave and...and...you can drop me off at my house. I'll be fine with that."

"Bullcrap, of course you're coming with us. We'll go out and get a winner's meal," Ethan said in a much lighter tone, startling us all. He stepped forward and smacked Chris on the shoulder. "No one cares about your ugly face at Burger King."

A small grin slipped onto Chris's lips. "Right back at ya, bro."

To my astonishment, Ethan had succeeded in taking the awkwardness out of the moment. Even his mother let go with a sigh. All this odd talk was probably due to the shock of finding her son beaten. I even noticed how her hands were shaking when she reached out to stroke Chris's good cheek. "I'm sorry. I shouldn't have yelled at you."

He accepted her apology with a nod and climbed into the car. We followed. As he started the engine and Beverly buckled herself in next to him, she said in a casual voice, "By the way, you're grounded for the next two weeks, buddy."

Chris stared at her, his mouth hanging slightly open, but he must have considered this a mild punishment, because he closed it without contradiction and drove us to Arroyo Grande.

Chapter 9

THERE WEREN'T MANY people at Burger King when we arrived. We must have missed the rush before a film started in the theater just around the corner, and I can't say I was sorry about it. While Chris and his mom lined up to place our order, Ethan and I claimed a table in the back. It was in front of a wall-to-wall window, but the light in this fast food restaurant was so bright, the only thing I could see when I looked at the glass was a reflection of the interior and my pale face. Music drifted from somewhere, just loud enough to notice but not to break any flow of conversation...which Ethan and I didn't really have right now.

He'd grabbed a bunch of straws on the way back here and started peeling the paper wrappings off them as he mumbled, "You okay?"

"Yes. Why do you ask?"

"You were so silent on the drive here."

I stole one of the straws and peeled it, too. My usually cold fingers had gone to ice status, which wasn't uncommon in situations of stress, but it made fumbling with the paper wrapping almost painful. "Well, everyone was," I replied, and that wasn't even a lie.

"Yeah, but still. You seemed a little concerned when Chris came out with that black eye."

"I was." I looked up, putting enough sincerity in my voice to make him understand what really unsettled me about it. "More because your mom seemed ready to pick a fight on such an important night for your brother. I hate fights." My voice dropped. "I get more than enough of them at home."

Ethan tapped a rhythm on the table with his straw. "Your parents fight with you?"

"Not with me, but they do shout at each other a lot." I cut a glance at the counter and saw that Chris and Beverly were headed our way, each carrying a tray loaded with wrapped burgers and paper cups. "Long story. Now is not the right moment to talk about it," I told Ethan.

He tracked my gaze and nodded.

Chris planted his butt next to me, and I knew I should have chosen the empty space beside Ethan instead of across from him. I mean, how was one supposed to enjoy a burger when the beguiling scent of Axe was clouding your mind and senses? Chris must've had a bottle of that stuff in his duffle bag and put it on again after his shower. Before the fight with Will. Thinking about it, I wondered what the guy had said that made Chris feel the need to put a fist in his face. No one mentioned it while we ate, but it had to be something really bad. I was curious. Maybe Ethan would find out later, and he could tell me tomorrow.

He and Chris were discussing the other team's tactics right now, which sounded like gibberish to me. How would I know what a *double dribble* was, or an *alley-oop*, and even weirder, a *backcourt violation*? But that reminded me to ask Ethan why he'd dropped basketball, once I got a chance to grill him alone.

After giving his all in the game earlier, Chris obviously had to recharge his batteries. As I warmed my fingers on my burger and munched with pleasure, he inhaled freaking *three*. And after he'd finished his fries, too, he stole a handful of mine.

Not being a big eater myself, I didn't mind. When only one fry was left, though, and his hand sneaked toward my tray once again, I quickly grabbed that last one and stuffed it in my mouth, turning to Chris and grinning while I ate it.

"Meany," he mouthed with a wicked smile.

"Hey, you can't promise to treat me for dinner, then eat half my meal," I teased. With a glance at Beverly, I assured myself she was occupied with talking to Ethan, before I leaned a little closer to Chris and added in a low voice, "Anyway, it's not my fault you gave away your chance at an unhealthy, half-pound steak that might have filled you up a little better."

"Ah, I don't care," he shot back and shrugged. "Ethan's steaks are much better, anyway."

"True," Ethan joined in our conversation. I wasn't aware he'd been listening. "You have to let me cook for you one day," he said to me.

"What?" I nailed him with a challenging stare. "Was that

an invitation for dinner next Saturday?"

"It certainly was. But I can't do it alone. Chris has to help me." He looked at his brother as if this was enough of a request.

Chris made a scrunched up face. "No, I don't like cooking for guests, Ethan. You know that." He stole a couple of his mom's fries and happily took the last bite of her double cheeseburger when she mercifully offered it to him.

"Oh, come on. Why are you always playing down your talent? She'll love it. You're an excellent chef," Ethan countered.

If the dessert Chris had prepared the other night was any indication, Ethan was right. And suddenly, I really wanted him to relent and cook for me, if only to give me an excuse to watch Ethan do something he loved. I tilted my head to Chris and tried for a teasing smile. "Pleeease?"

He laughed softly, seemingly touched, but still he shook his head. "No."

"Come on, don't be a spoilsport. I promise I'll eat up, even if it tastes terrible."

His flattered smile disappeared, replaced by a blood-searing look pinning me straight in the eyes. "It won't be terrible."

Suddenly, all I could manage was a hoarse whisper—how could he do this to me in only two seconds? "So you're going to cook for me with your brother?"

"Mmm"—he cut a musing glance into space—"nope."

Dammit. My hopes dashed, I sighed, but a second later I had one last brilliant idea. Struggling to imitate his blood-heating gaze from before, and most probably failing, I cooed, "You owe me."

Quietly, Chris studied his family for a moment and finally focused on me again, wiping his fingers with a napkin. "I do, indeed." He paused. "You're lucky I'm grounded and don't have anything better to do next Saturday."

That was the equivalent of a yes, and my mouth stretched into a grin.

"Ah, that's lovely," Beverly said. "But you have to make sure to come early to be around when they actually cook. Their meals are always delicious, but it's even more of a delight to watch them in the kitchen together."

I leaned back, dipping my head against the glass wall beside me, and locked gazes with Ethan. "Is that so?"

He waggled his eyebrows. "Well, if my mom says so, it must be."

"Are you finished, guys?" Beverly asked a moment later, stacking the empty cups and cleaning up the mess the boys had made with crunched paper wrappings and extra ketchup packs. She got up and swung her handbag over her shoulder, which might have been a little too peppy, because the bag knocked Chris straight in the face.

Clapping his hands over his nose, he yipped and squeezed his eyes shut, biting back his curse. "Darn it, Mom!"

"Oh, sweetie, I'm so sorry!" She dropped her bag and leaned down to her son, caressing his hair and patting his shoulder.

When Chris lowered his hands, his eyes had glazed over, which was normal when getting a punch to the nose. I would know; several elbows had knocked into my face since I'd started playing soccer, and there was nothing you could do about the tears welling up at such a moment. A streak of blood also crossed his fingers. "Fuck," he hissed and got up from his seat, heading at a fast stride for the restrooms.

"Ouch," I whined, feeling Chris's pain in each cell of my body.

"Ah, he just needs to learn to stay out of fights," Ethan joked, "or, by all means, away from *her*." With a nod at his mother, he gave me a conspiratorial smile. Grabbing the edge of the table and the backrest of his seat, he lifted himself up and climbed out of the booth over Beverly's place. "Anyway, I better go after him and make sure he doesn't bleed all over the place, or they'll call the police on Mom before we're out of here."

"We'll be waiting for you by the car," Beverly told him, clearing the table. She shoved the trays onto the stack by the wall and tossed the cups in a separate basket.

I followed her to the exit but changed my mind at the last second. "I need to wash my hands. I'll meet you outside in a minute." Beverly nodded, and I headed to the ladies' room. Pushing the door open, I heard Ethan's voice drifting from the men's. The only way I could tell it was him and not Chris was because he didn't sound like his nose was broken.

"You did this because of me, didn't you?" he said in a low tone, obviously feeling bad for what had happened to Chris. Curiosity kept me rooted to the spot and I strained to hear more of their conversation.

There was a pause and no reply from Chris, so Ethan added, "You know, you didn't have to do this."

"You're wrong," Chris snapped all of a sudden. "I did have to. And I don't regret it either. Will has been asking for an ass-kicking for a long time. But you, on the other hand, shouldn't have brought Susan home."

Leaning back, I narrowed my eyes at the stick figure on the door and made a funny *huh* sound, as if this little sketch had anything to do with it. Fortunately, there was no one else back here in this corridor to see me acting a little crazy.

"I don't know what you mean." Ethan's voice was small, guilty. I didn't believe him, and obviously neither did Chris.

"Don't play stupid, Ethan. You know what I mean. What do you want to prove with her?"

A thud on the door made me jump backward and I knocked into the wall behind me. Ow. Ethan must have tipped back against the door. He replied, "I'm not trying to prove anything. I like her."

Chris laughed. "The same way she likes you?"

"Maybe?"

"And maybe not."

At Chris's sardonic voice, goosebumps grew all over my skin like moss on the forest floor. He'd told me before that he didn't think Ethan and I were a good fit, but I'd thought it was only to irritate me. Now, as he confronted Ethan with the same accusations, I wondered how much truth there'd been in his chatter from the beginning—and if I wanted to find out after all.

This was probably a good moment to retreat and forget what I'd heard, but the masochistic side of me just couldn't miss out on a chance to know everything.

"Sue seems like a nice girl," Chris continued after a beat of silence. "You're going to hurt her if you don't tell her the truth soon."

"You know what?" Ethan growled. "I don't care about this shit. Come outside when you've stopped the nose bleed."

The door opened, and in a panic, I slipped into the women's restroom, hiding behind the wall while the door slid close. But before it shut completely, I heard Chris say in a stern voice, "Ethan. I'm your brother. I don't *care*." A short pause. "And neither does Mom."

That was the last thing I heard, because the door next to me had securely closed and all I could do now was go pee. But Chris's last words didn't leave me alone. What did he mean, he didn't care? Of course he cared about Ethan or he wouldn't have said all these things to him. So what was that particular thing that he *didn't* care about?

Washing my hands, I shook my head, cursing the moment I'd traded the movies for a darn basketball game tonight.

I got to the car before Chris. The nose bleed must have been worse than it looked. Ethan said nothing to me when I climbed into the backseat and sat next to him. He only looked out the window on the other side. Wondering if this was the end of our romance, and if all this had actually happened more in my head than reality, I pressed my forehead against the cool glass of the window and watched the streetlights flash by once Chris came out of Burger King and drove us home.

He found my house easily with my instructions at every crossing and parked at the curb to let me out. I thanked Beverly for the invitation and told Ethan to call me if he wanted to do something next week. He didn't look at me but nodded.

Now thank you, Chris Donovan, for ruining this for me! Even if it was all only ever a bubble, which had popped now. Gritting my teeth, I slammed the door shut and walked inside.

It was just shy of eleven and I found both my parents still awake—and not fighting for once. They were both watching TV and said hi when I came in. Forgetting about the confusing night for a moment, I just leaned against the doorjamb and looked at them. Mom had her socked feet stuffed under Dad's thigh. He absently rubbed her calf up and down while he focused on the screen, eating pretzels which they had placed in a bowl between them.

Why couldn't it always be like this?

"Is everything okay, darling?" my mother asked, ripping me out of my musings. Both their puzzled gazes zeroed in on me now.

I cast them a warm smile. "Sure. It was just a strange night. I'm tired. See you in the morning."

Mom blew a kiss my way before I headed for my room.

Once I was showered and dressed in my PJs, I crawled under the bedspread and fished for my phone, which I'd put on my desk. A text had come in, but it was not from Ethan, as I had hoped. It was from Chris again, reading: *Good night, sweetness.*

For a moment there, I felt the urge to throw my phone across the room and bang my head against the wall. Ethan had a secret. He liked me, but he was lying to me. And Chris obviously knew the answer, but he would only send me crap messages. How was that fair?

I considered sending Ethan a text and asking him about their chat in the restroom, but that, of course, was a dumb idea. He would hate me for listening in where I wasn't welcome, and if he kept things from his own twin brother, I was certainly the last person he'd tell them to.

But the conversation swirled in my head and kept sleep at arm's length. Frustration made me toss and turn and sigh at regular intervals—until I finally switched the bedside lamp on again and reached for my cell phone, my mind set.

Are you still awake? I keyed in and sent the message off to... Yeah, who would I send it to? Ethan or Chris?

My head dipped forward onto my bent knees and a sinister growl left me. Ethan would be the better choice for sure, just because it was about him and me, and we connected so easily over simple things like books and music. But the way he'd sounded earlier made me doubt he'd be happy if I confronted him about such a peculiar topic on the phone.

Chris, on the other hand, was a dick, and he would get a kick out of my texting him, but he seemed more ready to help me figure things out than his brother. Taking a deep breath, I straightened and sent him the message.

I am now, his reply came forty-five seconds later.

It was fifteen minutes past midnight. I should have checked the time before I texted him. But since I'd already woken him, I might as well go through with my plan.

I typed another message: *Can I talk to you about*

something?

You can call me anytime. ;-)

Agh, I'd been hoping for a "Sure, what's on your mind." Calling him seemed like such a bad idea that the hair at the back of my neck protested with a standing ovation. It was like he was teasing some sort of commitment out of me. But I wanted to find out the truth...

Swallowing hard, I steeled my nerves, swiped my thumb across the screen and called Chris.

"Hey, sweetness. What's troubling you?" Some leftover sleep resonated in his voice, but it wasn't too bad. In fact, he sounded positively surprised that I'd jumped on his offer and given him a call in the dead of night.

"Something that you did earlier," I confessed, carefully.

After a beat had passed, he drawled, "Starting with offering to give you a hickey, that could be many things." His soft laugh carried to me. "Could you be a little more specific?"

Why did he have to mention the hickey, for Christ's sake? Now a rush of goosebumps tingled across my skin as I recalled the sensation of his lips on my neck. Rubbing the spot absently, I sank back into my pillow. "I did something terrible tonight," I started, almost whining. "When you went to the restroom after your nosebleed, I did, too."

"Okay, that's really not a big issue, Susan. Everybody needs to pee sometimes," he mocked me.

I wished he was in my room, face to face with me right now, so I could flick his forehead for that. Since he was two miles way, all I could do was roll my eyes in frustration and explain, "I was outside when you and Ethan were talking in the bathroom. I heard you."

The silence that followed almost killed me. "Chris...?"

He cleared his throat, all amusement gone. "What did you hear exactly?"

Now that was a bit hard to explain. I didn't want to repeat their entire conversation, so I simply said, "There's something going on, and you know it. Since it's concerning me, I think you should tell me."

"No, I don't think I should." His answer was so curt, so absolute, that a shiver raced down my spine.

"Then at least tell me why you got in a fight with that guy—Will."

"Sorry, can't." The same determination as before.

Irritation started to gnaw at me. Chris was a dead end. "Fine. Then there's no need for me to talk to you anyway." I hung up without saying good night, but it only took him ten seconds to call me back.

"That was rude," he said as a second greeting.

"Keeping secrets from me when you know that I like your brother is rude," I snapped back.

"Fair enough, but I can't help it. It's not my business, as you told me so nicely the other day."

A deep sigh escaped me. I didn't like his cynicism, but he was right. I'd wanted him to lay off us earlier, so why in the name of sanity had I even considered asking him about it now? But I knew why. I was falling in love with his brother, and I needed to know the truth. "How about I take a guess, and you just say yes or no?"

"Nope." The sound of his chuckle warmed me. "It doesn't work that way."

Damn, this was getting us nowhere. Squeezing my eyes closed, I pinched the bridge of my nose and groaned.

"Do that again!" Chris's voice suddenly took on a whole new layer of raspy. "And I might ask you what you're wearing right now."

Realizing that I'd moaned right into the phone, my cheeks burned with embarrassment. "Chris, you're such a blockhead."

"Yeah, maybe. But you have a date with this blockhead in a week."

What the heck made him think that? "No I don't."

"Oh yes, you do. You're coming to my house, I'm going to cook for you, and we're eating together. Sounds very much like a date to me."

He couldn't really believe what he'd just said. Was he mocking me?

"And like it's customary for a real date," he continued, "I will kiss you before the evening is over."

"You're insane if you really think that."

"So? I've been called worse." He laughed softly, and I hated that the sound gave me pleasant shivers again. Moreover, it made *me* wonder now what *he* was wearing in bed. Agh!

"You should consider the possibility that Ethan, nice as he may be, just isn't the right guy for you," Chris added.

Well, with all their bullshit talk about me, they were actually forcing me to consider it. "But you are?" I snapped.

"At least I don't have dark secrets."

Jeez, so now Ethan didn't only have secrets, he had *dark* ones. What had he done? Killed his last girlfriend and buried her in the garden?

"I think it's late and time to end this conversation," I replied.

"Really? Shame." He didn't mean it. Or maybe he did, but he just made it sound like the worst teasing ever. In a drawl, he added, "Before you go, could you moan for me again?"

"In your dreams," I forced through gritted teeth, which only made him chuckle.

"I guess I'll be seeing you around. Night, Sue."

I hung up, shaking my head, and narrowed my eyes at the screen that said I'd been talking to Chris for sixteen minutes. But when I turned off the light again, a smile slipped to my face.

Chapter 10

AFTER SUNDAY LUNCH and completing my essay for school, I called Lisa and asked her if she wanted to hang out. I knew Hunter was with her, and that would give me an excellent opportunity to ask a few subtle questions that might get me some answers in the matter of Ethan Donovan.

Lisa told me to come to her place. They were watching *Iron Man 3*, but the movie would be over by the time I got there.

Since Lisa's house was like my second home, I jogged up the stairs to her room instead of waiting for her to come down to the door and invite me in. When I knocked, a muffled "It's open" drifted to me. Walking inside, I saw why that had sounded so dull. The couple was lying on Lisa's bed, she on top of him with her cheek pressed to his chest, Ryan's arms building a solid cage around her.

Immobile, because her boyfriend wouldn't let her go, she

murmured, "Make yourself comfortable. I'll get you something to drink as soon as the ogre here lets me go."

"Which will be about never," Hunter added and smirked at me.

The first week of December had started, so they'd been together for three and a half months now...and he still couldn't seem to get enough of her. My inner romantic lifted the back of her hand to her forehead and swooned. Sometimes, I really envied their lovely relationship. Especially since the day that I met and started to fall for Ethan.

"Never mind," I said, smiling back. "I'm not thirsty, and I know where I can get a glass of water myself." Apart from a queen-size bed in the middle of the right wall, Lisa's room was equipped with a desk, a wardrobe, and a futon next to the door. I lowered myself into the swivel chair by her desk and started spinning gently back and forth, glancing out the window. Some birds fluttered about building a nest in the tree outside.

"You've been hanging out with Ethan so much this week, I'm surprised you found the time to stop by today," Lisa joked.

I swiveled back to her, forgetting the birds. "We were out last night. I thought it was okay to take a break and squeeze in some time with my other friends." I stuck out my tongue in the same playful way.

"How did you like the basketball game?" Ryan asked me.

"Hm?" How in the world did he know about that? None of the guys had been there, and I hadn't told anyone yet. But of course, he would have heard it from Ethan or Chris. I tended to forget that they were friends, too. "Well, it was interesting, but nothing as good as soccer. The Sharks won, so I guess that's good."

"And dinner at Burger King afterward?" He chuckled, fully knowing just how well he could tease me today.

Still baffled, I glowered at him. And so did Lisa, as she wrestled in his arms for a little more space and planted her chin on his chest. "How do you know things about my friend that not even I know?" She tilted her head to look at me. "And when were you going to tell me about it?"

I raised my brows in a sheepish way. "Um...now?" Finding a pen on the desk and tapping it on my thigh, I briefed them through last night. Since Hunter already knew almost everything and would tell Lisa anyway, I also mentioned Chris's black eye and that I thought it had to do with Ethan.

"Why do you think that?" Lisa demanded.

"Because I overheard Ethan and Chris talking about it. The fight started with something this basketball guy, Will, must have said." I paused, with a quick look at Hunter. "You wouldn't know what that was about?"

Ryan released Lisa and sat up, leaning against the headboard of the bed. He cleared his throat. "Chris said he had to get some things straightened out between him and the team, but he didn't say what exactly."

Should I believe that? I thought not. He sounded serious, all right, but with his gaze lowered and not meeting mine, it triggered my suspicion.

"Did you know that Ethan was on the basketball team as well?" I asked him, and he nodded. "Why did he drop out?"

"I don't know for sure."

"Take a guess."

He heaved a sigh. Jeez, the guy was so hesitant about whatever he was going to say next that it felt like forever to get an answer. Why did everybody seem to know more about Ethan than me, yet no one wanted to spill?

Ryan rubbed the back of his neck. "I can imagine that it had to do with William Davis. They don't get on well from what I hear."

"That's it?" I grimaced in disappointment. "That's all you know?"

He pressed his lips together, hesitated a second, then nodded. Dead end, once again. Oh, how I loved this.

Massaging my temples, I closed my eyes and said to Lisa, "Since your clingy boyfriend released you, now would be a good moment for a drink, if you don't mind."

Lisa jumped up from her bed. "Of course. What do you want? Mineral water or OJ?"

"Whiskey would be fine, thanks."

Laughing, she hurried downstairs, probably not really hunting for the liquor. She'd been gone twenty seconds, when Ryan's soft voice dragged me out of my frustrated mulling. "Lisa said you kinda like Ethan. Like...*really* like him."

I lifted my gaze to him, scrutinizing his face for the length of a breath. There was something in it that could have been stolen right from Chris's expression when he talked about Ethan and me. Oh no, not Hunter, too. A sigh pushed out of my throat. "And now is the moment you tell me he's not the right guy for me?"

Ryan pursed his lips. "Would you listen if I did?"

"I would listen if somebody told me what the heck was going on for a change! Does he have a girlfriend? Because that's the only thing I've come up with in the past few days when I try to figure out the problem."

"No, Miller, he doesn't have a girlfriend." When Hunter laughed, a hint of irony rang in it, but the reason eluded me. He wouldn't say more on the subject however, because Lisa came back with my glass of whiskey-free orange juice. And from the look on his face, he'd already said more than he intended to, anyway.

A little later, I let them talk me into going down to Misty Beach with them, where Ryan's parents owned a beautiful little bungalow. Sam showed up, too, but instead of her boyfriend, she brought Nick, because Tony was on bussing duty at Charlie's, and she seemed to be as bored as I was. Lisa brought out a game of *Monopoly* from Ryan's room. We set it up on the oval kitchen table and engaged ourselves in a financial battle that lasted until sunset.

The many houses and hotels I owned and the growing pile of money in front of me proved one thing: Lucky at cards, unlucky in love.

When Nick rolled the dice and landed on *Park Place*, where I owned another hotel, he went bankrupt and threw his arms up in defeat. "Fantastic, Susan. Mission accomplished. Nick is game over."

"Aw, don't sulk, little boy," Sam said and patted him on

the shoulder. "You can beat her at *Twister* next time we play."

Yes, he probably could do that. But with my injured knee—though it didn't hurt anymore, it still had to be treated with care—*Twister*, as well as soccer, wasn't going to happen for a long time. Calling it a game after I bankrupted Lisa in the next round, we moved with our drinks to the front room, settling down on the white couch around a low coffee table. Hunter served us roasted peanuts. While I popped one after the other in my mouth, licking the salt off my fingers, my mind drifted to Charlie Brown and I totally spaced out for a moment.

Only when I got smacked on the forehead by a peanut that Nick had thrown at me did I manage to push all thoughts of Ethan away. Playfully, I whacked Nick's shoulder. "Hey, did your mama not teach you it's rude to toss food around?"

"She did." He chuckled. "But she also said it's rude not to answer a question."

"Hm?" I looked at the others and sure enough, everyone in the room was staring at me. "What did I do?"

Lisa was the first to burst into laughter, the rest followed suit. "Never mind, Susan," Ryan said and lifted his glass in a mocking salute. "I guess we got our answer."

Dammit if my face didn't get swamped with red. I took a sip from my mineral water to cool off and hoped the others would let me live this down.

Luckily, Sam changed the topic. "Can anyone tell me why there's no winter formal at Grover Beach High? There's been one at every other school in any other country I've been in. Why not here?"

"We had them in years past," Lisa informed her. "This year's an exception."

"Why?"

"Budget," Hunter said and shrugged. "At least that's what I was told."

Sam puckered her lips. "That's a shame."

And it totally was. This year I might have finally had a chance to go with a real date. The dances in the past had always been fun. I'd gone with a whole bunch of people, not caring who partnered with whom. But since my closest friends all had boyfriends now, it would have been nice to show up on a guy's arm as well. Ethan could have been that guy.

Or maybe not...

If only they'd spill what that freakin' secret was so we could all move on.

"Hey, I have an idea!" Lisa blurted out all of a sudden, sitting up straight and tucking her legs underneath her. She clutched Ryan's arm and looked him in the face. "We could do some sort of winter ball at your house."

He studied her with his head tilted and lips pursed. "Hmmn. For Christmas?"

"Yeah. Or for New Year's. That would be nice, don't you think? It would be like a party, but not really a party. Everyone has to dress up and stuff."

"Hey, we girls can wear ball gowns and get our hair done," Sam suggested with the same enthusiasm as Lisa.

Admittedly, the idea was nice. Somewhere in my wardrobe, my knee-length satin dress with the spaghetti straps would still be hanging. I'd only worn it once and now that I finally had curves, it would fit so much better.

Hunter started to grin. It was clear that he'd reached a decision, and he didn't hesitate to announce it. "That settles it. New Year's Eve ball at my house. Should be fun."

Lisa clapped her hands and cheered, "Baby, you're the best!" She gave him a sidelong glance, her eyes narrowed. "Just don't invite all of Grover Beach and the surrounding towns this time." We all knew where that had come from. Normally, Hunter's place burst at the seams on party nights. Three hundred guests wasn't unusual. "Small and nice, for once, what do you think?" she nudged him.

"All right. One hundred?"

She cast him a sheepish smile. "I was thinking fifty, maybe sixty."

"Really?" He made a face. "How can you call that a party?"

"I don't. I call it a ball just for close friends." She kissed him quickly on the lips and the deal was sealed. He could never say no when Lisa batted her huge green eyes at him.

"Fine. So it will be just the soccer team and then some. But you better make up for it and wear something backless that night, Matthews." He wiped her hair aside and kissed her neck. Keeping her at his side, he asked, "Who wants to play *Catch Phrase*?"

*

It was long after dark when I got home that night. After my

awkward chat with Hunter, we'd played *Catch Phrase* and *Pictionary* for hours. My cheeks hurt from laughing so hard; it felt like I'd lifted weights with the corners of my mouth all afternoon.

Unbelievable, how much a few enjoyable hours with friends could lighten up my mood. I'd really needed that to get my mind off Ethan and the issue surrounding him—whatever that was. Anyway, how bad could it really be? Hunter said he didn't have a girlfriend, and Hunter could always be trusted a hundred percent. And Ethan sure wasn't an axe murderer, going after the girls he dated. Was he? Oh man, I couldn't let that ridiculous slope of thinking take hold. I'd rather believe he was just gay.

I laughed at that idea...until it came right around and hit me straight in the face like an eighteen-wheeler.

Oh Jeez! Sit- -I had to sit down. There wasn't enough air in the room for me to breathe all of a sudden.

Ethan—gay. Could it be true? He was so nice, so polite and understanding. So charming and incredibly sweet. I whined as I covered my face with my hands. Could all these things be indicators? The fact that I truly felt so comfortable with him...like I did with a girlfriend?

No. *No!* I shot up and paced the room. Any straight guy could be just as sweet as that. I shouldn't jump to conclusions here. Especially not ones as grave as this. It just couldn't be. Ethan having a girlfriend? I could handle that. I'd just make him leave her and fall for me. Ethan being a serial killer? Fine. I'd wait until his jail time was done. But him not being interested in girls at all...? What could I ever do to change that?

My heart beat so fast, it would bring my house down any minute. My knees trembled. I sank into my chair and banged my head on the desk. Please, anything but that. "God, please, give me a fair chance at least..."

My cell phone dinged next to me and made me jerk up my head. Why I even let my hopes get high was inexplicable. Ethan wouldn't send me a text after ten in the evening. But Chris would, and I pushed out a sigh through my nose as I read it.

*Fancy another chat after dark? ^^*

Not tonight, I texted back. Really, I wasn't in the mood to talk to him right now, when my world had just shattered. Besides, temptation would be too great to ask him about the gay thing, and if I was wrong, I could never talk myself out of that situation. The only one who could set this straight for me was Ethan. And I wouldn't ask him on the phone. Too much chaos resided in my mind right now. Tomorrow at school would have to do. It gave me some time to come up with the appropriate words, because "Ethan, are you gay?" was hardly the right conversation starter.

But of course, another text came in. *Why not? I thought yester-night was nice with you. ;-)*

Because you're trouble of the kind I just don't want to deal with right now.

Gee, why did I even bother to send that back to him? Chris should be so easy to ignore. And yet I couldn't. He was a dick, goddammit!

My phone beeped again. *Aw, every girl loves a little trouble. And you shouldn't hate what you haven't sampled yet.*

You have no idea what you're missing out on, sweetness.

The memory of Lauren coming out of his room and Chris lacing his fingers with hers resurfaced. In a way, it angered me. It was an odd sort of anger. A hint of hurt resonated inside me. That was too weird to analyze, so I just typed away the first thing that came to my mind. *Seriously, you're like a sample bottle of perfume in a drugstore.*

My phone rang.

I sucked in a deep breath through my teeth and let it out in a long exhale. Finally, I rolled my eyes and answered, but didn't even get a word out.

"I'm *what*?" Chris snapped at me, half amused and half confused.

Since he hadn't really greeted me, I didn't bother to, either. "You know those cheap perfume bottles they put in stores for promotion? Every woman walking by sprays a little of that bland scent on her skin and in the end, they all smell alike. But not me. I'm very selective, Chris. I don't have to sample everything that's offered to me for free. And most of all, I don't like *bland*." I'd said what I wanted to and didn't give him time for a comeback. "Good night."

He didn't ring again, like he had last night. Hopefully, he'd gotten the message this time. I turned off the light and snuggled deeper under the covers. Three minutes later, my cell beeped and the flashing screen illuminated my room with a shade of blue.

Wrapping my pillow tightly around my head, I screamed.

Why couldn't he leave me alone? Just one night! Was that

asking too much? I reached for the phone and took it with me under the cover, reading in my personal cave.

You think I'm boring? Ouch. That hurt, Miss Miller.

Was he boring? I didn't think I'd used that word, and to be honest, Chris was anything but. He kept me on tenterhooks most of the time I was in a room with him and his stupid texts stirred me enough to answer every freaking time. So no, he was definitely not boring.

I said bland, not boring. There's a difference. One means you make me fall asleep. The other means each time you open your mouth I want to go on an exploration and delve deeper to find out if there's more inside that hollow shell.

His answer made me swallow and turned my body to a warm tingle. *You want to explore my mouth? Go ahead.*

Chris, do you ever hear what I actually say?

Of course. Your last text said you wanted to kiss me.

Stupid as it was, it made me laugh. I came out of my cave, fluffed up my pillow, settled back, and typed: *Excuse me, I need to go bang my head on a wall now and get that image out of my mind.*

That's what they all say...before they beg me to date them... :)

Hah! *I'm not going to beg you to take me on a date.*

cough* I remember a certain someone begging me to cook for her on Saturday *cough

That was— Holy crap, it was true. I deleted the message I'd started to write and bit my lip. How did he always manage to construe my words to his benefit? Let's see what he'd make of this: *You're delusional.*

A long pause. I thought it was over. Then another message beeped.

Yes, one of us is, definitely. Sleep tight, little Sue.

The serious sound of this final message and the time it took him to come up with a short answer like that made me wonder what he meant. Was it another jibe at me for being in love with his brother, who might not be interested in girls? Or was he just joking?

"Good night, Chris," I mumbled, but didn't send him another text. Heaving a deep sigh, I put my phone back on the nightstand and wrapped myself into the blanket.

Thank goodness, I'd slept so poorly the past few days that tonight, for once, I drifted off despite my troubles.

I even felt well-rested in the morning, and there was a certain order back in my mind.

One: find Ethan before first period. But I had no idea what classes he had in the morning, so I didn't know where to start looking for him. Option two was to ask Chris for help when I saw him in the hallway.

His black eye came in handy for telling the twins apart. He was fist-bumping a guy whose face looked like a horse had trampled over it. Will Davis, I guessed, and from what I could see, the guys had reconciled. Probably for the best. Playing on a team with someone you couldn't stand wasn't the best idea.

I walked toward him, but a redhead beat me there, drawing his full attention to her...or rather to her ample chest, which was threatening to spring free of her black top any second. Chris smiled when she said something to him. I couldn't hear what, because they were too far away, but when he put his arm around her shoulders and tugged her along as he came walking my way, all thoughts of talking to him evaporated. I didn't even say hello when we passed each other and gritted my teeth at his "Good morning, sweetness."

Go to hell, you bastard!

I don't know why seeing him with this girl really pissed me off. Maybe because it reminded me that all his charming me was nothing but show. A show that he put on for any other girl at this school, too. Now if that didn't make me feel a whole lot special today... I rolled my eyes, silently cursing him in all three of the languages I knew.

The morning passed a little faster when I tried to actually concentrate on my subjects, and before I knew it, I was sitting at our lunch table with Ethan opposite me. He greeted me with a reluctant smile which I returned.

And now what?

All the things I'd put together in my mind...I couldn't throw them at him across the table with all the guys listening. That would be really shitty of me. My best bet was to hold him up after lunch and talk to him alone. Yep, a way better plan.

Cornering Ethan alone when everyone went back to their afternoon classes wasn't a problem. In fact, all I had to do was stay put for another minute. He'd risen from his chair with the rest of them, but when he realized I was fixing him with a stare, he lowered again, lacing his fingers on the table.

"Susan?" Lisa shouted back at me, obviously unsure

whether she should wait up or just give us some privacy.

"I'll meet you in the locker room," I told her. Gym was our next class, and no one would mind if I popped in a little late for that, since I was doomed to watch from the sidelines for a few more weeks anyway.

"What's up?" Ethan asked me when our friends were gone. But there were still too many other students around to speak openly.

I cleared my throat and leaned forward, sucking in a breath, but stopped before any sound came out. Uncomfortably, I looked around and sighed. "We need to talk, Ethan."

"Go ahead." He didn't look stressed one bit. Did he have a clue what I was going to confront him with? I doubted it.

With another glance around the cafeteria, I shook my head. "No, not here. Can we meet this afternoon?"

"Sure." Now he did seem suspicious. "Want me to come to your place?"

Monday. Afternoon. Mom had two days off. Dad usually got home early on Mondays. No freaking way! "Uh, no. That's not a good idea. Mind if I come to your house again?"

"Not at all. Pop around whenever you want." He smiled and stood up when I did. "But one of these days you'll have to show me your room, too."

Maybe I would. But there were more important matters to get straightened first. "All right. I'll see you later." We separated at the double doors, and I headed off to my next period.

Chapter 11

ETHAN'S HOUSE HAD never looked more terrifying than this afternoon, as I stood in front of it wondering if I should ring the bell or turn around and just pretend I never came up with this idea of him not being interested in girls.

On the way here, I'd pieced a speech together in my mind that went something like: *Ethan, you've become a really close friend to me over the past few days. I love hanging out with you and I especially love beating you at* FIFA. *Nothing would change that*—with emphasis on this particular line. *So if there's anything you want to tell me, something you think may come between us, you should know that you can.*

Hopefully that wouldn't sound overly dramatic, but he needed to know that I could handle whatever it was. I would hate losing the chance to make him fall for me, but at this point, I'd rather know the truth. The end of my speech would go something along the lines of: *Is it possible that you're not interested in me because I'm a girl?*

Yes, that should be subtle enough. And if I was wrong, he could tell me so, kiss me to show he was serious, and help me name our future babies. Encouraging myself with a determined nod, I pressed down on the doorbell and listened to the monophonic rendition of the first line of *Ode to Joy*.

"It's open!" one of the twins shouted from inside.

After I'd closed the door behind me, I called out, "Ethan?"

"In the living room!"

Heading there, I went through my speech once more, but broke off in the middle because the two lookalikes sat on the couch, concentrating on a chessboard on the coffee table between them. One was wearing a white polo shirt, the other the same shirt in black, and neither looked up when I came in, so I couldn't see their faces. Ergo, I had no idea who was who.

"Hi, um...guys?" I stammered.

The one with the black shirt reached to the back of his neck and fished out a set of chains from under his collar, holding it up for me to see. *Yeah, thanks, Chris!*

Ethan moved one of his figures across the chessboard, lifted his head and sent me a welcoming smile. "Hi, Susan."

Waving at him in a greeting, I walked toward them and cast a look at the game, which sported glass figures, one side using frosty pieces, the other clear. From what I could see, Ethan was frosty. The clear queen had cornered the frosty king. If Chris moved his castle across the board to the far end now, he could checkmate Ethan, but he kept mulling with his chin in his hand, seemingly unable to come up with that move.

Leaning down, I grabbed the clear castle and set it in the right place. "Checkmate."

"Hah!" Chris straightened with a grin, throwing out his hands in a there-you-go-I-won gesture. Clasping my wrist next, he pulled me onto his lap, squeezing me in an excited embrace. "That's my girl!"

Too surprised to wriggle free at first, I squealed and laughed, one arm around his neck for balance. Now I could see his damaged face, too, the black eye turning bluish violet already.

Ethan, however, didn't find the situation as funny as his brother. He widened his eyes at me. "Why did you do that?"

My mind sobered and I pushed away from Chris's lap. "Because I need to talk to you. And it has to be now and not in twenty minutes." The truth was I might back down if I didn't get these damn things out in the next sixty seconds.

"Okay, talk in my room?"

I nodded and went ahead of him. As Ethan followed me, he warned Chris, "You did *not* win. We're going to repeat this when you'll be on your own. No cheating!"

Some serious anger resonated in his voice which made me wonder if this game was about more than just fun. Maybe there was a wager behind it? Ah, whatever. I couldn't let chess distract me now. I was on a mission and had to get my subtle speech out before I changed my mind.

Ethan closed the door to his room and went to lean against the edge of his desk. "All right, what's up?"

I sucked in a deep breath then folded my arms over my chest and blurted, “Are you gay, Charlie Brown?”

His chin dropped and he stared at me with eyes wide as saucers.

Yes...veeery subtle, Susan.

A multitude of thoughts must have raced through his mind, because they visibly flashed across his face, and one of them was certainly to kick me out of his house. But then the most unexpected thing happened. Ethan straightened, taking on a defensive stance, mirroring my crossed arms. His features became hard and his lips thinned for an infinitesimal moment. “So what if I am?” he snapped. “Would you run screaming from my house?”

“I, uh—no!”

“Would you be disgusted or make fun of me?”

“No! Don’t be ridiculous.”

“Then what? Would you *pity* me?”

“Ethan! Stop that shit!” My arms loosened and I tipped back against the door, maybe for support because the truth was sinking in like a stone tossed into a lake. I’d been right. There was no chance for us. “I wouldn’t pity you. And why the hell would I be disgusted? If anything, I—I’m...” I raked nervous hands through my hair. This wasn't how it was supposed to go and it was my fault. Why couldn’t I stick with my original speech, dammit?

“You’re what?” he spat.

“I’m...sad.”

“Sad?” A vicious laugh escaped him. “That’s the same as

pity."

"No, you stupid dumbass!" I snapped. "It's not because of you. I'm sad for *my* sake—*me*!" Oops. Maybe that wasn't the best choice of words again. But what could I do? He was totally missing the point.

Ethan didn't ease up, but he narrowed his eyes in a way that made me think he was curious about exactly *how* I was going to explain that.

Eyes closed, I took a deep breath and slid down the door with my back until I was sitting on the floor with my knees drawn to my chest. I looked up. He stood motionless, nailing me with the same hard stare. The wedge my blunt accusation had driven between us wouldn't go away for a long time.

"Listen..." That was all that came out for now, followed by a heavy sigh. How could I put this into words that made sense?

"I'm waiting," he said sharply.

Okay, okay. Pressuring much? Gah! "This isn't easy, Ethan. Would you please give me a second to sort my thoughts so I don't blurt the first thing that comes to my mind again?" I kneaded my temples and found it easier if I didn't look at his face. Focusing on my knees worked. "When we met that first day at soccer practice, it was weird. I liked you from the start. We seemed to have so much in common and all..." A pause to give me time and put together my next chunk of words. "I wasn't prepared for...for the feelings I found myself having for you. You're the first boy I've really been interested in and in the beginning, I thought you'd like me, too."

"I did," he stated. When that made me look at him with a

somewhat hurt expression, he added in a softer tone, "I *do*."

"So all this time, I was hoping that you were just shy and would sooner or later start to...I don't know...show more interest? But it didn't happen, and you kept me on tenterhooks wondering if you'd ever make a move."

Ethan left the spot by the desk and came toward me. I traced his every move until he stood half a foot from me. After a slight hesitation, he lowered to sit right next to me, his legs bent and forearms resting on his knees. He didn't look at me but at his fingernails. "The truth is, I kept myself wondering for a long time," he mumbled.

A depressing silence followed, but I knew now wasn't the right moment to say something. Finally, he swallowed hard and explained, "I suspected that something was different with me, when all my friends started to date those pretty girls and I just couldn't make myself be interested in any of them. I mean, I didn't avoid them. Two of my best friends in the past were girls."

I couldn't stop wondering if they'd felt for him what I did but he couldn't return the feelings with them, either. Ethan must have read my mind, or he read the unspoken question in my eyes when he tilted his head and studied me. He shrugged sheepishly. "It seems I made the same mistake with them I've made with you. I knew what they really wanted but ignored their feelings."

"On purpose?" There was no getting away from asking that.

"No. At least not the first time. And not with you, either.

There was something different when we met. It's like you said...we had so much in common and I really liked you. I thought, if I worked hard enough with you, I could make myself fall for you the way you obviously started to fall for me." He grinned. "I liked what you did with your hair when you tried to flirt with me. Twirling it around your finger..." For illustration, he reached up and picked a strand of my loose hair, winding it around his index finger. "And after that first day it really seemed to work. I was thinking about you all night and couldn't wait to see you again the next day."

Really? I gulped, because this was the closest to a declaration of love that I'd ever gotten from someone, even if it wasn't quite as straightforward as I'd have loved. Wrapping my hands around my ankles, I said, "So what made you change your mind?"

Ethan hesitated, a taunting grin sneaking to his lips. He looked away again. "That was actually your fault."

"How so?"

"You stood me up."

"And that's a pet peeve of yours, I take it."

He laughed. The sound took a huge lump of tension from me. From him, too, it seemed. "No, that's not it." He nudged my shoulder with his. "But you made me wait at Charlie's for almost an hour. *Alone*. I sat at the bar, keeping an eye on the door, and suddenly this guy pushed a bottle in front of me and said something like, 'The beer's on me if you tell me who you're so desperately waiting for.'"

"A *guy*? Who?" There was no one sitting with Ethan that

afternoon when the girls and I got to Charlie's. Well, no one but— "Oh my God, *Ted*?"

His cheeks flushed. "The bartender, yes."

A little hurt that he'd transferred his attentions so easily to someone else, I was about to say so, but I stopped. The guy had admitted he was gay. It wasn't going to change anything. Pushing my feelings aside, I teased, "So while you were supposed to wait for me, you were secretly gushing over him? That's rude, Ethan!" But boy, did it feel good to be able to joke about this. Because otherwise I might start running in circles or throw myself in front of the five o'clock train that ran through Grover Beach.

"I wasn't gushing," Ethan protested with an embarrassed moan. "But when he introduced himself and we shook hands, I kinda liked that."

"What?"

"How his hand felt in mine," he admitted in a low voice and grimaced. "Is that weird?"

"Heck, Ethan, I was dreaming about you touching me all week and totally swooning when you let me hook my arm through yours. So, *no*, that's definitely *not* weird." A shame for me? Yes. But that was my problem now, not his. I sighed. "So it was love at first sight for you, huh?"

"God, Susan!" He folded his arms on his knees and buried his face in them, the awkwardness clearly overwhelming him. "This is the first time I'm talking about this with anyone. *Ever*! Please, don't make me say things like *love* out loud."

Aw, poor darling. I laughed at him nevertheless. It seemed

like I could handle this topic a lot better than he could. That, aside from the rest of our unusual conversation, was a surprise.

"Okay, so how about we call it *attraction*?"

"Ugh, can't we just say I find him cool?"

"If that makes you feel better."

He turned his head to me, peeking at me with only one eye. "It certainly would."

"Okay, I'll take note of that. Next time you're telling me you find someone cool, I'll know you're totally into him."

"Knock it off, Susan!" Ethan shoved playfully against my shoulder, but his nudge was hard enough for me to tip to the side. Grabbing my arm, he pulled me back up and I leaned my head against his shoulder.

"Does your family know?" I asked after a while.

"No, I don't think they do. Well, Chris probably suspects as much, but Mom has no idea."

"I think you're right about Chris," I said, pulling a sheepish grimace. "I told you he was a bit too interested in what you and I did in your room last week. He made some allusions to me not being your type. Heck, I didn't know how he meant that."

Ethan lowered his legs to sitting Indian-style and took my hand, holding it on his lap. As he traced my lifeline with his finger, my hand twitched from the soft tickle. "Believe me, if I was into girls, you'd totally be it. You're smart and pretty. And you're an ace at *FIFA*." He smirked, as if that would somehow make me feel better. "But it just doesn't feel right."

"Yeah, it's a shame," I sighed. "Two years I've been waiting for these"—withdrawing my hand from his lap, I grabbed my boobs—"to grow, and now you're telling me they are the actual reason I don't appeal to you."

Dumbstruck, he stared at me...until we both burst into a freeing fit of laughter. Oh boy, he *was* my twin soul, just not in a romantic way.

"You know, my brother wouldn't mind those." His gaze dropped to my boobs once more. "And if it was only my good looks you're after—"

"Ah, shut up, you!" I smacked his upper arm, which he probably didn't even feel, but he gave me the satisfaction of making a hurt face. "Chris is a dick. His ego is too big for him to handle."

"Don't let him hear that, or he'll come after you faster than you can say *Down*! He's all about the challenge."

I wrinkled my nose. "I'm afraid it's too late for that."

"What do you mean?"

My cheeks slowly grew warm and I dared a quick, guilty glance at Ethan. "He's kinda been after me all week."

"He was? Why didn't you tell me?"

"Why should I? You had *your* dark secret," I teased, "and Chris may have been *mine*." I stuck my tongue out at him.

"So is there something going on between you two?" He didn't sound angry or hurt at all. That's probably how it was when someone really *wasn't* interested in you.

"No, there isn't. At least not where I'm concerned. Telling him I'm not interested doesn't help much, though."

Ethan laughed out loud. "No, it never has. I guess he just

can't imagine there may exist a girl that really isn't interested in him." He paused, deliberating, and frowned. "In his defense, I haven't met a girl yet that turned him down once he set his mind on her."

My mouth fell open. "What? You think I can't resist him?"

"Well." He grinned, mischief sparkling in his eyes. "Like I said, with our good looks and—"

"Yeah, yeah, big-headed much?"

"Nah, but curious," he taunted me. "You know what? I think this could be quite an entertaining show. I'll keep an eye on how things go between you two." When my face went slack and my eyes widened, he laughed. "What?"

"Chris said something very similar the day I came here for the first time."

He arched his brows. "Did he?"

I nodded slowly. "You two are scary." And I didn't want to discuss Chris with Ethan, anyway, so I rose from the floor and headed to his Wii, holding out a controller to him. "Care for a race?"

"*Mario Kart*?" he asked with a surprised edge to his voice.

I shrugged. "I think I'm getting better at it."

Ethan got to his feet. After he set up the video game, he made himself comfortable next to me on his bed. We played a couple games in silence, but at some point I just couldn't hold my tongue any longer and needed to know, "So, does Ted actually have a thing for boys, too? Do you think he...finds you *cool*?"

A chuckle rocked Ethan's chest. "I don't know. He was

really nice and we talked, but I was the only patron at the bar for a while and he was probably just glad for some distraction."

"We need to go there again and find out, you know."

"Yeah, right. Feeling like a matchmaker already?"

"Maybe?" I knocked my knee against his. "If *I* can't have you, what's the point in keeping you single?"

He laughed at that, and though I'd come to terms with my new situation astoundingly fast, I still wanted to kiss him when I heard that sound. Ethan noticed my intense gazing. He fell silent and sighed. "I would have never believed how good it feels to have you know the truth."

"I know what you mean. I'm glad I could tell you I was completely smitten by you, too. But you probably figured that out on your own."

He rolled his eyes in the sweetest way. "It was hard not to notice."

"Hey now, it couldn't have been that obvious!"

Lifting one eyebrow, he dared me to say that again.

"Fine. So when was the first moment you got a clue?" I demanded.

"Let me think..." He pursed his lips, stroking his chin with his thumb and forefinger. "That was between minute three and minute seventeen of our first meeting."

"No way!" I dropped my controller and Daisy crashed her tricycle into a tree, trying in vain to drive through the trunk.

"It was, I swear." Ethan laughed so hard at my thunderstruck expression that his Mario shot past the edge of a bridge and fell to his death. "When I caught you spying on me, your cheeks turned this unmistakable pink. You couldn't have attracted more attention if you put a bright red paper bag over your head." He pinched my cheek and winked. "Just like now."

OMG, this was too much to cope with. I climbed over his feet off the bed.

"Where are you going?" he asked, still with no control over his amusement as he came after me.

"Home," I snapped, faking chagrin. But the truth was, there was tons of homework waiting for me.

"No! Come here!" He grabbed my wrist and swirled me around so I banged against his chest and he had to steady me. "I'm sorry, but you asked for it."

"You could have come up with a white lie and granted me some dignity."

"You don't want me to lie again," he said. And he was right.

The sudden rush of an idea swamped over me, and I took a deep breath. Since nothing would be like before from now on, I wondered if I could dare to hug him. Just to get a kick out of it and see what it could have been like, if only... "Mind if I—" Lifting my arms, I showed him what I was about to do.

For a moment, Ethan looked the slightest bit hesitant before he put his arms around me and pulled me close. "Not at all."

Jeez, he was so warm and firm all over, and he smelled really good. Maybe this intimate hold evoked some of the same feelings in him? Tilting my head up, I searched his face and cast him a broad, toothy smile, squeaking, "Anything?"

With his lips pressed together and one side of them farther up than the other, he wiggled his nose once like a bunny. "Nope."

"Ah, it was worth a try." A giggle escaped me as he actually kissed me on the forehead. "If you want to hang out sometime this week, call me."

"I will," he promised, and I had a feeling that I might be coming back to this house tomorrow. As I crossed the room, he stopped me once more with a soft "Susan?"

"Hm?" I turned around and got caught in his intense gaze.

"This is my final year of high school. I really don't want to..." He broke off, but he didn't have to finish anyway.

"Don't worry, Ethan. I'm not going to tell anyone."

"Thank you." He only mouthed the words.

I smiled, nodded, and walked out the door.

Chapter 12

DEALING WITH THE shock of hearing the truth from Ethan wasn't as hard as I'd expected…because, frankly, once it was out in the open between us, it was a little easier. I had a crush on him, but he didn't have one on me. He only wanted to be friends. These things happened time and again, and we could make it work. It wasn't the end of the world…

I told myself exactly that as I closed my English textbook. Done with homework, I showered and just wanted to hit the pillow, but something was missing, even if I couldn't tell what exactly it was. Until a text landed in my inbox.

I had no idea what in the world made me smile, but I did as I reached for my phone.

Have fun with my brother today? He came out of his room a happier man. About time too, his cranky mood all Sunday was a pain to cope with.

We had the best date ever, I texted back to Chris. *Guess what, we played video games. :P*

His next text had a smiley face at the beginning that was scratching its head. *I'm starting to believe that playing* Mario Kart *is the only way to seduce you. Never done that before with a girl.*

Oh, you should try it. You might be surprised. And just because I was in a good mood as well this evening, I added: *Sleep tight, sweetness.*

You stole my line.  *See you tomorrow.*

Well, that might be inevitable...

*

Ethan's classes must've been at the very opposite end of the school building, because like every other day, I didn't see him until lunch break. By then, I'd come up with a totally reasonable explanation for the girls for why Ethan and I were never going to be more than friends. I told them I couldn't cope with the uncertainty any longer and had talked to him about my feelings yesterday.

Simone sucked in a breath and Lisa slapped a hand to her mouth in shock.

"No worries," I told them. "It's all good. He said he liked me. Really, really liked me and wanted to keep hanging out, but he just doesn't feel ready for a relationship at the moment. You know, with college coming, and him maybe moving away from Grover Beach, and all."

Allie and Lisa made sad faces. Simone wasn't one to give up so fast, though. "Wait until he's really gone. He'll find that he can't live without you and he'll be begging you to choose the same college as him before we graduate."

I smiled at her confidence. "Yeah, sure." Not. This was not something a little distance could change. But maybe he would want me to go to the same college one day, just for the sake of a great friendship. I smiled a little wider at that thought and sat down next to Ethan with my food tray in front of me.

"Hey," he said. "You're in a good mood today. What's up?"

"Ah, just thinking about college and stuff," I fibbed and quickly changed the subject. "How was your day?"

He told me about his assignment in history and how that would keep him busy for most of the week. But obviously there was always going to be enough time to squeeze me in together with a video game. "We didn't finish the race yesterday. Drop by later?"

"Sure."

When I caught Hunter's gaze on me at that moment, I hesitated a beat then sent him a smile that carried a message. He nodded and returned the smile, and I knew there wasn't any need for more to be said between us. I'd figured out Ethan's secret and whether Ryan knew or not, he realized I was in a better frame of mind now.

That afternoon, I did my homework right after school so I wouldn't be in a hurry to get home from Ethan's. Informing my mom where I was going on the way out, I decided not to ask for her car but to take a walk instead. It was the beginning of

December but still too warm. The soft pink hoodie I wore almost caused me to break out in a sweat. The sun heating my hair and back also added a happy glow to the neighborhood.

My path led me past the soccer field. The guys weren't practicing today, but the empty ground called to me. Once again, I found myself reveling in the days that I'd been playing with them. At the entrance, I stopped, leaning against the pole of the fence. A few soccer balls lay scattered in the grass, left and forgotten after yesterday's practice. One sat right in front of me and was downright begging for me to kick it.

No hard sports for ten weeks, and barely three had passed. Hopefully, Dr. Trooper would have some sleepless nights for giving me that sentence! But one soft kick wouldn't hurt, right? I could just dribble it over to the goal and take a quick kick. The doc never had to find out.

"Having a chat with the ball?"

I jumped at Ethan's voice and jerked around, but when I saw the beaten face of the guy leaning against the other pole of the open gate, I knew my mind had played a trick on me. Wearing his black leather jacket, Chris shoved his hands into his jeans pockets, feet crossed at the ankles.

"What are you doing here?" I demanded. There was a bigger chance I'd have sounded a bit friendlier if Ethan was standing in Chris's place.

"Tuesday's I have basketball practice. I was about to head home but then I saw you. Which brings on my counter question: What are *you* doing here?" The corners of his mouth tilted up in a warm smile that had nothing in common with his usual mischievous smirks. “Other than trying to move the ball with a telekinetic stare, that is.”

Shrugging one shoulder, I let go of a sigh. “I don’t actually know why I came here. Probably because I miss playing soccer.”

“Which you can’t do because of your hurt knee.”

He remembered that? And I thought nothing about this guy could surprise me anymore.

It must have been my severe frown that gave me away, because Chris added, “Yeah, I do listen sometimes, you know.” He pushed away from the pole and shuffled the few steps toward me but took a turn for the ball. “Hey, want to play some soccer now?” He picked it up and tried to bounce it like it was a basketball and the soccer field was a gym. “Rubbish,” he complained, when the grass reduced the rebound, so he spun it on his finger instead. “Which is your bad leg? You can shoot with the other. And I’ll stand in the goal.”

“I’m a righty, which is my bad knee, so that would hardly be fair on me,” I argued.

“Ah, don’t be shy.” Clasping the ball under one arm, he wrapped the other around my waist and made me walk with him. “I’ve never played soccer in my life, so that should pretty much even out your chances.”

“As far as I know, you’re grounded.” I lifted my brows at him. “Doesn’t that imply you should go home right after practice?”

“This is practice,” he replied. “If I get in trouble for it later, I’ll totally blame it on your sad puppy eyes when I found you at the gate.”

I hadn't realized I was looking sad when I stood there, but he made me giggle with that visual. Since he seemed determined not to give me a choice, I tied my hair into a ponytail with a rubber band from my pocket and said, "Fine. Let's play."

Chris tossed the ball at me, shrugged out of his jacket and threw it onto the grass. Only in a white muscle shirt now, he inspected the goal. Standing in the middle, his face paled a little. "Whoa, who defends this? A baby elephant and its mama?"

A snort escaped me. "Nick Frederickson is our goalie, and he does a darn good job."

Chris rubbed his hands together, then he slapped them on his knees. His body poised for action, his eyes pinned on me. "Okay, bring it on, girl."

Unsure if this really was a good idea, I set the ball on the mark for a penalty kick. The distance seemed too long for a left side shot, though, so I tipped the ball with my toe and moved it another couple meters closer to the goal.

With a knitted face, Chris straightened and asked, "Is that the right spot to put it?"

"Absolutely," I assured him, snickering to myself.

My first shot bounced off the crossbar. Chris didn't have to move at all, other than tilting his head to watch where the soccer ball made impact. For my second shot, I tried to aim a little better. Zeroing in on the left upper corner, I kicked with a little more power. Chris dived headlong for the ball but missed it by miles.

"Beginner's luck!" he called out when I did a victory dance on the spot.

"Why? You're the beginner," I shot back.

He kicked the ball back toward me. I caught it and set it on the ground in front of me once more. This time, I pretended to kick his way but went for the opposite corner and scored again.

Chris gave me a mocking grin. "I totally let that slip through for you."

"Yeah, yeah, keep on dreaming." Laughing, I shot a fourth time, because one, my bad knee wasn't troubling me at all, and two, it was fun.

He jumped up into the air and missed the ball again—but damn the move did give me a good glimpse of his flat stomach when his tee rode up. He picked up the ball and came forward, mumbling something about elephant goals and trampolines.

"Give up?" I teased him.

"You wish." He kneed the ball a few times and finally let it drop to the ground. "We play against each other now."

"Not a good idea." With a duh-face, I lifted my leg. "Knee, remember? I can't run."

"But you can jog. Slowly. Right? And I'll clasp my hands behind my back."

"You play soccer without your hands, smart ass."

"Fine. I'll do that *and* run backward. Is that better?"

He'd already tucked his hands into his back pockets and started to attack the ball. I was closer and easily maneuvered it out of his reach, not yet convinced by his altered rules. The way he engaged me in a battle, though, left me no choice. I slid it away from him a few times and jogged toward the goal, lightly dribbling the ball in front of me.

Amazing, how speedy and agile Chris was, even when he was moving backward. He cut in front of me, successfully stealing the ball, before he kicked it with his heel, trying to glance over his shoulder. We fought another battle for the ball right in front of the goal. This was more fun than I would admit to him, but my happy grin probably gave me away.

Because Chris couldn't see what was behind him, he didn't realize just how close we were to the left goal post. "Watch out!" I warned him, but it was too late, and with his attempt to get away with the ball, he knocked into the pole. A groan whooshed out from his lungs as he dropped theatrically to the ground.

A fit of laughter erupted from my chest, and I could barely hold myself upright. My tummy hurt. Yep, I was sure to pay for this with a sore stomach later, but it was worth it.

Chris lay motionless on the ground. Still clutching my belly, I strolled over to him. "What's up? Did the goal knock the air out of you?"

He didn't answer. With my toe I poked his ribs, my laugh fading into a chuckle. "Come on, I'm sure that little bump didn't hurt as much as Will's punch to your face probably had."

Chris didn't grin or move. His face was totally expressionless. I frowned. "Are you okay?" With still no answer, I lowered to his side and leaned over him, a little worried now. "Chris?"

His hand shot up so fast that I had no chance to escape. I shrieked as he grabbed my neck and pulled me down until mere inches separated our faces. Blue eyes bored into mine. "You laughed at me," he growled.

Shocked, I panted like a dog after a sprint, which made him smile.

"That will cost you," he promised.

Suddenly, I became all too aware that my hands were braced on his bare biceps and that his breath smelled of mint gum. The skin on his arms was smooth and warm, the muscles hard beneath my palms.

Struggling to anchor myself in the present and leave behind a dream in which I was trapped above a guy that looked every bit as stunning as Ethan, I managed a croak. "Let me guess. You want a date?"

"Sounds like a good idea to me."

With annoyance that I had to fake more than I wished, I replied, "Seriously, when are you going to lay off me?"

A determined glint warmed his eyes as his gaze trapped mine. "When I get what I want, sweetness. Or to put it in your words," he taunted, "when hell freezes over."

"That's not gonna happen, dude."

The next instant, he moved so fast, switching positions, that he startled me when he trapped me beneath him. He was way too heavy on me and I could hardly get air into my lungs. The little I managed to suck in, I used for another outburst of laughter—from surprise, I told myself, not because this was funny. "Get off, Chris! You're squishing me!" I wrestled my arms free from under him and flicked him on the brow.

He froze for a split second. "Oh, you shouldn't have done that, sweetness." Faster than I could blink, he grabbed my wrists and pinned them above my head. His voice and look adopted a sinister edge. "Remember what I told you last time, if you did that again?"

My mouth fell open. *A hickey the size of Ohio* rang in my ears. "No, you wouldn't..."

His brows lifted. "You bet."

I laughed, squealed, and squirmed all at the same time, but that didn't make him stop from dipping his head and finding a spot on my neck with his lips. "Don't you—no—don't—don't you dare suck on me!" My words came out choppy, interrupted with hiccups and chuckles.

Chris pressed his lips to my throat, moaning against my skin. He whisked his tongue in a slow circle on that spot. Shivers of excitement I'd never experienced before raced through me. My entire body tensed with a tingling feeling. Something in my gut wreaked havoc. If I had to give it a name, I would call it a lunatic butterfly.

"Agh! Take your slobbery mouth off of me!" I wanted to sound a lot angrier with him but, with all the hysterical laughter, it just didn't come out right.

His tongue moved farther up my neck until his nose nudged the spot behind my ear. "Why, that was just foreplay, Sue," he whispered. A sharp little pain followed. He suckled only for the length of a breath, but that would be enough to mark me with an ugly spot for sure.

"Ugh! You branded me," I whined.

Chris chuckled into my ear. "And you should show it proudly." He picked himself off of me and pulled me to my feet.

Frantically rubbing his slobber off my neck, I pulled up my

nose. "That was so..."—at a loss for a better word, I frowned—"eew!"

"Yeah, that was probably the reason you were laughing so hard, right?"

My face grew so hot, I wanted to dip my head in a water barrel. Chris bent down and picked up his leather jacket, stuffing his arms through the sleeves. He glanced at his watch, making a wry face. "Sorry. I'd really love to fool around with you some more, but I'm still grounded so I have to go home now." He walked a couple of steps, stopped and turned, waiting for me to follow him. "Where are you going, anyway?" he asked me, when I reluctantly caught up with him. "Can I give you a ride?"

If my aim had been anywhere other than his house, I'd have declined. But in this case, it would have been silly of me. "Actually, you can take me home with you."

A laugh ripped from his chest. "Oh, sweetness, you don't know how I've been dying for you to suggest that."

A frustrated groan escaped me. When would I ever learn? I pinched the bridge of my nose and sighed. "Let me rephrase: You can take me home with you, where our ways will part at the front door, and I'll spend a nice afternoon with your brother. How does that sound? Better?"

"Lame." He rolled his eyes, but took my hand—really took it, like we were a couple going for a walk—and pulled me along to the parking lot. His fingers felt amazingly warm against mine, but my cold hands had always been an issue.

Chris noticed, too. "Whoa, what are you? Frosty the

Snowman?" He squeezed a little tighter. It only took seconds for my hand to warm in his hold.

When my cell went off on vibration in my pocket a moment later, I pulled it out, checking who had texted me.

"Who's Charlie Brown?" Chris asked me, leaning over my shoulder and reading the sender ID.

With a laugh, I admitted, "Your brother." He didn't need to get the full explanation.

Chris furrowed his brows and shook his head. "You two are strange." After a quick pause, he added, "Do you have a name for me, too?"

Whoa, that was something I really didn't want to tell him. But my hesitation was answer enough. His eyes grew wide. "You do? What is it?"

"Nothing." I turned away and read the message. Ethan wanted to know where I was. He'd expected me at his house some time ago, but Chris had thwarted my plans of being punctual. *On the way*, I wrote back, and I was about to tuck my cell back into my pocket, when Chris snatched it right out of my hand.

"Hey! Give it back!" I tried to grab it, but Chris was too fast and pulled it out of my reach.

"Let's see," he drawled, holding my phone up in the air with one hand and fending me off with the other. Looking up, I could see how he navigated to the SMS folder and skimmed through my texts, easily finding the ones that were from him, because there were so many of them. Uh-oh...

Chris lowered his hand and took a step back, staring at me

with a dumbstruck expression. "'Arrogant Dick'? You can't be serious." From the sound of it, I'd hurt his pride but not made him angry. There glimmered, after all, some amusement beneath the layer of shock in his eyes.

I shrugged it off. "What can I say? That's what I got to know you by."

He leveled me a stern but still taunting look and held my phone out to me with a stiff arm. "You are so going to change that. Now."

"Nuh-uh. It is what it is."

"Fine, then I'll do it for you." He turned his back on me and worked on my phone. I tried to slip around him, but he moved away each time I started a new attack, until he had finished his job and handed me my cell with a satisfied grin. Snorting, I put it away, refusing to check if he'd really replaced the *Arrogant Dick* with his name, so we could finally head on to the parking lot.

Climbing into the passenger's seat of his mother's car and buckling myself in, I prepared for a terrible five-minute drive of taunting. What caught me unaware was Chris's silence. Soon, it made me uncomfortable, because his enchanting scent filling the car's interior was the only thing I could concentrate on.

After a while, I started picking invisible lint off my jeans, glad for any distraction.

"Do I make you nervous?"

My head jerked up. He watched me from the corner of his eyes. Weird as it might be, cocky Chris was easier to handle than silent Chris. I cast him a cynical grin. "You never give up, do you?"

"Not as long as there's a hint of a chance." He showed a quarter of an inch with his thumb and forefinger. Then he drummed his fingers on the wheel for a moment and his smirk subsided. "Can I ask you a serious question?"

I bit my lip, blinking in a startled way. "I'm almost certain you can*not*, but please, go ahead and give your best."

"Very funny." He smiled in spite of his faked hurt. "Anyway, tell me... Why would you go out with my brother, who's my absolutely identical twin and who told you yesterday that a romance was not in the cards for the two of you, but not with me?"

So Ethan had talked to him about us. Actually, it shouldn't have surprised me. They were brothers, after all, and Chris sometimes seemed to really care about Ethan, if nothing else. I studied him for a long moment, and in that time his eyes nervously switched back and forth between me and the windshield.

"You think it's only about looks, don't you?"

"No." He sounded like a sulking little kid; like he actually wanted to say *yes* instead. At the next instant, a boyish smirk bulldozed through. "I think I can also be quite charming."

I remembered the cream-dipped kiwi and had to grant him that. But frankly, his most charming moment had been when he didn't know I was listening. What he'd said to Ethan at Burger King—those things he'd said behind the closed door—that was what made me think Chris could appeal to me in some ways.

"Yes, you can be. If you want to," I admitted. "But it's not enough to make me want to go out with you. You may look like your brother, but other than that, you're two totally different people. Like day and night, really."

"So you'd rather kiss a guy who's shy and insecure."

"I thought we were talking about going out, not kissing?" I mocked him.

He waggled his brows in my direction. "That goes hand in hand."

"Okay then... I'd rather go out *and* kiss a guy, who doesn't date a different girl every day."

Chris contemplated that. It took him a few minutes to come up with a reply, and by that time, he'd parked the car in front of his house. Cutting the engine, he leaned forward, folded his arms on the steering wheel, and rested his cheek on them, locking blue eyes with mine. "Give me a reason not to."

My heart pounded a little faster, just enough to make me aware that his intense gaze affected me. I had to unstick my tongue from the roof of my mouth before I could get out an answer. "It doesn't work that way, Chris."

Holy Jesus, had I just given him an incentive to stop dating other girls? Because it really wasn't meant to come out that way.

He hesitated another immeasurable moment, like he was seriously considering the idea. Eventually, the left corner of his mouth went up in a challenging smile. "All right," he said in a rather low voice. "Let's do it your way."

I hardly had time to gasp as he got out of the car. With shaky fingers, I fumbled with the seat belt buckle, climbed out, too, and slammed the door. Chris went across the short front yard to the house, leaving me behind. He locked the car with the remote on the key ring.

"Wait!" I called, too confused to catch up with him. "That's not— Just— *No*!"

He unlocked and opened the front door before he turned to face me. As I reluctantly walked up to him, his gaze slid down to my neck and a smirk stole across his face. "Your rules. You laid them down, so you better stick to them."

I shook my head.

Chris nodded in determination.

He reached for my hand and pulled me inside.

"Chris? Is that you?" His mother's voice came from the living room.

He placed a finger over his lips, shushing me, then shouted, "Yes, Mom!"

What in the world was he up to? My thoughts were still running a little wild, so I totally forgot to protest when he dragged me to his room. Once inside, he pushed the door closed but didn't shut it completely. He probably didn't intend to keep me in here for long.

Stiff like a rock, I waited in the middle of his room while he went to fetch something from a drawer. A dark red bandana. With a frown, I watched him shake it out and fold it to a triangle. As he came closer, I took a wary step back.

My shyness amused him. "Hold still," he told me and came forward again. Gently, he tied the bandana around my neck. He hooked his finger into it and skimmed his thumb over the hickey. "You know," he said in a soft voice, "I wouldn't have done that if—for only one second—I'd had the feeling you weren't enjoying it."

My heart batted an agitated rhythm in my chest. Maybe I should have said something; maybe I should have ripped the bandana off my neck and thrown it at his face. But I did neither. Instead, I spun on my heel and walked out of his room, wanting to forget the entire past half hour with him.

Chapter 13

ETHAN DIDN'T ASK me why I was wearing his brother's bandana around my neck. He probably didn't even know that it was Chris's, but I had the worst conscience while in his room. I'd let the brother of my first real love bite me, and only one day after I found out Ethan and I weren't meant to be together. How terrible was that of me?

Or was it? I mean, Chris's mouth on my neck didn't feel so bad. And what he did for me on the soccer field was really sweet...in an odd way. If Ethan got a chance to hang out with Ted and have fun, he'd probably do so without a guilty conscience, right?

"Susan, is everything okay?"

I looked up and found Ethan's narrowed eyes on me. "Yes."

He lifted his brows. "Are you sure?"

"Of course. Why do you keep asking?"

"Because you haven't moved a single player of your team in like two minutes."

Crap. *FIFA*. What was up with me today? "I'm sorry. I'll pay more attention now."

Ethan paused the game and lowered his controller. "Do you want to talk about something? Maybe about yesterday? It was probably more of a shock than you'd thought at first, huh?"

"No! No... That's not it." I could handle gay Ethan. I just couldn't seem to handle nice Chris. Struggling for a happy expression, I joked, "As long as you're fine with still being the man in my fancy dreams, I'm all right."

He laughed out loud. "I'm totally fine with that. But one of these days you should go out with the guy next door. I think you two would make a stunning match."

My chin dropped to my chest. "What made you say that?"

Ethan looked at me as if he wasn't sure whether he'd said something wrong, or if I was just interpreting it wrong. He scratched his head and sucked in a deep breath, which was meant for encouragement, no doubt. "Um...he asked me something yesterday."

"Yeah?" A foreboding layer of goosebumps sprouted on my skin. "What did he want?"

Scooting away from my side and turning so that he was facing me on his bed, he crossed his legs and rested his forearms on his knees. "When he got all serious and told me he needed to talk to me, I thought he was going to ask me about...well, you know, about me and guys. I know he's been wondering for a while now."

"But he didn't ask you about it." It was a statement more than a question.

"No, he didn't."

Then what the hell did Chris want to know? I hated when people got all reticent about important things, and from the sound of it, this was something important.

"He asked me if I was in love with you."

Oh. "Why would he ask that?"

His eyes searched my face. "Because he would never date a girl I had true feelings for. He's kind of a player, all right, but even he has a line. And as it seems, that line is me." After a short pause and more intense eye contact, he continued, "He's developing a real interest in you, Susan."

Hah! He just wanted to add me to his damn list. If he scored, even better. Ethan's severe expression, however, stopped me from throwing that bit of sarcasm out. Instead, I asked him with the same serious tone, "Why do you think you're right about this?"

"Because he told me so."

I gulped. Boy, if only he would have recorded that conversation. I was ready to kill to hear what they really said. "Come on, Ethan, Chris is a playboy. You said it yourself. His interest will only last until after the first date."

"Maybe..." Ethan shrugged. "Maybe not."

"Anyway, *I'm* not interested, and you don't want me to talk about Chris while we're playing video games, do you?"

"Nah, not really." Chuckling, he came back to my side and

continued the game. But after a few minutes, he said, "Oh, one more thing, Chris asked me if I knew what kind of cake you like, because he intends to bake one on Saturday when we cook dinner for you."

A smile sneaked to my lips. Arrogant dick or not, that was sweet of Chris.

Later that evening, I sat on my own bed and began reading the last *Outlander* book. My gaze drifted to the clock above my door and I wondered if Chris would send me a text again tonight. It was eight fifteen. His messages usually came in around half past nine.

A couple of pages later, my mind strayed away from the written words to Chris and the soccer field. Unable to concentrate, I closed the book, reached for my phone, and typed a message for Ethan. *You can tell your brother I like cakes with cream and fruit.*

Three minutes later, a text came back, but it was not from Ethan. It was from someone who was saved as *Dream Guy Material* in my contact list. I burst out laughing. It took me a couple of minutes until I could finally read the message, because I was shedding tears of hilarity at the new name Chris had picked for himself.

LOL. Why didn't you tell me that yourself?

Oh shoot! I hadn't meant for Ethan to tell him about the cake *now.* Tomorrow or sometime this week would have totally done the job. Even though I was alone in my room, an uncomfortable flush heated my face. I rubbed my cheeks and growled, then texted back: *I didn't know if I'd reach you at an inappropriate moment. What if you were with another girl right now? For all it's worth, you're* dream *guy material.*

I'm glad you finally realized that ;-) But I'm grounded, sweetness. And you're the only girl coming to our house these days. No need to worry.

Was I worrying? Certainly not! Although I didn't like the thought of him kissing my throat and then kissing another girl with the same mouth on the same night. While these thoughts spiraled up and down in my mind, another text came in. *What's your favorite?*

My favorite what? I messaged back.

Fruit. For the cake.

Ah. *I like kiwi. :P* Chew on that, smart ass! I grinned to myself, wondering if he got the hint, though.

His final text—and I knew it was the last one for tonight because it ended with "Sleep tight, sweetness"—had a link to YouTube in it. The nerves in my stomach twitched as I clicked the link and waited for the video to load and play.

My eyes grew wide. I couldn't believe it. Sam Smith's "Stay With Me" was his answer to my kiwi. He actually remembered what he was singing when he fed me the fruit. A soft laugh rocked my body as I turned off the light at a quarter to nine. I didn't want to read any more *Outlander* tonight.

*

Wednesday after science, I headed down the corridor with Sam. She was the first, and for now the only, one of my friends I'd told about the odd incident on the soccer field with Chris. Wearing a turtleneck instead of Chris's bandana today to hide the traitorous mark on my throat, I pulled it down for a moment to show her the evidence.

"Whoa, that's gross. And you let him do that?"

"I...don't know. Maybe I did." Shamefaced, I lowered my head. Chris had been right. My laughter would have made any other guy believe as well that I was enjoying it, even if I kept telling myself I didn't. I mean, I usually laughed when I hurt myself, so why not when I got eaten, too?

We continued down the hallway, and suddenly someone's arm wrapped around my shoulders. It didn't feel quite like last time when Chris had caught me unaware to ask me whether his brother had kissed me. The size of this guy wasn't right, and neither was the smell. For a weird moment, I felt the pull of disappointment but abandoned the thought really fast.

"Hey, booklover," Hunter said in my ear, but not at all quiet and subtle. "Do we have another dream couple coming up?"

I frowned at him sideways. "What do you mean?"

"Well, Chris has been asking me a lot of questions about you. Any idea why?"

I did have an idea. He wanted to find out the easiest way into my pants so this stupid game could be over for him, but that wasn't something to be said out loud and in front of my friends. "I hope you didn't tell him too much," I whined.

"Only the very basics, I promise." When he laughed, I wondered what exactly the very basics covered.

Of course, when Hunter was here, Chris couldn't be too far, and around the next corner we ran into him. He turned and smiled when he heard us. "Sleep well last night?" he asked in a low, taunting voice, leaning a little closer to me after Hunter had taken his arm away.

I couldn't help the grin that pulled at the corners of my mouth. "With a catchy song in my ears, actually."

Mischief sparked in his cornflower-blue eyes. He opened his mouth to say something, but a female voice broke him off. I was sure I'd heard that voice before, but couldn't place it until I turned to look at Lauren. She was a little taller than me and her black hair shone like liquid coal with sunlight in it.

"Hey, Lauren," Chris said, not showing any hint of the irritation I suddenly felt in her presence. "What's up?"

With the back of her hand, she brushed her perfect hair over her shoulder and gave him a stunning smile. To her credit, the smile was warm enough to melt a snowball and it was directed at all of us, not just him. "You said you'd call me about tutoring you in Spanish again."

"Ah, right." He grimaced. "I totally forgot about that."

"Yeah, I noticed," she said with a soft laugh.

Chris rubbed his neck. "You see, it's a little difficult right now...because...I'm grounded."

"I don't mind if we study at your place." There was just this little bit of *offer* in her voice and I suddenly wasn't sure if I should turn and walk away. But none of the others around us seemed to feel that particular need to give them privacy, so I remained rooted to the spot. I might have been mistaken, after all.

"Ah, no. That's not a good idea right now," Chris murmured. Was he even aware that his eyes switched to mine for the tiniest moment? "In fact, I don't think I'll need extra Spanish lessons for a while."

Lauren's warm smile faltered. She blinked a couple of times. "Are you sure?"

Oh my God, it hadn't been a mistake. She was implying more than just studying in her offer. And Chris...the idiot had actually brushed this super hottie off. What had gotten into him?

Sam poked me in the ribs with her elbow, and I coughed. As all eyes turned to me, I felt the awkward urge to say something, so I murmured the best I could come up with. "Excuse me."

I didn't hear the end of the conversation between Chris and Lauren, because Sam hissed in my ear, "You were staring with an open mouth. Hunter's watching you. If you don't want to start rumors, you better get a grip."

I was just surprised, was all. Why would anyone take that the wrong way? But Sam was right and Ryan's gaze was moving back and forth between me and Chris. He was smirking. With a little effort, one could certainly hear things clicking together in his mind right now. I cleared my throat and wanted to tell him to shove it, but Lauren saying goodbye to all of us cut me short. She sent Chris a smile that held a fraction of the warmth of before and told him, "See you in Spanish." Then she headed away.

Hunter moved closer with drawn brows. "Did that really

just happen?" he whispered in my ear.

What? Chris declining an offer? I wasn't sure myself. Obviously not expecting an answer anyway, Ryan turned to the left down the hall. Chris didn't follow him but faced me instead. Hands raised in a surrendering gesture, he drawled, "Your rules."

What the heck—

He adjusted his backpack on his shoulder and walked off, leaving Sam and me alone.

Sam scrunched her face at me. "I have to go to history. See you later."

And I headed off to French.

After everything that had happened—the hickey, holding hands, and the misunderstanding about my *rules*—I just didn't want to run into Chris at his house that afternoon, so instead of hanging out with Ethan again, I talked the girls into Christmas shopping. I got my dad a key ring that bleeped when someone clapped their hands, because he tended to put his car keys in places where it often took him hours to find them again. For my grandfather, I bought a do-it-yourself fighter jet made of balsa wood in a crafts store. He loved building models. Mom was a hard nut and I'd have to go shopping for her again another day. Of course, I couldn't get presents for my friends when they were with me. At least their repeated "now look at that" or "aw, this is so pretty" gave me some good ideas.

When I came home that evening, a wave of animosity slapped me in the face and chased away all the pre-Christmas joy.

"I can't stop doing them! It's what pays best!" Mom shouted in the next room.

Ah no… An argument about night shifts again. I rubbed my temples and moaned.

"You're hardly home three nights a week," Dad complained. "How can we ever sort out our problems if you're gone most of the time? It's not working that way, Sally. I'm not going to take that from you much longer!"

Where were the times when we all watched TV in the living room together and no one spat venom at each other?

At lightning-speed, I smeared myself a peanut butter and jam sandwich and sneaked upstairs, the noise of their argument following me. With my headphones on, I read for a couple of hours and hoped the worst would be over by the time I went to bed. But the truth was, their fight when I'd come home had only been the opening round.

Shortly after nine, I had enough of their shouts. Sighing, I leaned out the window and closed my eyes in relief when I saw the lights were still on in my grandpa's bedroom. He loved to read as much as anyone else in my family. If I went over there now, he might even make me a cup of hot chocolate before going to bed. Right, I needed to be in a loving and peaceful place, and Grandpa gave that to me.

Pillow stuffed under my arm and my phone shoved into the pocket of my PJ bottoms, I padded downstairs. "Good night!" I yelled into the living room but didn't wait for one of my parents to come after me and bribe me into staying. Their promises to stop fighting when I left never kept up, so why would they now?

The grass of our small front yard was cold, but slippers had never been my thing. At a quick push of the doorbell, a shrill sound like an old alarm rang out. It went on for as long as you pressed the button.

Light went on downstairs and fell through the frosty glass in the door. Gramps opened it. He didn't look surprised, just very sad. "One of those nights, hm?"

"Days, nights, who pays attention?" I answered. "Can I come in?"

"Sweetheart, you know you don't have to ask." But only then he seemed to realize that he was blocking the door. Stepping aside, he let me in and flipped the key in the lock again. "Do you want anything before you go to sleep?"

A grin stretched my mouth to a half moon. "Hot chocolate would be awesome."

"With cream?"

"Mm-hm." I nodded, tossing my pillow onto the couch. Five minutes later, a cup of sweet, steaming cocoa sat in front of me on the coffee table. Gramps got one kiss on the cheek for that and another for good night.

He stroked my hair, which I'd tied into a messy bun. "One day, things will get better between them, you'll see," he said in a soft, deep, encouraging rumble. I liked his voice. It was the only soothing thing on such nights.

"I hope so. Sleep well, Gramps."

After he left and went upstairs to his room, I switched on the small lamp behind the couch and turned off the main lights.

The hot cup warmed my frozen fingers as I sipped my cocoa.

My phone vibrated on the coffee table with a brief beep. Half past nine. Why did the prospect of this message being from Chris make me smile in the midst of all of tonight's misery?

I opened the text. *What are you doing?*

Okay, someone was seriously bored. *Just moved in with my grandfather*, I typed back.

Want to explain?

No, I didn't want to. *Long story.*

You have three and a half hours. If I get less than six hours of sleep, I'm grumpy in the morning.

Ha ha—and I wrote that because it really made me laugh—*so we better make sure you go to bed early.*

I'm in bed now. I always am when I text you. Why aren't you?

Fine, since he was begging for the facts: *My parents are having a rather noisy argument. My grandpa lives next door, and I came here to sleep on the couch.*

Wow. You do that often?

Funnily enough, I'd expected him to reply with an offer that I could sleep on his couch, or better yet in his room, if my house wasn't good enough anymore. After all, that would fit right into his usual assortment of answers. If his message would have been anything of that kind, it would have guaranteed him a night full of silence from my end. But because he seemed seriously concerned, I typed another reply.

Sometimes. I'm used to it. So you go to bed this early every day, so you can text me? Drinking the rest of my hot chocolate,

I waited for his next text, and a part of me was getting impatient when it took him more than six minutes.

Yeah. I don't like being disturbed when I talk to you. ;-) How's the hickey doing?

Absently, I rubbed the spot on my neck. *Turning violet. How's your black eye doing?*

Turning yellow-ish. Makes me a whole lot more attractive, doesn't it? ^^

I like flawless. :P

I like ponytails.

I gulped. Was that a reference to how I had my hair up when we were playing soccer? For some reason, that last text gave me a warm tingle that crept all over my body, right down to my toes. Feeling bold after that rush of adrenaline, I replied: *I like charming Chris.*

I like kissing your neck. You taste like coconut cream.

Oh my freaking Jesus! Was he serious? I had to stop this conversation. It was getting out of control. Even though I knew his last couple of messages wouldn't let me rest for a long time. I pulled my knees to my chest and hid them under the thick wool blanket, keying in with slightly shaking fingers: *Body butter. I'll get you some if you like it so much. :P It's late. Have to go to sleep now, or I'll be grumpy in the morning.*

My heart beat a little faster than average-weekday-night pounding, and I wished I had a way to stop it. It finally managed to relax when Chris's final text arrived. *Sleep tight, sweetness.*

"You, too," I whispered and turned off the light.

Chapter 14

THE FOLLOWING NIGHT, I found myself texting back and forth with both Donovan guys, which kept me busy until twenty minutes to midnight. While Chris wanted to know how things were going at my house and if I was back in my own bed again—yes, I was—Ethan complained that we hadn't been hanging out at all these past two days. He must have grown used to us spending time together just as much as I had, which made me smile.

He demanded I meet up with him in town tomorrow afternoon. I was fine with that. And since it was Friday, he might even get to see Ted at Charlie's.

However, no such luck for him. Tony had taken over Ted's shift and served us the hazelnut latte and cappuccino we ordered. He didn't stop to chat with us because, as was usual for a Friday afternoon, the place was brimming with customers.

Ethan and I talked the hours away with topics like Obamacare and how far one would have to go to find the end of a rainbow. He also told me why he really quit playing basketball. Hunter was right, it had to do with William Davis, but in a way I wouldn't have guessed. Apparently, Ethan had been crushing on the guy for a while, and though he never made a pass, Will must have noticed. He didn't react well to it.

Obviously, Chris had threatened to drop off the team, too, if Will kept spilling crap about Ethan—which we now knew wasn't such crap after all. However, the threat kept the guy from starting serious rumors about Ethan being gay. That was really adorable of Chris, but talking about him didn't feel right at the moment, so I dipped my lip into the warm milk foam of my latte and after another sip, I said, "How's soccer practice going?"

Ethan leveled me a long look. Obviously, he'd gotten the hint and didn't bring his brother up again all afternoon.

When he drove me home later and stopped in front of my house, he turned off the engine and shifted in his seat to face me. "Shall I come pick you up tomorrow? I think we'll start cooking at three, so dinner will be around five. If you still want to watch the show, I can be here at two forty-five." He smiled. "Or earlier, if you want to play some video games before."

"Yeah, about that... Maybe it's not such a good idea right now. It's probably better if we cancel that dinner." I should have brought this up earlier, but I just didn't know how. Sending him a message later tonight had been my original plan.

Opening the door, I put one foot out, but Ethan grabbed my hand, stopping me. Interesting, how normal his touch already felt to me—like when my other friends took my hand and not at all like when an angel was caressing my skin.

"What's the matter, Susan?" he demanded. His frown warned me he wouldn't let me get away before he got an answer.

The problem was, there wasn't an easy explanation. Heaving a sigh, I shrugged. "I don't know. Things are just getting a little weird with your brother at the moment."

And I didn't only mean the sweet texts he kept sending me. Mostly, I meant my strange reactions to them. I hadn't smiled as much as these past few nights in a long time, and ninety-five percent of the time it was when I glanced at my cell and read another message from Chris. It was because of him that I'd grown my own personal hoard of butterflies in my stomach. And they felt so wrong there.

Logically, I knew he was a playboy that made about seventeen hundred and then some other girls pant after him. But in my heart, there was a small spot growing fond of Chris.

"Weird..." Ethan nodded. "He told me that he brushed off Lauren because of you the other day. He must be pretty hung up on you, if he stopped seeing that bombshell."

"Well thanks, Ethan!" I smacked him playfully on his arm.

He chuckled and tilted his head, casting me a stern glance. "You know that I think you look a hundred times better than her." He shrugged. "But she was sort of my brother's go-to girl for quite some time. I never thought they'd stop seeing each other for fun until one of them was in a serious relationship."

"And Lauren is still single?" I murmured.

"As far as I know."

I wrinkled my nose. "I don't want to become Chris's go-to girl."

"I didn't think that suit fit you anyway. Do you want me to talk to him about it? Tell him to lay off?"

"Thanks, but I guess I have to deal with him myself."

He nodded and let go of my hand. We said goodbye and I walked inside, kneading my temples to get the thoughts of Chris sending Lauren off because of me out of my head.

Reading some sixty pages in the bathtub after dinner helped ease the stress about Chris a little. I smelled like gingerbread when I came out of the bath and walked to my room, wrapped in a fluffy, white robe.

At five minutes past eight, it was far too early for a good-night text from Chris, but I checked my cell anyway. Bad habit, whatever.

My heart did a little flip in my chest when there actually was a message from him. Just one word. *Please.*

Please what? I typed and sent back without thinking too much about it. He always started conversations with cryptic things like that.

Please come tomorrow.

Oh no... A groan slipped past my lips. Ethan must have told him I cancelled the cooking show and dinner. Of course, I was going to tell Chris tonight, but I wanted to think of the right words first.

Five minutes of silent staring at the screen obviously exceeded the limits of his patience, because after that time, my phone went off. *Dream Guy Material* was calling. My heart began to flutter with panic. I realized we hadn't really talked since Tuesday and the thought of actually discussing my cancellation of what he liked to call our first date now turned my knees wobbly. Sitting on the edge of my bed, I stared at the screen until the ringing stopped.

Seconds later, another text arrived. *Pick up the phone!* Then it rang again.

Sucking in a deep breath, I swiped my thumb across the display and answered, "Hey." Crap, that came out a bit raspy.

Without wasting any time on a *hi* or *hello*, Chris demanded, "What's up?"

"Nothing."

"Yeah, sure. And my brother moved into the Playboy Mansion."

Damn Chris for making me laugh. He did it so easily these days.

"Come on, Sue. What's the problem?" he continued. "Why don't you want to come over tomorrow? And don't think I didn't notice that you haven't been at my house most of this week."

Okay, so he smelled that something was off. But how could I explain my reluctance to him? No way would he get the truth out of me—that I was scared of how his strange behavior this past week was affecting me. His charm, actually.

If he found out that his little messages caused happy butterflies to flutter in my stomach, he'd totally think he'd gotten me where he wanted me in the first place. Chances were, this was true. He might even kiss me. And then...?

He'd break my heart.

"Things have been a little stressful with my family these past few days," I fibbed, hoping he'd catch the hook.

"Oh." The pause that followed was long enough to make it clear he didn't quite believe me. But my alibi was cast in iron. "I'm sorry about that," he finally said. "But that's even more reason for you to come tomorrow."

"Is it? How so?"

"Because it'll take your mind off the trouble at home for a while."

From his point of view, it even made sense. The real problem was, however, that he was the trouble that concerned me, not my parents' everlasting fights. And spending time with him might make matters worse instead of better. But how could I argue? I'd led myself into this trap. Terrific.

"Come on, Sue," he pleaded after a couple of seconds. "Let me cook for you. It'll be fun and it'll taste good."

What could I say to that? After a deep sigh, I relented. "All right. Tell Ethan he can pick me up at two." If I was going over to their place, I could just as well give Ethan a run for his money at Wii Sports. "But you better not put any peaches in that meal," I teased Chris, said goodbye and quickly hung up with the ring of his chuckle in my ear.

His bandana still lay on my nightstand. I grabbed it and pressed it to my chest. Yeah, this was some deep shit I'd maneuvered myself into... Now, where was a lifeline when you needed one?

*

Ethan was dead on time on Saturday afternoon. He honked in front of my house and waited like a chauffeur to open the car door for me. "I'm glad you're coming after all," he told me when he got in on the other side and drove off.

"In the end, Chris's arguments were smoother than mine," I admitted with a grin. "It's hard to say no when someone is begging." And begging he'd been. There were seven messages on my phone this morning, all reading the same. *Please don't change your mind!*

He only stopped sending them after I wrote back: *Calm down, tiger. I'm coming, I'm coming...*

When we arrived at Ethan's house, Beverly welcomed me with a beam, but a second later she excused herself, because a difficult client wanted to see a house out of town. "Don't wait with dinner for me," she said and kissed Ethan on the forehead.

We headed to his room, but crashed into Chris on the way. Well, not both of us, only me.

Chris had come out of the bathroom, dragging a steamy cloud that smelled of shower gel with him. His hair was perfectly styled in a chaotic stand-up mess and he'd dressed in a white tee with a graphite-gray, button-down shirt thrown casually over it. The moment he caught my elbow to steady me after the bump, his mouth widened to a happy smile. "Hey now, look who found the way to our house again."

I let him hold my arm longer than necessary, fighting against a hoard of little fluttery fellows in my gut. It'd been too long since the last time we'd met, and facing him instead of reading a text made me all too aware of how much I'd actually missed his smile.

Pull yourself together, Susan. Now!

"Look who's dressed up for cooking," I teased back, glad I sounded normal and not squeaky or hoarse.

"It's how I dress up for a date, actually."

"Well, then you dress up nicely."

"Right back at you." He gave me a once-over, his eyes returning to the deep V neck of my snug-fit, soft green t-shirt. "I see there's no need for a turtleneck any longer."

He was right, the hickey was gone, as was his black eye. Almost. The softest layer of yellowish violet adorned his right cheekbone. It would be gone in another day or two, but it still reminded me of how he'd fought a battle for his brother. Tempted to reach up and brush the spot with my fingers, I resisted the urge and clamped down on my teeth instead. This moment was all but magical, and Chris found my staring very amusing.

"Bowling or baseball, what do you want to play, Susan?"

Glad for Ethan's distraction, I detached myself from his brother and headed to Ethan's room, clearing my throat. "How about golf for a change?"

He set up the game, but we didn't stay alone for long. Not ten seconds, in fact. Chris came in and flopped on Ethan's bed beside me. "Three players?" he suggested.

Ethan sent me a questioning look. I rolled my eyes but nodded—as if I could say no to his brother joining us—and a smile appeared with that...on my lips, not his.

All three of us played virtual golf for quite some time, and it turned out that Ethan and I didn't stand a chance against his brother. When it was my turn again and I took up my position, Chris stepped behind me and reached around my body, placing his hands over mine on the controller. "You're holding it wrong. It'll never work with that shot."

Whoa, his embrace made me shiver.

He blew my hair out of his face, reminding me of how he'd told me he liked ponytails. Maybe that was one of the reasons I'd tied my hair into one this morning.

Afraid he'd notice my pounding heart standing so close, I raced through seven different comebacks in my mind to make him go away. The one that made it was, "Please, this is so cliché, Chris." I waggled my shoulders to shake him off.

Laughing, Chris backed off. When he came around, I gave him a hard stare then shot. My ball landed in the pond between the two virtual islands. "Told you so," he taunted. "Anyway, it's time to stop playing and get to work or we'll be eating at ten tonight."

Ethan and I followed him into the kitchen, where several utensils were already placed in a nice order around the stove. The boys got some things from the fridge and cupboards, added oil to a pan and flour to a bowl.

I didn't know what was coming at me. Somehow, I'd expected them to dress up as chefs with huge hats and white aprons. Well, they didn't. Dressed like they were, they started chopping veggies and Ethan seasoned some steaks. What their mother found so special about that escaped me.

Until Chris turned on the radio.

A catchy song blasted through the kitchen with some Italian or Spanish lyrics I didn't understand, but the rhythm was infectious. The twins twisted from one end of the room to the other, getting what they needed, sometimes tossing things at each other and showing off how they could juggle veggies or the salt and pepper mills. My heart stopped when Chris tossed a vinegar bottle in the air, but he caught it behind his back like he was a trained cocktail bartender and this was a whiskey bottle.

I let out my breath. Thank God, nothing shattered into a million pieces during that stunt. At my horrified face, he only chuckled. Next, he beckoned me with a tilt of his head and patted the corner of the kitchen counter. Thinking I'd only be in their way, I shook my head and remained seated at the table, happy to watch from here.

Chris crooked his finger.

"No," I told him, but he wasn't happy about that. Exhaling an exaggerated sigh and rolling his eyes, he walked to me, took my hand, and pulled me to my feet. It all happened very fast, but when he swirled me around him and caught me to his chest, a startled laugh escaped me. Thank God for the dancing lessons we were forced to take in tenth grade—I didn't trip.

In a way that matched the samba rhythm of the song, Chris moved me to the kitchen island. He held my right hand up, wrapping his other arm around my waist, and never broke eye contact as he made me dance with him across the room. That was probably the hottest thing I'd ever done, and with one of the two hottest guys on the planet. Did he notice how deep I breathed in his scent when I was so close to him? Hopefully not.

The dance was over far too quickly. Dropping his hands to my waist, Chris lifted me onto the kitchen island, right where he wanted me to sit before. Feet crossed at my ankles, I clasped my hands in my lap and enjoyed the view from here.

Spicy smells wafted around us as Ethan fried the meat and bacon-wrapped veggies. From the other side, a sweet scent crawled toward me from where Chris was mixing a cream of yogurt and mascarpone.

When he was done, he stuck his finger into the cream and held it out to me.

"Seriously?" I grimaced. "Gross."

Laughing, Chris shrugged and stuck the finger in his mouth, sucking off the cream. Seconds later, he startled me once again as he grabbed my hips without warning and slid me along the edge of the island. The music muffled my shocked shriek, but he just wanted to get me out of the way so he could fetch a kitchen knife from the top drawer that I'd been blocking with my dangling legs. Really, he could have asked me to move. Instead, he placed his hands on my hips again and slid me back to my original spot. This time, I didn't shriek but giggle.

"I need the oven in a minute," Ethan said, filling a ceramic bowl with the meat and pouring some creamy sauce over it.

Chris went to retrieve a baking tray from the oven to make room for his brother's dish. From the look of it, he'd prepared a cake base earlier today. I loved the biscuit smell that crept up my nose when he placed the tray next to me on the counter.

After Ethan shoved his part of the cooking deal in the oven, he wiped his hands on a dishtowel and announced, "Half an hour."

Chris, who'd smeared the cream on the cake by now, picked a few oranges from the fruit bowl and juggled them, singing along to "All About That Bass," until one of the oranges dropped to the floor. Ethan picked it up for him while Chris grabbed a few other fruits. He dug a little deeper into the bowl and finally turned around to his brother, a frown on his face. "Where are the kiwis?"

Ethan sucked in a breath through his teeth. "Crap." He gave me a guilty look. "I completely forgot about them."

Annoyed, Chris suppressed a groan. "Go get me some, now."

Of course, he'd asked me about my favorite fruit, but I didn't see what was so tragic about not having any kiwi on the cake. As long as there were no peaches in my dessert, I was fine with any fruit. But Chris seemed to want everything perfect.

"How about you go get them yourself?" Ethan taunted him.

Chris braced his hands on the counter and leveled Ethan the same mocking look. "I'm grounded."

Grimacing, Ethan let go of a sigh. "Right."

"Hey," I said, drawing their attention to me. "I can go get them."

About to slide off the counter, Chris put a hand on my knee and held me back. "Ethan can go. *You* stay right where you are."

My heart knocked against the base of my throat. Last time I was alone with Chris, I ended up with a hickey on my neck. It would be wise to insist I run to the store. But Ethan was out of the kitchen before I even had a chance to argue. "Be right back," he shouted from the hallway. The sound of the front door slamming shut drifted to us.

Oh shoot...

Chapter 15

MY NERVES IN a sudden tangle, I eyed Chris hesitantly. To his credit, he didn't act as if he had any hidden motives or as if he planned to roast me and have me for dinner. No, he just turned off the music and fished for another stainless steel bowl in a cupboard.

In this one, he dropped several bars of dark chocolate and a chunk of butter. Heating the mass in a bain-marie, he stirred it nonstop with an egg beater. Every now and then, he dipped his finger into the melting chocolate and tasted it.

Strange that he wouldn't talk to me now that we were alone. It heightened my tension, but like hell would I let him notice that.

The next time he dipped his finger into the chocolate, he jerked back his hand, wincing. A stain landed on the collar of his white t-shirt. "Damn," he murmured under his breath, trying to wipe the chocolate away, but the dark spot remained.

He turned off the burner and pulled the bowl aside—the chocolate was probably hot and liquidy enough now. Shrugging out of his shirt, he pulled his tee over his head and tossed it across the room. It landed on one of the empty chairs.

I stopped breathing, my chest gone too tight at the sight of his toned body. Heck, did I need to wipe some drool off my lips? Hopefully not, but I couldn't guarantee. Chris certainly noticed my gaze on him. With a smirk, he pulled the dark gray shirt on again and buttoned it up, leaving only the top two buttons unfastened. His set of silver chains glinted against his skin.

Unaware he'd left me feeling a little woozy with his unintentional strip show, Chris calmly continued stirring the chocolate sauce, improving it with a splash of rum and some grated orange peels. A sweet, warm smell spread in the room, reminding me of birthday cakes and Easter candy.

Next, he peeled an orange and a banana and plucked some grapes from the fruit bowl. Between chopping the fruits on a board, he continued to stir the chocolate and occasionally tested the temperature with his finger. It looked so delicious, I wished he'd let me dip my finger into that bowl, too.

When he finally seemed pleased with the consistency, he retrieved a small plate of strawberries from the fridge and set it on the counter next to me. "Close your eyes and open your mouth," he said softly, his attention on the food in front of him rather than on me.

I did, but a moment later, I opened one eye again to scrutinize him. "You're not going to stick your finger in my mouth, are you?"

Glancing up, he laughed. "Now that would be a little *gross*, right?"

It would *so* be, but he'd offered me his cream-dipped finger before, so who could know with him? I closed my eye again but shot both open the next second. "And you're not going to kiss me, either?"

Chris, still working the molten chocolate with the egg beater, cocked his head and gave me a funny look. "I wasn't thinking about it." A short pause. One corner of his mouth tilted up to a crooked smile. "But now I'm wondering why you were."

Very funny. "You better play nice, if you want me to stay through dinner."

"I always play nice, little Sue," he promised with a touch of mischief in his voice. "Now close your eyes."

The back of my neck tingled, but I did as he told me.

I could hear when he put the egg beater away and I could feel the warmth of his body as he moved closer. He took his time preparing whatever he was going to put in my mouth, and with each second that ticked away, my heart galloped faster. My knees trembled, so I pressed them tightly together. If Chris saw my shaking legs...that would be the death of me.

"Open your mouth," he repeated in that same soft tone as before.

I parted my lips a little.

"You don't trust me?" There was a smile in his voice.

Warily, I opened my mouth a tiny bit more. When something touched my tongue, I closed my teeth on it and pulled it out of his fingers. The taste was a mix of sour and sweet, fleshy and juicy. It was kind of hard to figure out what exactly he'd fed me with my eyes shut, but in the end I knew. It was half an orange wedge, coated with warm, dark chocolate.

As a moan of pleasure escaped me, Chris asked, "Good?"

"Jeez!" Good didn't even begin to describe it. "This is *awesome*!"

He chuckled, but I didn't open my eyes yet. "Next one," he said and gently put another fruit into my mouth. This time, however, he didn't pull back his fingers fast enough and I closed my lips on them. With the speed of a shooting star, heat traveled through my veins and in that instant I was aware of him in every single cell of my body.

Chris dragged his finger across my bottom lip, leaving me vibrating when he pulled his hand away. Maybe now was the right moment to open my eyes and run from the room. But I was struggling so hard to just keep breathing, I couldn't manage anything else.

"Susan?" His voice was barely a whisper.

I swallowed the strawberry, then croaked, "Hm?"

His breath teased the skin on my cheek as he gently said in my ear, "What's the temperature in Hell right now?"

This time, my eyelids flew open and my jaw dropped, but all that came out was a shaky breath. From three inches away, we gazed into each other's eyes. Chris was so quiet, I wondered if he could catch the sound of my drumming heart.

Lifting his hand to my face, he brushed my cheek with only the tips of his fingers.

Jeez, he was going to kiss me, and I was going to let him, and then he would go break my heart, and I was going to regret it, but still I would let him kiss me now and, *oh my God*, please don't let there be strawberry bits left between my teeth, and of course I should jump off this kitchen counter and run as fast and far as I can, but heck... I closed my eyes.

Chris touched his lips to the corner of mine. And the butterflies were back. All ten thousand and then some.

"Are we getting close to freezing point?" he breathed.

As an answer, I turned my head slightly his way. Splaying his fingers, he cupped my cheek and he placed another gentle kiss on my lips. It felt so incredibly good that I wanted to press pause on this moment, call Sam, and tell her all about it. An excited squeak built up inside me. I was going to explode! But of course, I contained it all, even when Chris tilted his face a little and slowly molded his mouth to mine.

I'd never been aware that lips could actually feel so soft. And boy, when he made me open my mouth and touched my tongue with his for the first brief moment, my stomach became too small a place for the butterflies in there. I had the feeling all of them were pushing up and trying to escape through my mouth, nose, and ears.

Chris's other hand graced my right cheek. It moved to my neck until his fingers brushed the skin behind my ears and his thumbs stroked my cheekbones. This way he had total control and tipped my head up a little as he stepped in front of me, pushing gently against my knees until I opened them and let him stand between my thighs.

Unclasping my hands, I prayed they weren't coated with cold sweat. There was nothing I could do about their soft tremble, however, as I flattened them against his chest. My fingers dug into his shirt, needing something to hold on to.

His tongue came back for another sample of mine, this time not as fleetingly as before. In fact, Chris took his time feeling his way around my mouth and teased my tongue out of hiding. Everything was amazingly tender.

From the taste of his mouth, he'd been nibbling an orange while he fed me fruit. Maybe he could also taste chocolate and strawberries in mine? Chris deepened the kiss, seeming hungry for whatever I was ready to give him. In spite of a small voice at the back of my mind telling me that this was dangerous, insane, and stupid even, I didn't hold back.

The next moment, I was reminded that I'd grown a perfect pair of boobs since last summer, because they pressed against his chest—that's how close he was. The touch gave me chills of a funny kind.

I moved my hands over his shoulders, feeling up the back of his warm neck until my fingers slid into his cropped hair. A slight shiver traveled through him. His lips tightened to a smile, and he kissed a path along my jaw to my ear. "Hey there, Frosty," he teased.

A little shy, I pulled my hands away. I didn't want to give him chills with my cold fingers, but Chris caught my hands in front of his chest and led them back to where I'd touched his neck.

Bracing his hands on the counter on either side of my hips,

he nibbled the length of my throat. These small kisses didn't feel slobbery like when he'd given me the hickey. They were just warm and very, very gentle.

When I exhaled a sigh, he moved his mouth back to mine and traced my bottom lip with his teeth. Tenderly, he bit down and suckled with a sensual pull. He might've been sucking the life right out of me that way, because my head began to spin from the sensation. Eyes closed, I let my brow dip against his, surrendering with everything I had when he deepened the kiss once again.

I could have done this forever—*wanted* to do this forever. Except, Ethan chose that precise and utterly wrong moment to come back from the store.

Chris heard it first—the sound of a car parking in front of the house. He inched away from me, growling with irritation and a good deal of unsatisfied hunger, but soon enough a warm smile crept to his face. With the tip of his finger, he brushed a few unruly wisps of my hair out of my eyes. "Now...that wasn't so bad, was it?"

I licked my bottom lip, savoring the last taste of him there, and shook my head, grinning.

He stepped away from me and resumed stirring the cooling chocolate as if nothing at all had happened between us, just as Ethan walked through the door.

"Hey, guys," he called out. "Here are the kiwis." He tossed one after the other across the room at Chris, who put them on the counter with the other fruits he'd already chopped. With Ethan checking the meat in the oven, Chris cast me a half-smile and winked.

Once again, I clasped my hands in my lap, suppressing a smile of my own, but a wave of warmth surged to my cheeks. I couldn't hold Chris's gaze for long and lowered my eyes.

Ethan went to pull the scalloped fillets of pork out of the oven and prepared three fantastic-looking meals on white porcelain plates. Hopping off the counter, I helped him lay out the table for only the three of us, while Chris finished decorating the cream cake and put it in the fridge to cool for later.

"God, Ethan, this is delicious," I complimented him a quarter into my meal. Other than that, we didn't speak much as we ate, and I wondered if Ethan sensed that something was off. He sent me glances across the table, but so did Chris, and at some point I just didn't know where to look anymore, so I focused only on my plate.

Dinner over, Chris checked on the cake but told us, "It could do with another twenty minutes."

"Maybe we should clean up the kitchen before dessert," I suggested.

"Good idea," Chris replied. "Ethan can do it."

His twin brother crossed his arms over his chest and leaned back in his chair. "Why me?"

"Because you forgot the kiwis today."

"Well, I actually drove to the store again and got them. You clean up here."

The guys stared each other down in a tight match until they both said at once, "Let's play it out."

Like a couple of racehorses that could barely control their

energy, they stomped to the backyard and I followed them. Most of the ground out here was lawn and flowerbeds, but a square was paved right behind the house, too. Only a fifth of the size of a real basketball court, it had a basket mounted on an iron bar cemented into the ground. Ethan brought a ball from the little shed at the very back of the yard and the boys made me toss it in the air for an unbiased start.

I knew that Chris was a pro, fit for college basketball, no doubt, but it surprised me to see that Ethan could totally keep up with him. There was no way of telling which of them would win this game.

I watched them jump, run, dive for the ball, and dunk it for several minutes. Finally, I decided to contribute my share to today's date with the two of them and went inside to clean the kitchen myself. Rinsing and scrubbing the plates, pots, and bowls until they were clean enough to go into the dishwasher, the sound of their game drifted to me through the open window above the sink. The guys laughed and cussed all the way through it, and with Ethan's counting out loud, I knew the score at all times.

Once done with the dishes and wiping the cutting boards clean, I headed outside again, but something caught the corner of my eye and stopped me in the kitchen door. Chris's stained t-shirt still hung over one of the chairs.

Safe with no one here to observe me, I sneaked closer and snatched it from the backrest. Holding the fabric to my nose, a deep breath filled my head with Chris's enticing scent. Reminded of how the car had smelled of him after we played soccer the other day, I closed my eyes.

On a sad note, I wondered if I'd done the wrong thing when I let him kiss me. A while back, I'd told him that I could never kiss a boy without having some feelings for him. Today, I'd proven myself right.

Now, a nervousness crept over me that the deal was over for Chris. He'd finally gotten where he wanted with me. The challenge was over...he'd won. What was going to happen now? Would he walk away and find his next challenge?

If so, I had no right to whine about it. The rules of this game were clear from the beginning. The fact that I'd changed my mind had nothing to do with him. Well, no, that wasn't quite true. It had everything to do with Chris, but it didn't mean the new rules applied to him, too.

I sucked in another lungful of his scent and sighed. He'd succeeded. This past week, I'd gotten to know a side of him that had me utterly smitten...and confused. I really had fallen for playboy Chris Donovan.

At a subtle cough, I jerked around, abruptly dropping my hands with the shirt. My gasp of utter mortification echoed in the room.

Chris leaned against the doorjamb, arms casually folded over his chest, a taunting smile riding his lips. "Would it make you feel better if I pretend I didn't see that?"

In fact, the only thing that could make me feel better right now was a shovel in my hand so I could dig myself a hole and disappear. Why did fate hate me so? Hadn't I suffered enough yet?

"Hey now, don't look so bashful," Chris teased and walked toward me. "It was just a matter of time until you fell for my irresistible charm." With a gesture at the t-shirt in my hands, he added, "And scent."

From the sound of it, he meant it as a joke, but I knew better. He was right, it had only been a matter of time. I took a wary step back, not ready for any teasing, and knocked into the island behind me.

Trapped and with a pounding heart, I watched him prowl closer. Where was Ethan? He should come and save me!

"I won," Chris said in a lower voice than before and took the shirt out of my shaking hands, tossing it aside. I thought he'd read my mind and was referring to our challenge, but he continued, "Ethan has to do the dishes." Looking over my shoulder at the clean counter, he shrugged. "I see you already did his job. Nice." His gaze moved back to my eyes. "So we can go straight to dessert..."

He scrutinized me as if I was a piece of cake on his dessert plate. His hands lifted to my hips, his fingers hooking through the belt loops of my jeans. Slowly, he pulled me against him, the length of my body flush with his. Even our thighs touched, and I clasped his upper arms to steady myself.

"We have about twenty seconds for us," he purred.

When he dipped his head down a little and leaned his brow to mine, I sighed. Here I stood, about to make the second mistake today, and no one came to stop me. How was I supposed to protect my heart from this playboy if I kept stumbling into his kisses?

His lips had barely brushed mine when, down the hallway, the back door slammed close. "Make that five," Chris growled. To my absolute astonishment, he pressed a hard kiss on my mouth, then let go of me altogether and headed around the kitchen island.

I stood rigid, struggling to rein in my ragged breathing as Ethan walked through the door. He stopped at the sight of me, and I blurted, "Hi!"

"Hi," he replied, pulling his brows into a puzzled V. "Everything okay?"

"Yeah! Sure! Why?"

Obviously, Ethan was going to explain to me that my jumpy behavior was the reason for his wondering, but I didn't give him the ten seconds he'd have needed for it. Instead, I made my legs move and rushed past him, down the hallway, and locked myself into the bathroom, falling against the door with my back.

Breathe, I told myself. All is good. The light above blinded me as I gazed at the ceiling. This was not the best moment to panic over being kissed by the wrong guy. There was enough time to do that later, at home, where no one would notice.

But then, a small voice spoke up at the back of my mind. Maybe Chris wasn't the wrong guy after all. He wanted to kiss me again, which meant he probably enjoyed our first time...as much as I did, right? And if he liked it, maybe he wanted to repeat it more often. What if I was all wrong and maybe he'd changed the rules of our challenge for himself as well during the past few days? His text messages had become a lot more sensitive, and when he'd touched me today, it didn't feel like a meaningless brush-off.

I rubbed my hands over my face, adjusted my shirt and squared my shoulders. Walking back to the kitchen proved a long way with legs as shaky as mine. On the threshold, I stopped, casting a shy glance into the room.

Ethan was working the coffee machine, filling three cups with classy smelling cappuccino and adding a cream top to all of them.

Chris placed two plates each with a square piece of cake on the table. When he went for the third, he took a detour to where I stood, reached for my hand, and pulled me along with him to the seat I'd already deemed mine in this house. With a gentle push and a smile, he made me sit down before he headed for my dessert plate.

Kiwi wedges framed this piece of cake, and one half of a strawberry cut in the shape of a heart sat in the middle. The upper part was dipped in chocolate. I dared a probing sideways glance at Chris, which he returned with a half-smile before he cut a piece of his cake with his fork and ate it.

Grapes and strawberries formed a pattern on his piece, while banana eyes and an orange wedge grinned from Ethan's. Chris's creativity when it came to desserts was certainly unsurpassed.

"Thanks for doing the dishes, by the way," Ethan said to me. "You know you didn't have to do that."

"Of course. But between watching two hunky guys playing basketball or doing dishes..." I laughed. "Well, I guess I'm just weird."

"Only a little." Ethan smiled back at me. "I'll drive you home for it later."

"No. I can drive her home," Chris said around another bite of cake.

Ethan licked his fork clean. "No, you can't."

"Sure can."

"Nope."

"Why not?"

Flashing him an evil grin, Ethan stated, "You're grounded."

"Ah, fu—sh—*craaap.*"

Glad I didn't have cake in my mouth, I laughed out loud. Half an hour ago, when the guys were playing outside and he thought they were alone, he didn't bother to swallow his four-letter words like that.

Actually, I wouldn't mind if Chris was the one driving me home tonight, but I didn't want him to get in trouble with his mom later, so I happily accepted Ethan's offer.

Taking my plate and cup to the sink, I said to Chris, "Well, thanks. That was a very...interesting and delicious dessert." Ethan was in the room hearing every word, so I didn't say anything else. As long as things hung at the edge between Chris and me, I didn't want Ethan to know what had happened on this kitchen counter while he was gone. First, Chris had to come clean with his intentions concerning me. Maybe a text later or a chat on the phone would help clear the situation. Excitement gripped me at the thought of what he was going to write me tonight.

Chris nodded. He secretly stroked my hand with the back of his as I walked past him. "Good night, sweetness," he whispered so only I could hear.

Chapter 16

"ACTUALLY, THERE'S A reason I wanted to drive you home tonight," Ethan said as we climbed into his car. For a split second, I was afraid he'd seen everything and was cornering me for letting his brother kiss me, but only he cast me a sheepish grin. "You've been to my house so often now, I'm dying to see *your* room from the inside. Think it's okay if you show me?"

A queasy feeling churned my gut. Saturday evening. Both my parents would be home. There was a fifty-fifty chance we'd find my house in a peaceful mood when we arrived, but I didn't dare get my hopes high on that.

However, when we got to my place, Dad's car was gone. Maybe his boss had called him to an urgent meeting with clients. At times, Dad did work on weekends, so this wasn't all that strange. Tonight, I thanked God for the saving grace and welcomed Ethan to my house with a happy smile.

My mom was dying to meet him since she'd heard of our first date. I searched for her downstairs but she was nowhere around.

"Mom?" I yelled. No answer. A little disappointed, I turned to Ethan. "She's probably taking a bath. Come on." I quietly ushered Ethan upstairs to my room, not wanting to disturb her.

Ethan ambled around the room, marveling at my huge collection of books and CDs, then he plopped on the bed, feet dangling off the edge. "I like it."

"There's just no Wii or Xbox in here," I mocked.

"That's okay. We can watch a movie instead." He bounced on my bed, grinning. "It's cozy."

A car pulled up the drive to the garage underneath my window. A quick glance proved my suspicion right, my dad had come home. "Come on," I said to Ethan. "I want to introduce you to someone."

Ethan came to the window, too, and gave me a quirky look. "I've never been introduced to a girl's father. Is it weird that I feel uneasy now?"

I laughed, taking his hand, and pulled him to the door. "I promise not to use the word boyfriend. He'll leave his shotgun in the closet then."

"Ha. Ha. You do know how to make a guy feel comfortable, don't you?"

I opened the door and instantly froze. Mom must have heard him coming home, too, and she beat us downstairs. The first thing she shouted in a volume that could take down a house was, "You can't always run away when things get tough,

Richard!"

Filled with horror, I turned to Ethan. The shock in his eyes ceased the moment his gaze met mine. Embarrassment and pain surging through me, I let Ethan pull me back inside. He closed the door, but my parents' voices still carried to us like the walls were made of paper. Their horrid accusations slinging back and forth grated on my emotions. God, why couldn't they just be silent for once?

I didn't know what to do, but my shaky knees wouldn't hold me much longer.

"Susan—" Ethan said in a compassionate voice, stroking my forearms. "I'm sorry. But it's okay. It's not your fault they're fighting, and I heard worse when my father still lived with us."

"It's not—it's just—" Squeezing my eyes tight, I covered my face with my hands. "This is so embarrassing."

"Don't worry. I don't care, really." He sighed. "I shouldn't have insisted on coming here."

When his touch left my arms, I opened my eyes to see what he was doing. Checking the window again, he cast me a grimace over his shoulder. "It's not too high, I could escape this way, but I'd land on your dad's car."

He wanted to jump out? My awkward reaction must have shocked him more than my parents' fight. Was it that obvious I wanted him out of the house? But jumping...?

"Don't be ridiculous," I told him. "You'd break your neck."

"Mm, maybe. But I'm afraid you'll never speak to me again if we sit through their argument."

He might be right. How did we get into this horrible

situation?

Ethan took on a determined expression all of a sudden. He walked back to me, took my hand, looked me sternly in the eyes, and said, "You know what we should do now? We go downstairs, get out, and we'll go have a coffee. In a couple of hours, when you come back, things will have cooled down, and everything will be fine again."

He had no idea what he was saying. Nothing was going to be fine in this house tonight. I was going to sleep at my grandpa's place like I did so often, and worse, I would never again look at Ethan without feeling the shame I felt right now. But I let Ethan drag me out of my room and down the stairs anyway.

The shouting got louder the closer we got to the living room. There was no way we would get past them without being seen. Porcelain hit the wall. I don't know which of the two vases on the mantelpiece Mom had broken, but from the tinkling sounds, a sea of shards now covered the floor.

My first thought as Ethan and I stopped in the doorway was, *Aha, it was the white vase*. Then I met my mother's thunderstruck gaze and said, "Mom, Dad, this is Ethan."

Thankful for Ethan's hand holding mine at this moment, I squeezed it tight for support. He returned the pressure, stroking his thumb across my knuckles in a gentle, soothing way.

"Darling," my mother squeaked.

My father came forward, raking a nervous hand through his hair. His lips moved, too, but with the terrible ringing in my ears, I couldn't hear what he said. Swallowing hard, I pushed

Ethan on and out the door. With every intention to follow him, I only stopped when my mother cried out my name, sounding the worst kind of sorry I'd ever heard.

My hand slid from Ethan's and I turned back to her. Maybe everything after that wouldn't have happened, if he had held my hand tighter...

My chest quirked with shallow, painful breaths, and I fought against tears of shame and anger. "Why can't you behave like normal parents?" I screamed at both of them. "Just for one freaking night? Why do you always have to fight? Mom! Dad didn't kill Grams, for heaven's sake!" That must have hurt her more than anything my father ever said to her. I didn't care. I couldn't stop myself at that moment.

Ethan reached for my hand from behind, but I yanked it away and exploded once again. "And Dad! Why do you always have to give her reasons to be angry with you? Why can't you two talk things out like normal people? Did you decide to make my life hell on purpose? So I can't even have friends over? Because if so, you did a great job! I hate you!" Tears spilled over. "Both of you!" And for this very short episode in my life, I meant it.

*

Ethan held the front door open for me. I slipped through and tiptoed to his room. After the terrible argument in my house, going into town held no appeal. At my request, Ethan had driven us down to the ocean instead, where we'd strolled along the beach for what seemed like hours. He offered to take me home after that, but the truth was I couldn't face my parents just yet. As he randomly cruised through the streets, exhaustion beat at me and my eyes started to close. Ethan suggested it was best if I crashed at his place. That was at two o'clock in the morning.

We didn't make a sound, just kicked off our shoes, and Ethan stuck out his arm on the pillow so I could snuggle up to his chest for the comfort I needed not to fall apart. He pulled the bedspread over us and caressed my hair. I passed out within minutes.

Dawn was breaking through the windows when I woke up again.

Still lying on his back with his arm draped around my shoulders, Ethan quietly dozed next to me, his chest heaving and falling with deep, even breaths.

Gently, I shook him until he opened his eyes. "I need to go home," I whispered.

To his credit, he sat up, wide awake in seconds. "Why? It's Sunday. No school. And you texted your mom last night, so she knows where you are. At least stay for breakfast. I'll drive you home later."

"No." I shook my head, grimacing, and climbed out of his bed. "I don't want anyone from your family to find me here—it doesn't feel right."

Ethan frowned at me, but got up and put his shoes on, too. I was already at the door and sneaked out into the hallway. The coast was clear. Ethan followed me, whispering, "Not my family. You just don't want Chris to find out..."

Right. Maybe I shouldn't have told Ethan that Chris kissed me last night, but some things just come up when you walk along the beach together for hours. "I don't want him to ask stupid questions," I whined. Turning around, I touched his arm and gave him a pleading look. "This is really something I'd like to keep between you and me."

With a sigh, Ethan relented. "Fine. I won't say a word about it."

"Thanks, Ethan." And since I'd slept in his bed—more like in his arms—last night, there really was no barrier between us any longer. Flinging my arms around his neck, I buried my face in his shoulder.

He patted my back, then quietly opened the front door and led the way to his car.

*

Ignoring the apologies from my parents, my mom's tears, and my dad's sorrowful face, I ran to my room and locked the door. Right now, I didn't want to talk to them. Not after they'd destroyed what should have been the perfect ending to a lovely date last night.

Arms folded on my pillow, I hid my face in them and sulked. There was nothing that could have lightened my mood...

Or maybe one thing could.

I pulled my phone from my pocket and glanced at the screen. Still no new messages. My heart sank once more.

Chris hadn't sent me a single text last night. The first time, in two weeks, that he didn't tell me good night this way. I sniffed. Maybe he hadn't because he'd told me his usual finishing line at his house already. At the memory of how his hand had softly brushed against mine before I left, a small smile made it to my lips. There must be a reason why he hadn't texted me. Certainly he was going to message me again tonight.

But I didn't want to wait that long. Something had happened the previous week—something I didn't know how to deal with. For a while, denying it to myself seemed like the best idea. But when Chris had kissed me, and all these butterflies caused chaos inside me, there was no doubt left. I had fallen for Ethan's brother, and much deeper than I'd ever anticipated.

Proof was that not twelve hours had passed since the last time I saw him, and I missed him already. That was bad. More than bad. It was shocking.

What had happened to my solid "your charm will get you nowhere with me" attitude?

Oh, but I knew what had happened. Somebody coated it in molten chocolate and made me swallow the whole damn thing.

When all these sweet memories came up again, I chanced my luck and typed a message to Chris. *Good morning. Are you still asleep?*

Usually, he was fast with his replies. Not this time, though. Minutes ticked away and turned into half an hour. My attention continued to wander back to the screen, checking for new messages. Nothing. Curled up on my bed, I waited and my anxiety grew as the half hour dragged on into a couple more, me still staring at the damn phone in my hand. My heart had become a walnut in a nutcracker by that time.

He must have seen my text. So what kept him from answering? A lazy morning? Or was I just not worth any more of his time? He'd gotten what he wanted after all. Aside from teaching me a lesson in how irresistible he was and how he got every girl to fall for him, getting serious with one had never been his intention. He'd made that clear from the beginning.

I'd been a fool.

But hope dies last, they say.

Somehow I convinced myself he'd just send a text later today. In the evening. Yeah, at his usual time. To tell me good night and call me sweetness, like he always did. Feeling a little better, I came out of my room around noon to eat lunch with my parents.

As soon as they saw me, they came around the table and wanted to hug me or something, telling me how sorry they were for sure, but I held them off with a raised hand. "Don't! Really, I don't want to talk about it. Let's just eat. I'm hungry. And my head hurts. Mom?" I rubbed my temples. "Can I have a painkiller later?"

"Of course, honey." She gave my hair a caress when she set my plate of spaghetti in front of me. It was nothing as good as Ethan's steaks—or Chris's dessert—but I ate enough to keep me going for the rest of the day and night, because I didn't intend to come down again today.

The evening came and passed, it was just shy of midnight, and still there was no text or call from Chris. Not even after I'd sent him a good-night message at five to ten. If nothing else, this was enough to convince me that the only one who'd fallen for someone in the past few days was stupid me.

As punishment for being such an idiot, I should've prohibited myself from my beloved liquor-filled pralines, but to be honest, they were the only thing that kept me from bursting into tears that night.

Ethan had called me earlier to check how I was doing, but he'd said nothing about his brother. And I didn't ask.

After the silent treatment all Sunday, I almost didn't expect to see Chris at school on Monday morning. But he must've had a class close to mine first period, because this was the time when we'd met most often in the hallway in the past...and again today.

With my books under my arm, I walked to science, keeping an eye out for Sam or Nick. Distraction would do me one hell of good today. So, dammit, where were they?

Rounding the last corner and heaving a frustrated sigh because they were nowhere to be seen, I stopped dead with a sudden gasp. Only a few steps ahead, Chris was talking to Justin, a friend of Hunter's and somebody I'd gotten to know pretty well since I started hanging out with the guys.

Frozen to the spot, I just stared across the corridor. Walking up to Chris and saying something would have cost me an amount of bravery I couldn't muster after the weekend, but it didn't take long for Justin to notice me. He smiled and waved back when I did, which also made Chris look in my direction. For the length of a painful heartbeat, we gazed into each other's eyes, but no one moved or mouthed a single word. Chris pressed his lips together in annoyance, lifted his brows in a cool look, and turned back to Justin.

He didn't act like he didn't know me. He just acted as if…he didn't care.

My chest constricted. I sucked in a painful breath and made my heavy legs move, trudging on to my first class. Sam and Nick were already in there and beckoned me over to their table with a wave. *Now is a bit late for distraction, guys.* The catastrophe had already occurred.

But that incident wasn't even the thing that hurt most this week.

Because I didn't visit Ethan in the afternoons for obvious reasons, I didn't meet Chris, either. Several times, temptation got hold of me to tell him what a big, fat, and complete ass he was. It verged on a miracle that I didn't send the text off, even when my thumb hovered over *send* for almost half an hour on Wednesday night.

I hadn't told anybody about the kiss. Mostly, because it filled me with shame to see that I—in spite of better knowledge—had let myself fall for the worst playboy when all the warning signals had been there and so obviously, too.

At school, I tried to act my normal self in order to not give my friends any reason to grill me about my problems. I even bantered with Ethan and the others at lunch. Ethan asked me a couple of times how things were at my house, and he was the only one to whom I told the truth. That I wasn't speaking a lot with my parents and that they didn't speak a lot with each other these days, either. My outburst must have had some severe effect on them. Time would tell, though, what came out of it.

That same day, I dared to ask Ethan for the first time if Chris had said anything about me after that dinner on Saturday. The sorrowful face Ethan made gave me chills. "He seems to be avoiding me as much as he avoids you. I asked him what his problem was yesterday, but he got really aggressive and told me to f—to get lost. What in the world did you do to him, Susan?"

"Me? I did nothing." Other than letting him kiss me. But that was probably the whole point. "I can understand why he's no longer interested in me. He got me where he wanted me in the first place. But I don't understand what that's got to do with you."

Ethan shrugged. Neither of us had an answer.

Most nights, I slept with Chris's bandana tightly clasped in my hands, pulling from it what little comfort it would give me. Of course, I needed to return it to him soon, but I was just not ready to give away the only thing that I had from him. Nor could I bring myself to delete all the messages he'd sent me. I must have read them a thousand times over the week, but all they did was make me sadder than before.

Friday finally appeared, and I was glad I only had to battle through one more day before I could sulk an entire weekend in my room alone. I wandered from my history class to math on autopilot, focusing on my steps instead of on the happy people surrounding me in the hallways.

With a loud "Uff," I came to an abrupt stop when I bounced into someone.

"Whoops," a familiar voice said.

Please, let this be Ethan. Please, let this be Ethan. Please...

I looked up and gazed into a face that held the warmth of a Canadian winter. So much for "God hears every prayer sent to him." If he'd heard mine, he happily ignored it.

"Hi," I mumbled and added, "Sorry."

Chris stared at me so hard that I couldn't bear it much longer and lowered my gaze—which was the worst mistake I could have made. He was wearing the dark gray shirt which only a week ago I had dug my fingers into when he kissed me. Where the short sleeves ended, his tanned, smooth skin reminded me of how warm he'd felt. And his hands, his fingers that he'd hooked through my belt loops...they were leisurely laced through someone else's fingers now.

I swallowed so hard that the small group of students next to us might have heard it, too.

The girl at Chris's side was a stranger to me. Long, fair hair fell smoothly down her shoulders. Her slim legs were wrapped in mega-tight jeans. The moment Chris seemed to notice my appalled stare, he tightened his hold on the girl's hand, somehow forcing me to look up at his face again.

"Anything wrong?" he bit out in a cold voice that I hadn't heard him ever use before.

Slowly, I shook my head, horrified. My gut churned and I wanted to throw up right there. With bile rising in my throat, I stepped aside to let him and his new catch pass. I headed on toward math but took a turn for the head office instead. Telling a lie about having period cramps got me a pass to leave school early.

Mom looked surprised when she saw me walking through

the door, but not as surprised as I was when I found both of my parents home that morning.

I dropped my schoolbag on the floor, grabbing the backrest of a kitchen chair, and told her, "Afternoon lessons were canceled. Some teachers' conference or something." Casting my father a sidelong glance, I asked, "Why are you home? Don't you have to work today?"

"I took the day off." He hesitated, looking at my mom—for support, it seemed. What the hell?

My mother came to me and caressed my hair. In a soft, terribly foreboding voice, she said, "It's good that you're home, honey. There's something we want to discuss with you."

Both of them lowered to the metal kitchen chairs, their eyes on me. Their sad faces triggered a rush of adrenaline inside me. The urge to storm out the door and run over to my grandfather's house to check if he was all right took hold of me. Since there were no tears on my mom's cheeks, though, it couldn't be that.

Warily, I sank into the chair that I'd held onto until now, preparing myself for more bad news.

Chapter 17

"YOUR MOTHER AND I are getting a divorce, Susan."

My father's voice echoed like a clanging church bell in my mind. Over and over. Divorce.

They broke up with each other.

Holding my cold, sweating hand, Mom explained, "When you got so angry with us last weekend, we realized the terrible mistakes we've made these past months."

They broke up with each other.

"We were so self-involved that we didn't notice just how hard it must be for you, honey. All the shouting and arguing. You deserve a quiet home, Susan. A loving home, not a broken one like this is."

They broke up with each other.

"We both love you," Dad said in a very quiet voice and caressed my cheek. "We just don't love each other the way we should anymore. You finally made us realize that we can't keep doing what we're doing, or we're going to hurt you even more in the process."

Oh my God.

I was mistaken.

They didn't break up with each other...

I broke them up.

And I'd thought Chris was my biggest problem these days.

Unable to deal with the situation, I had to get out, or I was going to faint. There was so much to take, I could hardly stomach it in this moment. I needed to get fresh air in my lungs. Get some distance between us and get my mind sorted. Get to a place where I could break down. Without them around...

I rose from the chair and focused on the door, the only way out of this. Everything happened in absolute slow motion. Like someone had trapped me in a film and was making me live through the worst seconds in my life, dragging them out to last torturing hours instead.

"Susan," my mother called to me from very far away, her voice barely audible through the haze surrounding my mind. "Where...are...you...going?"

"Away from here." The words, like everything else, dragged on like rubber.

The last thing I heard was my dad's calming voice as I walked out of the house. "Let her go, Sally."

With no direction in mind, it was a miracle my legs even carried me all the way down to the ocean. Walking the same way I had with Ethan last weekend, the images of how we'd tried to sneak past my fighting parents and how I'd screamed at them played in front of my eyes. Time and again. I tried to figure out where I should have taken a different path that night so none of this would have happened. But the truth was, the course had already been set the night before.

If only I had stuck with my decision not to go on that date to the Donovan house. My family would still be a family, and my heart wouldn't have been broken twice this week.

I wished I could let myself fall someplace quiet and just cry. My throat was thick and tight, and my lungs hurt every single time I took a breath, but the relieving tears just wouldn't come.

And suddenly, I didn't want to walk on any longer. I didn't want to be alone right now. I longed for a shoulder to cry on, for someone's arms to hold me so all the pain would come out in a well of tears. More than anything, I wanted to be with Ethan right now. He'd already proven that he understood my hurting. He'd become my best friend; one I needed to hold me right now.

But my phone was in my schoolbag on the kitchen floor in my broken home, so I couldn't call him. School was over by now, so he should be home. Since I was closer to his house than mine, I headed that way.

Leaving the beach, I walked the last mile to his street. When the white façade of his house came into view, a surge of a different kind of pain swamped me and made me stop in my tracks. What if Chris was there? Not ready to face him, I didn't want to let that ache take hold, but it was at that moment that the first tears squeezed out of my eyes. I struggled to dab at them faster than they came, but the wet stream continued to flow. Everything put together was just too much to cope with.

Mustering all my courage and strength, I walked up to Ethan's door and rang the bell. I could break when he was there to catch me.

The door opened seconds later. In front of me stood a guy in jeans and a black hoodie, barefoot, his hair wet after a shower. It could be either of the twins.

I cleared my throat. "Hi, um—"

He folded his arms over his chest, successfully creating distance. "Chris."

"Right." Why had I even bothered hoping for this not to happen? My voice wavered. "Is Ethan home?"

"Soccer practice."

If things weren't already bad enough, I would have slapped myself for being so stupid as to forget that. Once again, a warm drop trailed down my check and I rubbed it away. "Okay, um—" I shook my head. "Never mind."

About to turn around and walk away, Chris reached out and tilted my chin up with his knuckle. "Susan, why are you crying?" he asked with such soft determination that I froze on the doorstep. The anger and distance were gone from his face, like a storm had wiped them away. No, not a storm. Sincere worry.

It was that look on him that shattered my control. My knees buckled. Chris must have seen it coming even before I did, because he grabbed my arms and pulled me against him before I fell.

When he hugged me tight to his chest, my own arms came

up, my fingers digging into the hood of his soft sweatshirt behind his neck. "I broke up my parents!"

"You did what?"

The feeling of his hand brushing tenderly through my hair gave me a little bit of comfort. The dam broke and I finally shed all the tears that hadn't wanted to come at the beach. "My parents are getting divorced. It's my fault!"

"Tell me what happened," Chris said in the softest voice.

I clung to him harder and tried to get some air into my lungs, which hurt. "I went home after third period today. My parents were both home." I sniffed and coughed, with more sobs escaping. "They told me they want to get divorced. They've been fighting for so long, and last weekend—" My voice broke on a hiccup. "...Last weekend, Ethan wanted to see my room. I showed him. But my parents started fighting again—they didn't know we were home. It was so embarrassing. I said some horrible things to them. Then I ran away."

Wiping my eyes on his hoodie when he wrapped his arms tighter around me, the rest came out in a hoarse croak. "They didn't fight after that. I thought things would finally work out. But it just got worse. They must have been plotting this all week. Today, they told me they didn't want to be together anymore. Because of me. Because of what I said to them. They said they don't want to hurt me with their fighting. But I don't want them to break up because of me."

Chris was silent all this time and just let me fall apart in his arms. Even now, when there were only sobs coming out and no more words, he didn't let me go. Embracing like this, we stood in his open door for what seemed like an eternity.

Eventually, he eased his hold and let me slip away so he could look at me and brushed the wet strands of my hair from my face with a few clumsy moves. He wiped the remaining trail of tears from my cheek with his thumb. Sternly looking into my eyes, he said, "Sweetness, you certainly did *not* break up your parents. They have some shit to deal with, but it's not your fault."

I didn't know why, but when he called me sweetness, I wanted to break down all over again. It was a good thing he took my hand and pulled me into the house, closing the door. That was enough distraction to help me keep my crap together.

Chris led me to his room, making me sit down on his bed near the window. Pulling the cuffs of my pink sweater over the heels of my hands, I rubbed my eyes dry with them. From a drawer in his desk, Chris fetched a pack of tissues and gave me one. After he watched me clean my nose and eyes, he ordered, "Don't go away. I'll be right back."

My throat felt dry, like somebody had sandpapered it. Words wouldn't come out anyway, so I didn't ask him where he was going but only nodded. As soon as he was out the door, it dawned on me where I actually was. An uncomfortable feeling crept into the pit of my stomach.

Chris had caught my fall, but too much stood between us after this week. The image of his fingers intertwined with those of a blonde made me stand up from his bed and find a more neutral place to sit. But truth be told, there wasn't a single corner in this room where I'd be comfortable, so I just walked to the window and gazed out into the backyard where he and Ethan had played basketball last weekend.

My life had been good. Maybe too good for too long. No serious trouble. Good friends to hang out with. Good grades to show off. And a first, amazing kiss that will always stay in my memory. But nothing was sunshine and roses forever. I should have known...

A soft cough beside me made me aware that Chris had returned. He put a steaming cup in my hand.

At my inquiring look, he told me with the shadow of a smile, "Tea is good for the soul."

The sweet scent of strawberry and vanilla drifted to my nose. I took a sip and warmed my hands on the cup for a while, letting my gaze wander back to the yard.

Chris remained at my side. He stood so close, our arms touched. Though it also hurt on a certain level, it felt good to be near him again. After a deep breath, he said, "You're lucky your parents still have that base where they talk to each other and to you about things like a divorce. When my parents broke up, they'd long gone past that point."

He didn't sound sad, like he was trying to come to terms with his own problems. No, he just sounded like he wanted to ease me into a conversation, give me a chance to get things off my chest. I tilted my head and studied him as he continued to gaze out the window. "How was it for you?" I asked a moment later.

"Well, it was pretty hard at first." He shrugged, casting me a sorrowful grimace. "I came home one day, and my dad was no longer here. No goodbye, no letter, no phone call. He was just gone."

Man, that sucked. For a brief moment, I did count myself lucky.

"The first sign of life Ethan and I got from him was after two freaking months, and I know he only called because Mom begged him to talk to us. She was the one who saw how we suffered every day, not him."

I took another sip of my tea, my eyes glued to the side of his face. "What did he say to you that day?"

"Something about how he needed time to sort out his life and shit. Well, he did sort it out pretty quickly. He moved in with his secretary two days after he moved out of here." When Chris laughed, it didn't hold that bitter sound Ethan had adopted when he'd first told me that his father wouldn't be home for dinner. To me, it seemed like Chris had found a way to deal with his parents living separated. Ethan might not have.

"Two years ago, I started seeing my dad again. Not often, just for birthdays and Christmas and maybe one or two other times a year. That's all right now. We have a comfortable relationship."

"And Ethan?" I just couldn't get around asking.

"It was harder for him. Ethan never forgave him. They haven't seen each other once since the day my dad moved out. I believe Ethan just needs a little more time. Maybe when we're at college, or just one day...whenever." After a quiet pause, Chris turned to me and hooked some loose strands behind my ear. "The fact that your parents talk to you about it and even try to do what they think is best for you means they care a lot for you. You're not breaking them up. If anything, you were the one holding them together. But you can't do that forever."

He took the cup out of my hands and placed it on the desk behind me, then he pulled me into another careful hug. "And know what the best thing about it all is?"

There actually was a good side to all this? I lifted my head, pressing my chin against his sternum, and scrutinized his face.

"The fights will stop," he said softly.

No shouting, no screaming, and no crying? A deep sigh escaped me at that prospect. But no matter what, I'd rather have both my parents in the same house with me. I just couldn't imagine a time when one of them wouldn't be around. Maybe I could plead with them to give it one more try...

Taking another deep breath, Chris's familiar scent filled my head, and for a second it felt like I could take a step away from my body and look at the situation from an outer angle. I wasn't crying any longer, but still, Chris was holding me tight. Something was completely wrong about that.

Carefully, I detached from his embrace and picked up the cup of tea once more to have something other than him to hold on to. Chris certainly noticed my subtle retreat. He stiffened and a muscle started to tick in his jaw at the same time a frown pulled his brows together. It was like only now he remembered he actually didn't want to talk to me ever again.

All of a sudden, I couldn't bear being in the same room with him any longer. "I should go," I mumbled, handing him the almost empty cup, and whirled around to head out. But

Chris held my hand, stopping me.

"Wait." His voice held a soft plea that actually made me turn back to him.

He looked at me for an immeasurable moment. The arctic cold from this morning was nowhere to be felt. In fact, his gaze was quite heated, giving me goosebumps of a warmer kind. There was something burning on his mind—maybe an explanation as to why he'd kissed me and kicked me to the curb the same night—only, he remained silent.

Discomfort grew inside me. "What is it?"

"I—" He turned away from me, putting the cup on the ledge, and stared out the window.

If it helped him not to look at me, all right, but would he spit it out already? Because his hesitation was making me uneasy. "*What*, Chris?"

From behind, I saw how his chest expanded as he took a deep breath with obvious bravery. For a tiny moment, I wanted to slip out of the room and run away. Whatever he had to say wouldn't be nice. And I'd had so much *ugly* already today.

"Fine!" he spat through gritted teeth and whirled back to face me. "Tell me one thing. Why did you let me kiss you last weekend and then sleep with my brother the same night?"

Sleep with his brother? Was he having a mental breakdown? I narrowed my eyes in response. "What bullshit are you talking about?"

His gaze hardened. "*You* tell me."

"There isn't anything to tell," I almost shouted. "I didn't sleep with Ethan. What in the world made you come up with something so stupid?"

"You came back that night with him—or should I say, in the morning?" he snapped with a cynical edge, folding his arms across his chest. "And you sneaked out before sunrise."

My mouth fell open. "How did you get that out of Ethan?"

"I didn't have to. I *heard* you."

Good. Ethan hadn't broken his promise. Funnily enough, I found myself mirroring Chris's stance after that. "And your point is?"

"Wha—" He huffed and cut himself off, throwing his arms in the air. "That you spent the night with him? Obviously. And *after* you kissed me the same day!" His accusation came out on a bark that made me back off a step. Realizing he might have taken it a notch too far, he calmed quickly. His voice became soft and a little sullen even. "I thought you liked it."

Oh my word, did I like kissing him? I'd freaking slept with his bandana the entire week, because I loved it so much! Suddenly, things clicked into place. He hadn't abandoned me because the challenge was over. He was jealous.

A surge of wonder along with anger rushed through me. "I spent the night here for the reasons I told you fifteen minutes ago. I had a fight with my parents and ran off. But I didn't have sex with your brother." Taking another step backward, I knocked into his bed and slumped down on the soft mattress, exhaling a long breath. "I can't believe that you'd really think that. And if you were so sure, why didn't you ask Ethan?" With more annoyance, I added, "For Christ's sake, why didn't you ask *me*?"

He decided not to answer that question, because we both knew all it would have taken was a reply to my text...which he had refused to do all week. When he did say something, his voice was low, like that of a hurt little boy. "Are you saying I hit rock bottom over nothing?"

Rock bottom? Was that the truth? He hadn't looked really miserable to me all of last week. "I'm saying, please, for once in your life, think before you act. Do you know what a horrible week I've had because of you?"

Chris stared at me with a blank expression. He leaned back against the windowsill, grabbing the edge. "What do you mean? I thought you were feeling miserable because of your parents."

Dammit, I shouldn't have let that slip. I wanted to bite off my tongue. Lowering my head and resting my forehead in my cupped hands, I mumbled, "Yeah, that too."

"So what did *I* have to do with it?"

"Nothing. Forget it." Now that he'd revealed the reason he was a dick all week, I didn't want to talk about my hurt feelings anymore. He had a way of exposing me that made me uncomfortable. But of course, he wouldn't let it go.

"Susan?"

"Hm?" Lowering my hands to my lap, I looked at them instead of him.

Chris hesitated a beat, then he asked in a soft voice, "Why did you go home after third period today?"

Of course, now, of all times, he would remember that little detail of my story. I didn't want to answer him, I really didn't.

"Susan," he pushed again, and even without me looking

up, his quiet footsteps revealed he was coming toward me. "Tell me."

I shook my head.

"Why not?" He hunkered down in front of me and tipped my chin up so I would look at him. I hated that he saw how my eyes had glazed over again. "Tell me why you left school after we ran into each other in the hallway today."

I shouldn't have had to, because he knew already. He knew that he'd hurt me, and now he was hurting me again by forcing the truth out of me. His hand slipped away from my face, his knees lowered to the floor, and he sank back on his heels. Even though the only broken person in this room was me, he suddenly looked like *he* was the broken one. With a sigh, he surrendered.

He reached out for my hands, and they felt cold against his. When he laced our fingers, I didn't protest because, frankly, I was too exhausted at this point.

"I'm sorry I hurt you," he said in a whisper so low that it was barely audible in this quiet house. "But she means nothing."

Who? The blonde? "Now that's a hell of a relief, isn't it?" The words burst out of my mouth before I could stop them. "As if any of them ever mean something to you."

He looked stricken, but he knew I was right. After a long pause, he started brushing his thumb in circles over my knuckles. "You do."

"Oh, do I?" A cynical laugh escaped me. "Obviously so much so that you couldn't wait to replace me with your next challenge right after you kissed me."

"I swear there's nothing going on between Rebecca and me. She's only a friend."

"Rebecca," I repeated bluntly. Great. Did he want to tell me anything else about her? Maybe rub it in that she was so much better to kiss, or that she was just a damn lot more beautiful or more popular than I was? "Maybe we come from two different places, Chris, but from where I stand, it does mean something when a guy laces his fingers with a girl's."

"Yes, it does." For emphasis, he squeezed my hands. "But not this morning." He blew out a frustrated sigh. "Heck, I was a complete douche, okay? I used my friend's girlfriend to make you jealous."

A gulp stuck in my throat. "You did what?"

"This entire week, you seemed so happy when you were with the guys...with Ethan. Oblivious to how I felt about you. It was a stupid thing to do this morning, but I wanted a reaction."

"And that was your plan?" I cried out. "To shove a random girl in my face?"

He shrugged, forlorn. "Well, it did work."

"If you only wanted my reaction, a phone call would have done, Chris!"

"Yeah, I get that... Next time, I know."

"Next time?" What in the world did he mean by that? I certainly wasn't going to let him kiss me a second time just to break my heart all over again! "There won't be a next time. Not with you and me, anyway."

"Why not?" he asked, looking a little upset. "Last Saturday was an amazing date, and we didn't even leave the house. Don't you think we should do it again?"

And here it was, oh my God—the offer to be his next go-to girl. How could he even think about it—after what he'd done to me! "No, I really don't. I'm not that type of girl."

He scrunched up his face. "What type?"

"The type that's available whenever you fancy a brief roll in the hay, or that you can send away when you're bored of her." The type like Lauren... The name hung like a flashing sign above us.

His voice became defensive. "You wouldn't be that kind of girl for me."

"No? I'm not sure you even know a different kind, actually."

"I do know how exclusive works," he answered bitterly.

"Really? When was the last time you had a girlfriend?" Whoa, did I really just suggest that this was what I wanted from him?

"It doesn't matter," he mumbled.

"It matters to me."

His blue eyes bored into mine as he ground his molars.

"See, I knew you didn't know how it works."

His gaze never wavered from mine. "Tenth grade. Amanda Roseman. We lasted seven and a half months. She broke my heart when she left me for my once-best friend. So I decided to take a little time off from being *exclusive*."

Boy, my mouth sagged open.

"That doesn't mean I'm not willing to try it again with the right girl."

"You think I am the right girl? Why? Because you had to wait two weeks before I let you kiss me?"

"That, and because I did stuff with you that I've never done with anyone else. Not in a long time anyway. Apart from you, my mom is the only girl who ever gets texts from me. And when I took random chicks to my room, I never cooked for them...or freaking played Wii golf."

"Oh, that justifies everything, does it?"

"The way I see it, yes, it does." He paused with a helpless expression. "Let's give this a shot. We could be awesome together."

That's what I'd thought when I walked out of this house last weekend. Except, here was the rub. "We didn't even last a day. How is that awesome?" With a soft shake of my head, I tried to smooth out my frown. "Seriously, I just don't think we'd work together." Finally managing the strength to pull my hand away from his, I rose from his bed and stalked to the door.

Chris was behind me in a second. "Where are you going?"

"I don't know." Out. Home. To the beach again. Wherever. I couldn't bring myself to confront my parents just yet, but I didn't want to stay around Chris anymore, either, thinking about how much pain he could have saved me the past six days if only he'd gotten over himself for once.

"Wait, please!" His fingers wrapped around my wrist so firmly that I was yanked backward before my next step. He spun me to face him. "I was an arrogant dick when we met, you were right about that. But I thought I showed you a different side lately. Someone you could actually like. I even played by your rules."

Taking a deep breath, my shoulders lifted and sank. Exhaustion came over me again. "You did," I said weakly and after a moment of thinking, I added, "I meant what I said the other day—that I probably couldn't kiss a guy without having true feelings for him. You made me believe you could be that guy. But it wasn't for real, Chris. *You* weren't for real. You said yourself, you played by my rules—you tried to be different for me. That's not what I want."

"What *do* you want?"

I looked at the ceiling, then turned around, and sagged against the wall behind me. "I want someone who is all that you showed me, but naturally so. Someone who doesn't have to force himself to be the kind of guy I want. Most of all, I want someone who doesn't come with the tag 'trouble.' Do you understand?"

His gaze didn't waver from mine as he seemed to contemplate my words for a long moment. Once again, he easily managed to create distance by just adding enough cold to his voice. "I do understand. You want someone safe and boring. Someone who doesn't give you that exciting tingle in there." His fingertip brushed across my stomach. Immediately, the gate to my butterfly container burst open and all the little fellows came out to play. "In short," he snapped, "you still want Ethan."

It was *Mario Kart* versus chocolate-covered strawberries. In a way, he was right. Ethan would have been my perfect match. We were compatible on a level that Chris and I would never reach. But that was not it. In a soft mumble, I told him, "I do like the exciting tingle. I just don't want the heartache that comes with it."

"Give me a chance to show you that you and I can work without heartache. I'm not Ethan—God, I'll never be like him." He rolled his eyes in a way that almost made me laugh. "But I can do *safe*. Give us a shot and let's start again."

For an infinitesimal moment, there was just Chris and me in this world. I considered an option that would let me say yes to that offer, but I also remembered the roller coaster ride it promised just because he was *him*. And with my family breaking apart, I didn't think I could handle trouble like him right now.

Slowly, I shook my head. Then I turned and walked away.

Chapter 18

IT WAS THE longest evening of my life. The conversation with my parents about the divorce wasn't something I ever wanted to have again, but it wasn't as bad as expected, either. Lots of tears—my tears—and hugs and vows that no one was going to drop out of my life just like that.

Apparently, they'd sorted it all out before they decided to tell me the *good news*. Dad was going to move out before Christmas. This weekend, actually. But he'd stay close. No running off to L.A. or San Francisco, he promised. His office was in the neighboring town after all, and that's where he intended to move. He'd already found himself a small apartment to rent, but he made sure the couch there was big enough for me to sleep on if I should ever want to crash at his place—which I totally intended to do every weekend from now on.

Strangely enough, this was the longest talk my parents and

I'd had in months without them shouting at each other. Maybe Chris was right. Even if most things about a divorce were just crap, there was a tiny part that gave me hope that with some distance my parents would be able to work at their relationship.

And finally, they made clear that I had nothing to do with them breaking up. "If it wasn't for you," my dad said quietly, "your mom and I might have hated each other in the end, and that wouldn't have been good for you."

"That's right," Mom agreed. "A breakup too late in a relationship is the worst thing that can happen. So don't be sad or feel guilty, honey. It was about time someone showed us the truth. And we're both glad it was you." She gave me such a genuine smile that I just had to believe her. And the relief coming with it was like...strawberry-vanilla tea. It was good for my soul.

When I returned to my room later that night, my phone blinked with several missed calls—most of them from Ethan. Since he could have already gone to bed, I decided to text instead of calling him. *Free for a chat?*

It didn't take ten seconds for my phone to ring. "Hey, Charlie Brown," I said, feeling sleepy, and sank into my pillow.

"Finally! Chris told me what happened. Are you okay?" At Ethan's anxiety, my sleepiness fled. No drifting off to the sound of his voice while on the phone. Shame.

"Yeah. I'm good now. Had the longest talk with my parents. My dad is going to move out this weekend."

A long pause followed. "I'm so sorry, Susan."

"I know. Thanks." It still hurt to talk about it, but not as much as it had earlier in the afternoon. "I think I'll be fine. We all will be. They promised they'll work it out." And for once, I believed them.

"Do you want to do something this weekend?" From the sound of it, he was asking that for two reasons. One, he really wanted to distract and help me. And two, he wanted to catch up on the time we'd missed this past week. Who wouldn't love him for that? But I already had plans this weekend.

"I'd like to, but I'm going to help my dad move. There's a lot to pack, and I want to spend some time with him, too. Maybe next week?"

"The offer doesn't have an expiration date." Ethan's voice held a softness that made me smile.

"See you on Monday."

"Yeah. And hey..." He hesitated. "Chris says good night."

At the mention of his brother, a knot pulled around my heart. I'd said some mean things to Chris today, but I never thanked him for breaking my fall. Remembering his fluffy sweatshirt drenched with my tears after our embrace, I heaved a deep sigh. "Tell him not to turn off his phone just yet," I said to Ethan before we hung up.

Apart from Ethan, Sam was the only friend I called tonight. When I briefed her about the divorce, she agreed to meet tomorrow morning and even help us move my dad's things if we wanted. After that call was made, I typed in a message for Chris.

Amazing how long it took me when in the end it was only three words. *Thanks for today.*

No answer. So we were back to the silent treatment?

Maybe I deserved it for turning my back on him, but how could I deal with dating a guy who came with a reputation longer than the red carpet? Just because he enjoyed kissing me didn't mean we were on the same terms when we said "we work together." For him, I was an interesting adventure because I was different from the kind of girls he usually hung out with. For me, he was my first real kiss, something you didn't brush off like a ladybug in the summer.

I'd been dreaming of it every night since last Saturday, even when I'd slept in Ethan's arms after the fight with my parents. And I would again as soon as I closed my eyes tonight for sure.

After ten minutes of waiting, I gave up hope for a response and turned off the light. Just as I rolled to the side and pulled the cover up to my chin, my cell beeped. It bothered me that a smile reached my eyes at that moment.

Taking the phone with me under the bedspread, I read in the illuminated blue cave with the cell against my thighs: *Ethan said you're feeling better. I'd like to make sure of that myself. Mind if I call you?*

All right, he was forgiven for taking so long to reply when his answer was as sweet as that.

Do you really think that's a good idea? I sighed and sent off the text. Common sense told me it was best to keep a distance so everything could go back to normal between us. Yet another part of me hoped he'd reply with a *yes*.

When my phone started to vibrate in my hand, it wasn't accompanied by the usual beep of a text, but the Harry Potter medley. *Dream Guy Material* flashed on the screen.

I picked up and quietly said, "Hey."

"Hi."

An endless silence followed.

The only sign that he was still there was his deep breaths. They were heavy and painful.

I tried to ease the tension with a soft tease. "I thought you'd say something stupid to make me laugh so you could hear that I'm fine."

After another short moment, Chris startled me as he said, "Ethan is gay."

At that statement, so calm and out of nowhere, I burst out in wild laughter. "Yeah? So what?"

"You knew."

"Yes, I did. Didn't you?"

"I assumed. Never knew for sure." If a shrug could be heard in a voice, it certainly was in Chris's now. "He told me today. You know what that means."

"No, what?"

"That you can't have him." He might as well have ended that with a "duh."

"True."

"I'm confused. Today you turned me down because you wanted him." I really wanted to see the frown on his face when he said that. Because he was so wrong.

"No, Chris, I didn't turn you down because of Ethan. I said I wanted someone a little more like him. That's all."

"Ah. Safe and boring. I get it now."

Total crap is what he got. "Ethan isn't boring. We talk a lot. He understands me. We can have fun without me having to worry that he's gushing over the next best girl."

He huffed. "Because he'd be gushing over the next best guy..."

"Chris!" An outraged laugh escaped me. "You're impossible."

"Yeah, I know." There was a smile in his voice. "But I think it's cool that he finally told me. And he's going to tell Mom, too. You're good for him in that way."

This genuine compliment took me unaware. Nobody saw it, but my brows lifted in surprise. "I guess he just needs someone who doesn't judge him for what he feels."

"I don't. He knows that." Chris sounded serious enough to wipe out all doubt. "I just wish he'd have confirmed my suspicion a little bit sooner. Like a *week* sooner."

Getting his innuendo, I asked, "What would have changed?"

"I wouldn't have been an ignorant dick. I would have come for another kiss the very next day. I wouldn't have messed us up."

"Us?"

"Well, the *possibility* of us."

Damn, he put it so nicely that the corners of my mouth twitched up. I could barely speak without making it known. "Dude...shit happens."

The rich sound of his laughter filled my head. "So I guess I'll have to show you."

"Show me what?"

"That I can be safe, boring, funny, a listener, a talker...and all on an *exclusive* basis."

I didn't see how he'd ever manage to pull off that stunt, but the promise gave me a warm feeling in my chest anyway. Nevertheless, tonight wasn't the time to return to that particular discussion, so I let him off with a chuckle. "In your dreams, Chris."

"Perhaps. Luckily, you'll be there as well tonight." If we were sitting across from each other, he'd have winked at me without a doubt. "Sleep tight, sweetness."

I closed my eyes and bit my lip when he didn't hang up after that. He was waiting for something. Something I hadn't given him yet when we talked on the phone in the past. Tonight it felt right, though. "You, too," I mumbled and clicked him away with a swipe of my thumb.

*

The weekend was hard—on all of us. I saw my mom crying more often than she wanted me to witness and didn't always let me comfort her. As wrenching as it was for me to see her broken over the end of her marriage, it was also relieving, because it proved one darn thing to me. They still loved each other. And even if they didn't live in the same house anymore, it would never be like with Chris and Ethan's parents, who couldn't find a nice thing to say to each other after their dad moved out.

Sam had been a great support these past two days. She'd

been there to catch me when emotions took over, and she was there to lighten the mood with stupid jokes when I could do with a laugh.

Gramps helped us pack some of Dad's stuff, too. The worry lines in his face had grown deeper, but he didn't seem as shocked about the whole breakup as I had been. Of course, my parents had talked to him before they'd told me and, in a quiet moment, he admitted, he was glad they finally worked up the bravery to make a change. If he thought it was for the best, it gave me confidence to put trust in their decision.

The apartment my dad moved into was cozy. That's the only thing I could say about it. Not big, but with a warm welcome clinging to the air. I slept at his place the first night, and he took me out for breakfast on Sunday morning before he drove me home—to my home, not his anymore. I hugged him for so long before letting him leave that his body might have bruised underneath his clothes.

"Hey, dinner at my place on Wednesday?" he offered with the loveliest smile. One I hadn't seen in a long time.

"Absolutely! We can cook together." The flicker of a memory crossed my mind, how Ethan and Chris had danced through their kitchen when they cooked for me. "I'd like that," I added on a softer note.

Dad nodded. He went to hug my mom, who was standing quietly on the threshold, and said goodbye to her, too.

If it was going to be like this from now on, things wouldn't be too bad. We could make this work out. Together. And for once, both my parents seemed to have set their minds on the same thing. That was actually nice.

Ethan came to my place on Monday afternoon, and he got the full introduction to one half of my family.

"It's nice to *really* meet you at last, Mrs. Miller," he said when he shook my mom's hand, biting down a funny grimace at his slip of words.

The awkward moment was gone fast, and Mom made us a cup of hot chocolate with cream, which we sipped while we watched *The Bourne Identity* in my room. I was glad he didn't make me talk about the situation with my family. Being distracted with a movie and just having him close to lean on totally did the job. For once, I'd even been glad it was Monday and school had provided some mild deflection, too. The only thing that had troubled me was dodging Chris.

Getting out of the house later than usual, I had to dash through the hallways to get to my first lesson, so there wouldn't have been any time to watch for him in the morning. Between classes, I kept a low profile. We met once between third and fourth period, but a feeble wave was the most I granted him as I walked by, even when he stopped in his tracks.

The less I talked to him or even saw him, the faster I'd get over this whole damn issue. It was December, he was a senior, he'd graduate and leave in less than six months...I could manage that. If only he'd take back the hoard of butterflies he'd sowed in my gut. They were a hard package to carry around all day when he was near.

"Want to watch another?"

Ethan's voice pulled me out of my reveling. "Hm, what?"

"Watch another film?"

With my gaze snapping to the TV, I noticed the end credits were running. "How about tomorrow?" I suggested and stopped the DVD.

Ethan sat up Indian-style on my bed and began working his fingernails. Recent chats with him had proven this was a surefire sign he was about to pick up an uncomfortable topic.

Please, don't let it be my parents or—

"Chris told me his version of the afternoon we cooked for you."

Of course he had. With a deep sigh, I put the DVD case back on the shelf and slumped down on my bed again, hugging my knees to my chest. "Yeah? So..."

"So, I just thought I'd tell you."

"Why? It was a one-time thing. We're not what one would call a good match, actually." A weak laugh escaped me.

It made Ethan look up with arched brows. "My brother begs to differ."

I gulped. "Does he now?"

"He hardly talks about anything but you these days. By the way"—Ethan gave me a funny look—"he's complaining that you don't come over to our place anymore."

"Yeah, well. I do miss Mario, but that's not gonna happen for a while, I think. A little distance will do both him and me a hell of good."

"You really want me to tell him that?" Ethan laughed. "The guy seems a little desperate to me right now."

He couldn't be more than I was last week. "Tell him

whatever you want. I think he's lucky I'm still talking to him"—well, texting to him as of right now—"after how he treated me."

"Okay." He got up from my bed and slipped into his shoes. "See you at lunch tomorrow?"

"Of course."

After Ethan left, I called my dad and talked to him for a while. It felt like this was going to become a routine in the future. Since I had his undivided attention on the phone, I thought I could live with that.

Sometime during that chat, my cell beeped with a message. Dad was priority, but after we hung up, I opened the text with a queasy feeling in my gut as to who it might be from.

Dream Guy Material wrote: *Seriously? Distance? How am I supposed to show you all the good sides of me then?*

What good sides, was the first thing I wanted to type back in a mocking way, but that would have been a little bit too harsh. *You can shine with your absence. ;-)* It was still a mean tease, but I couldn't resist sending him that.

And fade out of your mind? Clever girl. Guess what? It's not gonna happen, sweetness.

Was that a threat or a promise? Either way, soft tingles slithered down my spine as I read the words. Tempting as it was to contradict him in another text, I decided to give it a rest and put my phone away, spending the evening with my mom and Zac Efron on TV.

None of my friends came over on Tuesday, which gave me much-needed time to catch up with homework and studying for Winter finals. Sometime that afternoon, Ethan called me. I loved how he cared for me and always asked how I was feeling before anything else.

"I'm fine," I told him. "Doing homework. What's up?"

"Nothing much. I just thought, since you don't want to come play Wii with me anymore, we should go for coffee again. We haven't been to Charlie's in a while."

Ah...Ted. A smile curled up my mouth, but I didn't let it enter my voice. With some faked nonchalance, I answered, "Sure. Why not?"

"Cool. How about Fri—" A crackling sounded through the line, like Ethan had tripped and cut himself off. "Sorry," he said quickly and growled. "Some idiot left his basketball in my room."

The visual made me chuckle.

"Anyway, how about Wednesday? Would that be good?"

Ooh, someone wanted to see Ted really soon. Too bad... "Ah, sorry, no can do. My dad invited me to his place tomorrow," I answered with a hint of regret for his benefit.

"Okay, how about Thursday?" he suggested.

"That would work. I haven't had a caffé latte in a while. Should be nice."

"Cool. I'll pick you up at five." We hung up, but the smile remained pasted on my lips.

Three weeks ago, I wouldn't have dared to believe I could be so happy to see Ethan working up the nerve to chase a love interest other than me. Right now, I couldn't wait for Thursday to come to see how things turned out for him.

Chapter 19

FOR THE DATE with Ethan, which I only called a date because I hadn't been on one with him in a while, I picked a blue dress from my wardrobe. It was longer than the red one Chris had liked so much—the bell skirt almost covered my knees—and it tied with a narrow, black belt around the waist. With wide straps, it could be topped neatly with a white bolero cardigan that was just right for the mild December temperatures.

"There's someone waiting outside for you, honey!" my mom's voice carried into my room while I finished off my hair with a ponytail.

"Coming!" I slipped into my black ballerina flats and dashed downstairs. On the way out, I promised to be back before curfew and waved bye to my mom.

In front of my house, Ethan leaned against his blue Mustang, arms folded and ankles crossed. It seemed like we were on the same wavelength about color today, because he sported a denim jacket over a white crew-neck tee, which matched with his washed-out blue jeans. His blond hair stood out in spiky chaos, giving him a touch of cute as much as a touch of just-out-of-bed.

He looked so sweet that I couldn't hold back a tease. "Trying to impress somebody today?"

His gaze lingered on me longer than usual. It seemed he hadn't expected me to wear a dress to our casual date. Ethan reached for the shades in his chest pocket and put them on. "Are you?" He opened the door for me. Oh boy, if Ted didn't fall for his charm, I might again before the afternoon was over.

"Just every guy in town, other than you, since that's not working," I teased with a grin and got into the car.

"So you were with your dad yesterday? Have a good day?" he asked on the ride to town.

"It was awesome! I had him all to myself the entire time. We cooked and ate grilled chicken, and he even made eggnog for us."

Ethan gave me an encouraging nod. "I'm glad things are working out for you now."

At Charlie's, we claimed the same table we sat at the last time. Ted watched us coming in with an interested look, but he didn't say anything until he came to take our order. "A hazelnut latte deluxe for you?" he asked me, a notepad in his hand, though he made no move to write anything down.

"What do you think?" I taunted him with a roll of my eyes.

Ted turned around. "Ethan?"

Ethan cast me a quick look then stared at Ted. "Hmmn,

what?"

Oh dear, the boy must've been out of his mind with nerves. I gave him an encouraging look as Ted asked with a chuckle, "What do you want?"

"Um...a cappuccino. Thanks."

"Whipped cream, no foam, right?"

Ethan tilted his head to Ted and studied him for a silent moment. "Yes."

Once alone again, I leaned forward and placed a hand on Ethan's arm, trying not to grimace too hard when I told him, "Sweetcakes, flirting doesn't work that way. You have to smile, not scare him off with a stare." Then again, what did I know about flirting?

He studied me for an immeasurable time. Finally, he gave a quick nod. "Yeah, right."

"Hey, it's cool," I whispered, seeing he'd just figured out that I knew why he'd brought me here today. "I don't mind you using me for cover."

His brows knitted together. "What?"

I shrugged and waved a hand up and down his chest. "Look at you. You're gorgeous, all dressed up. Did you really think I wouldn't realize who you truly wanted to impress today? Actually, I knew when you mentioned Charlie's on the phone."

"You did?"

"Yes. And I'm fine with that. Now relax and show the guy what a great catch you are."

His face broke into a smug smile. "So I'm a great catch, huh?"

"Absolutely."

Ted returned with our drinks, and this time, Ethan held the smile until he was gone again.

"See? That wasn't so bad," I encouraged him.

He let out a long breath. "You actually have no idea."

"Don't worry. It's okay to be nervous. You'll get used to the butterflies. And at some point, you'll love them."

Leaning forward, Ethan propped one elbow on the table and rested his chin in his palm, his fingers on his lips. His gaze pinned on me, he began to smirk. "I don't make you nervous anymore, do I?"

Unless he kept looking at me like that... "No, you don't."

"Who does?"

At the mere thought of the answer hovering on my tongue, my cheeks warmed over.

"Chris?" Ethan probed.

"Well, he does...sometimes." My gaze lowered, though I had no idea where the bashful feeling came from all of a sudden. Ethan knew almost everything about Chris and me by now. "I'm working on getting that under control."

"So if you still get nervous when you see him, you haven't written him off completely." It was a statement, not a question.

Wondering how much truth it held, I let go of a sigh while I poured sugar in my latte. With a hoarse sound, I cleared my throat. "Any chance Chris asked you to grill me about him today?"

"Would you be mad if he did?"

"Not at you, of course." I looked up, my gaze stern. "It's

not your fault."

Ethan grimaced. "So you're mad at *him* because of it?"

"I won't say another word if you're going to run off to tell him again at the first chance you get—like you did on Monday," I scolded him, the touch of a tease in my voice still apparent.

"Okay, I won't tell him." He started scooping up the cream of his cappuccino. "But tell me why you don't want to give him another chance."

"That's a difficult thing to explain."

"When's your curfew?"

"What?"

"Home? When do you have to be there tonight?"

"Um—" I scratched my head, confused at the sudden change of topic. "Nine. Why?"

"That gives me about three hours to make sense of what you're going to tell me." He angled his head with a taunting quirk of his brows. "I think I can cope."

"Fine," I laughed. "But you have to promise that you'll never tell anybody about it."

He slapped a hand to his heart, expression serious. "I'll keep all the good stuff to myself, I swear!"

The foam of the latte felt warm on my lips as I sipped it. I licked my upper lip and wiped the rest of the foam away with my hand. "The problem is...Chris scares me."

Ethan looked like I'd shocked the hell out of him. "He does *what*? Why?"

What were the right words to explain? "You see, when I met him, he was this really arrogant...popular...lionized guy."

"Lionized?" He chuckled at that.

"Yes." No other word would describe Chris any better. "So, I just ignored him, because—duh!—I was head over heels for you. At some point, he decided he wouldn't let me ignore him anymore. I hated myself because he started giving me butterflies and managed to break through my defenses with stupid little things."

"Butterflies? That's sweet." His eyes gleamed with mischief. "So what where those little things that brought you around?"

A sigh escaped me. "Text messages, mostly," I mumbled. Ethan's soft laugh made me grimace. "That's not funny. I mean, me and the playboy? Come on, that's just not right."

"But you did fall for him." He shrugged. "That's cool."

"No, it's not cool. Because I kinda *really* did. And Chris is not the guy to take feelings seriously. Yet, I let you guys talk me into that stupid date at your house and it was...fun." I paused, dropping my lids to escape his gaze, but at the next moment, I searched his face again. "And then he stole my first kiss."

The awkward silence that followed made me curl my toes in my shoes. I knew exactly which little part of this revelation was actually news to Ethan.

He took a moment to gather himself, slowly sagging against the backrest of his chair. Finally, he pushed out a quick breath through his nose and said in a low, resigned voice, "That was your *first* kiss?"

I pressed my lips together. "Mm-hm." Inhaling deeply, I continued, "I don't know if you've ever kissed anyone. If you have, you know what that first kiss meant to me."

"I think I do." His voice was so soft that there was no room for doubt in his words.

"But please, Ethan," I begged, making a whiny face as I grabbed his hand. "Don't tell him that. For Chris, it was probably a godawful kiss, and nothing that he was used to from his other, more experienced girls."

A wry expression crossed his face. "Oh, you're so wrong."

"What?"

"When Chris told me about that kiss, he said he found it pretty *amazing*. I think you should believe him this one time."

Really? He'd said something like that to his brother? A smile sneaked to my lips, together with a warm tingle in my cheeks.

"All right, so let me recap," Ethan said half a minute later and started to tick things off on his fingers. "You had a crush on him. He gave you your first kiss. You liked it. He still gives you butterflies..." Cocking his head, he scrutinized me with a whole new interest. "What's the problem?"

"The problem is that I sort of take romance quite seriously. I might have been more into him than he was into me. I don't want to be his next go-to girl."

"Go-to girl..." he repeated, narrowing his eyes.

"Yes, you know, what you said about him and Lauren the other day. Even though I'm not one of those girls who want to wait until marriage before they...er...sleep with a guy"—my cheeks grew warm with that confession—"it doesn't mean I'll give it away to some arrogant womanizer either. I think the first time should be something special with the guy I love...and not just about a stupid challenge." Stirring my hazelnut latte, I focused on the swirling foam. "But I don't expect you to understand that."

Ethan lifted my chin with his finger. He grinned when I looked at his face. "Did you just say that because I'm a guy?"

In fact, I didn't know what had actually made me say it, but I was glad that he didn't finish his sentence with "or because I'm gay." Returning his grin, I fished a strand from my ponytail to my front and twirled it around my fingers. "Who can tell what's really going on in that head of yours?"

"It seems you have a completely screwed up view of us guys," he teased me. "Someone should show you one day. And I'm sure, if Chris was the one, he wouldn't mess that moment up for you. Believe it or not, I know he's done some serious thinking on that matter the past couple of weeks."

"Chris is thinking about getting in my pants?" I said with dry humor. "Why doesn't that surprise me?"

"Oh, come on. Give the guy a break." Ethan made a wry face. "You know I didn't mean it like that. He's really not that bad."

"What, are you trying to play matchmaker now? Please don't." My moan was torn by my laugh. "That's my job, anyway."

"Your job?"

"Yes. I think you brought me here for a reason."

"And that would be what?"

"Helping you get on with your own romance."

Utterly relaxed now, Ethan laughed. "I don't think I have a

romance going."

"Well, maybe not yet. But with a little push you might just start one today." I made a subtle nod at the bar, and Ethan followed my gaze.

He lowered his head, rubbing his neck. "He's staring at me, isn't he?"

Checking surreptitiously, yup, Ted sure was. "Well, I don't think he's staring at *me*."

Ethan seemed at a loss. I started to wonder if it was a good idea to come here with him after all. If he wanted to get closer to Ted, a girl on his arm was not the way to go. "Know what?" My tone was light enough to make a balloon fly. "I'll just pop to the loo and you go engage Ted in a nice chat. If it works, I'll call Sam to come hang out with me."

I rose from my chair, but Ethan snatched my hand. "No!" he hissed and narrowed his eyes to slits. "Don't leave me alone with him."

"Honey, it's okay. You talked to him an entire hour a few weeks ago." Laughing, I pulled my arm out of his panicky clasp. "He won't eat you."

"You can't know that."

Well if so, Ethan should count himself lucky, but of course that didn't come out of my lips. "Relax. I'll be back in a few minutes."

Ethan looked ready to anchor his arms around my waist to make me stay. Giving his shoulder one last pat, I told him, "Just be yourself, and no one can ever resist you." Then I headed to the restrooms at the back of the building.

My bladder was actually empty. The stalls were all open, and since there was no one in the restroom with me, I just leaned against the wall and glanced at my watch. Three to four minutes, that would have to do. If Ethan could get a chat running with Ted in that time, Sam would so have to bail me out of here. If not, the evening would be for Ethan and me alone. That was the plan.

Before I headed out, I prepped my hair in front of the mirror and pinched some color into my cheeks. Ethan still sat alone at the table. Phone in his hand, he keyed something in. Either a text or he was Googling away the time he'd been alone. "Oh Ethan," I muttered on my way back.

Ted eyed him from behind the bar, but Ethan seemed oblivious to it. Or he ignored it on purpose. Playing hard to get? Well, I had no idea how guys ticked, so maybe that was the way to go.

Reaching him, I leaned down and whispered in his ear, "Who are you texting?"

"Whoa!" Ethan almost jumped out of his chair. "Don't you sneak up on me like that, woman!"

"Why? Did you think it was Ted?" I teased.

He grimaced. "Not funny."

"Okay, sorry. So who are you texting?"

Pressing his lips together, he made a deliberating *hmmm* sound. "My brother."

"Why?"

"He asked how the afternoon was going."

Oh my God! "You did not tell him what I said before!"

Ethan began to smile, which made me glare at him. "Give me that phone and let me see," I demanded, reaching for his cell, but he pulled it out of my reach way too fast.

"Does the term *privacy of correspondence* ring a bell?" Laughing, he pushed his cell into his pocket. "Drink up, we're leaving."

"We are?" My hazelnut deluxe was only half finished. "Why the rush?"

"Things aren't working the way I'd hoped." His eyes flickered to the bar and back at me. "It wasn't a good idea to bring you for cover."

So my toilet time didn't get him anywhere. Shame. "Okay. What do you want to do instead? And don't suggest *Mario Kart*. You know I'm not going anywhere near your house right now."

Ethan rolled his eyes. "I wasn't going to suggest that. Let's just go find another place. There's a nice pub in Pismo Beach. We can grab some food, and they have great music." He barely gave me time to finish my coffee—I downed half the beverage in one go—as he'd already risen from his chair and tossed some money on the table.

"Bye, Ted!" I shouted, while being dragged out the door by Ethan.

"See ya!" his answer drifted after us.

Outside the café, I dug my heels into the asphalt and stopped Ethan, nailing him with a hard stare. "What the hell, Ethan!"

He spun around to me, one eyebrow lifted.

"It's okay if you don't want to sit in there with me, but you could have at least said goodbye to Ted. From his looks, he really could have a thing for you. Why do you want to ruin this?"

Three deep breaths later, Ethan was still staring at my face. Then he bit his lip and cut a glance at the sky. "You're right. I'm an idiot." He let go of my hand and walked back through the door.

"What are you doing?" I hissed after him.

He shrugged and glanced at me over his shoulder. "Giving him my number...I think."

Refusing to follow him and destroy his courage, I waited until the door opened again and he came out, wearing a smug grin.

My eyes grew wide. "You really gave him your number?"

A curt nod.

My mouth curved up with excitement. "Awesome! What did he say?"

"No way. I'm not talking to you about this," Ethan warned in a voice that spelled: *No further questions.*

Silently cheering for my friend, I respected his wish. Maybe he'd tell me more once Ted really called him.

He ushered me into his car and drove off without another look back.

On the way here, I hadn't noticed it so much, but the inside of the car soon started to take on a very yummy scent. A smell that even my butterfly friends remembered. "Did you borrow your brother's cologne?" I asked as we took a turn onto the road parallel to the ocean. "You smell like Chris."

Ethan cast me a quick glance, one corner of his mouth tilted up. "Good?"

My answer was a tiny nod.

His grin grew a little wider, self-assured. "You said the other day that you liked how he smelled. I thought it couldn't hurt to try it. You know...for Ted."

And now, all that good scent was wasted on me instead of him. What a pity. "Do you think he'll call you?"

"I don't know." Ethan shrugged. The sun was slowly dipping into the sea. The last rays breaking through the windshield made him squint. He put on his sunglasses and tossed me another cheeky look. "A text would be cool."

A cozy warmth came up with the memory of how Chris's texts made my heart flutter each time my cell beeped. It would be so sweet if my friend here could sample the same excitement. Hidden in the fabric of my skirt, I crossed my fingers for him.

The pub Ethan took me to was cozy. Spot lamps cast a warm glow over the entire place which was furnished in wood dark as bitter chocolate. Several lights were tinted in purple and blue but most of them shone in a friendly yellow. Right from the first glimpse inside, I loved it.

The actual bar at the right side and the dining area to the left were separated by a wide dance floor. A few couples twisted across the parquet.

"Agh," Ethan groaned as we walked around the couples, finding a place to sit. "Oldies night."

"What? I like it. And look at us"—I made my skirt sway a little—"we seem to have picked just the right clothes for it, too."

Sliding into a green upholstered booth, Ethan grabbed the menu. "I'm hungry. Are you?"

"You always are." I laughed and snatched the colorful, laminated card from him. Nothing on it jumped out at me. "I think I'll go with fries."

Signs on each wall said that this was a self-service place, so Ethan headed for the bar. He returned with a tray carrying two Cokes, a cheeseburger, and extra fries. Pushing the basket toward me, he started munching his burger and snuck a French fry from my side every now and then.

Done with the meal, he wiped his fingers on a napkin. "You're not really a big eater, are you? I noticed when you stayed over for dinner."

I took a sip of Coke and grinned. "I like to save up my quantum of calories for liquor-filled pralines. They're my soft spot."

"I thought I was your soft spot..." Ethan's voice was so low that I wasn't sure if he meant for me to hear that, especially when his gaze was focused on the empty fries basket instead of me. But he sure noticed my baffled stare when he looked up. He shrugged, pressing his lips together, and waggled his brows once in a sheepish way.

This date was starting to get a little weird. Not at all like what I'd expected. Something was on Ethan's mind, I could tell when he captured my gaze, but he wouldn't come out with what was going on with him. Instead, and probably to break the awkward silence, he reached under the table and pulled playfully on my skirt. "Does that swing?"

A startled laugh burst out of me. "What?"

Ethan rose from his seat, shrugged out of his jacket, and pulled me out of the booth. "They're playing your song. Let's dance."

I recognized the oldie that had just started to play, even though I couldn't put a name on it. Why this would be my song eluded me. "I—agh... Wait!"

But Ethan didn't waste a minute. Still holding my hand, he dragged me to the dance floor, where he twirled me under his arm and caught me in a light embrace.

"I can't dance. My knee. You know that. And why is this my song?"

"Don't get your panties in a twist. Just move your hips a little." With a cheeky grin, Ethan pulled me toward his hard body. "And because it's called 'Runaround Sue.'" One hand on my waist and holding my right hand with his other, he started to sway with me.

The catchy rhythm took only a second to grow on me. Leaving the lead to Ethan, I laughed out loud as he danced me across the floor. With a gentle push, he made me twirl away from him. Knees bent just slightly and legs far apart and teetering, he came twisting after me in the sexiest way.

The guy was...gay. *God, why do you hate me so?* As smoothly as possible, I twisted, too, loving how my skirt fanned out with that move. Ethan snapped his fingers and I clapped my hands left and right as he twisted in front of me. His gaze was hot on me as he crooked his finger, beckoning me to him. My hand stretched out, he clasped it, and we moved together once more.

His toned body grinding against mine was more than I could take. Mouth watering, I soon began feeling his skin where our hands joined. His hand was warm like Chris's, heating mine, too. And his smell today...I swear, I was falling in love with Ethan all over again.

It got worse when the groovy song ended and a slow one began. Ethan didn't let me slip away from him. If anything, he held me tighter, adjusting the movements to the new rhythm of "Stand By Me."

Somewhat shyly, I placed my hand on his shoulder, my cold fingers brushing over the warm skin on his neck. For a brief moment, he closed his eyes, smiling, and I could see a shiver slithering through him. When he looked at me again, his gaze never wavered from mine. The smile stayed, growing a little more intense coupled with that stare.

My breathing came faster. First I thought it was because of the way the twist had me worked up, but the truth was, it only had to do with being so close to this guy. The hand he'd put at the small of my back started to stroke over the fabric of my dress. A pleasant warmth spread out from there.

Moments later, Ethan lifted my other hand to his neck too, then let go, skimming his fingers down my arm and side until he held me around the waist with both arms. His forehead dipped to mine, and still he trapped me with his intense gaze. His warm breath caressed my face. Mere seconds, and he was going to kiss me.

"Ethan..." I whispered hoarsely.

"Where?"

"What?"

He quirked his brows. "Never mind."

My last thought was shot to hell as his lips touched mine. So tenderly and softly, like I'd imagined them to feel from the first moment I'd met Ethan on the soccer field. But I'd already sampled his brother's lips—they'd tasted like heaven to me. Nothing in this world could ever compare to my first kiss with Chris.

Guilt filled my chest up to the base of my throat. Even though I closed my eyes and welcomed how his mouth molded to mine, I knew I had to stop this. I shouldn't be kissing Ethan...but it felt so right.

Still swaying gently, my arms wrapped around his shoulders and neck tighter, my fingers sliding down his skin until they clasped the collar of his shirt.

Wait—what?

There was something beneath it.

Stiffening, I felt the set of silver chains. My eyes shot open. "Chris—"

He didn't lift his gaze to mine, but he reached for my hands, taking them away from his neck and lacing our fingers. "Don't think about it, Sue, just don't," he begged in a quiet whisper and placed another tender kiss on my lips.

My hands trapped in his, he held them prisoner behind my back. Caged in his arms and my body flush to his, I didn't know how to get out of here...and I didn't even know if I wanted to. My system was on alert down to the very last cell, my blood pumping hard and hot through my veins. I'd missed his touch, his smell, and his kiss so much the past two weeks that running from it now felt impossible.

Teasing my mouth open, Chris slid his tongue past the seam of my lips, tentatively stroking mine. Fireworks exploded with that little touch. I was in a whole different world, where no regret existed. No shame and no thought about tomorrow. Only Chris...me...and ten thousand butterflies.

Closing my eyes, I kissed him back.

Chapter 20

THE REALIZATION CAME with the end of the song. He'd deceived me. Lied to me. He made me say things…

Oh hell, he'd made me tell *him* about my feelings for him!

I broke free from the kiss. Chris still had his hands on my hips, but I yanked them off me and took a step back. For the length of time it would take a feather to drop, our gazes were still locked in that world where only the two of us existed. As he came toward me and slowly reached out, I left that world.

"Don't touch me!" I hissed.

His hand froze midair. "Sue—"

It was too late for that. Too late for any explanation. I spun on my heel and stormed out.

My dad's new apartment was across town. He could be here in five minutes. I had my phone out and rang him before Chris caught up with me on the street.

"Susan—please let me explain!"

The cell pressed to my ear, I swirled around. He held his jacket clasped in one hand—the thing that took him the five extra seconds to follow me.

"I don't need your explanation. You're a bloody—"

"Hello?" my dad's voice was in my ear.

"Dad? Hi. I'm sorry to bother you, but could you pick me up at the"—I lifted my head and read the sign above the door—"Merry Melody? It's a pub across town at..." Heck, where was a street sign?

"I know where it is. Are you okay, sweetheart? You sound stressed."

"I'm fine." Damn, and now Chris had made me lie to my dad, too. "Just a misunderstanding. I need a ride home."

"Stay where you are. I'll be there in a few minutes."

I hung up, still holding the phone for support as I turned back to Chris.

He looked at me with sad eyes. "You didn't have to call your dad. I can take you home."

"Do you honestly think I'll ever get into the same car with you again? You goddamn liar!"

"Please. It's really not what—"

"—it looks like?" I finished for him. Oh, how original. "Save me that! I'm done with you."

A muscle ticked in his jaw as he pressed his lips together. "Jesus Christ, why won't you let me explain? You gave me no other choice! All the things you loved about Ethan—" Helplessly, he tossed his hands in the air, the jacket flying. "I had to show you somehow that you can have them with me, too."

At his brother's name I stiffened, my blood turning cold. Just how deep did this betrayal run? Slowly and in a low voice, I asked, "Does Ethan know what you did tonight?"

His silence was clear enough. My eyes shut of their own accord when the painful truth sank in. So many things ran through my head, but I couldn't get one of them out.

The pub door opened again, and an older couple walked out, laughing and chatting. As they glanced at us, the woman gave me a compassionate smile of understanding. She probably thought it was a lovers' quarrel with the tension and anger vibrating off us.

Soon we were alone again, wrapped in utter silence. My gaze returned to Chris. "I'm sorry," he whispered.

"I don't believe you." My vision misted over, but I blinked the tears away fast. It wasn't too hard with the wrath brewing inside me. My hands fisted at my sides. Chris, for all it's worth, backed a step away.

His sigh sounded more like a pained moan. "What can I say to make it up to you?"

"You've already said enough. I don't care for more of your false words or actions." A well of heat rose within me. Suppressing my anger wouldn't work much longer. "Go away and leave me alone."

"Sue—"

God, how I hated that he called me that now. It had become something special, his pet name for me. Just like *sweetness.* Somewhere in this game, I'd come to like it. And now he'd ruined it for all time.

"Me not telling you the truth from the start was a mistake, I realize that now. I was going to tell you before the evening was over, I swear, but first you had to *really* see me. Nothing about this date was fake."

No, nothing... "Apart from your identity!" I screamed.

A car came up behind me and parked on the curb. Thank god. The engine running, my dad got out, his expression wary. "Hey, sweetheart." He put an arm around me and kissed my forehead. No matter how bad this situation must look to him, he still held out a hand to Chris. "Ethan," he said in a low greeting.

Expression guarded, Chris shook his hand. "No. I'm Chris. Hello, sir."

Suspicion marred my dad's face. "I see." He turned to me. "I believe you will explain that on the way?"

"Yes. Let's just leave." I hooked my arm through his and walked to the car. Without another look at Chris standing on the sidewalk, I climbed into the passenger seat and buckled myself in with my head lowered. Dad said goodbye to Chris in his friendly, paternal manner but, thank God, he drove off without hesitation.

Since the cell was still clasped tightly in my hand, I typed a message for Ethan. *You're in trouble.* After sending it off, and because I really didn't feel like dealing with any of the twins tonight, I turned off my phone.

*

The moment I strode into my room and slammed the door behind me, I snatched the dark red bandana from my pillow and tossed it into the trash can beside my desk. The past couple of weeks it had been lying on my bed, but no longer.

Stripping down to my underwear, I flung the damn blue dress across the room and it hit a wall. A scream erupted from my throat. In a frenzy, I pulled the hair tie from my ponytail and disheveled my hair with both hands until it fell all over my face. "Screw you, Chris Donovan!"

To hell with him for fooling me...for making me say all those stupid things about him in the café...for charming me in the pub and making me dance with him. With a wipe of my arm, the stack of books on my desk went flying. Damn him for ruining other guys for me. Tears stung my eyes. Back against the wall, I sank to the floor and buried my face in my folded arms. A sob broke free.

Screw him for being the one I wanted.

A knock rattled the door. "Susan?" my mother asked quietly. "Can I come in?" I wanted to tell her no, but she'd already popped her head in, and of course there was no going back from there. "Oh, honey." She hastened toward me.

I hid my tearing eyes in my arms again. The Bambi blanket was being draped over my shoulders. Mom pulled it together at the front and laid her arms around me, rubbing my back. "Your dad told me what happened. Do you want to talk about it?"

No. Heck, it was a miracle I could still talk when my dad drove me home. It must have been the anger that had made me spill all the details like a darn fountain in front of him. But now my voice had abandoned me. I shook my head.

Mom just sat there and held me until my feet had turned into ice cubes and it was no longer my sobs that shook me, but the cold. She helped me put on my flannel bottoms and handed me a sweatshirt and thick woolen socks. When I was dressed, she took my hand and led me downstairs where she parked me on the couch while she went to get me a cup of hot cocoa. With whipped cream topping...

"Thanks, Mom." I dipped my lip into the cream and licked it off. "Why are you home anyway? Isn't it a night shift for you again?"

"I called in sick. I think I'm running a fever."

Placing my cold palm on her forehead, I checked. No, she definitely didn't have a fever. But her eyes were swollen and her nose blotchy. From crying?

There wasn't a single day in the past three years that my mom had stayed home without a cause, such as tending to me after getting my appendix removed in ninth grade. Dad's leaving must have hit her harder than expected.

Curling my legs on the couch and holding on tight to the warm cup, I tipped to her side and put my head on her shoulder. She stroked my cheek and my hair, then pressed a kiss to my brow. "It's not easy to be seventeen, hm?"

"Doesn't seem like it's any easier at forty-two."

A quiet laugh came from my mom. "No. It isn't."

Soon, I fell asleep on the couch and didn't even notice when my mom covered me with a wool blanket, turned off the light, and snuck away.

In the morning, she woke me with a special breakfast of sausage, eggs, and hash browns. There was also a plate with a pile of pancakes and maple syrup waiting to be attacked.

Looking at the scrumptious meal, I heaved a sigh. "Mom, I don't want to go to school today."

"I know, honey, but I don't like you playing hooky. It's Friday. Don't you think you can cope until noon?"

"No." I would only run into Chris...or Ethan. And I didn't want to see either one of them today. "You ditched work last night. It's only fair that I stay home today, too."

Mom clicked her tongue and gave me a sheepish smile. "I knew you'd say something like that. That's why I made us a special breakfast. Fine. But only today." She pointed a strict finger at me. "On Monday you're going back, no matter what."

"Thanks, Mom. I promise." Kissing her on the cheek, I sat down and picked up my fork. But the hunger that should've risen with such an epic Friday morning breakfast remained hidden. I shoved the scrambled eggs around on my plate until a crumb fell over the edge.

Cutting her sausage but not eating, either, Mom sent me a sad look across the table. "You don't look hungry."

"Neither do you."

"Maybe we should call Grandpa. He'd loved to be served pancakes and eggs."

That's what we did, and with him in the kitchen, the mood crawled up a few notches. It was enough to make me force down half a sausage and a hash brown.

A little later, my mother got ready for work. She'd traded her shift with one of her colleagues and would work for the rest of the day. I trudged back to my room, turned on the TV, and switched to the Disney Channel. Donald Duck was the only guy I could stomach today. After some time, I remembered that I hadn't turned my cell back on since last night.

There were twenty-four missed calls—thirteen from Chris, six from Ethan, two from Lisa and Sam, and one from Hunter. Apart from that, seventeen new text messages waited in my inbox. Without hesitation, I deleted all sixteen from Chris, but read the one from Ryan he'd sent the night before. *Chris begged me to talk to you. Can I talk to you...?*

All of them were at school right now and certainly wondering why I hadn't shown up. I sent Sam a message to call me at lunch. Instead of following such a simple order, though, she decided to drop by herself. And she brought Tony and Nick.

Feeling a little awkward when I opened the door still in my PJs, I grimaced. "What the heck are you doing here?"

"We're the cheer-up commando," Nick announced, shoving past me and raiding the fridge for something to eat. Since they'd skipped lunch because of me, that was probably fair.

"Sorry, I couldn't shake them off," Sam mouthed, coming in with Tony. She sat down in a kitchen chair.

Tony straddled the one next to her. "So you really had no idea who you were with yesterday?"

"Tony!" Sam poked an elbow in his ribs.

His bluntness made me laugh, because I expected no less from him. At least now it was clear that everyone knew everything already. No need to play keep-a-secret. But a little subtlety wouldn't have hurt.

"Twins?" I replied with a sarcastic edge to my voice. "Identical? How do *you* keep them apart?"

Tony stole one half of Nick's sandwich as he joined us at the table and bit off the corner. Around the bite in his mouth he murmured, "Most of the time, it's clear from where I meet them. If I don't know, I just ask."

"Yeah, right." I blinked a couple times. "Because asking would have gotten me a damn lot farther with Chris last night."

A casual shrug. "Probably not. By the way, Ethan says"—he creased his forehead and made an intense face after he swallowed the bite—"Thanks for the message and then turning off your phone. If you don't answer it soon, he's going to toss stones at your window."

Yep, I expected something like that. "You'll see him at soccer practice today, right?"

Both Tony and Nick nodded.

"Good. Tell him he better have a really, *really* good explanation, or I'll never again answer my phone when he's calling."

"I don't know..." Sam lifted one shoulder in a shrug. "I liked his explanation. In fact, I like both their excuses for doing what they did." She heaved a romantic sigh. "Team Chris all the way."

Slowly, I turned my head toward her, my gaze baffled but hard as stone.

"Whoa, it's late!" she said quickly and jumped from her

chair. "We better get moving, guys, or lunch will be over while we're still sitting here." With a sheepish grin on her face, she pulled the boys up and ushered them out the door.

"Call me if you want to hang out this weekend!" Nick shouted over his shoulder as he was pushed by a dwarf that reached no farther than an inch beneath his collar bone.

"Will do." It was a halfhearted promise, but maybe some nice company could take my mind off the recent embarrassment in my life.

My phone rang a few more times that day. Most of the calls came from *Dream Guy Material*. At some point, I was so sick of that name that I changed it. So when Chris tried to reach me the next time, my phone read out the warning: *Don't pick up!*

Ethan's calls also went straight to voice mail. Talking to him just didn't fit my mood this weekend. The only two people I let into my life were my mom and Gramps. And I talked to Dad on the phone. He was seriously worried. From the sound of it, he doused the phone in spittle when he said, "I should drive to that guy's house and have a word with him."

"That won't be necessary, Dad." I laughed. "But thanks for offering."

His voice calmed. "Anything for you, sweetheart."

Really, anything? *Then come home*, I wanted to beg. *Let's be a family again. Mom's so sad because of you.* But of course, that would be the wrong wish to put into words because—for all it's worth—my dad might do it. And nothing would be different from how it was before. It was hard on everybody, but I was starting to believe that it really was for the best. I still had my dad, after all. And time would heal my mom's pain...like it would heal my pain over Chris.

That's what I kept telling myself the entire weekend.

Until I saw Chris again on Monday morning.

I should have been more observant as I walked to science, but seriously, how could I get my head clear when Simone and Allie were stereo-babbling in my ears about the New Year's Eve party at Ryan's? Like there was nothing more important than what to wear to that damn pseudo-ball.

"I'm not even sure if I'm going," I told them, pushing my schoolbag higher up my aching back. Lounging on the sofa for forty-eight hours with tearjerkers on the screen was murder for my spine.

"What?" Nick blurted behind us and startled me. "I was so going to ask you to go with me."

Slowing in my tracks, I turned around and made a sheepish face. He only suggested it because after Friday's lunch break he knew how down I was. "Nice try, Nick, but it won't work."

"Shame." He made a sad face, but it brightened quickly enough as a flock of girls passed us by. Nick's head turned as his gaze followed them. He spun back to me with a smile. "If you really don't want to go, I'll ask Jessica Markert. Think she'll go out with me? She's coming to all our games."

I had history with Jessa and Nick knew her from math. She was a nice girl, blond and shy, but she'd broken up with her boyfriend a couple of weeks ago. I seriously doubted she was back to dating anybody yet. Not to ruin my friend's enthusiasm about it, though, I forced an encouraging smile and held up my hands, crossing my fingers.

Simone grabbed my arms. "Why don't you want to go? A party will do you a hell of good in your current mood."

"Yeah, right. Like I need to be at a party where that douche is, too." Turning around, my mouth dropped open, because said douche had rounded the corner and stood right in front of me, stopping me dead. Thank God, he wore his leather jacket today, the only thing that gave him away.

"Hey, Sue," he said in a low voice. He seemed to be no less startled than me, although there might have been a little bit of happiness attached to his surprise.

Looking at his cornflower-blue eyes, which held a touch of pleading, a new surge of anger swamped me. There was only one way for me to evade kicking up a stink in the hallway of my high school. I had to get away, and fast.

Voice freezing like an arctic storm, I said, "Excuse me. I have to get to my class." I brushed past him and headed on, not caring if the girls followed me or not. Science was only two doors ahead. I slipped inside with a bunch of students, hoping for the bell to ring soon so class could distract me.

I didn't see Chris again all morning, but lunch didn't appeal to me much either, because Ethan would sit with us again, and there was no evading talking to him. Or maybe I could, if I held my head low and looked at no one.

Sam, Lisa, and I were some of the first students who got to the cafeteria. Our table was empty, except for Sasha Torres and Alex Winter. Not hungry, I headed straight to them instead of lining up in front of the buffet with my friends.

"Hey, guys," I said and lowered into my usual seat, grabbing one of the water bottles from the middle of the table. Taking a sip, I almost spilled the water on myself when someone pulled out the chair beside me, slumped down, grabbed one leg of my chair, and pulled me around to face him.

Leather jacket. "What the hell, Chris! Are you crazy?"

"We talk. Now."

"No."

"Oh, yes." He planted his legs on either side of me, caging me in. Leaning forward, he rested his elbows on his knees and fixed me with a stare. "You're mad at me, all right. Not answering your phone? Fine. But I'm not going until you hear me out."

"Didn't you get the message last time? I'm not interested." I screwed the lid back on top of the bottle and put it on the table.

More guys from the soccer team had come and joined us. Ryan sank into his chair across from me. "Hey, Chris," he said in an amused voice. "Showing up here? Respect, dude."

Chris ignored him. His gaze was still on me. "I don't buy it. You were interested from the very first minute you challenged me. You were interested when we played soccer together. You were interested when I kissed you. And you were interested when I fucking kissed you again. Don't tell me bullshit and don't brush me off. This is too—"

"Shut up," I cut him off sharply and rose to my feet, shoving my chair back. More students filed into the cafeteria.

Our table was now full with eleven people, one of them his brother. They all eyed us with growing interest. "I told you why it's not going to work with us. That you fooled me last week only proves my point." As Chris stood, too, venom crawled into my voice. "You're so full of yourself, it's disgusting! Now let me go."

"No." He was no longer trapping me with his legs, but he laid his hands on my hips, holding me in place.

"Don't touch me!" I hissed, reminding him of one of the last things I spat at him at the end of our miserable date.

Chris didn't let go.

"You call me full of myself?" he snapped. "Don't throw stones while in your little glasshouse, Sue. From the start, you tried to keep me away, simply out of principle. Because I wasn't who you expected to fall in love with. You kept denying your feelings for me, but I have proof of it on my phone. It's in every damn text you sent back to me!"

My hand shot out and left a red mark on his cheek as his head jerked to the side. He didn't see that one coming. Frankly, neither did I. On second thought, it was the one thing I'd wanted to do since the moment I'd figured out who had kissed me in that pub.

A collective gasp sounded around us. "Ouch," Ryan whined.

Grinding his teeth and blinking slowly, Chris turned back to me, the shock in his eyes apparent. "I certainly deserved that one," he said in a much lower voice than before, "but I also deserve a second chance, don't you think?"

Really? After spewing all these things in front of my friends? "I think I'm done with you. And I told you so already. Now get the hell out of my way." I grabbed my backpack and was about to head off, but Chris snagged my wrist and held me close to his side.

"Don't run away from me now," he begged quietly.

Turning so we were eye to eye, I lowered my voice too, but there was nothing at all pleading in it. "Let. Go."

Jerking my hand free, I spun around and stalked out of the cafeteria.

Chapter 21

I FORCED A happy face through PE and journalism, but as soon as the final bell released us from school on Monday afternoon, I escaped and was on my way home without another word to anyone. My throat still tight with unshed tears, speaking about Chris with my friends would have hurt on more levels than just emotionally. I didn't want to break down where *he* could see me.

At home, I flung myself into studying for Winter finals. With luck, I could keep myself distracted for the next couple of weeks. After that, my sorrow should have eased and winter break could once again be fun. Yep, that was the plan. Only, there was a tear sliding down my cheek...

I dabbed it away.

Halfway through my history assignment, the doorbell rang. Mom was at work and I was alone. Gramps wouldn't ring the bell, he had a key, so who the heck was disturbing me? Hopefully not the guys again. I really needed a break from everything and discussing whether or not I should go to Hunter's New Year's party was the one thing ranking lowest on my list of wishes.

With little hope that it was a salesman who would be easier to get rid of than Sam or Simone, I opened the door. And gaped. What the hell—

For a silent moment, I just stared at the guy outside. Heat and cold zoomed in a twist down my spine. I grabbed my unzipped hoodie and wrapped it tighter around me, leaving my arms crossed. Anger charged through me. My jaw hardened and my eyes narrowed. "Which twin are you?"

"Um..." Hands in his pockets, he bit his lip. His gaze darted uncomfortably from left to right and back as he slowly offered, "Da...gay...one?"

I wanted to grab Ethan by the collar of his blue shirt and shake him because he'd almost made me laugh when I so didn't want to in front of him. Keeping a leash on my giggle, I snapped, "What do you want?"

"Well, I'd love to play *Mario Kart* with you." He shrugged sheepishly. "But I believe there's a huge amount of apologies to be given before that's going to happen again."

I stood on the threshold and fixed him with eyes that had turned into glaciers. Ethan sighed. "Why won't you answer your phone, Susan? It was a lot of bull that happened last week, but for the sake of our friendship, you owe it to me to at least listen."

"I owe you nothing." I didn't even blink when the words flowed out of my mouth like ice water.

"Yes, you do. Now get out of the way and let me in. I have some explaining to do." As if him ordering me wasn't shocking enough, he put his arms around my waist and lifted me off the ground, carrying me inside so he could close the door.

"Ethan!" I cried out. "What are you doing?"

"Making sure you don't slam the door in my face, because that's what you were thinking about—and don't even try to deny it." He shoved me to the kitchen. "Now sit down, or do you want to go upstairs to your room so we're alone?"

"We *are* alone. My mom's at work."

"Good. Now sit."

At his order, I sighed heavily and dropped to the seat. Ethan slid into the chair across from me. "I understand that I messed this up. Even though—and we should both consider that"—his stern gaze held mine—"I only acted in your and my brother's best interests."

Folding my arms over my chest again, I leaned back in the chair. "How is getting played by twins in my best interest?"

"You and Chris are perfect for each other. Well, you're probably more perfect for him than he is for you, but I'm not stupid, Susan. You like him."

I lifted my brows, wanting to object.

"Okay...*liked* him," he corrected. "But that's not the point. He's been working a great deal on changing his ways since you walked into his life. That's weird because I haven't seen him like this in a really long time. From what I got, he seemed determined to make things work. Heck, he hasn't been so single-minded about anything or anyone in—no." Ethan shook his head. "Just *never.*"

A slight flutter got my heart in a tangle of beats when he said all those things about Chris, but the truth was, it justified nothing. "I don't care what his intentions were for tricking me into dating him. Why did *you* play along? I thought you were my friend."

"That's the whole point. I am your friend. It seemed like you needed a little push in the right direction to see what was going on with Chris. He actually begged me on his knees to help him." A grimace marred Ethan's face as if the visual with that memory was anything but pleasant. Definitely unusual.

"I said crap the other day about his go-to girls, I know," he continued. "I didn't want to make you feel insecure. Sorry. And I think if you gave him another chance, you'd be anything but. That's all he wanted with that date, anyway. A chance to show you that, if you looked past the things you knew about him, you could still like him."

"And you say that because he told you to?"

"I'm not talking to him right now, but that's what he said when he begged me to set up the date with you, yeah."

A growl forced up my throat. "So that was it? A little *blah blah* and he got you to play along with his stupid plan?"

"He sounded serious to me." Ethan paused, taking a deep breath. "And he gave me his basketball."

My chin dropped. "Sorry, what?"

His voice turned small. "It's signed by Kobe Bryant."

"And you fancy that guy?" It was the most ridiculous thing I could have blurted out, but my tongue was faster than common sense at times.

"No!" Offended, Ethan frowned at me. "He's just the Lakers' most valuable player and his autograph is on the ball..." Glancing out the window for a second, he fumbled for the right words to explain. "It's like Harry Potter's signature on a magic wand."

Okay, I grasped that comparison.

"And it's your fault anyway that I didn't own the ball already."

I pursed my lips. Should I have known what he was talking about?

Rubbing his neck, Ethan leaned forward. "Remember when you ended that game of chess for Chris and me with a checkmate? I think it was the day you called me out on being gay."

A small nod. It was a couple days after Chris's basketball game.

"Well, he offered me the ball if I won. Since you made me lose, I didn't only *not* get the ball, but I also had to truthfully answer him one question. That was the deal."

"You play chess with weird rules," I mumbled, though I wondered what that particular question was. "Did he ask you if you were—"

"Gay? No. I already told you what he asked me."

The memory of that one didn't come up, so I pulled my brows to a frown and shook my head.

"He wanted to know if I was in love with you," Ethan refreshed my memory.

"Oh..." If the ball was worth as much as Ethan had said, it made no sense for Chris to offer it to his brother just to find out about him and me. And giving it to Ethan to make him trick me into a date with Chris... This was insane.

Steepling my fingers under my chin, I propped on my elbows and gave him a level look. "So a date with me was more important to Chris than this stupid ball, but you chose the ball over our friendship. Is that right?"

Ethan lowered his gaze and traced the scratches on the metal table surface with his finger. "It kinda makes me an asshole, doesn't it?"

I just stared, letting him figure the answer out for himself.

He dragged out a breath. "Look, I'll give him the ball back today. I told you, we aren't really on speaking terms these days, but since he lost you in the end, I guess it's unfair to keep the ball." His eyes moved up until they met mine. "And I'd do anything to make you forgive me."

Oh boy, that look. How was a girl supposed to stay mad when someone as cute as Ethan batted his lashes? I was tempted to give in, but what good would it do me? Hanging out with the nice twin brother wouldn't help me much in getting over Chris. "I don't know..." I said after a long pause. "All this is really crazy and, for now, I'd rather keep a distance from both of you."

His gaze burned a hole into my skull. If I got a headache from it later, it was totally his fault. "Are you sure...?" he murmured.

"Yes." Shoving the chair back, I stood, the metal legs scraping on the tiled floor. "This is too much drama for me to handle right now. Not with everything else I have going on in my life."

Ethan rose, too. He pushed the chair back in and braced himself on the backrest, stalling for time. "I see why you're mad at me—and at Chris. But you really don't want to give him another chance? Even if we aren't talking to each other right now, it's painful how miserable he is. After all, he was just trying to show you how much you mean to him."

I told myself I didn't care. Chris made me feel miserable most of the time, so maybe that was divine justice. "Tell him if he really cares about me, he should stop sending me texts or calling my number. And most of all, he should leave me alone at school. He ruined whatever we could've had, and he can't change that."

After all, I wasn't the girl for a playboy. And my first boyfriend didn't need to be a damn liar, for Christ's sake. I deserved better than that.

Walking to the door and holding it open for Ethan, I made it clear this conversation was over.

"Okay..." Lips compressed, he crossed the room but stopped in front of me for a moment. "I'm really sorry about what happened. If you ever change your mind about *Mario Kart*, call me." He walked out and I closed the door behind him.

Returning to the table, I braced my hands on top and stared at the blank wall. Soon, the heaviness in my chest got too much and dragged me down. I hunched forward, leaning on my elbows, and buried my face in my arms. A whiny shriek made it out of my throat. Thank God, no one was home. I was sick of explaining myself to everyone.

*

The weeks until Christmas were strange. They were empty and passed fast. I did what I'd always done around that time of the year: decorated the house with mistletoe and Christmas bells, sprayed some artificial snow onto the windowpanes since we never got any real snow in California, and drank barrels of hot chocolate with whipped cream. In the past, I usually had both my parents to help me pep up the house and watch trashy Christmas movies on the weekends. This year there was only Mom and me. And she wore that sad look all the time.

She and Dad hadn't seen each other in a while. From what my father told me, they'd agreed to keeping a distance—at least for a few weeks, and if that worked, maybe extend it to a couple months. Phone calls were okay, but no personal contact. It would help them get over the breakup, or so they hoped. Only, Mom didn't seem to feel relief at that. If anything, not seeing my dad was making things harder for her. For once, I was the lucky one in this family triangle. I could spend time with both whenever I wanted to. No shouting matches attached to that deal.

Dad looked like he'd adjusted to his new single life fairly well and really fast. Occasionally, he asked me how Mom was doing, but he always had a happy smile on his lips when I dropped by his new apartment. On the other hand, he never said if he was going out much or seeing someone else. Maybe his happiness was just a façade? Was he a better actor than my mother?

Honestly, thinking about their breakup and a possible reunion kept me awake many hours of the nights. There was nothing I could do. This wasn't my fight. Not my problem. But a happy family for Christmas? Well, that was worth a wish.

Considering my misery with the Donovan twins, however, I had little to no hope that someone above would even think to take note of my wishes. Christmas time would be blue this year.

It didn't help much that Ethan and Chris were obviously following my demand and staying away from me. No texts in days, not one phone call from either of them, and when Chris saw me in the hallways at school, he lowered his head and walked right past me.

Although Ethan stayed with the soccer team at lunch, he'd moved a few chairs down the table so we wouldn't sit next to each other anymore. That was okay for the first couple of days, but after a week, I really started to miss him.

Boy...if that's how it felt when my wishes were granted, I'd have to rethink the one for Christmas again.

Thank God for my friends. Apart from Sam and Simone, who made me go present shopping with them every other day, Nick was a wonderful distraction and made me play *FIFA* with him a lot. First I had to force myself to leave my room and have a normal life after Chris and Ethan, but with days passing by and winter break getting closer, things took on that typical end-of-the-year smoothness that always put me in a softer mood.

When the Winter finals were done and I'd passed them all with no grade worse than a B minus, I even started to relax. It was Lisa and Ryan who told me on the last day of school that they were glad to see me smiling more again.

Was I really? I hadn't noticed. Although the biting pain in my chest whenever I thought about Chris—or checked my phone for messages even though I'd told him to stop sending them—had ceased to a dull ache. I tried not to think about him and our first kiss too much, but when I did, no tears stung my eyes anymore. That was some progress, right?

And dreaming about being kissed by him again was nothing I could really control. The human mind is a bitch at night, nothing could be done about that. But one day, I was sure, even the dreams about him would stop...maybe when he went away for college.

Only, that was a long time coming, and running into him after school on that last day before winter break threatened to ruin all my hard-earned composure. It might not have been an accident after all that we met outside the building. He looked like he'd been waiting for me and wanted to talk.

"Don't, Chris. Just don't say anything," I cut him off while he was still drawing in that breath for a lecture, a speech, another apology, or whatever.

That breath came back out on a deep sigh. "It's been so long, Sue. I did everything you wanted. I stopped texting you, didn't talk to you in the hallways. What else do you want me to do to convince you to give me another chance?"

"Why do you think I'll ever do that? Chris, we're done." It came out in a steady voice, but looking at his blue eyes and how his throat twitched when I said it, the strength within me threatened to collapse any second.

He frowned, tilting his head just slightly. "Are you dating somebody?"

"No." I folded my arms.

"Why not?"

What? "Because I'm not interested in anyone else." Duh.

He started to smile a little.

Wait—*what*? Damn! How did that slip? "I didn't mean it like that," I growled.

His smile grew wider and more confident. "Are you sure?"

"Yes! Of course." Or...was I? Gah, I'd been talking to him for only twenty seconds, and already there was a headache coming on—and yeah, maybe one or two tiny butterflies, too. Irritated, I rubbed my temples, lowering my gaze. "Can we stop this now? I want to go home." When I looked up again, Chris hadn't moved, but he was holding something out to me.

"What's that?"

"Your Christmas present," he said in a low voice, the smile wiped away from his face. "I was hoping this chat would go differently. Since it didn't, I doubt you'll let me see you for Christmas to put it under your tree myself."

Nope, I most definitely wouldn't agree to that. And I didn't reach out to take the gift, either.

"Girl, you're one stubborn little thing," he snarled and took my hand to put the small box in blue wrapping paper into my palm. "Merry Christmas." He blew out a ragged breath and walked away.

Maybe I should have thrown that little present after him and knocked him out with it, but I didn't. My gaze focused on the little silver bow. Whatever was in this box, Chris had put a lot of effort into wrapping it up neatly, and I knew it'd been him and not a shop assistant or his mother, because there was so much transparent tape on it that one could hardly feel the wrapping paper anymore. It was such a boy thing to think about safety rather than elegance.

Still, I'd never gotten a prettier present—and where that thought came from eluded me.

I shoved the box into my schoolbag and walked home. It would not go under the Christmas tree. If anywhere, it might land in the trash.

But holding it above the trash can in my room, I couldn't let go. Instead, I pulled out my phone, took a picture of the gift, and sent it to Sam with the caption: *Guess who from!*

OMG! Wait. I'm there in ten minutes. That was her answer, but why she wanted to come over she didn't say.

Sam stormed through my door in even less than her announced time, gasping. "Did you open it?"

The gift? "No." I frowned. "What's wrong with you? Did you run all the way through town just to see the present?"

"No. I was still at school. Tony wouldn't let me go after AVE, because we had to do this project and he wanted—ah, never mind." She waved a hand. "Where is it?"

I pointed at my desk and sat down on my bed, giving her a

moment to inspect it. When she looked up, her face was all smiles. "Damn, isn't this the sweetest thing ever? He must have spent hours sealing it like this."

"I bet it's even waterproof," I joked, but then I merely shrugged.

"Open it?" she prompted, slumping down next to me and holding out the little package.

I took it from her and twisted it a few times in my lap. It was the size of a ring box, but Chris certainly wouldn't give me one of those.

When I kept staring holes into the package instead of tearing off the wrapping, Sam's face went puppy-like with a disappointed look. "You don't want to know what's in there?"

I did want to know. In fact, it was killing me not having a clue, but I shrugged it off with forced nonchalance.

"Okay, it's too early to open it anyway. Put it under the tree and open it with the rest of the presents on Christmas morning."

"Yeah, as if." Making a wry face, I stood and walked to my desk where I pulled the bottom drawer open. The perfect place was at the far back. That's where this damn little thing would go.

"Aw. Really?" Sam pouted, bouncing on my bed. "I'm sure Chris got you something totally sweet...and lovely...and adorable. Something you would never want to put away again once you saw it."

Maybe. Maybe not. "It's probably just some crappy thing, like a stupid eraser or...whatever. I don't care for any present from Chris."

Her head cocked, she scrutinized me for a long moment. In the end, she curled her lips, waggling a finger at me. "You don't fool me, Susan. All this time you try to smile, but you always have this sad frown on your face when you talk about Chris. You do want to be with him."

I opened my mouth to protest, but nothing whatsoever came out. Heaving a sigh, I flopped backward onto my bed. "It doesn't matter what I want, because I'm not going to get it. Chris isn't the right one."

"Then who is? Nick? He'd date you in a heartbeat, I swear. Or Ethan? Somehow I don't see you two doing anything other than playing Wii. While Chris..." She swooned, lying beside me, and gazed dreamily at the ceiling. "Did you know that you get static electricity when he's near you?"

I laughed out loud. "What?"

She tilted her head to me. "I swear. When we met him in the hallway the other day, and I touched you, you totally zapped me."

"That's bullshit and you know it. Coincidence."

"Maybe." She grinned. "But your eyes sparkle when you see him. Is that coincidence, too?"

"What exactly are you trying to say?"

"Nothing." She sat up with an innocent smile and rose from the mattress. "I have to go now. Tony's waiting for me." She was out the door before I could get up and corner her about whatever she'd alleged here. That monster. She knew exactly how she could make me think. But I refused to. The liar Chris

Donovan had hurt me and wasn't worth another thought. Period.

Scowling at the bottom drawer of my desk, an angry snort pushed out of my nose. I grabbed a book for distraction and banned the guy from my mind for the rest of the day.

*

December 24th was a bit of a jumble. I spent the afternoon with my dad in his apartment. He had a mini Christmas tree with a couple of presents underneath. One was for me. The other had a tag with 'Sally' on it.

"Would you take this home and give it your mom?" he asked me when he caught me spacing out at the sight of it.

I lifted my head to him. "Sure. But will you call her at least? She's really depressed nowadays." Okay, that was a fib. She'd been feeling down ever since the day he moved out, but I didn't want to rat her out.

"Tonight. And tomorrow in the morning. I promise." A smile appeared. Only he could look so happy when he heard about my mother's depression. I knew exactly what it meant to him. It was the same reason Chris had seemed pleased to hear I'd left school after running into him with *Rebecca*. I rolled my eyes at that memory.

Rising from the floor and sitting down on the couch, I handed Dad my presents for him together with a kiss on his cheek. While he opened them, I started to unwrap what was mine. A planner in green leather and two tickets to the movies.

"I thought you and I could go to a movie together during your winter break," he offered.

"Of course. Thanks, Dad." I flung my arms around his neck and kissed his cheek again. Then I let him get up and change his old key ring for the one I'd just given him. Next, he placed the picture frame with the seashells I got a while back on a shelf close to the TV. Three happy Millers smiled from the photo. It had taken several days for me to finally find one of the three of us that I thought could remind Dad that we could be a happy family again, if only everyone put a little effort into it. He stared at it for a long time, seemingly forgetting that he wasn't alone. Absently, he stroked his thumb across the picture.

A smile pulled at the corners of my mouth when I saw that it wasn't the whole picture he caressed, only the part with my mom in it. I wanted to go hug him and tell him that everything was going to be all right. With them—with us. One day, we would be a complete family again, I just knew it. But for now, I remained on the couch and gave my father a couple more minutes in his private little world.

Later, we drank a cup of eggnog and around five he drove me home to my mom. Since it was Christmas and he knew she was having the blues because of him, he wanted me to spend the evening with her. He'd planned to drive out to his parents near San Francisco and spend the next couple of days with them anyway. At least he wouldn't be alone.

Mom and Gramps had set up a beautiful dinner table when I got home. The turkey Mom made was a great deal smaller than the usual one we had on the twenty-fourth, but we were also short one big eater tonight, so that was okay.

The three of us watched *A Christmas Carol* at Grandpa's house after that delicious dinner and later just sat together around the coffee table with cookies and hot chocolate and talked about how nice it would be to have actual snow for Christmas. It was close to midnight when Mom and I went home. She locked the door, turned off the lights, and went upstairs to her room after a long hug that I'd desperately needed.

But before I went to sleep, too, I sneaked downstairs again to put the present for her from Dad under the tree. With no light to guide me, I knocked into the couch, which pushed a snort from my chest. Feeling my way over to the corner where the tree was, my toe caught on the coffee table. I bit down a moan and a curse, but when I nearly poked an eye out on a protruding twig of the Christmas tree, I decided no surprise was worth this torture.

Switching on the light, I set the package from Dad next to mine for Mom. We'd done a great job decorating the tree this year. It was a pity Dad couldn't see it. Remembering the lousy excuse of a Christmas tree he'd gotten just because of me, I was glad he was spending the holidays with his family. Nana and Grandpa Seth always had the most beautifully decorated house on their street. Their tree would be big enough to house a clan of squirrels and probably a stork, too. Dad was going to be in a warm place...probably much warmer than it had been in this home for years.

I stroked one of the red baubles on a twig, catching the reflection of my nostalgic face in the shiny surface. A deep sigh escaped me. All the presents were here now. All but one. Chris's gift for me still sat in the drawer of my desk. Should I go get it and put it with the other presents?

Say I did, what would that mean? That I forgave him? Because that certainly hadn't happened. He'd done too many cruel things to get back on my good side so fast. Oh my *freak*, all the things I told him at the café...things about us. About him being my first kiss and how he gave me the romantic chills. This couldn't be brushed off, not even with a Christmas present.

Dragging my feet along, I trudged back to my room, closed the door, and slumped with my back against it. My gaze on the bottom drawer, the tiny voice inside my head tried to bribe me into giving in to my curiosity and just opening that damn package. Sam had almost gotten me to open it the other day. She was one curious little monster.

I'd refused back then, but tonight was Christmas Eve. And this was a Christmas present. If I didn't open it now, I might never. I stalked to my desk and pulled the drawer open. There it was, small and blue, and oh so sweetly wrapped up.

I swallowed. Chris had hurt me. More than once. The incident two days ago after school changed nothing. I'd been doing so well, I could go on distracting myself and finally I'd forget him. And all would be good. I just had to tell myself this often enough...

Slamming the damn drawer shut, I changed into my PJs and went to bed. As I turned off the lamp on my nightstand, a small blinking light on my phone made me aware that there was an unread text. It must have come in during the past ten minutes while I'd had a one-on-one with the Christmas tree, because the cell had been silent all evening.

A message so late at night? None of my friends would do that, and all of them had sent me texts earlier today, and some just called, or I rang them. It wasn't unusual for Chris, however, to send me a text this late...but did I really hope it was from him?

The stutter of my heart said *yes.* The grumpy voice in my head shouted *no.* The sudden tremble of my fingers said, *you can't handle a text from him right now.* And the small, red-skinned devil on my left shoulder said, *you'll never find out if you don't read it, stupid.*

Shaking my head, I swiped my thumb across the screen to open the message. It was from—my heart sank a little—Charlie Brown.

Neither of us dared to call you today, even though we both considered driving to your house for a Christmas hug at least three times this evening. Anyway... There was a link to YouTube attached here and beneath it stood: *Chris and Ethan.*

Wow, that was a surprise. And what a nice one, too, when I clicked the link and "We Wish You a Merry Christmas" played out. It made me smile and think of a possible reply. But did I really want to go down that road? That I even considered it must have been a side effect of the cheesy movie I had watched earlier. A moment later, I'd typed a message for Ethan. *Merry Christmas to you, too... And to your family.*

Noncommittal. I wouldn't name Chris specifically, but Ethan would pass on my message to all of his two family members for sure. My mind drifted across town to their house. Christmas Eve must be wonderful there. Warm and cozy, with a great meal and dessert. The guys laughing together with their mom while they sit around the tree. Tight hugs for everyone.

If I was there, would Chris catch me under the mistletoe for a kiss?

A sigh escaped me. I missed his smile. And his bright eyes, too. The laughs he gave me with his witty comebacks and the banter he used for getting close to me. But most of all, I missed his goddamn texts every night.

Why did he have to ruin it all?

I put my cell away and went to bed hoping for a happier Christmas next year.

Chapter 22

TWO DAYS AFTER Christmas, Ethan reached the limits of his patience with me. *Either you come over and play Wii with me now, or I'll come to your house and blow it down. Your call.*

Ethan the big bad wolf? The thought coaxed a smile out of me. *Coming*, I texted back. Panic swamped me only after I hit send. What if Chris was home, too? Running into him during my winter break, which had been fairly nice so far, wasn't an appealing idea. But we'd be in Ethan's room the whole time. No trouble. Right?

Trading the flannel bottoms that I still wore at three o'clock in the afternoon for snug-fit jeans and a yellow sweatshirt, I grabbed a hair band from my desk and tied my hair into a high ponytail.

"Mom, can I use the car?" I asked, running down the stairs.

"Sure, honey." She forced a smile as she handed over the

keys. "Have fun."

Hopefully more than she was having, since the book she'd been reading had obviously moved her to tears. Or was she thinking about Dad again? I longed to comfort her, but the last time I'd tried, she'd brushed it off as nothing, so I let it rest. "See you later."

Grover Beach seemed deserted today. Most people were probably visiting family out of town, or they stayed in, enjoying a lazy afternoon in front of the TV. No stop at a single crossing, this must be my lucky day. At the Donovan house, I parked the car behind Beverly's, then walked up to the front door and rang the bell.

Nervous seconds passed. I wrung my hands. Odds were two to one that it wasn't Chris opening the door. Two to one was good. I could live with that. Today was my lucky day. He wasn't going to—

The door opened. It took me only one glimpse at those surprised blue eyes, and there was little doubt the powers above had plotted against me. My heart stopped, then restarted with a panicky drum roll. "Hey," I said to Chris.

"Hi." He scrunched his face in wonder, holding on to the door with one hand. His white tee rode up on that side and revealed a thin strip of skin above his jeans. Just enough to make any girl's mouth water. A happy glow wormed into his gaze. "Why—"

"Ethan," I cut him off...and destroyed his budding hope that I might have come to talk to him.

"Right." A muscle ticked in his jaw. After another second,

Chris stepped aside and let me pass, his gaze focused on the floor rather than me. "He's in his room."

Without a *thank you*, which certainly hovered on my tongue but wouldn't come out with my throat gone dry, I headed that way. Halfway down the hallway, I broke into a run. There was no time to knock. I fell into Ethan's room without warning and closed us off from the rest of the house with my back pressed against the door.

"Susan!" Ethan jumped off his bed.

"Hi, there." Panting, I tried to get rid of the queasiness in my stomach. "Set up the game. I'm ready for a race."

The thundering sound of another door slamming shook the entire house and made me jump, a tiny gasp escaping me.

Ethan squinted at the wall as if he could see right through it. He laughed as he came to me. "Ran into Chris, did you?"

I shrugged helplessly and nodded with a grimace.

No asking, no warning, no sign of his intentions next, he wrapped me up in a tight embrace that knocked the rest of the air out of my lungs. "Merry Christmas, Susan. I'm glad you're here."

"Yeah, me too...I think."

Ethan held me at arm's length again and studied my face with a smirky look. "You think?"

"Me, too." *Period.* I smiled and kissed him on the cheek. "Merry Christmas back at you."

He led me to his bed, making me take up my usual place in his room, and set up a game of *Mario Kart*. Boy, did it feel good to be with him again. Nick was great at *FIFA*, but he hated

Mario Kart. I'd missed racing Ethan these past weeks.

"So, are you going to talk to Chr—"

"Not one word about him," I cut Ethan off quickly. "I mean it. If you make me talk about your brother, I swear I'm outta here before you drive over the finish line."

The game paused. Big blue eyes stared at me. Ethan pressed his lips together and grinned. "Gotcha. Not a single word." He continued the game and kept his promise. Good for him, because I would have made good on my threat in an instant.

An hour later, my hand was cramping from pressing the buttons on the controller. I put it down. "Let's stop here, or my thumbs will fall off."

"Want to do something else? Watch TV or play chess or something?"

In fact, being here for an hour was probably long enough for a reset of our friendship. "Maybe next time."

"Next time?" Ethan smiled in anticipation. "I'll nail you down on that."

Nodding, I climbed out of his bed. I did intend to come back here...someday.

"Need a ride home?" he offered.

"No, I drove my mom's car."

"Good. So, I guess we'll see you at Hunter's New Year's party?"

My chest slumped inside at another mention of that party. "Nah, I'm not going."

"Why not?" His brows knitted together shortly before his

eyes widened. The penny dropped. "Oh."

I gave him a dry smile. "Exactly."

"Okay. Then just call me if you want to hang out again."

"Will do." With Ethan on my heels, I opened the door and walked out into the hallway.

Beverly's voice drifted from the kitchen. I hadn't wished her a Merry Christmas yet, so I made a detour. In the threshold, I froze. She sat at the table, her back on me, and said, "If she means so much to you, then don't give up. She's here. Talk to her, love."

Across from her sat Chris. He looked up, his face paling like that of a snowman. When his mother turned around to me on that cue, her eyes widened. "Susan! We— I was—" She rose from her chair and came over, her mouth tweaking in a warm smile as she regained control over her stammering.

"Happy holidays," I murmured, letting her squeeze my hand. My gaze was stuck on Chris the entire time. Leaning back, his expression appeared so defeated. His eyes were fixed on a plate with a piece of cake that was damaged beyond recognition. While Beverly obviously had enjoyed hers, he must have stabbed at his with the fork.

The desperation he emitted churned my stomach. Could the reason for this really be me?

"Why don't you come in, sweetie?" Beverly tugged at my hand. "Have a cup of tea with us."

I yanked my hand out of hers, startling her, which wasn't my intention. "Sorry, but I can't. My mom's waiting for me. I have to go." Lie, lie, and truth. I really needed to get out of here.

Working up the strength for a polite smile, I whirled around and dashed to the door.

Ethan caught up with me in the next moment. He must have been behind me all this time. "Wait," he said in a low voice and spun me to face him. "Will it always be like this from now on?" He grimaced. "Because that's really awkward."

My knees shook. "I'm sorry for that. Maybe I shouldn't have come at all." Not as rude as before, I pulled my hand out of Ethan's and slipped out through the door, heading for the car.

"Don't forget to call," he shouted after me. I assured him with a nod but didn't look back. *Go, go, go,* my mind urged me. I could think about everything later. When I was back in safety. Far away from Chris...who'd looked every bit as close to crying as I'd so often been recently because of him.

*

That night, I sat on my bed with my phone in my hand. I'd typed a message. For Chris. *Want to talk?* But I couldn't make myself send it off. It would have been so simple—just pressing that damn little button. But it seemed impossible every time I started to think past that moment. What would happen if he really called me? What would he say?

Would he sneak his way back into my heart?

Probably.

Did I want this?

Maybe.

Was that good for me?

Definitely not.

He was a liar. A damn jerk who coaxed my deepest secrets out of me and played me for a sucker. At the memory of that particular date at Charlie's and later in that pub in Pismo Beach, my stomach rolled with betrayal once again. How could this be the base of a fair friendship? Or a possible relationship?

Something warm slid down my cheek. I dabbed at the tear and deleted the stupid text.

*

In the following days, I made it a point not to be home and drown in self-pity. Hunter's place at Misty Beach was a nice distraction when most of the guys came to hang out. Sam told us about her Christmas with her aunt and uncle, and how she and Chloe finally sorted things out between them. It was weird to think of Chloe as an actually nice girl with issues, but we were all happy for Sam. Especially me. A functioning family was worth everything.

Only when the conversation took a turn to the approaching party did I find an excuse to slip out since I wasn't planning on going.

When not hanging with the guys, my alternative plan for not thinking about Chris was to read. Luckily, it worked. Most of the time. Sort of... *Gah*! Who was I fooling? I checked my damn phone every half hour for a new message. Nothing. All those days, the stupid device remained silent, except for the calls from the girls.

Well, I could deal with that. It's what I wanted after all. Right?

Since everyone seemed overly excited for the New Year's party, I decided to spend the day in an exclusive cloud of pampering at my house, so there wouldn't even be a flicker of regret that I wasn't going. After sleeping in, I took a two-hour bubble bath at noon, paid extra attention to my skin and hair with beauty products, and afterward settled down with tea and a new book in front of the fireplace.

Wrapped into my fluffy white dressing gown, I rocked back and forth in the rocking chair and warmed my bare feet at the fire. Mom had to work until nine, so the house was all mine. Amazing, how fast I'd grown used to the silence in here. But there were moments when I really missed my dad's voice...like right now. On the positive side, I could just call him.

"Hey, Dad," I said when he picked up.

"Sweetheart, how are you doing?"

"I'm all right. Are you still at Nana's place?"

"Yes. I'll come back tomorrow. We can have a dinner for two again—" He broke off at the ring of my doorbell. "Who's that?" he asked.

"I'm not sure." Scrunching my brows, I got out of the rocking chair and went to answer the door, but kept talking to my dad. "Can't wait to cook with you."

"Your Nana's packing a jar of cookies for you, too," he continued, but I wasn't listening anymore. On the doorstep of my house stood a bunch of girls, all wearing an evil grin.

"That's great. Tell her thanks," I said absently to my dad,

my eyes wide like saucers, focusing on my friends. "Um, hey, the guys are here. Can I call you later?"

"Sure. Love you, sweetheart."

"Love you, too, Dad." I hung up and my hand dropped. "What in the world are you doing here?"

"Surprise!" Sam shouted and led the rest of my friends into the kitchen, looping her arm through mine to pull me along.

Did I say I don't like surprises? Especially not when they came with a conspiratorial smile and Simone wearing her *I'll-do-your-makeup* face.

"We know you don't want to come to the party tonight," Lisa began.

"But we don't give a damn about what you *think* you want," Sam added. "You're going and we're here to make sure of that."

Allie was the last to come in after all of them. Both arms loaded with bags, she moaned. "Hey, people, is the word *burro* tattooed on my forehead? There's still stuff in the car. Can somebody get that, please?"

Lisa jogged outside and soon returned with more bags and boxes.

"What is all that?" I demanded.

"Our ball gowns and accessories," Simone stated. "What did you think we would be wearing tonight? Slacks and a hoodie?"

Well, obviously not. She ran her fingers through my still damp hair. "Good, you already took care of that. No need to dump you in the tub then." With a snicker, she pushed me down onto one of the chairs at the kitchen table. "Now let me finish this."

As her silent helper, Sam retrieved a hairdryer and curling iron from one of the many bags. The next instant, warm wind was blowing around my face and ears.

"Hey," I protested over the noise of the hairdryer once I'd found my voice again. "Don't I get a say in this, too?"

"No!" all four of them shouted back. And obviously, for them, this settled it.

Making a face like Grumpy the dwarf, I folded my arms over my chest. There was little else I could do while my hair was pulled and twirled around a huge circular brush.

Happy with my defeat, Sam smiled up to her ears. "Anybody want a cappuccino?" After helping my dad pack and move into his apartment two weeks ago, she knew her way around this kitchen and set us all up with a steaming cup. I took a big gulp to quench my irritation with a shot of caffeine.

When my hair was dry and Simone was working some more curls into it with the curling iron, she said in a casual voice, "Did you know that Chris doesn't want to go tonight? He wants you to have a nice evening—without him."

"Really?" Why did that news hurt inside my chest? I should've been relieved, since there was no way for me to escape the plotting bunch of girls in my house. But knowing Chris would be without his best friends tonight—on New Year's Eve—because of me wasn't something that brightened my mood.

"Mm-hm." She put the curling iron away. Next, she began

winding up bunches of my hair and fixing them with barrettes on top of my head. "You know, the guy likes you. And he wants you to relax and be happy."

I tried.

The hours flew by with all of us getting dressed up and Simone doing our nails and putting some decent makeup on our eyes and lips. Sometime that evening, my tension and grumpiness eased, and I found myself laughing more often than scowling at someone. Around nine, when my mother came home, we welcomed her with a pile of pizzas we'd ordered. Careful not to stain our gowns, we ate them and later lined up before my mom to show her what we'd made of ourselves. Okay...we showed her what mostly Simone had made of us, but the result was quite presentable.

Lisa wore a stunning, white, multiple-layered silk dress that played around her ankles but left her back bare for a nice glimpse of skin. Vaguely, I remembered that this was part of her deal with Hunter about the party thing, and he wasn't going to be disappointed.

Simone had chosen a Jessica-Rabbit style dress that glittered like a thousand diamonds in the light. A necklace with a garnet heart and long gloves in the same red as her dress finished her outfit. Sam and Allie were both wearing babydoll dresses, one soft pink and the other as black as Allie's hair.

Mom complimented them all, gushing with excitement for us "true beauties" as she called us. But it was me who her gaze lingered on the longest. She walked closer and ran her hands over the ice-blue satin dress that hugged my figure and fanned out from the waist downward.

Since Simone vehemently objected to the ballerina flats I wanted to wear tonight, my feet were now clad in a pair of her strappy silver sandals with just a little bit of heel. Walking in them proved to be somewhat of a challenge, but soon enough I got a feeling for them. I twirled in front of my mom. "What do you think?"

Her eyes glazed over. She pulled her cell from her handbag and took a picture of me. "I think your dad would want to see this."

"Mom." My voice went hoarse as I touched her arms. "Do you want me to stay home with you tonight?"

"No, honey. You go. I'll be fine with Gramps." She cast me a genuine smile that promised this was not just a lame excuse to let me go so she could break down and cry. Because I knew Granddad planned to come over and bring a deck of cards tonight, Mom would be in good hands.

"Are you guys ready to go?" Lisa asked and put her own phone away which had buzzed while I had my moment with Mom. "Ryan wants to know if we're ever gonna get there," she said, laughing.

I stepped back from my mom, took a deep breath, and turned with a smile to my friends. "Okay, let's do this."

Chapter 23

ENTERING HUNTER'S HOUSE was like walking onto the *Frozen* film set. My breath caught at the beauty of the decorations. I knew the girls had spent a lot of time here recently, to set it all up and create the perfect atmosphere for a winter ball, but this was amazing. Snowflakes cut from white and blue cardboard hung from the ceiling, a chain of lights wound around the stairs' handrail, and artificial snow covered shelves and tables.

Several elegantly dressed couples were swaying to music that wasn't as loud as it usually was at Hunter's parties, and also the number of people—though nothing close to the fifty or sixty that Lisa had demanded—was only a third of the amount that usually came here on party nights.

An expectant beam appeared on Sam's face when she noticed my surprise. "You like it?"

"Are you kidding? You guys outdid yourselves!" I blurted, twirling on the spot to get a glimpse of the rest of the house. It was then that I found Ethan leaning against the doorjamb to the pool room. Simply stunning in his black tuxedo, a bow tie kept his collar closed. Smiling when I noticed him, he came over and gave me a one-armed hug.

"I'm glad you came," he said in my ear. "Wouldn't be the same without you. And hey, I could use some mental support tonight."

He inched back and grinned, prompting my next question. "Support? What for?"

Cutting a glance to all sides, making sure we weren't overheard, he lowered his voice. "I think I have a date."

My mouth dropped open like all the muscles in my face had given out. "You don't say. Ted?"

Ethan blushed a little and nodded, rubbing the back of his neck.

"How did that happen?"

"I don't know, really," he murmured, like everything had happened too fast for him to grasp. "I got a text from him today—and don't ask me where he got my number from, because I have no freaking idea. He asked me what I was up to tonight."

Oh my God. A chill ran down my arms. I knew who gave Ted Ethan's number, but this was certainly not the time to blurt out this bit of information.

"So I told him I was going to Hunter's party," he continued with a grin. "And well...he's going to be here, too."

I squeezed his hand with sheer joy, resisting the urge to jump from happiness. "Good luck! You've gotta tell me all about it tomorrow. Promise!"

"Since you're the only one I can really talk to about this, you'll certainly get the details in the morning." Suddenly, his face paled like Caspar the ghost as his gaze skated to the door. "Oh *God*, I think I need another drink."

Casting a subtle look over my shoulder, I saw Ted had just come in. "No, you're not running away now," I hissed and gave him a gentle push in the right direction. "Go talk to him."

Ethan moaned, but he walked toward Ted with his hands in his pockets. I looked after him, nervous on his behalf, until my gaze got snagged on someone else standing close by. All of a sudden, my heart beat out of control. Blood rushed to my head so fast that I almost got dizzy from it.

Without thinking, I shot around and stalked back to my friends, nailing Simone with a hard stare. "You said he wasn't coming!"

Baffled out of her chat with Nick, she asked, "Who?" Then she dared a glimpse over my shoulder and smirked. "Oh, Chris. Well, to be correct, I said he didn't *want* to come. Ethan took care of that, though."

"What?" I should strangle that girl with her own hair.

"Relax, hun. We couldn't let him spend New Year's Eve alone. And the house is big enough for two. You don't have to cozy up to him...unless you want to." She taunted me with a wink.

I blew out an exasperated breath that made even Nick

laugh. "You guys are so funny, aren't you?" Only, the fun got lost on me as my heart banged against the base of my throat.

Leaning against the banister behind me, I chanced another look to the chest-height table near the entrance. Chris hadn't noticed me yet. Good. One hand in the pocket of his black pants and a drink in the other, he was talking to some of the guys from his basketball team. Lauren and three other girls were with them. At least they were all keeping a safe distance from him.

Safe for whom? my mind chided me.

Ignoring that voice inside my head was easier than keeping a leash on the first tiny butterfly that had just awoken in my stomach at seeing Chris. The sleeves of his white dress shirt were rolled up to the elbows; it didn't surprise me that he hadn't shoved the hems into his pants or topped it with a tux. The casual style was more like him, and the sloppy black tie hanging loosely from his neck rounded out his cool appearance.

One of the girls must have said something funny, because the small group erupted in laughter, two guys even saluting her. Still cheerful, Chris's gaze wandered to the side and found me staring at him from behind my friends. His laugh ceased as he tilted his head a little and blinked. When his gaze traveled down my body to my toes and back up, I wondered if he liked my outfit as much as I liked his.

It was such an awkward moment, staring at him across the room, protected by my friends, that, to my total astonishment, my hand lifted in a feeble greeting. I didn't know if he took it as a sign of forgiveness or just a chance at talking things out, but his mouth curved in a slow smile and he subtly nodded once to beckon me.

I shook my head. It was too much and too soon. Lowering my gaze, I turned away, trying to forget what his bright blue eyes looked like in the dim party light.

"Let's dance," I said to Nick instead and bulldozed him to the dance floor with my arm looped through his. He didn't object and swirled me under his arm. We danced to a few slow songs and some fast ones. All that time, I kept watch of Chris, so that I could adjust our position to be out of his path. Noticing my effort, Nick questioned my motives with a cocked brow. I didn't explain, but from his look, that wasn't necessary anyway.

When the next song ended, he led me to the line of tables that held the punch and other drinks. He poured me half a champagne flute of sparkling wine and filled up the rest with strawberry juice. Set with our drinks, we retreated into the pool room that was—for once on a party night—empty.

I leaned against the pool table and sipped my drink.

"What's up, Susan?" Nick asked in the most serious tone I'd ever heard him use. He must have dug it right out of his grandmother's attic for just this one occasion. "I've never seen you act tense like this before. Like you've got a stick up your ass."

I almost sputtered a mouthful of my drink at him, my eyes growing wide.

"What?" he said. "You know it's true. What did this poor guy do to you that you turned into this wary badger? And where has all your happiness gone? He messed up, all right, but he's really sorry about it."

Setting my glass on the felt-topped table behind me, I shrugged. It wasn't Chris alone. The breakup of my parents and my mom being sad all the time added a great deal of gloom to my mood, but Nick was right. Most of it was due to how I just couldn't let go of Chris, even if I tried to...night and day. Every time I thought I was over that hump, I ran into him and totally reset the game. The truth was, I was starting to get sick of how I felt about Chris. Why didn't love come with an off switch?

"Things are a little more complicated than that," I told Nick. "There's just too much going on in my life right now. Chris picked a bad time for his stupid game."

"Yes, he did." Lisa's voice drew our attention to the door where she stood with Sam. The two walked in and joined us at the table. "But it's the end of the year," Lisa added. "Maybe you should let go of the anger now. Time to get over it and start a new book."

Sam nodded in agreement.

With a sigh, I braced my hands on the edge and hoisted myself up to sit on the table, legs dangling. "And what if I do? How can you guarantee he's not up to another of his little tricks? Or that he won't get bored of me in just a couple of weeks and break my heart all over again?"

Lisa gave a tiny shrug. "It's a chance we all take if we like someone enough. I wouldn't be with my boyfriend now if I hadn't stopped thinking the same thing you do now."

"And your boyfriend wouldn't be such a happy guy tonight," Ryan teased as he sauntered into the room, sliding behind Lisa and kissing her bare neck. Arms looped around her waist, he looked at me over the pile of curls on her head. "Chris isn't such a bad guy really. You would be surprised what you'd find if you only let it happen."

Moaning, I tipped back until I lay on the tabletop and studied the spotlights in the ceiling. "Not everyone is granted such a happy love story as yours."

"Happy?"

I turned my head to look at the latest newcomer to our cozy group. Tony came in, followed by Alex and Simone, and squeezed in between Sam and Lisa. "If I remember it right, there were some obstacles even in their love story," he said with a wink at Lisa.

She poked him in the ribs with her elbow. "Right. You were one of them."

Everyone laughed but Hunter, and that fact coaxed a chuckle from me. Propping on my elbows, I cut a wry look at Simone, who'd snuggled up to Alex on the couch. "Was that your brilliant plan? To bring me here so everyone could toss their pieces of wisdom at me and make me change my mind?"

"Absolutely not." She snickered. "You just have awesome friends who only want the best for you."

Now I was the only one laughing, and it was drained of all humor. "And the best for me is Chris?"

"Yes." A collective answer.

"What did he pay you to say this?" I demanded dryly.

"Nothing." They all shook their heads. Apart from one.

"Well..." Sam murmured, her cheeks turning slightly pink. "He promised me a cherry-vanilla sundae for a teeny tiny favor."

All eyes turned to her. "What favor?" I growled.

She grimaced. "Can't say."

"Oh yes, you can, you little witch," I blurted, sitting up again.

Panicky, Sam sucked in a breath, turned to Tony and pulled at his arm. "I think you owe me a dance, remember?" She ushered him out of the room, disappearing in the crowd. That vixen! How did she always slip away so fast after dropping one of her bombs on me? I could only stare after her with an open mouth.

Lisa rubbed my arm. "I'm sure it's nothing too bad."

I turned a questioning look at her. "Say that again?" Sam could be a monster, and we all knew it.

Lisa snickered, but the sound died when her gaze got stuck on something behind me. A sudden hush fell over the room. With a chill running down my spine, I slowly turned to the door. Chris was leaning against the frame, hands in his pockets, lips compressed.

I had to give credit to my friends, they put my wish above what they thought was best for me. Nick and Hunter stepped in front of me, facing Chris as he slowly walked closer.

"Hey, buddy," Hunter said in a friendly but determined voice. "I'm not sure this is the best moment to show up. Susan will come when she's ready."

Thanks, Ryan! If Lisa wasn't his girlfriend, I'd totally have offered myself to him after that. He was my hero.

Chris, however, seemed unimpressed by the two guys blocking his way. Gaze lowered for a second, he cleared his throat. When he lifted his head again, his first look was for me, then he focused on Hunter. Not even taking his hands out of his pockets, he only tensed his muscles and suddenly looked ten times more dangerous than a German Shepherd ready to attack. Shit. Goosebumps sprouted on my skin.

"I get that you want to protect her...from assholes like me," he said in a low, controlled voice. "I appreciate it, because you're her friend, and I would do the same." He paused. Next his voice turned lethal. "But now get the fuck out of my way, Hunter, and let me talk to my girl."

I gulped. What the hell— Did he just call me *his* girl?

A silent beat passed in the room with the guys just staring each other down. All of a sudden, Ryan began to laugh. "All right." He clapped a hand on Chris's shoulder. "Good luck, my friend. You'll need it."

Chris's features eased. He nodded.

"Come on, everyone," Alex called out, rising from the couch and dragging a swooning Simone with him. "Let's give the kids some privacy."

As they left, Nick and Ryan followed. What the hell? I cast Lisa a pleading look. She wouldn't leave me alone right now, not her! But she gave me a sheepish grimace and shrugged, following her boyfriend out of the room and sliding the door closed behind her.

Dammit!

I had no time to get off the pool table. Chris stepped in front of me, put my glass out of the way, and placed both his hands flat on the cushion next to my hips, caging me in. His eyes were level with mine and I could feel his raging breath on my face.

With an angry edge in my voice, I said, “Let me go, Chris. I don’t want to talk to you.”

He didn’t move an inch. “You’re not going anywhere until we’ve sorted this out. I don’t care if you’re my friend or my *girl*friend when you leave this room again, but you’re going to stop acting like I ruined your life. And you’ll stop it right now. Are we clear?”

My mouth slacked open. He’d really said girlfriend, didn’t he? It caught me off guard, but I regained control fast. “You’re hardly in a position to give me orders.” I slid off the table, about to escape this conversation, but Chris didn’t budge, his hands still gripping the cushion. My body flush to his, I was trapped between him and the pool table. His hard abs pressed against my stomach. My knees turned weak.

A sneer on his lips, Chris drawled, “Am I not?”

I gulped. Pushing at his chest didn’t get me anywhere. For a lack of better choices, I quietly hoisted myself onto the table again and scooted back a little, so my nose wouldn’t brush against his. Feeling like an obedient middle schooler, I clenched my teeth.

The sneer still in place, his eyes turned dark with humor. “Good choice.”

Yeah, glad I could make him happy. Remaining silent, I folded my arms and snorted. It was enough to propel him on to speak his mind. Fine. Let’s get this over with.

“Listen. You had every right to be angry at me. You were

right to yell at me, and I even deserved the slap—though I wish you had chosen a private moment for that." Wrinkling his nose, he rubbed his neck and lowered his gaze to my lap for a second. "The guys will never let me live it down."

"You're embarrassed because I slapped you in front of them?" I snapped.

Eyes lifting, he nodded.

I flashed an imitation of the sneer he wore before. "Good. So you know how I felt when you ratted me out—in a full cafeteria!" The last bit came out with hysterical vehemence.

"I'm sorry about that. I didn't think the situation would"—he frowned—"escalate. I just wanted you to listen and understand."

"You want me to understand?" Struggling to adopt a cooler, more controlled voice again, I growled, "Why don't you try it first? Can you imagine how it feels to know I told you all those private things about *you* when I thought you were Ethan?"

His eyes narrowed with true concern. "Why is that such a problem for you, Sue? It's not like you told me some weird fantasies you had of me that day."

At that my face heated as if I were sunbathing in August in Texas. "No, I just told you about the most personal moment of my life. My very first kiss, ever. With *you*."

"And I told you how amazing that was for *me*. So what?" No blinking or moving his gaze away. He stared straight into my eyes, cementing the truth of his words. It really wasn't such a big deal for him. *Gah*! *Boys*!

But it wasn't the kiss alone he'd heard about, and he

certainly wouldn't forget the rest. "I told you about the butterflies that came with your texts," I whined.

A suppressed smile tightened his lips. "And I've never heard anything sweeter than that, I swear."

When I felt the heat crawl up to my hairline, I covered my face with my hands, whining, "And I practically said I wouldn't sleep with you because you're a womanizer."

His fingers curled around my wrists, pulling my hands away. As I looked up, he narrowed his eyes at me. "Yeah, that hurt a little." With his next thought, his brows smoothed out again. "But in the end, it only made me fall for you harder. I wanted to be that special guy for you. Still want to be. Sue—" He stroked my cheek. "For me, you'd never be a simple go-to girl."

Oh God, how could he react so sweetly and totally miss the point?

"You don't understand. You were never meant to hear those things. That's just wrong."

Several seconds ticked by. Chris was so still, he could have passed for a marble statue as he scrutinized me with sharp eyes. After some time, understanding changed his features to a quizzical expression. "This is what it was all about? You were just feeling embarrassed because you confessed some silly things to me?"

I scooted farther backward on the table. His enchanting smell was driving me crazy and my head needed to stay clear for this conversation. "You find them silly. To me, they're very serious."

"I know they are. You actually gave me a great deal to think about."

Thinking about the fastest way he could get into my pants? I got it.

Chris made a wry face, tilting his head dramatically. "That is *not* what I was thinking about."

Damn him, could he read minds? But my cynical snort must have given me away. "It doesn't matter if it made you think or not."

He put one foot farther back, stemming his hands against the table, head hanging. Poised as if he wanted to move the table against the wall, he said in a low voice, "Tell me *what* matters, Sue, because I really don't know how to set this right with you."

His tousled blond hair tempted me to run my fingers through it. I'd dreamed of it for so long, and now he was only inches away. How was that fair? Taking a deep breath, I clasped my hands in my lap. "You tricked me that day. All evening you lied to me, and that left me completely exposed. You know about all my feelings. And I know nothing about yours."

He remained in that defeated position, but his head tilted up and he frowned as he locked gazes with me. "Are you kidding?" Genuine puzzlement rang in his voice. "From the day you walked into our kitchen and let me feed you that kiwi, I couldn't have been more obvious how I felt about you. How very much I wanted *us* to be exclusive. Do you think I lied to you every time I talked to you? Or in all those texts I sent?"

"Not exactly lying, but you made it clear I was nothing but your next trophy." My voice sounded shaky.

"Did I? When?" He straightened and folded his arms over his chest. "When I gave you that hickey and afterward covered it with my bandana for you so no one would ask silly questions? Or when I kissed you while we were alone and didn't mention it to anyone because I thought you wouldn't like that? And believe me, that was one helluva kiss I'd have loved to brag about."

My throat dried out. I swallowed to keep it smooth, but there was nothing I could have said.

Chris reached out, gently placing his fingertips on my cheeks, and moved a little closer, his eyes capturing mine. "Or did I treat you like a *trophy* when you let me comfort you after your parents' breakup? Is that really what you think I had in mind?"

Chills raced across my skin at his words. And if what I read between those lines was true, he'd just evened out the situation between us, because whether he said it out loud or not, he'd just confessed he'd kind of fallen for me the same way I did for him. Did he not?

Dragging my hands down my face, I groaned, "I don't know what to think anymore." All this time I'd missed him so much, even when I was mad at him. And a tiny part of me agreed with Sam, that his reasons for tricking me into that date were kind of adorable—but I wasn't ever going to admit that to anyone!

A while ago, I forgave Ethan, so maybe it was time to forgive Chris, too. I started to really consider that option, when I remembered the gloss on my lips. I might have just smeared it all over my chin. Terrific.

Hands lowered, I saw there certainly was a pink smudge on my fingers. Mortified, I wiped at my chin, but Chris stopped me, pulling my hand away, and chuckled. He dragged his thumb beneath the left side of my bottom lip, very slowly. I was stunned, like a bunny caught in a trap.

"There, all gone," he said softly. His finger came away with the same pink color, but he simply rubbed it off on his pants. "I like you better without makeup anyway. You're a natural beauty."

Heat rushed to my cheeks at the compliment. I lowered my gaze, but Chris tilted my chin up with his knuckle. He moved in really close, whispering, "And here's a secret. Kissing glossed lips is annoying as hell."

I sucked in a startled breath as he placed a quick but tender kiss on my lips. When he broke away a moment later, he ducked his head and squeezed his eyes shut. I sat frozen, unable to move from surprise, but his scrunched up face made me giggle.

Inching one eye open, he asked wryly, "You're not going to slap me?"

For the kiss? "I don't think so, no." Dang, I sounded almost as uncertain as he did.

As he straightened, a relieved breath escaped him. "Good." A smirk began to play around the corners of his lips and mischief danced in his eyes. "Can I do it again?"

A grin tugged at my lips so hard that my skin felt like it might pop if I suppressed it any longer. Before I knew what I was doing, my hand wrapped around his tie and I pulled on it a little.

"I believe that means yes." His burning gaze switched back and forth between my eyes and mouth. With the slowness of a lazy cat, Chris rubbed his thumb across my lips, wiping away the rest of my gloss. The move was enough to cause my heart to gallop. His thumb wasn't yet gone when he tilted his head and kissed me again. Longer this time, gently and slowly.

His warm hand stroked my cheek. Taking my bottom lip between his teeth, he tickled it with his tongue. A smile parted my mouth and he invaded. A little surprised, I pulled him closer with his tie. Chris moaned with pleasure.

With a firm grip on the back of my neck, he yanked me harder against him, and suddenly the kiss burned with intensity. Whoa, did the lights just go out? There was no time to think, I only knew I missed him. Responding to his passion, I moved my tongue in a swirl and let it dance with his.

Easing the hold of his tie, I slid my hands around his neck and closed my eyes. My actions seemed to have ignited a shudder in him...or was it my cold fingers? Chris chuckled against my mouth. "We really need to do something about that sometime." He reached behind his neck, intertwined our fingers, and brought my hands behind my back, warming them and pulling me closer to him at the same time. He kissed me deeply, eliminating any fear that this might be the last time I found myself captured in his arms.

With his lips still brushing against mine, he whispered, "Say yes."

I struggled to catch my breath, my mind still reeling. "To what?"

Inching back only so far that he could gaze into my eyes, he said, "Do you want to be my girlfriend?" The hopeful half-smile curving his lips pledged he was dead serious about it.

I don't know what made me hesitate, because I'd already made the decision the moment he kissed me. My mind was probably still hung up on that hot kiss and longed to continue where we'd stopped, but Chris stared at me, holding my hands in my lap, and waited for my official answer. At some point, I obviously took too long and he slowly started nodding with a suggestive tilt of his eyebrows.

Smiling, I began to mirror his nod. A long breath pushed out of his lungs. "Dammit, girl, you know how to put a guy on the rack, don't you?"

I giggled. "You totally deserved—"

Chris cut me off with his tongue roaming my mouth again. His hands were on my cheeks, his eyes closed, and he kissed me like I was the incarnation of his best dream ever.

Did this make me feel good? Hell, yes!

Surrendering completely, I sampled a little more of his taste, getting high on his scent. Now I wondered *who* was the incarnation of *whose* dream here?

Far too soon, Chris broke the kiss with a smirk. He stepped back, shoving his hands in his pockets. "Since it's official now, we're a couple"—he pulled his right hand out again—"I guess it's okay to give you this."

What the heck— My chin dropped to my chest. The small blue package that should have been in a drawer in my desk at home now sat on his palm. "How did you—" But realization struck fast. "*Sam*!"

Since she was the only one who knew about the present—and where I kept it—she must have stolen it this afternoon and given it back to Chris. The favor in exchange for a sundae?

"I'm sorry!" the little monster's voice drifted through the closed door. Oh my God, they weren't all outside, pressing their ears to the wood to catch our conversation, were they? Did none of them have any decency?

Chris must have thought the same thing. Laughing, he cut a glance to the ceiling. "Guys, go away!"

"Okay!" That was Simone's voice torn with a snicker. "But don't stay in there for too long. It's almost midnight. We're moving to the garden!"

A glance at my watch—it was ten minutes to twelve. "Think we should go with them?" I asked Chris in a far lower voice now to keep the things between us actually *between us.*

"Open it first." He handed me the present.

Dying to finally find out what he got me for Christmas, I ripped off the bow and started picking at the tape. It was hard to see where the crazy thing started and where it ended, so most of the time, I just turned it over and back again.

Chris frowned, taking the package out of my hands. "Heck, I'm starting to wonder if the reason you never opened it is actually because you simply couldn't." He glanced up with a teasing grin. "I did a darn good job with the wrapping, eh?"

I laughed. "It certainly wouldn't get ripped by accident."

He went behind the small bar in the room and took a red pocketknife out of a drawer. Flicking it open, he sliced through the tape and blue paper, then he closed the knife again and put it back into the drawer. With his hip, he pushed it shut and returned to me, proudly holding out a small box made of stiff, black cardboard.

I opened the lid and found a pretty little bag of blue velvet inside. Just another wrapping. At the effort he'd put into securing the gift, I shook my head and laughed again. Hopefully, this one was holding the actual present, or we'd be doing this the entire night.

Turning the bag upside down, I poured the contents into my open palm. My heart stopped and I sucked in a sharp breath of amazement.

Chris's present for me was a delicate silver charm bracelet with charms attached to three dangling loops. I examined them all, stroking my finger over one at a time.

A basketball.

"That's a reminder of our first unofficial night out together, when you tended to my bleeding wound and defended me in front of my mom," Chris said with a low, intense voice. Certainly, he was dying to hear how I liked the present.

When I smoothed out the second item, a strawberry, he continued, "That's a symbol for the most amazing kiss ever."

I glanced up, warmth flooding my face as he smiled at me.

The third item on the bracelet was a small Super Mario. "That one's from Ethan," Chris explained with an eye roll. "He wanted to add something to your present, too."

This was, hands down, the loveliest thing anyone had ever given me. I loved the design, I loved the little charms, and most of all, I loved the thought Chris had put into it. Now I wished I had something for him, too. But he looked like he would be happy enough if I only accepted his gift.

A small smile on my face, I offered him the bracelet, the silver chain dangling from my fingers. He took it, frowning. Uncertainty crept into his gaze. To release him from his worries, I held out my hand to him. “Help me put it on?”

There, my favorite smile, which was actually the smirk that made his cornflower-blue eyes gleam, appeared, and he fastened the bracelet around my wrist. With a kiss on his cheek, I breathed the words, “Thank you. It’s adorable.” Then I shook my hand, admiring the beautiful present.

We both glanced at the clock on the wall at the same time. Three minutes until midnight. Though there was still music drifting through the door, all sounds of voices outside were gone. “We better join them in the garden, or we’re going to miss the celebration,” I reasoned and slid down from the pool table.

Chris nodded and held his hand out to me. I took it, aware that I’d be doing this a lot from now on. The thought came with a cozy feeling in my chest and the return of ten thousand butterflies in my stomach.

Somewhere on the way through the house, Chris intertwined our fingers and squeezed my hand tightly.

Chapter 24

"FOUR....THREE...TWO..."

We reached the garden as everybody was counting down the seconds until midnight. So many people stood by the gazebo that it was impossible to make out my friends, but I still hurried across Hunter's lawn to reach them in time, dragging Chris with me.

"*One*!" the crowd yelled and many of them blew party poppers.

A hard pull at my hand and suddenly I was in Chris's arms. I gasped as I fell against his chest. He hugged me tight, dipping his forehead to mine. "Happy New Year, sweetness."

"Back at you, *Dream Guy Material*," I teased.

As the people behind me started singing "Auld Lang Syne," Chris began to sway on the lawn, holding me under the stars. "I think we should change that name in your phone again."

"To what this time?" A lonesome firework exploding in the dark night sky reflected in his eyes. I winced at the sudden bang but turned around in his arms and more explosions followed above our heads. Usually, we didn't have fireworks in Grover Beach for New Year, but somebody must have set up a celebration down by the beach, and everyone in Hunter's garden craned their neck to watch the small, colorful spectacle.

His arms still wrapped around me in a tender embrace, Chris didn't stopped swaying, even with my back against his chest. "To *Boyfriend*," he answered my question, his mouth brushing my ear.

The sound of it gave me goosebumps of a special kind. I tilted my head back, resting it on his shoulder. "What did *you* save me as in your contacts?" I could absolutely imagine that "Little Sue" flashed on the screen every time I replied to his texts.

One of his arms dropped and I angled my head, looking down as he reached into his pocket. He pulled out his phone, swiped his thumb across the display several times, then held the cell up for me to read.

"Oh my God—you can't be serious!" My body shook from laughing so hard.

"Totally am." Chris planted a kiss beneath my ear as I read the line on his phone again: *She's The One*.

When the screen's light faded and he tucked the phone back into his pocket, I turned around in his embrace, looping my arms around his neck. "That wasn't your name for me in the beginning, right?"

His gaze burned with humor. "No. Not from the beginning."

"So, what did you call me?"

"Not saying."

"Come on, I want to—"

"Here they are!" Nick's voice intruded into our own little world and cut me short.

Turning around, I found the small group of my friends headed toward us, each of them carrying a champagne flute and a smile wider than Broadway. Lisa and Ryan handed us a glass, too. "Here's to an epic New Year!" Ryan shouted and lifted his glass. We toasted and took a swig with him, then he flung his arm around Lisa's middle and yanked her closer for a hot kiss.

More couples started kissing, but not all of my friends.

Allie and Sasha Torres danced on the spot, Allie flinging her head back and laughing when Sasha whispered something in her ear. Nick and Justin lay in the grass with Jessa between them, watching as those people down at the beach pumped a small fortune up in the air. Sam stood on her toes, placing a chaste kiss on Tony's mouth, before she handed him her drink and skipped off to a group of girls nearby. I recognized Chloe Summers with Brinna, her best friend, and some others there. Sam hugged her cousin tight.

I was glad the two of them were a family again, but damn, it was weird to see them together. The Christmas celebration in Chloe Summers' house clearly had changed a lot for the two girls.

My gaze drifted over the crowd in a nearly hopeless

attempt to find the one I was looking for. Was it my straight spine and craned neck that gave me away to Chris? I had no idea, but he pointed to my left and said, "He's over there."

Following the direction of his pointing finger, I found Ethan standing by the guys he'd spent lunch break with before he changed tables and started sitting with us. It didn't surprise me that Ted was with the group, too. They didn't hold hands or even stand next to each other, but every once in a while their gazes would meet and chemistry sparked between them. Perhaps that was only my wishful thinking, though...

Ethan cracked a smile when he noticed me staring at him.

"Let's go wish him a happy New Year," Chris said, lacing our hands, and pulled me with him over to the guys. When the twins stood face to face, Chris held out his fist and Ethan bumped it with his own. They hugged briefly with a smack on each other's back.

"So what's the deal?" Ethan asked, cutting a quick look at me with a wink, and focused back at Chris. "Can I hug your girlfriend without you going shark attack on me?"

Keeping a protective arm around me, Chris pulled me against him. "Nope," he said in a playful tone.

"Chris!" I slapped his chest and laughed, wrestling free. He chuckled as he released me. Giving Ethan a bear hug, I whispered in his ear, "How are things going?"

He certainly knew that with "things" I meant him and Ted. "We'll see," he replied under his breath.

Then out loud, I said, "Happy New Year, Charlie Brown!"

Ethan let me slip away as some of the guests started to

move back into the house. A casual arm draped around my shoulders, Chris led me inside, too. "When do you have to be home?" he asked me before we joined the others.

"One thirty." Which was far too early to go home on such a beautiful night. But my mom would freak if I stayed out much longer than that.

"Okay, I can't drive you home because I had a drink or two earlier, but if you like, I can walk you."

Although some of the party guests were already saying goodbye and leaving, I was sure Chris wasn't someone who disappeared early from any party. "That's not necessary," I told him. "One of the guys can give me a ride." Simone's curfew was the same as mine, and Alex always drove her home, so it surely wouldn't be a problem for him to drop me off at my house.

Chris pouted. "But I want to."

Heck, who could resist a sweet look like that? Definitely not me. I gave him a small smile. "All right. But we have to leave soon. It's two miles."

Nodding, he pulled me along to say bye to Hunter and my friends. "Awesome party," I told Ryan and hugged Lisa.

"Tell me everything tomorrow," she whispered.

"Promise."

Sam and Tony were engaged in a tongue battle I didn't want to interrupt, so I just waved at the rest of the group and followed Chris out the door.

Hand in hand, we walked down the street, my heels on the pavement the only sound for a while. Chris started swinging our arms between us. The jingle of my charm bracelet added to the clacking of my shoes.

"It's weird, don't you think?" I asked him in a low voice when we'd covered half the distance to my house.

He cut me a sidelong glance. "What is?"

"This." I held up our joined hands. "You and me, walking here, in the dead of the night." My brow creased with a little frown. "Being together."

Chris contemplated this for a second. "It isn't weird at all." He released my hand and tugged me to his side with an arm around my shoulders. As he pressed a tender kiss to my temple, my eyes closed of their own accord, though we kept walking.

"It's not?" I murmured in the dark night.

"No," he told me softly and pulled me against him tighter. "I think it's perfect."

September 19th

I sat in my room on my bed, an open book in my lap, but the words had stopped making sense a long time ago. One hundred and sixty-seven minutes ago exactly. That's when Chris had sent me the last text. *Leaving now. See you in a bit, sweetness.*

I hadn't replied, because I'd been downstairs getting a drink when it came in, and when I read the message five minutes later, I didn't want to distract him from the road. It was a long drive from L.A. to Grover Beach. Three hours and nine minutes—so said Google.

Ah, my heart in a permanent rave-like pounding, I glanced at the clock on my phone for the thousandth time this evening. Maybe I shouldn't have declined Nick's offer to drop by his house and play some video games. But I wanted to be home when Chris arrived. I hadn't seen him in eleven days. Hadn't hugged him or kissed him or just breathed in his mind-blowing scent. Okay, the last one was a lie. He'd given me a blue t-shirt that he'd worn all day before he left for college. Keeping it in a box, I only took it out when the longing for him overwhelmed me and made a normal life without him hard. I sniffed the t-shirt in those moments, once or twice, and put it back quickly to save as much of his scent as possible.

Chris had laughed at me when I told him what I intended to do with his shirt, but his eyes had warmed with this loving gleam, telling a story of their own.

Another glance at the clock. One hundred and seventy-two

minutes. Boy, I was a wreck. Banging my head against the wall behind me, I moaned. How much torture was a girl supposed to take? And then I heard a noise.

Was that a car door? Jerking off my bed, the book in my lap went flying and landed with a thud on the floor. Hands braced on the windowsill, I pressed my nose against the glass and peered down. A silver Honda—Chris's graduation present from his dad. My breath went out of control and fogged up half the window before I could make him out walking toward the front door.

Squealing like a guinea pig, I skipped out of my room and around the corner into the hallway, where I skittered to an abrupt halt. *Relax*! Two deep breaths... Ah, what the heck, one more couldn't hurt. Chris was always the epitome of cool, and I didn't want to run him over like a derailed tank engine.

My mom must have heard him coming, too, and answered the door before he could ring the bell. "Happy birthday, Sally," his voice drifted up to me. This was so much better than just hearing him through the phone.

When I felt calm enough to face him—or it could've been that my legs just wouldn't hold still any longer—I walked down the stairs and stopped at the landing between the floors. Mom had caught him in a brief hug. Damn, he looked so gorgeous in that white sweatshirt, the sleeves shoved up to his elbows, and the washed out jeans I liked best hanging loosely on his hips. His blond hair was the usual mess, standing on end. My mouth watered and I wanted to eat him alive.

"Thanks, honey," my mom said. "Now tell me, how's

college?"

"It's great." Chris released her and smiled. "But I really miss Grover Beach." Then his gaze wandered across the hallway and up the stairs to me. As our eyes met, time stopped for an infinitesimal moment. "And you..." he mouthed.

Screw those calming breaths and the crap about keeping a grip on my excitement. I let go of the handrail, flew down the stairs, and ran into his arms. Chris caught me, lifting me off the ground, and hugged me so tight, breathing wasn't possible for a whole ten seconds. "Hey, baby," he said in a low voice, meant for me alone.

I never wanted to let go of him again.

But we had plans for the evening, and since his last college classes this Friday had lasted until four thirty, he'd just made it in time. Wearing the blue dress he'd seen me in on our first date—the one that started as a tragedy—I was ready to go out. On the floor stood a black duffle bag, so he probably wanted to change clothes before we headed off to a restaurant in Arroyo Grande to celebrate my mom's birthday together.

Taking his hand, I dragged him upstairs with me and closed the door when we reached my room. After he put the bag on my bed, he bent down and picked up my book, cracking a smile. "Left the room in a bit of a rush, did you?" he teased.

I snatched the book from him, cheeks hot like baked potatoes, and stuffed it into an empty spot on my shelf. In the meantime, he pulled open the zipper of his bag, and the first thing that appeared was...my green tee? *Hello, my friend*! And here I'd wondered if the washing machine had eaten it when I couldn't find it the past couple of weeks. That rascal had taken it without a word. And after laughing at me for borrowing his shirt, too.

Chris tossed the t-shirt at me without an apology for stealing it. The only thing he said: "Wash it, wear it, and give it back to me before Monday."

There was a sexiness to his commanding tone that made me smirk. "What do I get in return?"

He pulled his UCLA sweatshirt off over his head and tossed that at me, too. Staring at his toned abs and pecs, I sniffed the sweatshirt and sighed. Ah, a girl's heaven. I put it into the box in exchange for the blue shirt, which vanished into his duffle bag. Chris had dressed again and was now wearing the graphite gray shirt that I still considered my favorite, unbuttoned over a white tee with some rock band's logo on the front. Zipping his bag closed again, he walked toward me, placed his hands on my hips, and pulled me in for a really hot kiss that was all tongues and craving. About time! I'd started to wonder if he wanted to wait until after the celebration.

When he let me come up for a breath, I leaned my brow against his, my arms loosely draped around his neck. "How are Justin and Ryan doing?"

"They're fine. Hunter misses Lisa." Chris swept his tongue across my bottom lip. "Talks about nothing else all day." He kissed me again, briefly. "And Ethan says hi."

I'd talked to Ethan on the phone this morning. He really seemed to love life on campus. "So many *cool* guys, I swear this would be your dreamland," he'd said jokingly. Yeah, he and Ted hadn't worked out, unfortunately, but the whole thing had boosted his confidence in a way none of us would have thought possible. He stepped right into his brother's footsteps with flirting once Chris was off the market. Only Ethan's target group usually wore a five o'clock shadow. Coming clean with his family and close friends was the best thing he could have done. Now I hoped he'd find his own Mr. Right one day so he could be as happy with him as I was with Chris.

The orange glow of the setting sun sneaked through the window, reminding me that I couldn't kiss Chris all evening—much to my regret. "We better go now," I breathed against his lips.

"Do we really have to?" he groaned and moved me backward against the door, taking my hands and pinning them above my head as he nibbled my neck. "It's been so long..."

I giggled, enjoying every stroke of his tongue on my skin, but eventually I pushed myself free. "We have a reservation, remember? And your mom's waiting, too."

"Fine." Chris pouted, but in a voice etched with mischief, he added, "I just hope this evening goes by really fast."

Me, too.

Looping his arm around my waist, we walked downstairs. Mom grabbed her handbag and locked the door as we headed out to Chris's car. He'd offered to be our driver tonight.

Mom climbed into the backseat, giving Chris the opportunity to hold my hand during the ride. Our first stop was his house, where Beverly was already waiting on the front steps. Chris got out and hugged her tight to his chest. "Hi, Mom," we heard him say through the open window.

Beverly kissed him on the cheek before she got into the back with my mother. They'd become really close friends the day Chris and I had introduced them to each other. Their chatter started the moment Beverly slammed the door and ended when we halted in front of the restaurant in Arroyo Grande. I didn't mind being kept out of their conversation. Seizing the chance, I enjoyed watching Chris the entire time. Every other minute, he'd cut me a taunting look or a smile, and sometimes he just squeezed my hand a little tighter.

As we entered the cozy restaurant and the waiter showed us to our table by the window, my mom stopped for a brief moment and sucked in a deep breath. I knew what was on her mind. This was the table that she, my dad, and I sat at together every year for her birthday. It's been a tradition no one ever questioned for so long.

This year, however, one person was missing to make this evening perfect. My heart stung for her...and for myself.

Mom and Dad were still keeping their distance. They talked on the phone once a month or sometimes even two or three times, but other than at my important soccer games, they never saw each other—and my last game had been before the summer. Why they still avoided personal contact, I didn't understand, because it couldn't have been clearer that they missed each other if they'd tattooed each other's names on their forearms. With big, fat hearts around them. Clearly, I got the best end of their breakup deal—I could see both whenever I wanted.

Rubbing my mom's shoulder, I gave her a warm smile. "He's going to call, you'll see. He won't forget your birthday."

Mom nodded, forcing the corners of her mouth up, but it looked little like a real smile. She'd given up hope of him remembering what day it was sometime in the afternoon. And really, I'd started wondering, too. What kept him so long? He hadn't forgotten...had he?

While Chris pulled out my chair, the waiter helped seat our mothers. He lit the candle in the middle of the white cloth-covered table and took our drinks order. Afterward, he handed us the menus and headed off into the kitchen. When someone walked up behind my mother and me two minutes later and reached around my mom to her front, I thought it was the waiter again, bringing our drinks, and I lowered the menu wrapped in blue velvet. But this hand wasn't holding a glass of club soda.

It was holding a red rose.

At Mom's gasp, Chris and Beverly looked up from their menus, too, their faces breaking into wide grins. They didn't look surprised, just happily entertained.

Mom and I whirled around. The velvety book slipped from her fingers and clattered on the marble floor, certainly leaving a dent in my big toe, but I couldn't care less.

"Dad!" I gasped at the same time my mother breathed, "Richard!" She rose from her chair, gripping the edge of the table and the chair's backrest for support. Oh my God, she was shaking just as much as I shook when Chris cornered me in Hunter's pool room on New Year's Eve.

Dad gently took her hand and pulled her one step away from the table, very obviously drinking in her delicate shape clad in a white halter dress cinched with a slim black belt. "Happy birthday, Sally," he said in a low voice, stroking his knuckles along her jaw with the flower still in his hand and cracking a half-smile that made her cheeks turn red.

I knew she wanted nothing more than to throw her arms around his neck and crush him in a long-needed hug, but the waiter returned with our drinks, stealing that chance from her. Placing the glasses in front of us, he asked my dad if he should get a fifth chair for him. My father didn't reply, but the look he cast my mother held a small question. Mom nodded her head vigorously at the waiter, but her smile was for Dad alone.

When everyone was seated again and even the flower had found a place in a slim vase the waiter had fetched from behind the bar, Mom introduced my dad to Beverly. I took the chance to lean across the table toward Chris and whisper, "You don't look surprised. Did you know he was coming?"

With a broad grin, Chris leaned closer to me, keeping his voice as low as mine. "He called me sometime last week and asked me if I knew whether you and Sally planned on coming here tonight."

"That's why he didn't call her," I concluded with a frown. "It was all set up."

Chris nodded and leaned back, enjoying a sip of his Coke, his roguish eyes fixing on me over the rim of the glass.

The birthday dinner was one of the happiest evenings I'd had in a long time, and that's saying something because since

Chris and I got together, he'd taken me out on many happy evenings. Tonight, we ate and drank, we made jokes, and heck, sometime between the main course and the dessert, my father had started stroking the back of my mom's hand in an inconspicuous manner. She didn't pull her hand away. My heart did a double flip for the two of them.

After Dad had taken over the bill and we were getting ready to leave the restaurant, he whispered something into my mom's ear. Gazing into his eyes, she gave a small nod. As if there was any reason to, she asked me whether it was fine with me if Dad took her home in his car.

"Of course that's fine with us," I hissed, almost bouncing on the spot like a preschooler that needed to go to the toilet.

We left the restaurant together but parted at the parking lot. After kissing my dad goodbye, I climbed into Chris's car. First, he dropped his mom of at his house, then he drove us to mine and came inside with me. I loved when he spent the weekends here. Falling asleep in his arms as he caressed the back of my neck was the best thing ever.

When he helped me out of my dress and dragged me with him into my bed, I knew his first year at college was going to be hard on both of us. "All these long periods of not seeing you...how will I ever stay sane until next summer?" I whined, sinking against his chest.

"Maybe that's the wrong way of dealing with it. Don't think about it as a whole block of time. Instead, focus on staying sane for the next couple weeks until I come home again." His lips pressed against my brow. "That's what I'm doing."

"But still…an entire year."

"Yeah, but there's Thanksgiving, and winter break, and spring break, and who knows what else. You'll see, I'll be home more often than at campus." His teasing didn't manage to lift my spirits. He wrapped his arms around me, his warmth seeping through my skin. "And before you can count to three, you'll be at college with me and we can share a room."

That prospect, on the other hand, made me smile.

Any thought about college and the future slipped away when Chris started kissing me, and I closed my eyes, giving in to the temptation of my sexy boyfriend.

*

The sounds of a car engine pulled me out of my sleep. I listened carefully, but only silence remained. It took me a few seconds to adjust to the dark room. Cautiously, I lifted Chris's arm off of me and slipped out of bed. Sneaking to the window, I chanced a quick peek outside. My dad's car was parked in front of our house and I could see the shadow of my mom through the passenger window.

Heck, it was after one o'clock in the morning. Where had they been so long? Did Dad take a detour all around California to get her home?

Warm hands touched my sides and made me jump with shock. "Chris!" I hissed as I turned to face him. The moonlight breaking through the window caught on his smirk.

"What are you doing?" he asked.

"Nothing. Go back to bed."

"I will, if you come with me." He glanced over my shoulder, out onto the street. The breath of his chuckle caressed my neck. "So they've finally come home."

"Yeah, a bit late, don't you think?" I whispered.

"Why? You should be happy. They were probably having a nice birthday."

That's what I hoped. But leaving them alone after so long could backfire. They hadn't had a chance to fight in a while. What if they caught up with that now? It was killing me not to know what they'd been talking about—and were still talking about. Neither of them got out of the car.

"Come on, sweetness, give them some privacy," Chris taunted me and pulled me away from the window. Maybe he was right. This wasn't my business. But when a car door slammed outside and another a split second later, I yanked my hand out of his and rushed back to the window, pressing my face against the glass.

Excitement made me shiver as they both walked toward the house. Squealing, I pivoted to Chris and grabbed fists of my hair, my eyes and smile wide. "They're holding hands!"

"Yeah?" He smiled, too. "Things happen. Now don't think about going downstairs. Nosy as you are, I won't let you ruin their evening." Dammit, he knew me too well. He crawled back into bed and held the covers open for me. "Come here."

Well, that was an invitation I could not possibly reject. Snuggling up to him, I let him warm my fingers and feet. He got a soft good-night kiss—and a second and third, and just one more for good measure.

"Sleep tight, sweetness," he whispered in my ear.

I did.

And you know what? Dad's car was still there in the morning.

Epilogue

THE TIME BEFORE Christmas was my favorite of the year. I couldn't help it, it just reminded me of the days when Chris and I had started dating. Hah, well, *dating* might be stretching it a bit, but it was the time when I first fell in love with him, and that's not something a girl ever forgets.

Staring out the window of our two-story house that—since last night—had been decorated with chains of lights, I tried to catch a glimpse down the street. Chris should be home any minute. He'd called me from the restaurant earlier, telling me to stay where I was. Today, he wanted to come with me to my important meeting with Dr. Lois Tallaware. In fact, he was taking me everywhere these days.

"You know what the Dr. Lady said," he argued with me every time I insisted on driving the car myself. "You have to be careful."

Yeah, I was probably going to hear that warning more often in the future. And as annoying as it could be at times, his overprotectiveness only made me love Chris more. If that was even possible.

A smile dented my cheeks when his car rolled up the drive. Quickly, I pulled up my hair, which was a lot longer than it had been back in high school, and fastened it into a ponytail with the rubber band I always wore around my wrist. Grabbing my coat and purse, I hurried outside and locked the door. When I turned around, Chris stood right in front of me.

Like every other time he came home and I hadn't seen him for most of the day, his roguish cornflower-blue eyes and the sexy smile took my breath away. But more than his looks, the kiss he surprised me with right now was devilish and hot, like the chili he'd cooked us last night.

"Hey, sweetness," he breathed, running his hands down my sides. I jumped as he pinched my butt. "Ah, happy to see me, are you?" he teased.

I smacked him on the shoulder, but he only chuckled, intertwined our fingers, and led me to the car, holding the door open for me and helping me inside. I gave him an eye roll that read: You're so overdoing it, baby.

One hand on the headrest and one on the dashboard in front of me, he leaned down and kissed me again, softer this time. "Just being careful," he whispered against my mouth.

Funny, how fast he'd adapted to the new situation. When we got the test results four weeks ago, he'd gone pale as the little vampire he turned into each time he sensed a chance to nibble my neck. And frankly, so had I.

Outside the doctor's office, we'd both looked at each other, no one speaking during the drive home, still in shock. Hours later and after baking a double-decker chocolate cream cake—cooking had become his stress-release button—he'd sat down beside me on the porch and started rocking us softly on the porch-swing. "I want you to stop playing soccer," he'd said then.

Soccer wasn't my life nor was it a career I'd chased after high school, but I still loved playing a friendly game twice a week with the girls from the town's team. It was fun and balanced the hours I spent in an office chair as an editor at a publishing house.

"Promise," Chris pressed when I hadn't given him an answer. "The damage is done and I don't want you to risk anything now."

"The damage?" Both my eyebrows had gone up at that.

I still remembered how Chris had rubbed his neck and dipped his head back against the backrest, his gaze moving to me. "You know what I mean."

He hardly ever asked anything from me, so this was clearly important to him. He only wanted the best for me, and that's why I'd relented in the end. "Okay, I'll stop until everything is back to normal."

His look had filled with an unspoken message. It didn't take much to understand. Nothing would ever be back to normal again. A diagnosis like that out of the blue would do that to a couple who'd graduated from college two years ago and just started to lead a normal life.

"What are you thinking about?" Chris's voice broke my train of thought when he halted the car in front of the doctor's office.

I managed a smile. "Nothing. Let's go inside."

"Wait." With that order, he ran around the car and opened the door for me again. Apparently, I couldn't do that on my own anymore, because my condition was tying my arms to my side, making me a complete and utterly helpless invalid. I grunted a sigh. We really needed to have another chat about that tonight. His wry grimace told me—yep, he'd read my expression correctly.

Doctor Tallaware's practice was inside a neat, yellow bungalow, part of which was her home. I'd never seen anything past the waiting or examination rooms, but if this part of the house was any indication, the rest must be a warm and cozy place, too.

"Hello, Mrs. Donovan," the receptionist with the black bun on top of her head greeted me across the frosty glass counter. "You can go right in. The doctor is waiting for you." Then she smiled at my husband, her cheeks turning a little flush. "Mr. Donovan, would you mind signing a card for my nephew? It's his tenth birthday on Saturday and he's one of your biggest fans." She must have been hoping that I'd bring Chris today, because she held out a basketball card with his picture on it.

Though Chris had stopped playing basketball last summer in order to be home more and was now working at his brother's restaurant, the kids in town all loved and remembered him. He could deny it all he wanted, but the gleam in his eyes every time someone asked him for an autograph spoke volumes.

He signed the card with his smirking face on it for the receptionist's nephew and afterward followed me into Doctor Tallaware's office.

"Ah, Susan," the woman with short chestnut hair and freckles said and shook my hand. "I see you brought support." She offered Chris a stool next to the examination table.

Cutting Chris a wry grin, I laughed and told her, "Yeah, he barely let's me go anywhere alone since we left your office the last time."

"Just taking care of the little bump," Chris murmured.

At the defensive but also caring expression that crossed his face, my heart melted for him...and for the little bump, too. I squeezed his hand as I reclined on the examination table and mouthed, "I love you." He started to rub his thumb over my knuckles, his gaze going tender.

"All right, let's see how this darling is doing," Doc Tallaware said while she squeezed a cold liquid from a plastic bottle onto my tummy and ran her ultrasound device over my lower belly. After a few seconds, she pressed a little harder and a clear picture emerged on the screen in front of her. The monitor was turned so that also Chris and I could see what was going on.

Using her finger to point, the doc explained what exactly the light and dark gray images on the screen were. "You see, this triangle is the cone of the ultrasound. Here's your uterus, Susan, and this"—she smiled at both of us—"is the little Donovan that will soon move in with you."

My heart started to pound at the sight of our baby, even if

it was no bigger than a strawberry right now. Chris held my hand tighter. When I shot him a glance, he gave me a proud-as-hell daddy-smile.

The doctor moved the device on my lower belly again, trying to catch the strawberry from a different angle. As the picture on the screen changed, she suddenly stilled. Moving the ultrasound around and around, her gaze was glued to the screen. And so was mine.

"Is…is that normal, Doc?" Chris asked in a concerned voice that gave me uncomfortable shivers. When I looked at him again, a frown marred his brows and I knew I was mirroring it. We both focused on the lady in the white coat as she cracked a smile.

"Well, it certainly happens more often than you would think. Congratulations, Susan. From what we can see here, you're going to have twins."

"Twins…" The word left my mouth in an appalled whisper. "This—this is— I didn't plan this!"

"Few ever do," Doc Tallaware replied, amused.

My chin dropped to my chest. When Chris's hold of my hand eased and finally slipped away, I tilted my head to him, preparing for the shock in his eyes to make this even harder to cope with. Slowly, he dragged his hands through his tousled, blond hair and down his face. When they came off, he began to laugh so hard that he startled both the doc and me. What the heck? He thought this was funny?

"Well," Chris choked out through continuous fits of laughter, "Uncle Ethan and William are going to love that." He got up from his stool, turned around, and headed out the door without another word to me or the doctor.

Through the window to my left, I could see him walk to our car and bang his head on the roof. Twice. His laughter never ceased.

- THE END -

Playlist

Far East Moment ft. Justin Bieber – Live My Life
(Outside her books)

Ed Sheeran – Thinking Out Loud
(A ruined birthday party)

Sam Tsui & Christina Grimmie – Just A Dream (cover)
(Alter ego?)

Volbeat – Still Counting
(The wrong room)

Sam Smith – Stay With Me
(Caffè latte & dessert)

Lilly Wood & The Prick and Robin Schulz – Prayer In C
(Basketball)

Ricky Martin – Le Mejor De Mi Vida Eres Tú
(Soccer backward)

Vito Lavita ft. Toni Tuklan – Danzare
(Cooking for Sue)

Disney's Frozen – Let It Go
(What's the temperature in hell?)

Leona Lewis – Run
(Falling apart)

Christina Perri – Jar Of Hearts
(He had his chance)

Dion and The Belmonts – Runaround Sue
(Twisting on a date)

Ben E. King – Stand By Me
(The kiss that shouldn't happen)

Kodaline – High Hopes
(Chris and Beverly)

Tyler Blackburn ft. Golden State – Save Me
(Get the fuck out of my way, Hunter!)

love
ANNA KATMORE
The Trouble with
Dating Sue
GROVER BEACH
TEAM 5

"When hell freezes over!"

Chris Donovan can't believe that Susan Miller just brushed him off like a fly in midsummer. He certainly wasn't looking for a girlfriend when he followed her into detention. All he wanted was to show this little smart-mouth that no girl can resist his charm when he decides to woo.

It's a plan that thoroughly backfires.

No matter what Chris does to crack through the snappy nerd's barriers, she blocks his every advance. Worse, she only seems interested in his quiet twin brother, Ethan. But Chris never walks away from a challenge, and Sue's stubborn resistance only makes him try harder.

To put a hickey on her delectable neck during a friendly game of soccer is one thing. To make hell freeze over and snatch a kiss is another. But when a strawberry and some molten chocolate lead to five hot minutes in his kitchen, the stakes of this challenge unexpectedly rise...

Also by Anna Katmore

PLAY WITH ME
RYAN HUNTER
T IS FOR...
DATING TROUBLE
THE TROUBLE WITH DATING SUE

TAMING CHLOE SUMMERS (a spin-off)

*

SUMMER OF MY SECRET ANGEL

*

NEVERLAND
PAN'S REVENGE

ABOUT THE AUTHOR

ANNA KATMORE prefers blue to green, spring to winter, and writing to almost everything else. It helps her escape from a boring world to something with actual adventure and romance, she says. Even when she's not crafting a new story, you'll see her lounging with a book in some quiet spot. She was 17 when she left Vienna to live in the tranquil countryside of Austria, and from there she loves to plan trips with her family to anywhere in the world. Two of her favorite places? Disneyland and the deep dungeons of her creative mind.

For more information, please visit her website at annakatmore.com
Or find her on Facebook: facebook.com/katromance

16119674R00235

Printed in Poland
by Amazon Fulfillment
Poland Sp. z o.o., Wrocław